Described in the *Irish Times* as 'one of our foremost writers for young people', Sheena Wilkinson has won numerous awards for her eleven novels, including the Children's Books Ireland Book of the Year for *Grounded* in 2013. Her historical trilogy about young women coming of age in early twentieth-century Ireland has been widely praised for its 'formidable narrative and ... acute sense of historical justice' (*Belfast Telegraph*). Her short stories and memoir essays have won or been shortlisted in many competitions, including the Fish and the Bridport, and she was awarded a Major Award from the Arts Council of Northern Ireland in 2012. *Miss McVey Takes Charge* is her second novel for adults, and the much-anticipated sequel to *Mrs Hart's Marriage Bureau* (HarperCollins, 2023).

Sheena is a Royal Literary Fund Fellow, and teaches writing at postgraduate level at Trinity College Dublin, as well as in settings ranging from prisons to healthcare settings to schools. She mentors on the Irish Writers' Centre's National Mentoring Programme and is an Arvon tutor. Sheena lives by the shores of Lough Neagh with her husband, stepson and two dogs.

I0587329

Praise for *Mrs Hart's Marriage Bureau*

'A riotously funny novel ... In beautifully authentic language true to its time and setting, along with mischief and irony, this is a gem. Kate Atkinson fans will love it.'
Anne Cunningham, *Irish Independent*

'A briskly witty delight, reminiscent of the best interwar popular fiction.'
Irish Times **– Great Holiday Reads, June 2023**

'Really ... funny, without being frothy ... a real treat of a book.'
Simon Thomas, *Stuck in a Book*

'I absolutely adored this. It's an intelligent and nostalgic read, with depth and surprising plot twists.'
Sue Leonard, *Irish Examiner*

'Mrs Hart's Marriage Bureau has been dubbed a "witty romantic comedy" but it's smart too.'
Áine Toner, *Belfast Telegraph*

'I loved this book! It's alive with the hopes and dreams and heartaches of women in a 1930s Northern town, and its twists and turns are a constant delight.'
S.J. Bennett, author of the bestselling 'The Queen Investigates' series

'Impossible to put down. The writing and story are so compelling. I thought the ending was absolutely perfect.'
Emma Pass, author of RNA-award-shortlisted *Before the Dawn*

'Charming, unexpected, and a really great sense of time and place.'
Emily Hourican, author of *The Glorious Guinness Girls*

'Full of heart ... a gorgeous, uplifting and sincerely charming read.'
Mairéad Hearne, *Swirl and Thread Reviews*

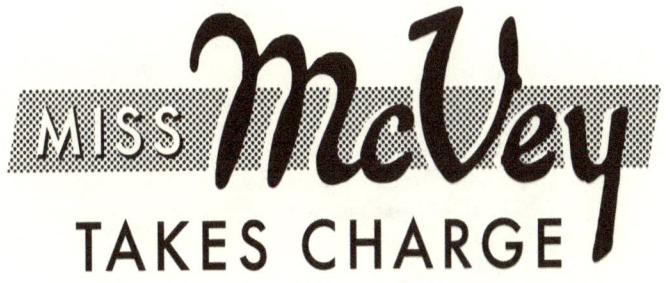

MISS McVey TAKES CHARGE

SHEENA WILKINSON

First published in 2025
by Writers Review Publishing
www.writersreviewpublishing.co.uk

Cover design by Niall McCormack
Typesetting by Michelle Griffin

A CIP catalogue for this book is available from the
British Library

PRINT ISBN 978-1-0685264-4-2
EBOOK ISBN 978-1-0685264-5-9

For Sarah Lucy Cooper,
who's not averse to a bit of taking charge herself,
with much love.

One

'I have rather an unusual request.' Miss Margaret Teal chewed her lip, folding and unfolding the cuff of her heavy beige cardigan.

April wondered why Miss Teal hadn't made more effort. Normally when people – women especially – consulted the True Minds Marriage Bureau they put their best foot forward. April was often touched by their efforts to look attractive, even for the preliminary interview when there were no prospective suitors in sight. Miss Teal seemed oblivious of her appearance. Yet the girl was very good-looking if you looked past the lumpen clothes and scraped-back hair: her skin was clear, her eyes dark, and she had fine bone structure like Katharine Hepburn, April's favourite actress.

Whatever she looked like, she was far too young to have resorted to a marriage bureau – twenty-one was strictly their age limit, and Margaret Teal couldn't be much more. People didn't consult True Minds until the normal well of ways to meet the opposite sex had run dry. And April was not one to turn away business, but all Miss Teal really needed was someone to help her present herself more favourably. Why, a pretty frock and a flattering hairdo and the young men would flock to her! What was her mother thinking? Mammy would have had something to say if April had gone out looking so frumpy.

She searched for a tactful way to say this, but tact was not her strong suit. And what if the wee girl said she was thirty? Now that April was over thirty herself and religiously did daily exercises to prevent her chin from sagging – apparently it could creep up (or rather down) on you when you weren't looking – she'd be thrilled to be thought younger, but one of the things she had learned since taking charge of True Minds was that not everybody thought as she did. Which was just as well for business, given that April had no interest in marriage for herself.

'You're grand and fresh looking, Miss Teal,' she said.

Miss Teal looked surprised. 'Well, I'd hope so,' she said stiffly. 'I'm only eighteen.'

'Eighteen? But' – but you dress like a fifty-year-old librarian. 'Miss Teal, we can't take anyone under twenty-one.'

'Oh, it's not for *me*,' Miss Teal explained. 'That's why it's unusual. It's for my brother.'

'But we can't …'

'Isn't that what you do?' She looked puzzled. 'Colonel Lucey's always talking about the *fine young gel* who found him a wife. That's you, isn't it? And no disrespect to the Colonel, but he's sixty if he's a day and, well …'

April was fond of stout, red-faced Colonel Lucey, whose gratitude to True Minds expressed itself in various kindnesses – trout from his stream, roses from his garden, and the last time his best spaniel bitch whelped he had been very keen for April to have a puppy. Pets made Felicity, whom she lived with, wheeze, so she'd had to refuse. Still, Miss Teal had a point.

'We're not only here for the young and attractive,' she said. 'It wouldn't do if we'd all the same qualities.'

'Oh, I know,' Miss Teal said. 'But Charlie's quite a catch. He's thirty-seven. *I* think he's handsome, though obviously I'm not the best judge. He's got a grand cottage and a steady job – he's groom to Colonel Lucey. Oh!' Her eyes blazed. 'Is it because he's a groom? Don't you take servants? But he's not the boot boy or the scullery maid.'

'Miss Teal.' April summoned up all the dignity of her status as senior partner of the True Minds Marriage Bureau. (There was no junior partner, just Lily, who did the donkey work, but she liked the title.) 'There's no prejudice against your brother's occupation, but we can't take clients on without their say-so. If *he* makes an appointment, we'd be delighted to try to suit him.' The part of her brain that never stopped matchmaking was already riffling through the files in her mind. That young woman last week: she hunted three times a week. No – too posh. Miss Dalrymple? She'd been trying to suit her for ages. Or …

But none of them were any good unless Charlie Teal came in of his own accord.

'He *won't*; he's hopeless,' Miss Teal wailed. 'He'll just fester up there with his blessed dogs and I'll worry, and it'll spoil everything and I'll end up coming home to fester beside him and ruin my life too.' Her eyes filled with tears and she looked suddenly like the young girl she was.

April, who had done a fair bit of festering at home in Northern Ireland until she had escaped to Easterbridge two years ago, felt a kick of fellow feeling. 'Why don't I send for tea,' she suggested, 'and you can tell me all about it?'

'Thank you.' Miss Teal fumbled in her skirt pocket for a handkerchief. 'Maybe it's a silly idea, but it'd be easier to go to the other side of the world if I thought he was being looked after.'

'Your brother's a grown man,' April began sternly, crossing the room to the door. 'Lily!' she called upstairs.

She disliked roaring like a fishwife, but one of Lily's peculiarities was an inability to hear a bell, though she responded to her name like a co-operative dog. She looked quite like a dog too, April thought as Lily lolloped downstairs, her sandy hair escaping its pins and her mouth half open: a Golden Retriever, big-boned, eager to please, but not quite in control of its limbs.

'Can we have a tray please? Tea for two,' April asked.

Lily looked startled. 'We've no biscuits,' she said. 'You said nowt about tea.'

'Tea will be fine. Don't worry about the biscuits.' April tried to hide her indignation. The biscuit tin had been half full that morning, and they had had no clients before Margaret Teal. Not for the first time, she regretted employing Lily. But as she re-entered the interview room she was smiling calmly, all her attention on this client-who-wasn't.

'Now,' she said, 'where were we? You mentioned travel?'

The girl nodded, her eyes brightening. 'I'm going to be a nun.'

April swallowed. 'I can honestly say that you're the first nun to consult this marriage bureau.'

'I'm not a nun *yet*.'

'And why does a wee girl like you want to join a convent?' April asked. 'I don't mean to be pass-remarkable, but you're so young.'

'I have a vocation,' Margaret said importantly, balling her handkerchief in one hand and looking younger in her intensity.

April was about to ask, 'How can you *know*?' when she remembered how irritated she had always been when people refused to take seriously her determination not to marry. Everyone said she would change her mind. *Wait until you meet the right man*. But they had been wrong.

4

Except, she supposed, that she had met someone – Felicity.

'It seems such a difficult life,' she said. 'Don't you have to give up all your possessions and do what you're told?'

'Oh yes, but that's nothing compared to what it'll give me! Dedicating my life to God. And being part of a community. Belonging.'

'Aye, I know what you mean.'

'I've always been the odd one out,' Margaret said frankly. 'I was the cleverest at the village school, *and* a Catholic. But the master found out about scholarships to a convent in York – and I won. I boarded there for four years and I loved it.'

'But if you don't mind me asking' – two years in England had taught April that the English were as obsessed with class as her own people were about religion, and she had heard that nuns could be desperate snobs – 'was it not hard being at a posh convent school?'

'If anyone was beastly, I just offered it up.' Margaret's face took on a pious cast that robbed it of its attractiveness, though that wouldn't matter once she took the veil.

'So where—?'

'I'm going to the mother house in Dublin.' Not quite the other side of the world, as she had claimed, but in her next breath Margaret said, 'It's a missionary order, so I hope to be called abroad eventually – Tanganyika, probably.'

Her excitement was palpable, and April wondered how much her vocation was for the religious life and how much for adventure.

Lily galumphed in, balancing a tea tray at a precarious angle. Before April could rescue it, Margaret leapt up and took it, and Lily, sniffing loudly, backed out of the room. She would have to go. April was all for giving people chances, but it would have been all the same if Margaret had been a real client.

She sighed, lifted the teapot from its surrounding puddle, and dried its bottom with a handkerchief before pouring. Lily had spilled so much there was barely a cup each.

'I'm sorry about Lily,' April said. 'She was keen to try office work, but she's not quite cut out for it.'

'I'm so lucky to have a vocation,' Margaret said. Then her face clouded. 'It's just leaving Charlie that bothers me. It's quite lonely, our cottage – about a mile from Shippardsholme, up on the moors. Apart from the Colonel's place, there's only a few farms nearby.'

'You left him to go to school.'

'I was home for holidays. After I'm professed – and if I get to Tanganyika …' She sighed. 'We've been on our own since Mam died. And even with the scholarship, there were things to buy: uniform, tennis racquet, books. It can't have been easy, but Charlie managed. He even sold his best dog! And now I'm repaying him by going as far away as possible.' She bit her lip.

'Look, Margaret,' April said, 'I can't find Charlie a wife unless *he* asks me to. But I'll give you one of our brochures – there's no harm in telling him you've consulted me. He does sound an interesting fellow.'

Honesty and loyalty fought it out on Margaret's face. 'I don't know about *interesting*,' she admitted. 'All he talks about is his dogs.'

'Och, the Colonel was the same. Does Charlie have spaniels too?' She had a mental image of a man in a checked cap and gaiters, striding across the moors with his faithful spaniel and his shotgun. Plenty of women would go mad for the like of that!

Margaret shook her head. 'Greyhounds. They're all he lives for – them and the Colonel's horses. He's bred a few litters since Mam died – Mam wouldn't have had one near the place – and they've never done much apart from the one he sold to help me. But he's got one bitch now; he says she's a champion. She's won at the local flapper track, but now he says she's ready for Leeds or Barnsley.'

This was double Dutch to April, who had a mental picture of flappers dancing the Charleston. Still, the new sport of greyhound racing was very popular, and not only with men.

She gave Margaret a brochure and a registration form. 'Maybe we'll see him here one of these days,' she said. 'And I promise to do my best for him if he does. Now off you go and try not to worry – you've done *your* best. You can do no more.'

Margaret said, without a trace of embarrassment, 'Yes, I can. I shall pray for him. For a special intention. And of course, Miss McVey, I'll pray for you.'

An unorthodox valediction for a marriage bureau appointment, but April smiled and said, 'Thank you, Miss Teal. Fair play to you.'

Two

Maybe there was something in the power of prayer after all. Two days later the afternoon post brought an envelope the thickness of which made April's heart thump with anticipation: a filled-in registration form. As she unfolded it, noting that the handwriting was untidy but characterful, one word jumped out from the *Hobbies and Interests* section: *horses*. Charlie Teal already? Well done, Margaret!

But no, it was a young woman: a Miss Barbara Firth. She was twenty-eight and loved the countryside and old horses! How odd to like specifically *old* horses, but how perfect for Charlie! April checked the address ... why, she even lived near him. Margaret had said their home was near Shippardsholme, and Miss Firth lived between there and Easterbridge. She was pretty too: the enclosed photo showed a young woman with a sleek dark bob and a sweet face. Any man would be delighted to be matched with her.

Your loss, Charlie boy, April thought. You don't know what you're missing. Still, maybe Barbara Firth was only the first instalment of Margaret's prayers being answered. The very next day could bring Charlie himself. April wasn't a great one for prayer herself, apart from when she was really in a fix, but as she cycled home through a spring shower, she found herself sending a few thoughts in a vaguely heavenwards direction: *How could it not be your will to bring these two people together? Sure, wouldn't it set young Margaret's mind at rest and her about to become a nun and do your work for the rest of her life? Och, come on now, God – fair's fair.*

She had a sudden memory of the few nuns she had seen in Lisnacashan, her hometown. They seemed to glide along the streets as if they had no legs. April and her pal Evelyn had once followed two from the Catholic church all the way to Doran's Loanen, where the poor Catholics lived, trying to work out what exactly was under their heavy long robes. Mammy had smacked her when she found out. She didn't hold with nuns herself, being Presbyterian, but that didn't mean she wanted her daughter being disrespectful. 'It's that bold chit Evelyn Brady leading you astray,' she'd said, which was exactly what Evelyn's mammy said about April. They used to dare each other to go into the Catholic church too, this being the most forbidden place they could think of. Old Father Quinn knew rightly they weren't in his flock, but he never seemed to mind.

Changing gear for the climb up Riverside Road, looking forward to the meal Felicity had promised to have waiting, April smiled at the memory of Evelyn – what eejits they'd been! – and then sobered, remembering the tragedy that had befallen her old friend: her little son had been killed in a farmyard accident last year. April had tried to keep in touch, but there were only so many times you could send a kind note without getting a reply. When she did write, she always ended, *And if you need a change of scene, come to me. We've a spare room and you're always welcome.* The offer might never be taken up, but it made her feel better to make it.

It wasn't even quite true that they had a spare room. More often than not their attic was occupied by Jewish

9

refugees from Nazi Germany. The Schneiders had left a fortnight ago to join relatives in Leeds, and though April had grown very fond of them, she loved being alone with Felicity. After dinner they could listen to the wireless without feeling antisocial. Felicity could sit on the floor and lean back against April's legs and April would massage her shoulders, tight from being hunched over her typewriter. Or they would sit on the settee together and Felicity would rub April's feet, which often ached from cycling. They didn't *have* to hide these intimacies from their lodgers, but April never felt comfortable. Felicity laughed at her prudishness and told her about the clubs in Berlin and London where women danced together and held hands and even kissed. But there was only one place in Easterbridge where April could do such things, and that was eleven Riverside Road. Home.

She wheeled her bicycle round to the shed and let herself in the back door. It led through a tiny scullery into their big, bright, not-always-tidy kitchen, and today she noticed seven cups piled in the sink. So Felicity's writing was going well. No plate – that meant she had forgotten about lunch. No smell of dinner. April sighed. Felicity worked as hard as she did; April didn't expect to come home to her dinner on the table, as Daddy had always done, but this was her busy evening. She had barely an hour before going back out to the girls' club she helped run at Shaw's Mill, a community centre run by Sybil and Henry Barrett, the first couple she had ever introduced. Surely it wasn't too much to hope that Felicity might have shoved something in the oven – a couple of potatoes baked in their jackets would have been better than nothing.

She opened the kitchen door and shouted upstairs, 'Felicity! I'm home!'

'You can't be! It's not time!'

'It is. I'll make us something quick for dinner.'

'Dinner?'

'Aye, you know that thing people eat in the evening?' That thing you promised to make. 'I used to call it my tea before I took up with you.'

'Oh lord – hold on!'

She heard Felicity's chair scrape back from the desk and then her feet patter and then she was flying down the stairs and into the kitchen in a rush of apology which ended in a fit of coughing.

April frowned, turned on the tap, rinsed out one of the seven cups, filled it and handed it to Felicity. 'You're still not over that cold.'

'It's nothing.' Felicity sipped the water, and her breathing returned to normal.

'Sit down and I'll make us something – it'll have to be toast.'

'That's fine. I'm not hungry.'

Well, I am, April thought, taking bread from the breadbin and starting to prepare a quick Welsh rarebit. Never mind, she could get a cup of tea and a bun at Shaw's Mill. The girls in her Thursday club took turns to make and serve supper. They were doing crafts this evening: Miss Dawson was showing them how to make over old hats into Easter bonnets.

As they ate, she told Felicity about Margaret Teal and her brother.

'Why don't you ask him to do a talk at the mill, like that young policeman who spoke about road safety?' Felicity suggested. 'You always say it's hard to get boys involved – greyhound racing might appeal.' She frowned. '*I* don't approve of it, though – surely dogs wouldn't race round a track if they had the choice, and then of course there's the gambling …'

'The lads might like it.' April helped herself to a spoonful of chutney. 'The wee fellas come for woodwork, and the men have their five-aside football, but it's hard getting the older lads in.'

'There are more of them hanging around the streets than there used to be.' Felicity cut into her Welsh rarebit. 'You see them outside the Queen's Head.'

'What Mammy called corner boys. Sure the unemployment's desperate.' April might not have Felicity's political awareness – sometimes she couldn't bear to read the newspapers because things seemed so worrying – but she knew that much. She liked Felicity's idea: Charlie might not want a wife, but he could make new friends if he came to the mill, and at the very least he could do them a good turn. How could she engineer it? Would it be too cheeky to ask the Colonel to ask him? It was different with PC Armstrong: young, keen, recently transferred from another force; it had been part of his job to raise awareness of road safety.

'Which makes them so vulnerable to gangs and organisations,' Felicity said, and April, lost in thoughts of Charlie, the Colonel, greyhounds and PC Armstrong, blinked stupidly. 'When they hear the poison Mosley and his lot spout about foreigners taking the jobs and Hitler having the right idea … And talking of Hitler—'

'Don't,' April said.

'You don't know what I was going to say.'

'You're going to say it's time we had another refugee.'

'It's been a while since Otto and Frieda went.'

'I know.' April's voice was small.

'There are so many in need.'

'But it's so nice having the house to ourselves. I'm awful busy, with the bureau and the mill – thon Lily's as useful as a chocolate teapot.'

'It's not much extra work. They always look after themselves. Look at Frieda – we couldn't stop her cleaning! And Otto did a wonderful job sorting out the shed. You know they always want to repay us somehow. And when you think what they've come from—'

April didn't want Felicity to start her litany of the evils of Nazism. Of course she agreed, but she was tired, still hungry, and had exactly ten minutes before she had to be jolly Miss McVey at Shaw's Mill with the gaggle of girls who thronged there on Thursdays. And she hadn't seen Felicity all day and it would have been nice for her to have agreed that *she* liked having the house to themselves. April admired Felicity's zeal and commitment, but sometimes she would have liked her to be a bit more … she couldn't think of the right word. More *mine*, was the closest she could get. Which was selfish and what Felicity called reactionary.

'It's you I'm thinking about mostly,' she said. 'You haven't shaken off that cough. And you're working too hard. You could do with a wee break.'

'I'll take *a wee break* when we've defeated fascism,' Felicity said, her blue eyes sparking. 'Or should I ask the refugees to take a break from being persecuted until it's more convenient?'

'Don't be an eejit. You know what I mean.'

But that was the trouble. It was all very well loving someone, knowing you wanted to spend your life with them, but Felicity didn't always know what she meant, and April didn't always understand Felicity.

'We'll talk about it when I get home,' she said, 'or when we're less busy.' Which was what they always said, only they never got less busy.

Three

Beyond the fields, the hills had darkened to shadowy humps fringed with the last of an orange-blue sunset. It would be dark before Charlie got home, and by the time he had settled the dogs, lit the fire and had a bit of supper, the evening would be well on. He could have waited for the last bus, but he would rather walk the three miles cross-country than hang about town for two hours. He had offered to escort Margaret all the way to York, where she was to spend a week on retreat before travelling to the Dublin convent, but she had refused.

'It's the same trip I've always done. Change at Leeds and don't talk to strange men,' she had said. 'I don't need a chaperone, Charlie – I'm a big girl now.'

'You'll always be my baby sister.'

'Don't be daft!' But she clung to him on the platform, and though she walked away with her usual jaunty air, the hand gripping the handle of her old suitcase looked very small. Settled in the train, she pulled down the window and called, 'Don't be lonely.'

'How'd I be lonely with the dogs?'

She looked unconvinced. 'Don't be sad, then. Get yourself out. Get yourself a wife.'

'Don't be daft!' He'd been astounded when she had presented him one day with a brochure for, of all things, a marriage bureau. 'What would I do with a wife? And I'm not sad.'

And he wasn't, but now, as Charlie climbed the stile beside Shippards Wood for the shortcut to the village, he couldn't have said he felt happy. Margaret had always known her own mind, but this wasn't the life he'd have chosen for her. Though his mam would have been pleased. And maybe he was being selfish. Margaret's vocation was a gift from God: he should be happy for her.

It felt strange, walking without the dogs. He kept looking back as if expecting Tippy to be at his heels or Tansy to slink from behind the darkening trees or the pups to start scrapping. He quickened his pace: they'd need emptying. They didn't like to soil their beds and it wasn't fair to keep them waiting. Usually he had a few hours off before evening stables and walked them then. He'd called at Yeadons' farm earlier to ask if young Sam could see to them after school but, unusually, there'd been nobody about.

The snicket emerged beside the churchyard at St Luke's Church at the top end of the village. Now he had to walk all the way down the main street and over the bridge, but then he could cut across Yeadons' meadow to the end of his own lane. He hurried past the village shop: if Miss Batley spied him, she'd dash out to ask him to join the bowls team or tell him about a new line in caramels or condole with him about Margaret's leaving and tell him her door was always open. And she would blush and finger the lace collar she always wore over her floral shop coat. Charlie was not vain, but he had not needed Margaret to tell him that Miss Batley had a pash on him. The only woman who did. Apart from Tippy, who adored him with tail-wagging, headbutting intensity, pushing her long nose into the crook of his arm when she walked beside him, gazing up with mild brown eyes. Tansy, independent and aloof, was more her own dog, as well as being the one he had high hopes for, and ridiculous dreams.

He was imagining leading Tansy to the winner's podium at Elland Road, with the crowd cheering, her bright eyes shining under the lights, her black-and-white flanks heaving, a laurel wreath around her neck, when he became aware of a whining behind him. Not a dog, the bus. It chugged past him and pulled up at the stop beside the Blacksmith's Arms. So he'd have been home no sooner if he'd taken it. His neighbour, Joseph Yeadon, emerged from the bus.

'All right then, Joseph?' Charlie said, pleased to have company. 'What you doing in town on a Friday? It's not market day.'

Joseph looked poorly, as if he'd been up all night with a cow. 'It's Florrie. She's having the baby.'

Charlie felt himself blush, which was daft – he had no bother talking about bitches whelping or mares foaling, and he'd helped Joseph deliver more than one calf.

'That's grand,' he said. 'I didn't realise she was, um ...'

Joseph gave an awkward laugh. 'We never expected – at our age! And by the time we realised there was a baby on the way, Florrie was five months gone. Oh, we did get a shock! But we've not said owt, in case, well ...'

'But everything's all right?'

'No,' Joseph said bleakly. 'It's too soon. Only Florrie started with pains this lunchtime, so I called for the doctor and, well, baby's coming. They've sent me home. They said I'm only in the way.'

'Where is she?'

'St John's. Maternity wing.'

'Well, they'll look after her, won't they?' Charlie knew babies were normally born at home; there must be

16

something to worry about if they'd taken Florrie into the hospital. Joseph's first wife had died, must be four years ago now, leaving him with two children; it would be a terrible blow if anything happened to Florrie.

'Oh God, Charlie, I hope so. Only she looked so frightened. I'll never forgive myself if – if anything …'

Charlie's repertoire of reassuring noises was limited, so it was a relief to see the gates of Yeadons' farm approach, the grey stone house square and stolid in the dusk.

Joseph's steps slowed. 'Well, here I am,' he said, reaching for the latch on the gate. Then he turned. 'I don't fancy being on my own. The kids are at my mam's. Would you come in?'

'Can't,' Charlie said. 'I've dogs to see to.'

People didn't always understand that Charlie's life and routine revolved around the animals – his own dogs and the Colonel's stable of hunters – but Joseph was a farmer. 'Well, why don't I fetch a bottle of Florrie's blackberry wine and we'll take it up to yours?'

'Aye, all right.'

Joseph's old sheepdog, Nell, slunk out from a shed. She padded after them on stiff legs, heavy plumed tail waving, and kept with them all the way, tongue lolling.

'She'll not win any races,' Charlie said.

'No, bless her; she must be fourteen. But she's a grand lass.' Joseph reached down to scratch behind the old dog's ears. 'Let's see these champions, then,' he said as Charlie's cottage came into view.

They went straight to the old stone shed out the back, the dogs already barking a welcome. He'd divided it into four good kennels and a whelping pen, with a small yard.

'You've a grand set-up here,' Joseph said.

'I gallop them in the paddock. It's a bit rough, but it gets them fit. Come on, lasses.' The two bitches, fawn Tippy and black-and-white Tansy, pranced out of their kennels and snaked round the men's legs before dashing out to the yard and relieving themselves.

'Only two?' Joseph asked. 'I thought you were in a bigger way of going. What about that big black dog? They were saying down the Blacksmith's that he was a champion.'

'Ted.' Charlie lit the lantern he kept on a hook on the door. 'I sold him to Eddie Blythe.' Preparing Margaret for a life of poverty hadn't been cheap. Eddie Blythe was a big trainer in Leeds with deep pockets and an eye for a good dog. Someday Charlie would have to watch Ted win for Eddie.

Charlie opened the kennel shared by the brindle pups and they streamed out, striped and dappled in brown and gold. Tippy trotted off to the corner of the yard, keeping a cool eye on the frolicking pups as if she remembered too well their nipping mouths and scrabbling paws.

Joseph laughed. 'She's glad to be rid.'

'Aye, they're six months old now.'

'Any good?'

The two men leaned over the wall and watched the dogs in the gloaming. Charlie set the lantern between them. 'Too soon to say. You don't do much until they're about a year old. Then you see if they show interest in rabbits in the fields, then take them for a trial.' He kept his voice casual. There was so much that could go wrong – a bout of distemper could wipe out a litter in days, and survivors were likely to be weaklings. Even if the dogs thrived, they mightn't make it. There were dogs who wouldn't chase the mechanical hare, dogs who fought, dogs who couldn't be bothered, and of course dogs that simply weren't fast enough. He'd even had one that used to turn himself round in the trap so that he came out arse first, and by the time he righted himself the race was over. So it was best not to count any chickens. 'The sire was a champion. I took Tippy here all the way to Durham to get served. She was no world beater, but she was a decent sprinter before she broke her leg. So, well, you hope, don't you? It's all you can do.'

Joseph sighed. 'Aye,' he said.

Charlie knew he wasn't thinking of dogs.

A bird had started to build in the hedge that hugged the wall: blackbird probably. It wasn't finished, but already the little cup of twigs and earth was recognisably a nest. Tippy and Tansy were back at the shed door now; it was past feeding time. Charlie whistled for the pups and showed Joseph how to put on the little sheepskin coats they wore at night, while he mixed their meat and biscuits. He could happily have stayed there all evening with the soft huffs and snuffs of his dogs, their simple single-minded focus on eating and then curling up to sleep on their beds. Easier than trying to find reassuring things to say about wives and childbirth, about which he knew nothing. But once the dogs were settled, he could drag it out no longer.

'I'll fix us something to eat,' he said.

He had grown used to an empty house, but he still disliked that first moment of homecoming, when the room struck dark and chill and the chairs at either side of the kitchen range were big empty shadows. But he soon had the lamps lit and the fire raked into life, and a supper of bread and cheese on the table. The blackberry wine, though not something he would have chosen, was cheering, the second glass going down easier than the first. Nell slunk under Joseph's chair and settled into a heavy sleep punctuated by soft snores. Margaret had left an apple tart in the larder – she must have baked it that morning when he was at work. He wondered if she had had to wait long for her connection in Leeds, if she was being well fed in the convent, if she was homesick. He cut two large wedges of pie and Joseph tucked in as if his wife had been away a month rather than a day. Anxiety wasn't putting him off his grub, which was just as well given how he was putting away the wine.

'You'll miss your Margaret,' Joseph said.

Charlie nodded. 'I will, aye.'

'Strange life,' Joseph said.

'A useful one,' Charlie said. 'And Margaret's always known her own mind. Even as a little lass she was stubborn, set on her own will. Not pious; I'd no idea she had a vocation until she was leaving school.'

As was generally the case with Protestants, Joseph shied away from such talk. 'And she's – what? – nineteen years younger than you?'

'Aye, about that.'

'It'll be a big gap between my two and the baby. I mean, if the baby – if everything's all right.'

'D'you think they'll be jealous?' Best to speak as if the impending birth was a foregone conclusion, with nothing to worry about.

Joseph shook his head. 'I don't think so. They both took to Florrie – it was hard on them when Kate died.' Again, that bleak, terrified look so that Charlie, for want of anything more constructive to do, poured them both another glass. 'Sam's only interested in farming, follows me round like old Nell here.' The dog stirred in her sleep though she was surely too deaf to have heard her name. 'I think Sally imagines something like a pet lamb.'

'Well, I suppose it is,' Charlie said, relieved to have the talk safely back on four legs. Though lambs often became pets because the ewe had died. 'A lamb'd be quieter than a baby. Margaret used to scream the place down.'

'Your mam can't have been young,' Joseph said. 'But she was all right?' His eyes bored into Charlie's, desperate for reassurance.

Charlie hesitated. 'Well – she'd just lost my father, and she'd had the Spanish flu – that's what he died of – so she wasn't *exactly* all right. But that doesn't mean Florrie won't be.'

'Kate died in childbirth. Baby and all. I wouldn't mind so much about the baby this time, as long as Florrie …'

Oh God. What was he meant to say? 'Well, at least she's in the hospital. They wouldn't have sent you away if they'd been really worried, would they? And Mam was bad for a long time, and baby Margaret was a sickly scrap, but they were both grand in the end.'

Even so, it had been the end of Charlie's own career. 'Don't come home,' Mam had insisted. 'Your work is too important. I'll manage.' She had been so proud of him, doing something she could boast about at Mass and down the shops. Prouder than she ever was of him as a groom, though she'd been grateful for the cottage that went with his job. His father had been Colonel Lucey's batman during the war – 'helped me out of no end of a tight spot,' the Colonel said, and he had wanted to help his widow and son, even though Charlie was a city boy, with no knowledge of country life. Flu, widowhood and pregnancy had left Mam weak, but the upland air suited her. Charlie discovered an affinity with horses, and it had been easier than anyone knew to give up his original plans.

He told Joseph a little of this now. Not the whole story: that would have taken more than a few glasses of blackberry wine. He said only that he had been away from home, studying for a job and had had to change his plans.

'I don't regret it,' he said. 'I love these moors, and my work. You know where you are with animals. And the Colonel's a decent boss. Lends me his Bentley shooting brake to take the dogs racing. Not many bosses'd do that.'

Joseph grunted. 'Aye, he's not the worst. Eccentric old bugger, mind.'

'He is that.'

'He's met his match now!' They both smiled, thinking of the Colonel's recent marriage. Thomasina Longbottom – now Lucey – was a fierce tweedy lady of indeterminate age and boundless energy, generally flanked by English setters. She had moved into Lucey Hall with her dogs and two flashy chestnut mares, Scarlet and Carnelian, who carried her with the Shippard Valley Hunt twice a week during the season. It was Charlie's job to exercise them when Mrs Lucey was too busy with her dogs, her good works or accompanying her husband on motor tours in their big Crossley.

'You know they met through a matchmaker?' Charlie wouldn't have said this if he had been quite sober, but he wanted to get Joseph away from worrying about Florrie. And he was breaking no confidences: the Colonel was thrilled that Thomasina had been introduced to him by the marriage bureau in Easterbridge. 'Splendid gels,' he told anyone who would listen. 'Took them a while to find my Thomsy, but by God she was worth the wait.' And Mrs Lucey showed no embarrassment either. 'Damned sensible,' she said. 'I shouldn't have had a notion where to find a chap.'

'Actually,' Charlie admitted now, 'our Margaret wanted me to sign up with them too! Can you imagine me in a marriage bureau?' He laughed. This blackberry wine was grand stuff when you got used to it.

'The True Minds Marriage Bureau?' Joseph looked sheepish. 'I, er, know it.' He smiled into his glass.

It took Charlie a moment to catch his meaning. 'You and Florrie?'

Joseph nodded. 'Aye. I knew pretty quick after Kate

died that I'd wed again. I couldn't manage the kids and the house as well as the farm, and it was so bloody lonely.' He rushed on. 'I read about the bureau in the *Easterbridge Recorder* and they found me Florrie. We liked each other. The kids took to her and that was it.' He went off into a rhapsody about Florrie – how loving she was, how good with the children, how she had changed his life …

Charlie sat back, sipping the last of his wine.

It was so bloody lonely.

Don't be lonely.

He wasn't lonely. As he had told Margaret, how could he be, with the dogs? There was always something to do, somewhere to take them, some hope to keep you going. And the daily routine of caring for and training them left you with no time to wonder whether or not you were lonely.

And he wasn't. You didn't miss what you'd never had. It was different for the Colonel – he'd struggled with civilian life, especially after his old mother died, and he needed someone to look after him. Different for Joseph with kids to bring up. Joseph's rhapsody took a darker turn as the level in the wine bottle went down: how Florrie had saved him, how he hadn't believed there could be happiness like that again, how proud he was of her for giving him another child, how he'd never forgive himself if …

But he, Charlie, was grand. He was used to this quiet room, the tick of the clock on the mantelpiece bringing him closer to the dogs' bedtime empty, the crackle of the fire. And then he became aware of an alien sound, a sort of rusty sobbing. Joseph was crying. Tears rolled down his ruddy face.

'Oh lord, Charlie, I'm sorry, but I bloody love her. I can't lose her – not again.'

The naked agony in his voice made Charlie glance away

into the flames, and to shiver despite the heat in the room. He had never loved anyone enough to cause that terrible, searing fear of loss.

'Come on, Joe, lad.' He stood up and took Joseph's glass from him. He had never called him Joe. 'You've had enough. I'll set you home.' He patted his shoulder.

'But I—'

'You'll be better in your own house – they'll telephone, won't they, when there's news?'

'Aye, they will.' He sniffed and wiped his face.

'Well, you need to be there. Come on.'

Joseph was a heavyset man who had consumed a lot of wine; Charlie had to do a fair bit of hauling to get him to his feet and outside. But finally he set off on his way with old Nell limping ahead, a denser darkness in the spring night.

Four

The child is dead.

Well over a year later, the words still twisted themselves round every thought, and the reality, the fact of it, was there, always.

The child is dead.

Evelyn had heard Maurice say the words, and one part of her brain registered his meaning, knew he would not lie, not about this, but still she could not believe it. Children weren't meant to die. Sickly, poor children, maybe – there were plenty of those in Lisnacashan, snattery-nosed, bandy-legged scraps – but not bonny, strong lads like her wee Robbie. One minute running about the yard, then—

Maurice had carried him in from the barn, and Jamesie the farmhand had run for Doctor Liddell, but it was too late.

Her child. Her life. The one thing that was hers.

And it was her fault.

That was the part nobody knew. If they did, they would stop being so kind with their apple tarts and lamb stews, their prayers and kindly-meant reassurances: *she was young; she would get over it; please God*, the more tactless ones said, *she could have another child.*

And over and over again, wanting to make her feel better: *it was an accident. It could have happened to anyone.*

Farms were dangerous places. Children were curious and wee boys had no sense of danger. She could only have taken her eyes off him for a minute. A moment. Nobody blamed her. She was a good mother. Even Maurice's old witch of a mammy said that. 'You were a grand wee mother, Evelyn.'

Only Evelyn hadn't been. Not grand enough to keep her child safe. And now she wasn't a mother at all.

The neighbourly concern had dried up as the weeks became months and the seasons turned, and then it was a year and more. Oh, she knew fine well what they said now: *surely it was time young Mrs Kenny was getting over her tragedy.*

She sat in the dark kitchen, not bothering to put the light on, not bothering to clean. She didn't read or listen to the wireless. She just sat. He had died on the twentieth of January, and exactly a year later, on his anniversary, the king had died too. *Fancy that*, people said, as though she should get some comfort from it. But there was no comfort to be had: the king was an old man of seventy and Robbie had been four. The king had died peacefully in his bed, while Robbie—

No. Don't think about the details.

The king had been replaced instantly – Edward VIII had been declared king the very next day – whereas she would never have another child, whatever people said about how young she was. She didn't feel young.

Maurice carried on as though nothing had happened. Worked the farm. Went into town with his cronies on a Saturday night, where he never had more than two glasses of Guinness. Went to church on Sunday mornings and didn't argue when she refused to go too. He never mentioned his son's name.

On Easter Sunday morning, when Evelyn dragged herself up to the range to cook his breakfast, Maurice cleared his throat and said, 'Mammy thinks it's time you came back to church.'

'Does she now?' She dropped the lard into the pan where it started to sizzle.

'Come on, Evvie. People would like to see you.'

'Well, I don't want to see people.' She threw in two sausages, a couple of rashers.

'It'd do you good to get out of the house. Get some fresh air.'

She snorted. 'I'd not get much fresh air in church.' She hadn't set foot in First Lisnacashan Presbyterian since the funeral. A coffin wasn't meant to be that small.

'You know what I mean. See about you. A wee change of scene.'

He was so bloody patient and reasonable; she would have preferred him to rant and rage and *react*.

'It's a grand day. I could put the hood down on the car; you'd get plenty of fresh air that way. We could take a wee drive afterwards.'

'It's too cold.' The rashers were starting to curl; she flipped them over and squashed them up to the edge of the pan to make room for the potato farls and soda bread. Ugh. She could boke at the thought of a fry.

'You could wrap up. Mammy'd like to see you.'

'Sure she's only across the yard.' Their bungalow had always felt too close to Maurice's home place, the big stone farmhouse where Mona lived alone now. She reached across him to the egg crock. 'One or two?'

'Two.' Maurice loved his fry.

So seen on him, Evelyn thought, feeling her lip curl at the sight of his belly pressing against his good navy waistcoat. She cracked the eggs into the pan. One of the yolks broke, bleeding bright yellow slime into the fat. She stifled a retch.

She tossed the food out on to a plate and set it on the table. 'Don't spill that on your good suit,' she warned, and handed him a clean napkin from the dresser drawer. She wet the tea.

He sat down and obediently tucked the napkin into his shirt collar. He thanked her and said it looked great. He didn't complain about the broken egg or the fact that the bacon wasn't as crispy as he liked. In fairness, Maurice wasn't one for complaining. He never hit her. He didn't drink much or gamble. He hadn't been a catch, exactly: older than her, already running to fat and baldness, but he was a decent man with a good farm, all his now his daddy had died. They hadn't been *un*happy. They had had Robbie.

And now they didn't. Now there was nothing between them, and too much between them, and Robbie was not to be spoken of, and the other thing was never to be spoken of. They could say *one egg or two?* and *thank you for the fry*, but they could not talk about the truth.

'Are you not having anything? You've gone very skinny.' He would not have let his cows get so thin.

'My stomach's sick. I'll drink the tea.' She lived on tea, strong and black; the smell of milk turned her. Sometimes, when he was out on the farm, she added a wee tot of Bushmills. She was never drunk. It didn't dull the pain, it was just a habit she'd started. The bottle was nearly done; it was one Jamesie McAlinden's mammy had sent last Christmas to thank Maurice for keeping poor Jamesie on, even though there wasn't much work in him. Maurice was good to him. He was a good man. In his own way.

'A jaunt to church would lift you, love. And it's Easter Sunday.'

She stiffened when he called her *love*. But the tea was settling her stomach, and the sun was shining through the streaked kitchen window. If she stayed at home, she would sit and look at the dirty windows. The bungalow had once been her pride and joy, polished and shining and new; now she didn't care how smeared the windows were. She might as well go and sit in the church and look at the windows there.

The windows in First Lisnacashan Presbyterian were stained glass, depicting bible scenes. Jesus balancing precariously on the prow of a boat. Jesus holding out the loaves and fishes. *Behold, I am with you always* in blue and red glass. Well, that was a lie. God wasn't with her. And he hadn't been with Robbie the day he'd let him die.

No, Evelyn, that was your job.

Miss Connaughton, who kept the haberdasher's, caught her eye and smiled. It was a kind smile, but Evelyn looked away and concentrated on Reverend McClure. He gripped the pulpit and words flew out of his mouth. She tried, not very hard, to catch them, but they dried up in the stuffy air.

Reverend McClure had called to see her after the accident. He had said the death of a child was hard to accept, but that the Lord had his ways and it was best not to question. He said that Robbie would be saved because he had taken the Lord Jesus Christ as his personal saviour.

'Robbie was four,' Evelyn had spat back. 'He barely knew who the Lord Jesus Christ was.'

The minister had sucked his teeth and said he was sure that wasn't the case at all, coming from a good Christian home. She wasn't to worry.

'Ah, that's grand, then,' she had said. 'I'll not give him another thought.'

He had looked at her very strangely and had spoken for a long time to Maurice at the front door.

Maurice sat beside her now in the box pew, eyes half closed as if in private prayer, big farmer's hands clasped over his belly. She saw, with a tiny spike of meanness, that there was a very faint egg stain on his waistcoat after all. He had not been as careful as he had tried to be.

Her mother-in-law, Mona, sat on his other side, her bulk buttoned tight into her heavy black wool coat, her bible clutched in black-gloved hands. 'I have known loss too,' she was fond of telling Evelyn. 'My Robert.' Robert, Maurice's daddy, had died three years ago aged seventy-eight. It was not the same. Evelyn's own father was dead and her mammy had gone out to Canada to her sister, and those were losses, but they were not the same either. They had not torn her heart out. Mona was giving her funny looks, her mouth so pursed her lips had disappeared. What's wrong with me? Evelyn wondered. She hadn't washed her hair for weeks; could Mona smell it, even though it was under her hat? Was it her clothes? Her Sunday coat, bought on a shopping trip to Dungannon two Septembers ago after a good harvest, was a rich cherry colour. She was never allowed to wear red as a child – *not with your hair!* Maybe that was why she had fallen in love with it. She must have worn a black coat for the funeral; she thought maybe someone had lent her one. She couldn't remember. Was Mona disapproving of the red coat because it was unbecoming or because she deemed it unsuitable for a woman who had lost a child? Did *she* smell? She had not been washing much of late. She gave a little sniff to see if she could detect anything, but she had had a sickly smell in her nose for weeks now so she couldn't tell.

Washing. That was what Reverend McClure was talking about. Being washed in the blood of the lamb. Robbie loved the lambs on the farm. He loved the calves and the chickens and the sheepdog and all the wee kittens in the barn.

It was very strange that the space inside the box pew should be getting smaller, but it was. There were only three people where there once had been five, and yet the pew was shrinking. There was no room for her. Was it Mona and Maurice? They were neither of them thin, but no, they had not grown that much. It was her. Her grief was expanding, swelling like a balloon. Maybe it would burst. Maybe she would. She was burning. She wished she could take off her coat. What was she wearing underneath? She couldn't remember dressing. She touched her neck and her fingers closed reassuringly on something silky. Ah! Of course she had dressed. Her black and grey rayon frock. That was all right. But she couldn't take her coat off in church. She felt a giggle burble up at the very idea – the people who wanted to see her would see more than they bargained for! – and then the swelling giggle burned her throat, a familiar wave of icy horror drenched her, and she knew, because it happened often these days, that she was about to be sick.

She pushed past Mona and Maurice, hand clamped to her mouth, and dashed for the door. She heard her heels clatter on the tiles and a little moan in her throat and somewhere, inside her head only, but deafening, a desperate prayer – Don't let me boke in the church, oh please, dear God, whatever you do.

Door, porch, stone steps, air, oh God, the blessed cool air! She made it almost to the gate before bending over to vomit into the grass. And after all that drama, it was no more than the tea she had had for breakfast, sour and burning. A dizzy weakness made her sway and she grabbed the nearest headstone for support, trying to take in big clean breaths of air, as if she could purge the sickness in her with pure clear air, leaving nothing inside. Slowly the dizziness settled, and she straightened up cautiously, noticing, with bleak amusement, that the grave she had boked over belonged to Jim McVey, her old friend April's daddy. Her own daddy was buried in this churchyard too. And Robbie. Maurice had planted bulbs on his grave in the autumn; now – she could see it from the corner of her eye – daffodils waved and danced, but she couldn't make herself go over.

She closed her eyes and held her face to the cool spring sun, still taking in those big clean breaths. Her heart was pounding. From inside the church, the Reverend McClure's voice thundered and fell, thundered and fell.

'Mrs Kenny? Evelyn?'

She opened her eyes.

'I don't want to intrude, but would a mint settle your stomach?'

It was Miss Connaughton, a stout, freckled woman about fifty. Evelyn knew her from the shop, had often gone in for wool and fabric and bits and pieces. Miss Connaughton rummaged in her bag and produced a bag of mint imperials.

Evelyn accepted one with shaking fingers: a sharp burst of freshness, clean and cool in her mouth. 'I'm grand,' she said presently. 'It happens a lot.'

'Och, you're hardly grand, Evelyn.' Miss Connaughton's voice was as matter-of-fact as if she had been telling a customer she was sorry she had no grey darning wool. 'Not after losing your child.'

Her directness was so startling that Evelyn's eyes filled with tears. She hadn't cried much. Tears might be a relief and she didn't deserve relief. Besides, they were an embarrassment to others. But Miss Connaughton was looking at her with undisguised sympathy, and no awkwardness.

'He was a grand wee fella,' she said. 'I mind your mammy bringing him into the shop in his pram, before she went away, and he was fascinated by the wool – I suppose it was all the colours. I mind him staring with his eyes like saucers, and pointing and saying, "Look at the rainbow, Granny!" Och, he was a great wee cub altogether. But you don't need me to tell you that.'

'I didn't know,' Evelyn said, 'about the wool.' She sniffed and dashed her hand over her eyes. It touched her that, even as a baby in his pram, Robbie had had a life away from her, had sparked memories in strangers. Evelyn had not known about the rainbow wool, and Mammy had never mentioned it – or maybe she had, and Evelyn hadn't taken it in, absorbed in something else, not realising that there would come a time when memories of her child would be all she had.

Miss Connaughton gestured towards a bench beyond the row of graves. 'Will we sit a wee minute?' She didn't make further conversation, just sat and let Evelyn weep, a stolid presence, content to sit and look at the daffodils along the edge of the path and the silent neat graves. Only when Evelyn started to fumble for a handkerchief did she move, to produce one of her own from her large brown bag. Miss Connaughton sold fancy lace handkerchiefs in the shop, and Evelyn gave a damp giggle at the unlikely plain serviceable white square.

'I must look an awful sight,' she mourned. She took off her hat and ran her hands through her damp, greasy hair.

Miss Connaughton eyed her judiciously. 'You look like someone who's suffering,' she said. 'But' – becoming practical – 'you've plenty of time to sort yourself out. The Reverend McClure looked like he was settling into one of his hour-long specials. You know what he's like on high days and holidays.' Indeed, even here, the rumble of his sermonising reached them. 'Caroline used to say he should do the opposite – keep it short and sweet on those days, when people turn up who don't come all year round. That way he might tempt them back to the fold, instead of putting them off for another six months.'

'Caroline?'

'Miss McGlone. She died two years ago come May.'

'Yes, of course. I'm sorry.' Miss McGlone had been Miss Connaughton's companion. They had shared the flat above the haberdashery for as long as she could remember.

'When she died, people didn't know what to say,' Miss Connaughton said. 'They crossed the street to avoid me.'

'I know what that feels like.' Not that losing a friend, however close, was the same as losing a child.

'And when they *couldn't* avoid me – because of the shop – they made sure to talk about everything *but* Caroline. The price of wool. The new fashions in sleeves.' Miss Connaughton sighed. 'And actually,' she went on, 'I *wanted* to talk about Caroline. I liked it when people shared memories of her.'

Evelyn couldn't think of a single memory of Caroline McGlone. She had simply been a fixture of the town, like Miss Connaughton herself. She had helped in the shop, but mostly she had kept house, so she was seen about the town more than her companion, doing the shopping. She had had very dark hair, Evelyn remembered, which had turned grey in dramatic, badgery streaks. That didn't feel like something she could share, so she said instead, 'People don't even mention Robbie now because I'm meant to have *got over* it. So when you said about the wool it was … it made me cry, but it was nice.'

'Good.'

'People said they were sorry for my loss. And that the accident could have happened to anyone. But they never talk about Robbie as a *person*. Not even Maurice.'

Miss Connaughton offered her another mint, taking one herself, and they sucked companionably. Evelyn replaced her hat.

'I feel sorry for men,' Miss Connaughton said at length. 'I think, in general, they find it harder to talk. Have you good friends?'

Evelyn shook her head.

'You were great pals with the wee McVey girl, weren't you? I mind the two of you coming into the shop for hair ribbons. She was a bright wee thing.'

Evelyn smiled. 'That's April all right.'

'And what's she doing now?'

'She's in England. She's in charge of a marriage bureau.'

'Dear bless us! And is she married herself?'

Evelyn shook her head. 'Not yet. She lives with a pal. Like you and Caroline.' Though April was pretty and lively and must meet men all the time at her work, so she would be bound to marry soon.

'Could you go and visit her, maybe? A change might do you good.'

Evelyn shook her head. The idea of making a decision, of having to pack and travel – trains and boats and strangers – was exhausting enough to bring back the nausea. And – her heart squeezed – how could she go and leave Robbie? Not so much his grave, but his wee room, full of the things he had loved and touched, and the fields and yards where he had run and played. On the other hand – to get away from Maurice. From Mona. From Lisnacashan. From the barn and the memories.

'I don't know,' she said. 'Actually, she does keep inviting me, but she's just being polite. I haven't been great at keeping in touch.'

Miss Connaughton patted her hand. 'That doesn't matter when you're truly friends. It's just an idea – a week or two away. And it's none of my business, of course, but' – she looked slightly embarrassed – 'is there any special reason why you *shouldn't* travel?'

Evelyn looked at her stupidly.

'You said you've been sick a lot. I wondered if …'

'Oh!' Evelyn felt her face burn. 'No. I just can't eat.'

'All the more reason to get away for a change.'

'I couldn't leave Maurice. It wouldn't be right. People would talk.'

'And that bothers you?'

'No,' she realised. After all, where was Maurice now? It must have been obvious that she was ill, in distress, yet he had sat on smugly in his family pew with that old bitch Mona. She heard, above the gentle voice of Miss Connaughton and the constant accusations of her own inner voice, April's firm tone. *Never mind Maurice*, she was saying, *or his old ma. Let them run on to hell.*

Let them indeed. For the first time since it had happened, Evelyn felt her mouth stretch into the beginnings of a smile.

Five

'She's just another kind of refugee,' April pointed out. 'I don't understand why you don't want her.' She turned back the top sheet over the blankets and folded it in neatly. They were changing the bed, their usual Saturday morning chore.

Felicity sighed. 'I never said that.'

'But ...?'

'There isn't any but.' Felicity pushed her pillow deeper into its case and set it back on the bed with a thump. A single feather floated out and she stifled a sneeze. 'I'd heard about a man from Munich – a friend of Erich and Hanna's, a teacher – and I'd hoped to have him next, but – this would only be for a few days?'

April took Evelyn's letter from her pocket and skimmed it, though she knew it off by heart. 'She says *a wee while*. But it's quite a journey from Lisnacashan. It wouldn't make sense for less than a week or ten days.' She lifted the counterpane from over the back of the chair and threw it across the top of the bed.

Facing each other across the bed, they smoothed the embroidered counterpane over the blankets. It was, like most things in the house, Felicity's, a Bavarian folk design, bright and jolly, but worn and thin in places.

'That old bedspread's near had it,' April said. 'We should treat ourselves to a new one. They've lovely stuff at the mill. A wee woman from Coaldale weaves them – they're dear but we could go halves.'

'I like this one,' Felicity said. 'Hanna bought it for my first Christmas in Bavaria. And stop changing the subject. I don't mind Evelyn coming, I'm just saying that I wouldn't want it to interfere with our refugee commitments.'

'Does it matter *who* we help, so long as it's someone who needs it? Surely it will be easier to have Evelyn than strangers.'

'Easier for *you*. She's your best friend.'

April felt stung. 'That's not fair. Sure half the time you and the refugees jabber away in German.'

'That's not the same.'

'And she's hardly my best friend these days – I hadn't heard from her in ages. But when her wee boy died I felt so bad for her. So if coming here might help …'

Could Felicity possibly be *jealous*? She knew, of course, that Evelyn had once been the most important person in April's life. But that was when they were girls. Decades ago. Evelyn was married now. April lived with Felicity. It had never been *romantic*, not even in the days when they roamed Lisnacashan all day and sneaked out to each other's houses in the evenings. But it had been intense, the way girls sometimes were. She and Felicity had not had that intensity for ages. There was always something in the way: refugees, housework, meetings, Felicity's writing, April's work at the marriage bureau and Shaw's Mill. Their conversations were more likely to be about who had time to pick up some groceries, and the damp spot in the hall.

But the mention of the dead child seemed to stir something in Felicity. She pushed her hair back off her face. 'No, you're right. How dreadful to lose a child. If we can do anything to help, we must. Write and tell her to come as soon as she likes. For as long as she likes.'

'And why don't we do something nice today?' April suggested. 'We've hardly seen each other lately. We could take a picnic up Shippards Hill' – Felicity frowned; she wasn't a big fan of the outdoors – 'or call and see Martha and Fabian? We've hardly seen them either.'

Martha, who owned the bureau, had married Felicity's brother Fabian a year ago.

'It's the third Saturday,' Felicity said. 'Anti-Fascist League meeting in Leeds. I can't miss it. There's no shortage of things to discuss, between Germany and Italy – and I don't like how things are going in Spain.'

I don't like how things are going in eleven Riverside Road, April thought.

'You should come with me,' Felicity went on, 'if you'd like us to spend more time together.'

April screwed up her face. 'When you're in an office five days a week, the last thing you need on a Saturday is a meeting.'

'And when you live in a fascist state three hundred and sixty-five days a year, the last thing you need is for the outside world to forget about you,' Felicity shot back.

'I know.'

'And it's not just Europe.' Felicity could never let things lie. 'There are fascist organisations all over England. I've heard rumours about the back room of the Black Horse. It's everywhere. I'm thinking of starting an anti-fascist league here in Easterbridge. Possibly just for women.'

April leaned across the bed and kissed Felicity. She touched her cheek. 'You go and save the world, love. I'll write to Evelyn.'

***

April stepped off her pedals, took the envelope from her bicycle basket, and dropped it into the postbox beside the bridge. The spring air warmed her hands and cheeks and she decided to take a wee spin up past the park to see if Fabian and Martha were in.

They were delighted to see her. Martha showed her into the conservatory where they had clearly been in the middle of a game of a chess. 'It's *just* warm enough to sit in here,' she said. 'I'll make some tea.'

'You've saved me from ignominious defeat,' Fabian said. 'Or at least postponed it. By the time we resume, she might have forgotten whatever dastardly scheme she was concocting.'

April laughed. 'Felicity's tried to teach me chess,' she said. 'But I'm too impatient. I thought I'd mastered thinking *one* step ahead, but it turns out you need to be about four, and my brain doesn't work that way. It's ages since we've played anyway. We never have time.'

Fabian looked at her closely. 'I shouldn't make personal remarks, April, but you look tired.'

'I am,' she admitted. 'I never stop working.'

'And that's partly my fault. For taking Martha away.'

'It is, aye.' True Minds belonged to Martha, who had set it up in 1924 as a young war widow, but she trusted April to take charge of the day-to-day running and all but the biggest decisions. Which was flattering, but exhausting. 'But sure, yous are happy as Larry.' Something in his face made her say, 'Don't tell me there's trouble in paradise?' She thought of Fabian and Martha as *her* couple: two lonely, widowed people who had brought each other such joy, and who would never have got together without April.

'We're splendid,' Fabian assured her. 'We're enjoying the car; lovely drives out at weekends, and Martha's learning to drive it too. But during the week I wonder if life's too quiet for her. After the cut and thrust of the matchmaking world.'

April laughed. 'I don't know how you imagine the True Minds Marriage Bureau,' she said, 'but I can assure you there's not a lot of cutting or thrusting going on. I miss Martha, I won't lie. Thon Lily's neither use nor ornament, but I haven't the heart to sack her.'

'What's this about sacking?' Martha returned with the tea tray.

Fabian lifted the chess board carefully from the table and set it on the broad stone windowsill.

'Lily's not up to the job. I have to double check her filing and you daren't let her answer the phone. But I promised her six months' experience, so I'll have to keep her until June. And her mammy's glad of the few shillings – she's seven of a family and Lily's the wisest.'

'Oh dear. That reminds me of when I was looking for an assistant. I was so lucky to find you.'

'You were, aye.' Nostalgia pricked her: those early days in Easterbridge; she and Martha working side by side in the cosy office, making plans together, rejoicing at their successes. But there had been lonely days too, adrift in a new town, trying to fill empty evenings and making quite a few professional mistakes. Lord, the blunders she'd made! Martha hadn't always been looking at her as fondly as she was now, smiling over the china teapot, offering her a slice of homemade ginger cake.

'Your first girl was jolly good, wasn't she?' Martha asked.

'Clara. Yes, very efficient.' Annoyingly so. She had been full of her own opinions, and April had never warmed to her. It was a relief when Clara had taken her opinions and her superior typing skills off to a big educational agency in Leeds where there would be more scope for her talents.

And when April had realised she couldn't run the bureau alone, she had engaged an assistant who was really only a clerk. Someone who wouldn't dare challenge her. Who would let her be in charge. She had her own arrogance to blame for Lily and she knew it.

'But how are things otherwise?' Martha asked, when they were settled with tea and cake. They never minded talking business with Fabian present: as a solicitor he was almost ridiculously discreet.

'Grand. I had this very horsey woman, she practically neighed, and I introduced her to a vet from Bramham. He's more used to cows but he fancied getting more experience with horses. And luckily he fancied her too.'

Martha laughed. 'Excellent.'

'And you remember thon nice wee police officer who was transferred from Newcastle? Constable Armstrong? He gave a talk at the mill about road safety.'

'Oh yes. Tall chap. Rather shy. Has he signed up?'

'Not exactly. But I told him about us, so I'm expecting him to get in touch any day.'

Martha smiled. 'Nobody can fault your optimism, April. But you have to stop seeing every unattached person as a potential client.'

'I wonder who I got that from?'

Martha sighed. 'I did love it.' She took a thoughtful nibble of cake. 'But what about *actual* clients?'

'The Honourable Augusta Wyndham-Howard signed up yesterday,' April said, giving weight to every impressive syllable. 'She's a pal of Sybil Barrett's from finishing school.'

'Splendid. Have you anyone in mind?' Martha looked suddenly serious. 'I know you're rather modern about class, especially since you took up with Felicity, but please tell me you don't plan to introduce her to a gamekeeper or – or a clerk?'

42

April laughed. 'How did you know?' she asked wickedly, but relented when she saw the alarm on Martha's face. 'Ah, don't worry, I've a couple of swanky fellas up my sleeve. No, I can't tell you any more than that.' The swanky fellas were not as far up her sleeve as she would have wished. They existed, in fact, rather more at arm's length. Or indeed in her imagination. But she was hopeful. 'And wait till I tell you about the wee nun,' she went on.

'A *nun*? How could even you—'

'Ladies, I'll take my tea into the sitting room and do some paperwork,' Fabian said.

Both women laughed, and Martha caught his hand affectionately as he left the room.

April told her about Margaret Teal. 'But not a dicky bird from the Charlie boy so I doubt he's interested. And I've someone on the books who'd be *perfect*.' She sighed. 'Mind you, I've a Plan B for him if he doesn't sign up, but I haven't had time to do anything about it.'

Martha looked slightly frightened, as someone with experience of April's Plan Bs. April could almost see her fighting with herself not to interfere.

Instead she said, 'Give him time to really miss his sister. Oh dear, does that sound calculating?'

'Once a matchmaker, always a matchmaker.'

Martha sighed and looked wistful.

For dear sake, April thought, why didn't she just come back to True Minds? Even a few days a week? All right, it wasn't the thing for a solicitor's wife to work, but when it was her own business …

But she had vowed never to put pressure on Martha, so she changed the subject. 'Well, the big news is from Miss Murrell – Mrs Yeadon, I should say. Remember she married thon big farmer fella?'

'Of course. She was lovely. They both were.'

'She's had a baby!'

'How wonderful.'

Martha clasped her hands, and April wondered, not for the first time, if she and Fabian hoped for a child. She was forty, younger than Florrie Yeadon; it wasn't impossible. Like Florrie, she was a stepmother, to Fabian's teenage daughter Prudence, and had never mentioned wanting a baby. But that didn't mean she wouldn't like one. It was something they never discussed, April having no interest in babies beyond a vague appreciation that they were generally considered a good thing. She was grateful that she didn't have the urge for a child of her own, which was certainly what brought many of their female clients to True Minds.

'Aye. The wee cratur was early; they thought she mightn't do, but she seems to be thriving now. Dorothy, they call her. Wee Miss Dawson's already got the knitting needles out.' Miss Dawson, a former neighbour of April's, had come out of retirement to teach handicrafts at Shaw's Mill. She was close to eighty and struggled with walking, but her fingers and mind were as nimble as ever and she loved nothing better than a baby to knit for. Sally Yeadon attended her handicrafts class, which was enough of a connection for her.

'I must send a note,' Martha said. 'I wonder if I can still crochet. I always think of our bureau babies as very special.'

'I've sent a card,' April said, 'but I've no time to make anything. I hardly have time to turn round these days between the bureau and the mill.'

'And Felicity?'

'You know Felicity.' April kept her voice light.

'Fabian worries about her. She seems to choose such difficult paths in life.'

'You mean living with me?'

'Not at all!' Martha shook her head and refreshed April's cup without asking. 'He's thrilled you and she chummed up. Thinks you're a steadying influence.' They both smiled at the irony. 'No, it's her involvement in radical politics, all those rallies she goes to, and protesting about fascism and bringing such odd people home.'

'They're not odd, Martha. They're just not lucky enough to come from a decent place like this.' She pushed firmly down the memory of what Felicity had said about fascists meeting in the Black Horse.

'I know. And it's very good of you to take them in. You make me feel as if we should be doing something. We have plenty of space. But Prudence ...'

Prudence was what Martha called *rather difficult*, and Felicity called *a ghastly brat*.

'She's well improved,' April said. 'She was a great help with the sports day we had at the mill before Easter. Bossed the wee ones like mad but they loved her. She's promised to do some country dancing with my Thursday girls.'

'Oh, she's terribly keen on that. Bless her. She's so grown up lately,' Martha said. 'Sixteen going on thirty.'

April felt thirty going on sixteen – or sixty sometimes.

'And she's working jolly hard. Miss Ingleby, her headmistress, is very pleased with her. She's set her heart on Bedford, the physical training college, and Fabian says he'll send her *if* she passes Matric well. It's not simply a matter of being good at hockey and tennis and gym, as she fondly supposed. But she's had enough disruption, losing her mother, and all those boarding schools, and then having to get used to a stepmother.'

'Och aye, you couldn't expect her to deal with strangers in the house,' April said. Felicity would have said, *Let her live as a Jew in Nazi Germany. Then she can talk about disruption.*

45

Which reminded her to tell Martha about Evelyn's impending visit.

'You must bring her for tea,' Martha said. 'Or perhaps I could take her out one day when you're at work. I'm rather good at driving now and she might like to see the countryside. Or if she'd be too shy with a stranger, we could all go one evening. The clocks go forward this weekend.'

April was suddenly hit with the enormity of entertaining an Evelyn she hadn't seen for well over two years. An Evelyn, moreover, who'd suffered this shocking, devastating loss. 'Oh Martha, I hope we're doing the right thing. Her wee boy died over a year ago but she sounds ... not herself. And what do I know about what she's going through?'

'You know everything about being a good friend,' Martha said, 'and that's all she needs.' She smiled at April and helped herself to more cake.

'But should I mention the kid or not? How were you when your Gordon was killed?'

Martha chewed her cake slowly before saying, 'There was a war on – I was by no means the only woman who'd lost a husband. It didn't make the loss easier, but people weren't so embarrassed by it. But no, we didn't talk about it much.'

'Did you want to?'

Martha considered. 'I'd have liked to talk about Gordon with someone else who'd known and loved him. If he'd had a sister, maybe. But I was busy nursing and we'd so little time together – we didn't have mutual friends and I hadn't got close to his family. There was nobody to mourn him *with*.'

'I barely met Robbie,' April said. 'He was a tot when I left.' She wrinkled her nose. 'I don't mind tiny babies, but toddlers – ugh! All waddling and sticky.'

'Maybe don't say that.' Martha took another bite of

cake, looking thoughtful. 'I tell you what I think odd: Evelyn *does* have someone who suffered the same loss – her husband. Yet she wants to go away alone.'

April thought about Maurice Kenny at his wedding, and the few times she had seen him since – he was always busy round the farm when she called: a quiet man, about ten years older than Evelyn, with a reputation for decency and hard work. Far from the romantic hero Evelyn had fantasised about as a girl, but she had seemed content enough. He was kind, she always said, and steady. Her infrequent letters had all been about Robbie, with barely a mention of her husband.

'I suppose he can't leave the farm,' April said fairly. 'And it was well over a year ago – it's not like it just happened.'

Which reminded her that she herself would have to work full time during Evelyn's stay, and Felicity couldn't be trusted not to get lost in writing and politics. If Evelyn could be jollied into coming to Shaw's Mill, it might be a distraction at least. And Martha, bless her, would clearly help.

'Don't worry so much,' Martha said. 'You've a great talent for people. Your own instincts and your years of friendship will guide you.'

Martha's faith was cheering, but even so, April couldn't help worrying that Evelyn's visit would be a disaster.

Six

April was shocked at Evelyn's appearance. From a distance, when she saw her walking towards her on the platform at Leeds station, and then break into an awkward, suitcase-encumbered run, her old friend looked the same – slim, not very tall, with red hair showing beneath her smart navy hat. But as she grew closer, every step revealed more of the ravages of grief, and when they met, and Evelyn set down her brown leather case and they hugged, April felt the bones of her shoulders beneath her cherry-coloured wool coat. They stood back and stared at each other, still clasping hands. Evelyn's felt cold.

'You look the same,' Evelyn said. 'Still got your hair bobbed.'

'And yours is still long.'

'It's desperate,' Evelyn said. 'I took the pins out because they were digging into me, and now it's streeling down. I must look like a ginger witch.'

'Don't be daft.'

But *ginger witch* wasn't a bad description. Evelyn looked maybe ten years older, her skin dull and pale, her cheekbones sharp. Her coat was more modish than April's old grey tweed, but it hung on her, the rich cherry-red a cruel contrast to the pallor of her face, where the only colour seemed to be her pinkish eyelids and a purplish tinge to the skin under them. And her hair, as bright and silky as ever, drained her even more. April hugged her again. 'We've a lovely big room ready. I've been lighting fires in it the last few days to get it cosy, and there's a hot water bottle in your bed.'

'I don't want to be a bother,' Evelyn said.

It was lovely to hear an Ulster accent again, but her voice was flat, all the music sucked from it. 'How was the crossing?' April asked.

'Rough. I didn't sleep, and I was scared to sleep in the train in case I missed my station. I've never travelled on my own.'

April picked up the case and tucked her arm through Evelyn's.

'Come on. Our train's not for half an hour. We've time for a cuppa and a bun. You look like you could with them.'

It was going to take a lot more than a cuppa and a bun.

Evelyn could not have been said to be any actual trouble. At first she rarely left her room. But her sadness seemed to permeate the house.

'Try not to worry,' Felicity said, when April fretted that Evelyn must be starving. 'She's had a terrible experience. Remember how some of our German guests were at first.'

'I know. Frieda couldn't speak for a week. And thon wee fella whose mammy was killed in front of him.'

'Julius.'

'Aye.' A silent boy of sixteen, who jumped at every noise and watched them with dark suspicious eyes that had seen God knows what. He had stayed a month and then Colonel Lucey, of all people, had found him a job in Scotland with his cousin, looking after pheasants. 'I don't even know what happened wee Robbie. Mammy just said

49

a farm accident. That was all she knew. But it was over a year ago. Is it normal to be so …?' But April didn't have a word for how Evelyn was.

'Who's to say what's normal? She'll tell us if she wants to,' Felicity said.

'I'll bring her up a cuppa and see does she need her hot water bottle refilled. It's not too warm up in thon attic.'

'I'd leave her,' Felicity said.

'I know you would, love.' She touched Felicity's cheek lightly. 'You hide away when you're sad too. Like a cat. But I'm not like that. And neither's Evelyn. At least – she didn't use to be. I'll see does she fancy anything to eat – Martha sent round some lemon biscuits.'

But when she climbed the stairs to the attic, Evelyn seemed to be so deeply asleep, her red hair streaked across the white pillow, that she hadn't the heart to disturb her. April hovered, hoping Evelyn might sense her presence, but her friend slept on, one thin hand hugging the eiderdown, her gold wedding band loose on her finger. April pulled the rug up over her and set the tea on the nightstand. Maybe Evelyn would rouse and take the tea when April left. Two years ago, when April had come to Riverside Road as a lodger, before she and Felicity fell in love, the attic had been hers. She had loved its cool white paint and airy privacy, so different from the dark, tense rooms she had grown up in. Since then a succession of refugees had found shelter there. April had sometimes been lonely in this room, and sometimes worried, but as she looked at her friend, her cheekbones sharp and her eyes, even tightly shut, bearing the evidence of tears, she knew that, compared to Evelyn, and to people like Frieda and Julius, she had never really suffered.

That night she floated in and out of sleep, alert for sounds from the attic. Once she jerked awake at what she thought was sobbing but was Felicity suppressing a cough.

'Sorry,' Felicity whispered. 'Didn't mean to wake you.'

April struggled up, reached for the glass of water on the nightstand and handed it to Felicity.

'Thanks.' She snuggled down again.

'Take an extra pillow.' April slipped her own top one under Felicity's back. 'That usually helps.'

Felicity patted her hand. Hers was hot. 'You're a darling,' she murmured, and was asleep again almost at once, her breathing deepening and steadying, while April lay wide awake until it was time to get up for work.

Even Lily noticed that she seemed distracted. 'Eeh, Miss McVey, you do look poorly,' she said and actually put the kettle on without being asked. It was true that she brought April a chipped cup which she should have thrown out last week, and that she hadn't put the lid back on the tin properly, so the biscuits were soft, but her intentions were good.

April yawned over the post. It was one of the jobs she should have been able to delegate, so that Lily could sort out what needed April's personal attention, what could be dealt with by popping a brochure into the post, and what could be ignored. But she could not trust her after Lily had carefully placed ten brochures into an envelope and posted them by return to a patent medicine company who had sent them an unsolicited advertisement for laxative powders.

There was nothing special in this morning's post, though she did cross her fingers at a request for a registration form from a Mr Clarence Taylor-Scott, who sounded very top-drawer and whose name she fancied she had seen in the *Tatler* that Martha always passed on to her for the downstairs room where they met clients. (April was sure she bought it specially for the bureau in fear that

April might bring in Felicity's *Daily Worker* or *Labour Monthly*.) Something to do with a Hunt Ball or a charity cricket match? Perhaps he would do for the Honourable Augusta. He was probably a bit posh for Barbara Firth. She popped a form into an envelope and addressed it with a dashing hand, setting it on the desk for Lily to post later.

She had an important meeting at eleven, introducing a retired Anglican clergyman to a widow. On paper, it should have been a likely match: he was a missionary, recently returned from Kenya, and she cited *church activities* and *travel* as her main interests. But it was clear from the start that there was no sympathy between them. The Reverend Waters was a frail-looking man with blotchy yellowish skin; he had had to leave the mission field because of ill health. Ada Thompson was a lively, no-nonsense woman, and the second time the Reverend Waters was obliged to excuse himself to use the lavatory, she had said, 'I'm sorry, Miss McVey, but I can tell you here and now there'll be no match. I spent ten years nursing my poor Percy. I don't intend to start over again with another invalid. I'd be better with a dog.'

April didn't blame her.

Anyway, she had more important worries than matchmaking. Turning into a Riverside Road that seemed to have grown steeper recently, she couldn't suppress a gnawing anxiety about Evelyn. For all Martha had said about friendship and instinct guiding her, she didn't feel she was being guided very well. Their friendship seemed to be more past than present. April could barely imagine having a child, let alone losing one. Was it normal to be laid so low for so long? Should she call in a doctor?

So it was a surprise to push open the back door and find the kitchen full of light and chatter and the smell of one of Felicity's German stews. Pichelsteiner, she recognised, its aroma reminding her of her early days in this house. Felicity and Evelyn were seated opposite each other at the table with a pot of coffee between them, Evelyn fully dressed and drying some spoons. It soon became clear that most of the chatter was coming from Felicity, and that the spoon drying was desultory.

Still, it was such a relief to see Evelyn out of bed that April burst out, 'Och, look at you!'

Felicity said, 'I'm indoctrinating Evelyn into the evils of strong coffee.'

'She's welcome to it.'

April remained a committed tea drinker. In fact, Felicity was already getting up to set the kettle back on the hob for her.

Evelyn made a face as if she agreed. 'I never knew Felicity was such a famous writer,' she said.

If you'd bothered to write to me before you wanted something, you would have known all about her. This was the very unkind thought that popped into April's head, but gone (mostly) were the days when to think a thing was to say it, so she simply smiled and said proudly, 'Her Forest Fay books are very well thought of. They're about to be published in America. And two of them have been read on *Children's Hour.*'

Felicity looked appropriately modest and Evelyn, once as keen a bookworm as April, appropriately impressed.

'Why don't you read one while you're here?' April suggested. 'They're really for children but lots of adults like them. Mammy loves them. They're very innocent and cheering. Like Milly-Molly-Mandy. I mean' – because Felicity hated her books being considered *sweet* – 'they're good comfort reads. Nothing too bad happens. Oh, except in the most recent one, but there's a happy ending.'

Evelyn frowned. 'I haven't read a word since …'

It was the closest she had come to mentioning Robbie.

Felicity and April exchanged glances. Should they brush over the reference or face it? Leave the wound alone or rip off the plaster? To April's surprise, Felicity spoke first.

'Did Robbie like reading?'

Evelyn stared at her as if she couldn't believe Felicity had said his name. Then, slowly, she shook her head. 'Och no,' she said. 'He wasn't one for sitting still and he wasn't even at school yet. He was a typical wee boy, running about the farm, following his daddy. He liked me reading to him. Winnie the Pooh and Beatrix Potter. He liked *The Two Bad Mice* best.'

'I gave him those books,' April remembered. 'They were old friends.'

'It was very good of you,' Evelyn said. 'I remember asking you why you didn't keep them for your own children.'

'Sure didn't I tell you I didn't want them.' April kept her voice light. She remembered Robbie's birth and, though she had cuddled him and agreed he was the most gorgeous baby ever born in Lisnacashan, what she had mostly seen was another nail in the coffin of their friendship. Evelyn married had already gone somewhere April couldn't follow, but now, completely absorbed in her baby, she was removed to a different plane altogether.

'Well, you could have the books back now,' Evelyn said. 'I mean, if you ever have a baby – it's not too late. You never know.'

Felicity laughed. 'Unless it's a virgin birth, there'll be no babies in this house.' She spooned tea into the pot as the kettle started to sing.

April looked at Felicity and then at Evelyn. She had never spelled out the nature of her relationship with Felicity, but she hadn't thought she needed to. I suppose, strictly speaking, we *are* virgins, she thought, if you think of sex as between a man and a woman. How odd. Because of course we aren't. She felt herself blushing. For dear sake! What a thing to be thinking of! In front of Evelyn!

But it occurred to her, as she watched Felicity take her favourite yellow cup down from the rack, and as Felicity caught her eye and smiled a slow, comfortable smile, that she need no longer feel that Evelyn, in marrying, had entered a world she couldn't follow her into.

Seven

At first Evelyn was so exhausted that she was barely aware of her surroundings. Just a vague sense of a quiet white room at the top of a tall house with bookcases stuffed into every available space. April, when she wasn't at work, was often dashing about, singing in the bathroom, pounding up and down the stairs for something she'd forgotten, or yelling to Felicity to remember to turn the oven down. Felicity spent hours in her study, writing: from upstairs, Evelyn was distracted and then lulled back to sleep by the constant tat-tat-tat of her typewriter. They both, in their different ways, worked very hard, and yet she didn't feel in the way. The shabby old house itself seemed to welcome her, as if it was used to being a sanctuary. *Come in and rest,* it said. *You'll be safe here.*

April was, in some ways, the same as ever, bright and fervent, but she was different too. Well, she was older, they both were, but she seemed more ... more *herself*, Evelyn thought, though she couldn't have said exactly what she meant. At home in Lisnacashan, April had been an exciting, demanding friend. Always restless, fizzing with madcap schemes. *We'll go to Belfast and work in a newspaper office,* she would say. *Or – no! Dublin! Maybe we could go on the stage? What about London?* Every book they read gifted her a further horizon. *We could go to Austria, where the Chalet School is, and yodel and climb mountains! Ah, wouldn't it be great to go to Prince Edward Island?* It took her a long time to accept that she ran the office of a small garment factory in a small town in the middle of Ulster, and that she would probably go on doing that until she married. Her eyes had burned with passion for – she didn't know what, but *something*.

She always included Evelyn in her schemes. When Evelyn, terrified she would never meet anyone better, started walking out with Maurice, she had advised April to do the same. April's mammy and daddy were *awful*; if she didn't marry, she'd never get away. But April had got away. Easterbridge, from the little Evelyn had seen, certainly wasn't as exotic as London or Prince Edward Island: it was a stolid stone town, hilly and higgledy-piggledy, its yellowish-greyish stone warm against the bruise-coloured moors above. It was funny that April, who had always claimed she would never marry, was in charge of a marriage bureau.

'I love the work,' she said after dinner on the first evening that Evelyn felt up to joining them.

They were having coffee in the sitting room: at least, April was having tea, and Felicity was once again encouraging Evelyn to join her in a strong-smelling coffee. If Easterbridge wasn't exotic, Felicity was. She was like nobody Evelyn had ever met. Sipping the coffee, trying to like it, she sat back and observed her friend's pal. Felicity had a thrown-together look, as if her mind was above such things as tidy hair and matching colours. Her stockings were wrinkled, and the bright purple paisley-patterned shawl she'd pulled round her – the room was draughty, though warm by the fire – clashed with the rust and orange check of her frock. *Bohemian*, Evelyn decided. Beside her, April, with her neat fair bob and her brown linen skirt and jacket, looked every inch the businesswoman, though she had kicked off her brogues and curled her feet under her in an attitude of relaxation. The light from the fire touched her hair with golden lights. She had always been coltishly attractive, but now she had grown into herself: she looked handsome, and sure of herself, her face glowing as she explained why she loved her work.

'It's so satisfying,' she said, 'when you find just the right person for someone. You see them afterwards, happy as Larry, and you know they wouldn't have managed that on their own. Some people need a wee push.'

Felicity smiled at her. 'People can be awfully dense about what they need, can't they?' she said, and April gave her a little shove.

Some private joke, Evelyn supposed. It was odd, seeing April with another close chum. At school in Lisnacashan, they had been casually pally with a gang of other girls, but she and April had always been an exclusive unit slightly on the edge. They were smarter than the others, more bookish, more imaginative, more ambitious.

And look where it's got us, she thought. Me: a husband I have nothing in common with, and – she made herself think it, though it felt like she was scratching off her skin – a dead child. And April? Well, she had a job she obviously liked, but she didn't seem any closer to getting married herself. Maybe she really was content to be a working girl, living with a pal. While Evelyn had dreaded spinsterhood, April had always said she'd be happy that way. She certainly seemed it. Mind you, in her line of work she was well placed to meet fellas: one of these days, some man would walk in, she'd take a fancy to him, set her cap, and that would be that. If she, Evelyn, had been brave enough to leave home like April when she was single, she might have met someone very different from Maurice. A soulmate.

'Of course, matchmaking's not April's only work,' Felicity said, pouring more coffee for herself and asking, with a tilt of her eyes, if Evelyn would like some too.

Evelyn shook her head.

'Has she told you about the mill?'

'A linen mill?'

April and Felicity laughed.

'No,' April said, 'it's a community centre. It used to be a woollen mill – it's just down the road; I pointed it out to you the day you came.'

Evelyn barely remembered the journey, only being cold and seasick and scared of getting the wrong train; the buzz of unfamiliar English accents around her; April materialising at the other end of a long station platform and the familiar, forgotten clasp of her embrace and the sound of her voice. And then, for the first time in many, many months, hours and hours of sleep.

'It's owned by friends of ours – actually, they were my very first match! Sybil's stinking rich – sorry to be vulgar, but she is – and Henry is a carpenter. Well, more a cabinet maker. He has part of it for his works and they use the rest for, och, all sorts of things! I run a girls' club, like the one you used to help me with at home. Felicity takes writing classes when she has time.'

'I'd grandiose ideas,' Felicity said, 'of nurturing working-class writers – you know, like the WEA?'

Evelyn nodded sagely though she had no idea what this meant.

'I imagined discovering wonderful authentic stories. But mostly they need help with the basics.'

'And there's sports, and handicrafts, even a wee shop for people to sell what they've made. Och, it's a grand scheme to be part of.'

April sounded proud and for a moment Evelyn felt ...

jealous? Felicity and April seemed to have such a sense of purpose, to be so busy and important and *needed*. The only person who had needed Evelyn in recent years was Robbie – and she had failed him.

'I helped April with her girls' club at home,' Evelyn said, partly to dispel thoughts of Robbie, and partly to show Felicity that she wasn't just some domestic drudge. 'We'd some craic, hadn't we? Remember when we took them to Cookstown to see *Alice in Wonderland* at the cinema and Millie Nesbitt sneaked off with a boy for a wee court in the back row?'

April smiled. 'Och, the girls here are the same. Eejits. But nice eejits.'

'Could I come and visit?' Evelyn asked tentatively. 'I wouldn't want to be in the way ...'

April's face broke into the wide smile Evelyn remembered so well. 'Of course! I wanted you to, but I wasn't sure if you'd be up to it.'

'I'm not an invalid.' But as she said it, she was aware of how much like an invalid she had felt for so long. Her sickness on Easter Sunday had not been an isolated incident, though she had managed, most of the time, to conceal her feeble condition from Maurice. But since leaving home she felt better. As broken by grief as ever – she could not imagine that ever changing – but that gnawing sour biliousness which had been a constant companion seemed to have subsided and for that she was grateful. Maybe it was getting away from Lisnacashan, not having to look at Maurice, not having to brace herself for Mona's visits. Not having to see the barn. Maybe it was the long restoring hours of sleep. Whatever it was, she felt a willingness to be distracted.

'The club's on tomorrow evening,' April said. 'They're having country dancing and a supper. Felicity's coming and a few other friends. If you're sure it won't be too festive …?'

'No, it'll be grand,' Evelyn said. 'I can't hide away forever.'

At first it seemed a huge mistake, and hiding away for a hundred years would have been preferable to surrounding herself with the boisterous spirits and enthusiastic galumphing of twenty adolescent girls. They were indeed, despite the Yorkshire accents, very like the girls in Lisnacashan. Very like how she and April had once been. Their wild swoops from earnestness to exuberance made her homesick for her own youth. Nothing was expected of her except to watch from the sidelines while a strident girl in a grey gym frock yelled out instructions to lines of dancers whose enthusiasm made up for their lack of finesse. Felicity and April were dancing together – neither seemed expert but they were obedient and knew left from right, neither skill over-developed in the younger dancers.

'Evelyn? May I?'

She turned to see a dark, handsome woman about ten years her senior preparing to sit beside her.

'Of course.' She shifted to make room and the other woman sat down.

'I'm Martha Carr,' she said. 'April's business partner and Felicity's sister-in-law.'

'Och, yes. I've heard about you.'

'That's my stepdaughter bossing them.' Martha made a humorous face. 'She's rather overzealous.'

Evelyn smiled. 'She's just keen.'

'I was very sorry to hear of your terrible loss last year,' Martha said. 'I hope we manage to give you a little respite.'

'Thank you,' Evelyn said. 'It's a great place you have here.' This was a safe topic and they chatted pleasantly about the mill, the work it did and its great sense of community.

'And much of that is thanks to April,' Martha said. 'She's so good with people; it's a real gift.'

'She always was.' She couldn't help smiling at April who, dancing in a short blue frock, her fair hair bouncing, looked almost as young as the girls.

'So many people come here who might otherwise have very little to get them out of the house.' Martha beckoned to an elderly lady shuffling along on the arm of a very solid girl, clutching a brown paper parcel. 'Miss Dawson!' She raised her voice. 'How nice to see you!'

Miss Dawson tottered over, her wrinkled face wreathed in smiles. 'Mrs Carr! Isn't this lovely? Many of the girls are in my handicrafts class and they were so keen for me to see them dance, bless them! Thank you, Daisy dear. I'm fine here. You join your pals. They'll be missing you.'

The inappropriately named Daisy stomped off to wait for a break in the dancing. Martha introduced Evelyn and Miss Dawson.

'And you've been friends with April all your life?' Miss Dawson asked. 'Well, I'm not surprised. She's one in a million. I'd be sitting alone day and night in my room but for her.' Evelyn smiled and didn't admit that she and April had almost lost touch until recently. 'And her companion, Miss Carr, is so clever!' Miss Dawson went on. 'You know she writes books?'

Evelyn nodded.

'So nice to see them enjoying themselves.' Miss Dawson's head bobbed in time to the music. 'They work so hard. Oh, talking of work – I've brought these things along for Mrs Yeadon's baby.' Miss Dawson handed Martha the package.

'I can run them up to the Yeadons for you in the car,'

Martha said. 'I'd like to see Baby Dorothy myself. But why don't you come? I'm sure you'd enjoy a run out.'

Miss Dawson sighed. 'Oh, I would! But it's right up above Shippardsholme, isn't it?'

Martha nodded.

'I couldn't manage to sit in the car for so long, I'm afraid. My old bones seize up. I can manage to come here for my classes – Mrs Barrett very kindly sends her car for me, and it's such a comfortable one, but of course that's only a few minutes' journey.' She patted Martha's arm with a gnarled hand. 'Old age, my dear – not for the faint-hearted. But what a blessing to have somewhere like this to come. And I can still knit and crochet.'

'I meant to ask you about crocheting: I don't think I'm joining my wool properly,' Martha began, but was interrupted by the ringing of a bell and April announcing a supper interval.

Evelyn turned to see a long trestle table at the back of the hall, laden with the sort of spread she had last seen at Robbie's wake, when neighbours had kept appearing with traybakes and sandwiches. She swallowed, appetite deserting her. Someday, she thought, every little thing won't remind you. She couldn't imagine when that day would be. But in the meantime, she could make herself useful by fetching supper for her companions, letting them enjoy their chat. She stood slightly self-consciously in the queue, glad to be joined by April and Felicity, both glowing with exercise, Felicity suppressing a cough. Progress up the queue was impeded by the many red-faced, damp-haired girls who bounced up to April to tell her what fun they were having.

'Did you see me and Beryl in "Rufty Tufty", Miss McVey?'

'I nearly fell over, Miss!'

'Did you see Rosanne go the wrong way?' Much collapsing into giggles.

Evelyn noticed that, while they looked with respect at Felicity, it was April's attention they craved. And she gave it willingly, joking with them and then sending them grumbling good-naturedly to the back of the queue, leaving a strong smell of perspiration behind them.

April turned her attention to the supper table. 'You've been busy baking, Primrose,' she said to the middle-aged woman presiding over the table with the help of a couple of older girls.

'Ooh, and that looks like Hanna's Anisplätzchen!' Felicity said.

Primrose beamed. 'It is indeed. The whole house smells of aniseed – it's lovely.'

Evelyn felt that maybe she could fancy a little something after all.

'Our friends Hanna and Erich lodge with Primrose,' Felicity explained. 'Why don't I fill a plate for us to share and you two fetch teas for everyone? Hello, Primrose, I thought Hanna was coming to help you tonight?'

Primrose paused in pouring tea into a waiting line of white china cups and looked slightly embarrassed. 'She's tired. She was on her feet most of the morning baking.'

'I see.' Felicity looked wise and said to Evelyn in an undertone, 'Hanna's expecting. Primrose thinks it's terribly vulgar to mention it.'

'Oh, Felicity!' Primrose blushed. 'That's not true. But I'm not one to talk about people's private business.'

'Hardly private much longer,' Felicity said. 'She's like a ship in full sail. I think it's twins – Erich has twin brothers and they say it runs in families. I don't know where you'll put them, Primrose. You'll have to empty a couple of drawers.'

Everyone smiled, even Primrose, but something kicked Evelyn's heart. Twins. Two babies! Two babies to be joked about so casually.

'Well, she can't send them back,' April said and then seemed to see Evelyn's face, because she said quickly, 'Primrose is right. We shouldn't be gossiping. Ooh – one of those, please, Primrose.'

Primrose busied herself in selecting a particularly good biscuit. 'Just for you, April,' she said, and Evelyn could see that here was another of April's conquests.

They really all did seem to *love* her.

Evelyn wasn't jealous – that would be stupid; she was glad that April had made good here and was so popular. It was just ... *I* was always the lucky one, she thought. The one with the happy family, the loving home, and then the husband and the lovely new bungalow and the child. All April ever had was the energy and the dreams.

And this was what energy and dreams – yes, and hard work and her own personality – had brought her. Respect and affection in a town across the sea. Well, fair play to her. She deserved it. She, Evelyn, was not going to be one of those bitter women who let loss eat them up and make them begrudge other people their happiness.

Which is why, when they were all settled with tea and biscuits, and Martha said, 'Why don't you come up to see Florrie Yeadon with me tomorrow evening, Evelyn? It would be a chance for you to see our countryside,' she did not say, 'I can think of nothing worse than visiting a stranger's baby when my own child rots in a cold grave across the sea.'

She paused, finished chewing her aniseed biscuit, and said, in the heartiest tone she could manage, 'That sounds lovely.'

Eight

The visit escalated into an expedition, and Evelyn began to regret her decision to go. April was to come too, and Felicity was invited. 'The country air would be so good for you,' April suggested, but Felicity said she didn't know the Yeadons, and would feel silly, and besides, she had a story to finish.

'All that talk of twins,' she said, 'has given me an idea for a serial about a doppelganger.'

'What's a doppelganger?' Evelyn asked.

'A double self – someone that looks exactly like you, but isn't you.' And Felicity disappeared up to her study.

'*I* don't know your friends either,' Evelyn said as they waited on the front step for Martha to pick them up, dressed similarly in light frocks and warm cardigans, but April said that was totally different, *she* was a guest being shown the local sights.

'We can say we're taking you up Shippards Hill for the view,' she said, 'and are leaving in the gift in passing. So she needn't feel she has to ask us in. Look, here's Martha. Isn't it funny to see her driving a car!'

Their destination was a farm outside a village called Shippardsholme, up on the moors. Florrie Yeadon, a dark, plump, pretty woman, who answered the door of the old stone farmhouse herself, was delighted to see them and insisted on their coming in.

'Mind the dog,' she said as they stepped into a dark stone porch, where an ancient collie snored on a rag rug. The porch led into a big, low-beamed kitchen with a large, scrubbed table and a couple of worn, comfortable settees facing each other in front of a big range. Florrie set the kettle to boil and sent a little girl to fetch cups from the oak dresser. 'The good ones, mind, Sally, love. And some of those rock cakes Miss Batley sent.'

She was thrilled with Miss Dawson's offering: a soft white shawl in the finest wool and four pairs of lemon bootees.

'She made them all the same because the baby's bound to kick them off and lose them,' Martha explained.

'How sensible. And how kind. Really, people have been so wonderful. You know, I can hardly believe this is my life now! *Three* children.' She smiled at Sally.

I can hardly believe this is my life now. *No* children, Evelyn thought. Please let the baby be asleep upstairs, not to be disturbed. Please let that wooden cradle beside the settee be empty. And please let us leave soon. It had been a terrible mistake to come.

Sally, busying herself with cups and solemnly piling a plate with rock cakes, asked, 'Would you like to see our baby?'

Of course everyone said yes, and Florrie reached into the wooden cradle and lifted out a bundle tightly wrapped in a pale lemon shawl. Her face softened as she looked at the child. 'She's fast asleep,' she murmured, 'and she should stay that way, as long as we're very gentle. Who'd like to take her?'

Evelyn held back and April said, 'Och, I'm always scared of dropping the wee craturs,' so Martha held out her arms.

They were regaled with the life and times of the infant. Her name was Dorothy, she had been very early and small but was now thriving. Sally adored her and Sam pretended to be indifferent but had been spotted hanging over the crib with a devoted expression.

'That's boys for you,' Florrie said. 'He's off round the farm with Joseph now, checking fences. He can't wait to farm, bless him.'

My Robbie was the same.

She couldn't say it. For so many reasons.

Evelyn had sat opposite Martha so she wouldn't have to see the baby's face. She looked round the room instead, noting its similarities to her mother-in-law's farm kitchen, itemising things as she often did in an effort to detach herself from company. She could smile and look normal, even contribute the occasional *hmmm*, while her mind inventoried safe impersonal objects. Eleven blue-and-white plates on the dresser; eight blue-and-white cups. They must have twelve of everything, since one plate had already been pressed into service for cakes and there were four of them for tea, which Sally was making with anxious competence. Sally mustn't be taking tea herself. Robbie didn't either; she would never have let him be one of those toddlers you saw in Doran's Loanen, bottles of tea hanging out of their mouths and bare bottoms sagging low from sodden nappies. And every one of those scabby brats was thriving, while her Robbie—

Perhaps this inventorying wasn't as successful as she had hoped. There was a trellis pattern on the wallpaper, with roses every few inches; she would count those instead. One, two, three, four – odd colour, she had never seen a real rose that shade of pink, but the paper was old and faded – five, six …

'There's not enough milk, Mam,' Sally said. 'Shall I fetch more from the dairy?' She sucked the end of one plait.

'I'd better go,' Florrie said. 'The big jug's too heavy for

you. And be careful with those cups. They're too near the edge of the table.'

Off she went, leaving the visitors alone with baby Dorothy, whose gentle snuffling Evelyn was trying not to hear. And damn, the interruption had broken her concentration. She would start again on the next row – oh, that was only half a rose at the top; should she count it or not? Maybe not. So that was one, two, three—

Smash!

Only a cup hitting the stone-flagged floor, but Sally burst into tears and baby Dorothy woke with a whimper that rose to a volley of outraged shrieks.

'Oh no! The best cups!' Sally bent down to pick up the pieces.

'Mind you don't cut yourself.' April went to help.

Baby Dorothy kept shrieking. Martha looked down at her helplessly. 'Oh dear,' she said, and gave her a hard jiggle, which made the infant cry louder. 'Hush, baby. Mummy will be back soon.' She held the bundle as if it was going to explode.

Instinct made Evelyn reach out her arms.

'Here,' she said, taking the baby and swinging her gently, as she had always done with Robbie. She offered her finger and Dorothy gave a couple of hiccupping cries and then latched on to it. When Florrie returned with a big jug of milk, Dorothy was quiet again, sucking placidly on one of Evelyn's fingers and grasping another in a little pink hand. She looked up at her with big blue-grey eyes and Evelyn could not stop herself from smiling down. 'Ah, you're a wee beauty, aren't you?' she murmured, though Dorothy, having been premature, had a slightly goblin cast to her features. Evelyn breathed in her hot sweet scent and closed her eyes.

'You're a genius, Evelyn,' Martha said. 'I was useless.'

Evelyn shrugged, gently so as not to disturb Dorothy. 'You just learn what to do when you ... when you have one.' The words hung in the air, making everyone glad of the distraction of tea and rock cakes and some gentle ribbing of Sally for breaking the cup.

'I'm usually very careful,' Sally said, frowning.

'You are indeed, love. You're a great help,' Florrie said quickly. She glanced at the clock. 'Nearly eight. Aren't the long evenings lovely? Joseph should be back by now – he's probably run into Charlie, our neighbour. They're thick as thieves these days and Charlie often rides out in the evenings at this time of year.'

This meant nothing to Evelyn, but April perked up like a dog hearing its name.

'Charlie who works for Colonel Lucey?

'Yes – his groom. Charlie Teal. Do you know him?'

April, to Evelyn's surprise, blushed. 'I've met his sister. Er, what's he like?'

'Oh, he's a grand fellow. Very quiet, keeps to himself.'

'I like his dogs,' offered Sally, who seemed recovered from the plate smashing. 'He said he's going to take me and Sam to see them racing.'

'We'll see,' Florrie said. 'I'm not sure a greyhound track is the place for a little girl. I can't help thinking it's cruel, too.'

Evelyn had no interest in this talk. Baby Dorothy had gone back to sleep, so she placed her carefully back into her cradle and concentrated on using the tea, which was excellent, to chase down the rock cake, which was not.

'We want to show Evelyn the view from Shippards Hill,' April said, 'so we ought to get going while there's light. We should catch a lovely sunset.'

'I'm not too confident about the country roads just yet,' Martha admitted. 'They're so steep and narrow. I'm always afraid of meeting something coming the other way – especially one of those big tractors.'

'Oh, nobody round here's got one of those yet,' Florrie said, 'but there's a shortcut from behind the farm anyway. Leave the car here and walk. It's a bit of a pull but worth it for the view. It's only twenty minutes. Sally, you'll show them the way, won't you?'

Flushed with importance, Sally agreed, and ten minutes later saw them all, apart from Florrie and the baby, climbing a stile into a steep, dry-stone-walled field. Sheep with lambs grazed its slopes, some of them resting on their front knees, the better to reach the grass, exactly like the sheep at home. Evelyn couldn't help smiling at them. A rough track ran up the side of the field, close to the wall. Sally took April's hand and they led the way, Martha and Evelyn following. The old collie came with them for the first few minutes, after which she turned and padded back down the hill to the yard, as if content that she had set them on the right path.

'Are you fond of country walks?' Martha asked, which made Evelyn feel she was in a Jane Austen novel.

'I've lived on a farm since I was married,' Evelyn said, 'and walking in the country's just a way of getting round. We have a car, but Maurice drives it.' It felt strange to talk about Maurice in the present tense, even though he was, so far as she knew, alive and well in Lisnacashan, having his dinner at his mammy's every night. 'I walked for miles when I was younger,' she said. 'April and I used to tramp the roads looking for, och, any sort of craic.'

Martha smiled. 'I can imagine.'

'But when I got married, there was no time for that kind of thing. Sure, you know yourself – didn't April say you only got married last year?'

'I did,' Martha said. 'But funnily enough I've found the

opposite. Time sits rather more heavily on me now.' She was quite posh; she probably had servants. No wonder she found time heavy. 'I do a lot of baking, and I help out at Shaw's Mill with some of the administrative tasks, but that only adds up to a few hours a week. I was used to running a business, taking charge.'

'I was only footering about at home, helping my mammy. And then ...'

Well then, though not as soon as she'd hoped, along had come Robbie.

The late April evening was cooling fast, and she pulled her cardigan more tightly round her. Ahead she could hear April and Sally chattering. April seemed to be saying something about having cycled up this hill a couple of years ago, and the little girl was looking impressed.

Sally turned back and called to Martha and Evelyn, 'Let's race to the top.' She broke away from April's hand and tore up the hill, plaits and skirt flying. April joined in gamely, and Martha and Evelyn followed more sedately, Evelyn annoyed to find herself breathless before Martha, who was ten years older.

Sally, reaching the top first, waved and jumped up and down. 'Daddy!' She turned back to them, beaming. 'It's Daddy and Charlie,' she said. 'Oh goody, I'll get a ride home on Bobby.'

Two horses appeared over the brow of the hill. Their riders halted them and greeted the visitors. Evelyn recognised Joseph from the wedding photo on the kitchen wall, a thickset man in a tweed cap and leather gaiters. She couldn't see Charlie properly, because his horse, a flashy chestnut, was slightly behind Joseph's sturdy black farm cob.

Sally introduced the visitors with grave courtesy.

'Well, of course,' Joseph said, 'I remember Miss McVey and Mrs Hart.'

'Mrs Carr now,' Martha said.

Propped up in front of Joseph was a boy in a cap the same as his father's.

'My turn, Sam!' Sally said, and Sam grumbled, but scrambled down, the cob seeming not to notice.

The chestnut titupped forward and gave a snort which made Martha and April step back, but not Evelyn, whose years on a farm had made her confident around big animals. She knew little about horses, but she could see that this mare, arching her neck, ogling the intruders with flared-nostril suspicion, was no farm horse. The chestnut snatched at her bit and tossed her head, as if aware of being admired, and Evelyn saw her rider for the first time: a wiry, strong-looking man in his thirties. His lean face had the hardened look of one whose life was spent outdoors. He nodded at the women, then busied himself untangling his horse's silky blonde mane, frowning in concentration. His fingers were long and strong, the backs of his hands lightly freckled.

He's shy, Evelyn thought, and then, he's *gorgeous*. Good lord, where did that come from? She was married. Her child was dead. How could she have such a thought about a stranger? What sort of woman was she? Mortified, she turned her face away from Charlie, from the easy way he sat on the horse, from the length of his legs in worn, whipcord breeches, and especially from his face, shadowed by his tweed cap, the high cheekbones and the straight nose and the firm lips. She looked back down the hill to the farmyard, safe and sleepy, its old stone barn golden in the last rays of the evening sun. She swallowed, feeling the rock cake lodged somewhere it shouldn't be, and turned back to the others. Sam had given Sally a leg up on to the cob in front of her father and she looked proud.

'Bobby likes me better'n you,' she said.

'Bet you fall off,' Sam said, and he and Sally stuck their tongues out at each other.

'Time you'd your own pony, isn't it, Sam?' said Charlie, and Sam nodded vigorously.

'Not a pony,' he said. 'A hunter like Scarlet here.'

Both men laughed. 'You may start saving now, lad,' Joseph said, 'and hope there's gold buried somewhere on the farm. You need money for a horse like Scarlet.'

'Charlie's got no money,' Sam said, and Charlie laughed.

'You're not wrong there, Sam, lad. Right – best get her ladyship back before dusk.' He nodded at them all and started to ride off alone down the hill, not the path the women had just taken but a rough track to the left.

Evelyn tried not to watch him go, but there was something compelling about horse and rider, their movements fluid against the still, rough landscape. Beside her, Martha was saying something about valleys and woods and St Luke's spire, and she remembered that she was meant to be admiring the landscape.

Charlie turned back, just once, and seemed to be looking at them – at April, most likely. Evelyn saw her, for a moment, through Charlie's eyes: tall, confident and relaxed, hands plunged into the pockets of her long cardigan, little strands of fair hair wisping round her pink-cheeked face. She had smiled and greeted him warmly – in fact, she had been very effusive. But now, because she had a lot more sense than Evelyn, she was being careful not to look at him at all, but at her friends. Evelyn was impressed. The old April wouldn't have known how to play with a man like that. How could he fail to notice her and be attracted? And why shouldn't he? April, unlike her, was as free as a bird.

Nine

Charlie couldn't understand why he felt so rattled. It wasn't as if he had never met a pretty woman before. But he hadn't expected, on his evening ride, to run into three of them at the top of Shippards Hill – one dark, a little older, obviously married; one tall and fair and eager-looking; and one pale and red-haired, with a fragile air. He hadn't known what to say to them. Thank God for Sally and Sam and their nonsense. And his lovely Scarlet. He smiled as he rode down the hill, shifting his weight back fractionally to free up the mare's forehand, and patted her warm red neck. Both Mrs Lucey's horses were well-schooled and willing, but Scarlet, with her gay head carriage and high-stepping action, was his darling. And as Charlie told the Colonel, she might look dainty but she would hunt all day and tackle the biggest fences; she had the heart of a Grand National winner.

'A drop of blood's worth a ton of bone,' he would say and the Colonel would *tush* and suck his moustache and say he didn't know what Thomsy wanted with such a weed. His wife would counter this by saying that Hadrian, his own favourite hunter, a stolid, roman-nosed bay, was next door to a carthorse. This segued into an argument about the merits of English setters (her choice) versus the spaniels her husband favoured. This rivalry was the main currency of their relationship; it sounded exhausting to Charlie, but it seemed to serve them well, and what would he know? He'd never really been with a woman, apart from long ago in a different life. He'd been, in so many ways, a different man then. A boy. But there was no need to think about that now, just because a beautiful woman had greeted him on a spring evening.

And definitely no need to think about Joseph, his daughter sitting proudly in front of him on the cob, his son at his side, and wife and baby waiting in that cosy farmhouse.

The rough track gave way to the main road, and he reined the mare in and waited until he was sure there was no traffic approaching. There was half a mile of road now before he would turn off on to the Colonel's land, and though he was tempted to trot to beat the fading light, he needed to bring Scarlet home dry and cool. Otherwise, he would be the one waiting around until she was settled enough to rug up for the evening, and he still had the dogs to empty. Most grooms finished after evening stables, but he never minded working late: he appreciated having time off every afternoon to exercise the dogs, and riding in the evenings made him feel less like a groom and more like a gentleman exercising his favourite horse. He would have liked Tippy's company, but he couldn't trust her to stay at heel like a carriage dog or a gun dog. She was bred to chase, and one sight of a hare or a rabbit – or a child's puppy or a kitten or a lamb in a field – and she'd be halfway across the county. Her racing days might be over, but she would always be a greyhound.

Usually, riding home, he planned the next few weeks' races. Tansy was too good now for the flapping track at Easterbridge, which was a pretty amateur affair. But tonight, it was the bright eyes and hair of the woman he had just seen that pushed into his thoughts, the shape of her body that her cardigan failed to disguise, instead of the shiny black and white coat and lean muscles of his best dog.

Daft, he told himself as he turned into the Colonel's gateway, absolutely ridiculous! He wasn't likely to see her again and a woman as pretty as that was likely to have a sweetheart anyway.

To distract himself he slowed down to have a nosey at the gate lodge. It had been uninhabited ever since Charlie had come to Shippardsholme, and had gradually fallen into disrepair. But over the last year the Colonel had had it renovated – Charlie suspected that Thomasina had brought a few quid to their union – and now it stood, small, square and empty, windows glinting in the last of the sun, door and fascia boards freshly painted white. And there was the Colonel, two liver-and-white spaniels at his heels, coming out of its little garden. He greeted Charlie with a wave, and Charlie slowed the mare to walk beside him up the long drive.

'Lodge is looking well, sir,' Charlie said. 'Have you decided what to do with it?'

The Colonel shook his head. 'One thing's for sure, Teal, there'll never be another gatekeeper. When I was a boy, those gates were kept closed; it was the gatekeeper's job to open them for visitors. And for servants.' He smiled, his mouth disappearing into his bushy moustache. 'Woe betide any servant who dared sneak in or out after nine o'clock. Changed times, old boy.'

Charlie wasn't sure if he was meant to welcome or lament this fact, so he said, with respectful neutrality, 'It would make someone a grand home.'

'Indeed.' He took in a big gulp of air. 'Feel that, Teal – straight off the moors. Sharp as champagne.'

Charlie had never tasted champagne, but he nodded wisely.

'There's no healthier air in the whole of England. Trouble is' – the Colonel lowered his voice though there was no one to hear but Scarlet and the spaniels – 'it cost rather a lot to renovate.'

'Everything costs more these days,' Charlie agreed.

'We ought to sell it or let it, really. Silly to have it empty. But you don't want just anyone on your land, do you?'

'I suppose not, sir,' said Charlie, whose chances of owning land were considerably less than one of Tippy's pups winning the Greyhound Derby in a few years' time. He supposed he should feel grateful the Colonel had considered himself and his family worthy to be on his land. Though it was his father's service to the Colonel which had earned that. He was a decent old bird, really; he couldn't help coming over a bit lord-of-the-manor.

And thinking of the dogs, he had a favour to ask.

'Tansy's running in Leeds next Saturday night,' he said. 'Would there be any chance of borrowing the Bentley? You know I'll take care of it and clean it after.'

'Of course, my dear fellow! Do it good to have a run out. I must come and see these champions of yours run some evening. Grand sport, I'm told.'

'It is that, sir.'

They parted at the stables; the Colonel went into the house and Charlie saw to Scarlet, which didn't take long as he had already prepared her feed, hay-net and deep straw bed. She had cooled on the slow ride home and her hooves were clean, so after a quick onceover with a body brush, she was ready to be bedded down, whickering a low greeting to her friends but more interested in the contents of her manger.

The stables were homely and restful, with their herringbone brick floors and the soft munching and shifting of the horses in their straw. He could have stayed for longer, enjoying the peace, putting off his own empty fireside, but he had dogs to see to, so he set off home, diligently thinking of those dogs and looking forward to Margaret's last letter, which had arrived this morning and which he'd kept to open this evening. He let in no other thoughts at all, and it was better that way.

But as he watched the pups sport in the paddock, and sorted out a sudden quarrel between Tansy and Tippy over a smashed blackbird's egg that had fallen from the nest in the hedge, he couldn't help thinking, Well, what would be the harm? It wasn't as though he was bound by any vows of chastity.

Ten

Things came to a head with Lily. For the past few weeks she had been worse than ever – arriving late, bursting into tears if you looked at her sideways, and drooping about so languidly that April wanted to give her a good shake. She had long ago arranged that Lily have minimal contact with clients, but the Wednesday after the visit to the Yeadons' farm, there was a crucial meeting between two clients April was desperate to match, which would necessitate Lily bringing in the tea tray designed to help everyone feel at ease.

April wasn't a snob, but it was no harm for the bureau to have grand clients. She had worked very hard to set up this morning's meeting between the Honourable Augusta Wyndham-Howard and Clarence Taylor-Scott. Both loved golf and Switzerland; both were ready to settle down and start a family. Both had family money but liked keeping busy – she helped in a home for blind war veterans, and he administered his family's property all over the county.

April had asked Lily to give the interview room a good redding out yesterday, but this morning there were two cigarette butts in the ashtray on the coffee table, and the door handle was greasy. Thank goodness she had checked, and not trusted Lily! Where was the girl? It was gone half nine. April sighed, emptied and cleaned the ashtray and gave the door handle a good polish. Then she opened the window wide to air the room – thankfully it was a warm, bright morning. She could close it before Augusta and Clarence arrived at ten. *Augusta and Clarence*: their names sounded perfect together, the match was as good as made! She laughed as she went back upstairs to her office. As if it was that simple! Still, work seemed to be the easiest part of life at the moment. Tomorrow she was interviewing a man who sounded absolutely perfect for Barbara Firth. His photo suggested that he wasn't as handsome as Charlie Teal, who had, since Friday evening, materialised into a real person in her mind, but at least Douglas Grant was interested in meeting someone and trusted April to take charge of that for him. And he wasn't the only one: she had no fewer than four prospective clients to see tomorrow. Something about the spring air seemed to make people more inclined towards matrimony. But she was happy to be occupied, and proud of how well True Minds was doing. The only awkward task on her work To-Do list was: *Speak to Lily (again) re. her manner/ dress/punctuality.*

If she had dared make a list of things to tackle in the rest of her life, she'd only have to look at it once to have palpitations:

Persuade Felicity to see a doctor about her cough. Or at least ask her to slow down and take things easier.

Ask Evelyn how long she plans to stay.

A short list, but one she dreaded tackling. Felicity was working too hard, which was nothing new, but that lingering harsh cough was exhausting her. Exhausting April too, because when it woke Felicity, it woke April, and then she lay worrying. And now she had Evelyn to worry about too. She had thought she was getting better, coming to the club, showing a bit of interest in life. She'd even started to talk a wee bit about Robbie, which could only do her good. So April had hoped that her trip to Easterbridge was helping after all. But since the visit to Yeadons' Farm, she had gone backwards – snappy and listless, her eyelids pink and swollen as if she was crying in secret, playing with her food as if it turned her. Probably seeing Baby Dorothy had been too painful. Evelyn had a delicate look she'd never had as a girl. Only her silky red hair, which April had always envied, was as bright as before. And now Felicity was asking April to find out when she was leaving so that they could see about a new refugee. And April didn't want another refugee, but she felt guilty about that, so maybe they were as well with Evelyn? But she was so *difficult* ...

And so it went on. No wonder True Minds was her escape.

Lily arrived moments before the ten o'clock appointment, pale and smelling of sweat. April felt the last remnants of her patience shred.

'No,' she said, when Lily opened her mouth to make some excuse. 'I haven't time. Just bring in the tea tray in ten minutes. I've left it ready. You have literally nothing to do but boil the kettle and wet the tea. And put five bits of shortbread on the plate. Can you manage that?'

Lily's eyes filled with tears. 'But, Miss—'

'There's the bell! That'll be one of them now.' She smoothed her hair and checked her stockings were straight. 'Now don't let me down, Lily. It's only a tea tray, for dear sake. And eat a mint. There are some in my drawer. Your breath would stop a train.'

That was cruel (though true), but True Minds wasn't a charity: Lily, who had attended Felicity's writing class, had wanted to try office work, had sworn she would do her best, and she couldn't even come to work with clean teeth.

But it wasn't fair to blame her. It had been April's own fault, thinking she knew best, thinking a wee girl from Townsend Street could make good. And then *she* would get the credit. Well, she would have to bear the blame instead.

But right now she had to smile and talk and listen and be charming, but not *too* charming, because this was all about the clients, letting them get to know each other in as relaxed a setting as possible. Letting them shine. These meetings were when she most missed Martha's calm good sense and natural empathy. She was good at it herself, she knew she was, but she could still feel gauche and bog-trotting, especially with people like Clarence and Augusta, who spoke exactly like the new king. Augusta's fur would have cost more than April spent on clothes in a decade, and her earrings, which caught the light every time she nodded, looked like real diamonds.

They were both nervous. Clarence covered it with bluster, Augusta with an affected cold reserve, looking round the room as if she had never seen anywhere so humble. Thank goodness April hadn't trusted Lily's cleaning! But April was used to nerves and engaged every weapon in her professional arsenal to put them at ease. By the time she heard Lily's familiar galumphing on the stairs, they had relaxed into talking about their respective schooldays: Augusta had been educated at home, and then at finishing school in Switzerland, where she had fallen in love with all things Swiss, but her brother Algernon had, it turned out, been to Rugby with Clarence. At least, he had been a junior when Clarence was a prefect, and Clarence *thought* he remembered him fagging for him: 'Wyndham-Howard. Chubby little chap, could never get my rugger boots clean.'

April, as so often with the English upper classes, felt she had entered a parallel universe.

Augusta laughed. 'He's not chubby now,' she said. 'He's a rowing blue at Oxford.'

'I say, good show. Which college? I was up at Balliol myself.'

'Magdalen. Reading Greats.'

This clearly met with approval – 'My cousin Percy went there!' – and soon they were rabbiting away about the people they knew in common, who all seemed to be called Bunty and Minty and Plumps.

Honestly, April thought, they could have met without True Minds!

But they hadn't, and they were paying good money, and were even saying what sport this was, and how they would jolly well tell all their chums to sign up, so she smiled and nodded and thought of all the posh business coming their way. April wanted to bring in a scheme where they reduced their terms for the less well-off, and a few top-drawer clients would subsidise that bravely.

'Here's tea,' she said, going to the door before Lily could knock, which April had never succeeded in getting her to do gently. This was a crucial stage in proceedings. She would serve tea to the couple and, if things seemed to be going well, retire discreetly to give them privacy. Often, at this point, they would declare their intention to meet again under their own steam.

Lily blundered in, bashed the tray down on the table and stood back nervously, pulling at one grubby cuff. April saw that she had forgotten the milk jug.

'Lily,' she said, 'would you fetch the milk please?'

'Oh lord,' Lily said and stared, bog-eyed, at the clients. 'D'you *want* milk?'

Clarence and Augusta looked confused.

'Well, yes, I'm afraid I do,' Clarence said apologetically. 'If it's not too much trouble.'

'The milk, Lily.' April failed to keep the chill out of her voice.

Lily clumped back out with a sigh.

'I'm so sorry,' April said. 'Lily's not quite suiting, as you can see.'

'Oh, it's frightfully difficult to get staff,' Augusta said. 'Mother has a fearful time of it. Girls don't seem to want to go into service these days.'

Let them think of Lily as the maid, April thought. It could do no harm.

She had poured the tea herself and seen them furnished with Martha's home-baked shortbread before Lily reappeared, paler than ever, almost green. She handed over the milk with a grimace.

'Sorry,' she said, 'but the smell makes me gip.'

She gave a loud belch, covered her mouth, then grabbed the wastepaper basket and was noisily sick into it, while the Honourable Augusta Wyndham-Howard hid her face in the *Tatler*, and Clarence Taylor-Scott said, in hearty tones, 'Oh dear. Better out than in, as Nanny used to say,' and produced a large spotted handkerchief.

Really, April thought wearily, you had to hand it to the upper classes.

There was no point being angry with Lily. April blamed herself for not noticing sooner.

'So you're expecting,' she said, when everything had been cleared up, the clients had left, and they were up in the private office, where she had made Lily a cup of tea, without milk, and got her to sit down

Lily burst into loud, wet sobs. 'I must be. I'm sick every morning. And things turn me up – milk and the smell of my mam's stew. Other things I can't get enough of.' She

85

reached out for a third piece of Martha's shortbread.

'And your monthlies?'

Lily shrugged. 'I've missed a couple.'

'I didn't know you were courting.'

Lily stared at her, mouth hanging open, breathing heavily through her nose. 'I'm not exactly courting,' she said. 'Not regular. There's a couple of boys ...'

'And whichever it is will get off scot-free,' April told Felicity later, 'while poor Lily bears the shame.'

'If her mother doesn't throw her out,' Felicity said.

'Her mother didn't seem overly shocked when I brought her home and explained,' April said. 'She can only have been about that age when Lily was born. I think they'll just sort of absorb the baby into the family. Though God knows where they'll put it. Or how they'll feed it. The daddy's on the dole and the mammy works shifts down at the sweet factory when she can get them, and Lily's wee sisters keep house. I've sacked her but I'll give her a month's wages.'

'Don't get involved,' Felicity said sharply. 'You always take on too much.'

April laughed. They were sitting in Felicity's study – April had rushed up to tell her as soon as she got home – and as always, her desk was piled with writing, and stacks of pamphlets and letters and papers. 'Oh Felicity! You're one to talk! What about you, with your writing and your anti-fascist leagues and your refugees and—'

'I know. We're a pair.'

April felt a rush of affection. 'We're that all right.' She leaned forward and hugged Felicity tightly, stroking the unruly brown curls, enjoying the weight of her head on her shoulder, breathing in her familiar scent of ink and coffee and coal tar soap. 'I wish we had more time to just *be* a pair.'

'Oh! Sorry.' Evelyn filled the doorway. 'I was ...' She gestured vaguely in the direction of downstairs. 'I thought I'd make a cup of tea.'

'Oh yes, please,' April said, moving reluctantly away from Felicity. 'I've had quite a day.'

'And me,' Felicity said. 'And I have to get this article finished and in the post. It's about the rise of local fascist groups and how they target the vulnerable with false information, so it's very important.'

'We'll give you peace.' And, because Evelyn had already seen them hug – and sure, she wasn't stupid, she'd been staying with them for over a week – she gave Felicity a quick kiss. 'I'll make us a nice dinner and we can all relax for once.'

'Thanks, my love.' Felicity brushed her hand with hers before turning back to her desk, while April followed Evelyn to the kitchen.

'Felicity will want coffee as usual,' she said, locating the coffee pot on the shelf. 'She hasn't had much luck trying to get you on to it, has she?'

Evelyn wrinkled her nose. 'It's too strong. It'd nearly turn you.'

'Aye, it's not to my taste,' April agreed. Something nudged at her as she watched her old friend fill the kettle and warm the teapot. Evelyn had made no secret of feeling nauseous off and on; her appetite was capricious and her mood even more so. She was as wan and droopy-looking as ever poor Lily had been. Was this simply grief, or could *she* be pregnant too?

And if so, surely this was the best possible news?

Time was when April wouldn't have thought twice about bringing up any subject with Evelyn. But that was years ago. She didn't feel she could ask her straight out as she had asked Lily. Instead, when they were settled in the kitchen with their tea, April having brought Felicity a cup of coffee and begged her not to work too hard, she said gently, 'Evelyn, I hope you don't mind me asking, but you seem, these last few days ... not yourself. And I wondered if there was anything more than, well, losing Robbie.'

Evelyn looked at her in surprise, her greenish eyes pink-rimmed and dark-shadowed. 'What could be *more* than losing a child?'

'I-I know.' She didn't like to say that it had been a long time ago. Clearly, to Evelyn, to any mother, probably, it was no time at all. 'But you don't seem well. You're barely eating, you look desperate' – oh dear, that wasn't tactful; no wonder Evelyn was looking at her like she could slap her – 'I wondered if there was more to it than grief?'

'*More* than grief?' Evelyn shook her head, and said, slowly, as if she was talking to someone not half wise. 'You haven't a clue, have you? You never could have.'

She sounded, April thought, as if she actually *despised* her.

'Because you're not like other women.' Evelyn's eyes flashed with something like disgust. 'You're not normal.'

'What?'

'I saw you. Just now. You and Felicity.'

'Oh.' April clasped her cup tighter, the tips of her fingers almost meeting. 'But you must have known. We've never pretended ... For goodness, sake, we share a bedroom!'

'You said *friend*. You didn't say' – Evelyn seemed to search for the right word, her face working – 'fancy woman.'

The absurdity made April laugh in spite of herself. '*Fancy woman*?' She waited for Evelyn to laugh too, to say och aye, she didn't mean that, she meant *partner*, or *companion*. Even *lover*, though a wee bit racy, would at least have been accurate.

She thought of Felicity upstairs at her desk, inky-fingered as always, her messy curls and the shapeless linen frocks that were somehow endearing now because they were Felicity's; Felicity frowning as she tried to find the right word for a story, or storming at the latest injustice from Germany, or passionate with plans to help refugees, or the unemployed; Felicity relaxing against April's legs as they sat together in the evenings, turning to rest her chin on April's knees, looking up at her as April told her about her day, her curls soft in April's fingers; Felicity dancing with her at the mill last week, light and springy, the rare chance to clasp hands and hold each other in a public place; Felicity waking from a bad dream, cuddling into April's back, the warm huffs of her breath as she gave herself back to sleep, safe again.

'Felicity is not my *fancy woman*,' she managed to say.

'Whatever you call it. It's unnatural. It's disgusting.'

'Well, you'll not want to stay in a house of unnatural passions, then, will you?' April said. 'I was going to ask you when you were leaving. I'll assume now that it'll be first thing tomorrow.'

And because she no longer felt remotely like laughing, and quite a lot like crying, and she could not bear Evelyn to see that, she stalked out to the scullery to fetch potatoes for dinner, jaw clenched, hands jammed into her pockets, so that Evelyn would not see them shake.

As she rummaged in the sack, taking a long time over choosing the right potatoes, she heard the front door slam.

Eleven

The very first thing Evelyn saw, as she almost ran down Riverside Road, was Shaw's Mill looming ahead, its rows of windows glinting in the early evening sun. Music streamed from an upstairs room – a folk tune played on a piano, and the steady drumming of feet, with occasional shouts: a dance class in progress. And punctuating that sound, the high-pitched yells of children playing, which made her stomach clench. As she passed the gate, she couldn't resist looking in, and sure enough there was a shrieking game of football in progress, and a gaggle of girls skipping in the yard. One of the after-schools clubs April had told her about. She rushed past and crossed over to the riverbank side of the road in case she might see anyone she would have to speak to. Anyone who might want to engage her in conversation about the wonderful Miss April McVey and all her good works. If they knew!

Plying her trade as a marriage broker when all the time she had set up home with a – Evelyn didn't believe she had even *thought* the word before – a lesbian! It was disgusting: women carrying on like men! Women who couldn't *get* men, that was what was wrong with them! What would the grand Martha Carr think if she knew the truth about her precious, trusted Miss McVey?

Then, as she approached the Queen's Head pub, her

steps slowed and she started to feel very stupid. Of course Martha knew. She remembered her, on Friday night, asking April why Felicity hadn't joined them, saying how good the country air would have been for her. Explaining to Evelyn that Felicity was her sister-in-law, 'and I think of April in that light too'. Evelyn thought it was just Martha's way of saying she considered April to be as close as family. Even that ancient wee Miss Dawson talking about April's *companion*! Everybody knew. Except her.

Why was *she* always the dupe? The last to know? The one who had to find out for herself? She saw again that kiss, that light, affectionate brush of hand against hand, and she felt …

Jealous.

She stopped, pressed her hands to her heart, which was fluttering like a thrush in a birdbath. She took some shuddering breaths and leaned on the iron railings which divided the road from the steep riverbanks.

Had she always been jealous of April? She frowned, trying to be honest, trying to work it out. *She*, Evelyn, was the lucky one: the one with the happy family, and then the husband, home and child. She had rehearsed this in her head so often. Yes, she had felt some envy of April in the last few days, because she seemed so settled and confident now, and maybe a little because Charlie Teal had looked at her with such interest on Friday night. Her cheeks burned at the absurdity of this – a stranger, whom they would never see again! And it was even more absurd now that she knew April wasn't even *normal* in that way. Or could the attentions of a real man – and such an attractive one – pull her away from the path of perversion?

Or was that April's true path, and Evelyn was mostly jealous of her for walking it so bravely? For having the courage to be herself?

I don't understand any of it, she realised. Not April, not myself. What am I doing here? Standing alone in a street she barely knew, in a strange town in a new country. She had neither hat, nor coat, nor purse, she had left in such a storming rush. Thank goodness it was a warm day, with May around the corner, the few trees overhanging the riverbank heavy with blossom, though darkness lurked low in the sky.

She wasn't ready to climb back up that hill, knock at that door and apologise. *I assume you'll want to leave first thing tomorrow*, April had said, so icy and dignified.

She had not bought a return ticket.

Two children skipped past, a boy and a girl about seven, probably on their way to the mill. They looked at her keenly, giggling behind their hands, and she thought what an eejit she must look, standing opposite the pub, leaning on the railings as if she couldn't stand up. Maybe they thought she was a drunkard! She would have to keep walking for a while, give April the chance to calm down – though April had not been the one to lose her temper. All right then, since she was trying to be honest, to give herself the chance to work out what to say, what she thought, how she felt.

With a new sense of purpose, she strode on past the Queen's Head, breathing in the sour, familiar, comforting smell of alcohol. Those days when she had pacified herself with whiskey! But her child had been killed, she had hardly known what she was doing, she could not be blamed.

That's not entirely true.

It was the same inner voice that had just accused her of jealousy. But she would not listen to it. All the same, it was a relief to realise that she had not touched strong drink for a fortnight. She had barely thought about it until now – proof that she had not had any unhealthy dependence on it; it had only been a crutch.

By now she had walked all the way down Riverside Road, crossed the bridge over the River Easter, and was in the centre of town. It was so unfamiliar, with its greying yellowish stone and hilly, cobbled streets, the shop signs bearing names that seemed so foreign: Oldroyd, Widdop, Hinchcliff, which she read at first as *Heathcliff*. She had only been to England once before, and that had been to London with Maurice, which had had its excitements – the theatre, the Underground, the wonderful shops – but had been rather frightening too, not least because, away from home and the farm and Robbie (and how *could* she have left him behind with his granny? If she had him now, she wouldn't part with him for a second!), she and Maurice had found little to talk about. Mona had paid for the trip – 'a second honeymoon,' she said, their first having been three wet days in Portstewart. Evelyn had suspected that Mona was hoping to encourage another grandchild along. Well, so much for that!

The chime of a church bell made her jump and she stood for a moment counting its tolls: six o'clock. The church, of unassuming grey stone, was, according to the wooden board outside, called St Anthony's. A bicycle was chained to the railings, the door was slightly ajar and without thinking further, she went in. She never thought of the English as being anything other than Protestants, so it was a surprise to find herself in what was unmistakably a Catholic church, with its ornate remote-looking altar, the plaster saints – St Anthony, she presumed, and of course the Virgin Mary, in blue and white robes – and the dark, eye-pricking smell of incense she remembered from the times she and April used to sneak into St Brigid's in Lisnacashan. She unfocused her eyes to avoid the gruesome figure of Christ hanging on the cross near the front, his hands and side pierced and bleeding. Honestly, why would anyone want to look at that? But she knew the answer, even though she was a Protestant: to make you feel guilty. They didn't go in for that sort of thing at First Lisnacashan Presbyterian. *I shouldn't be here*, she thought, but as she breathed in the dusty exotic air, blinked in the dim candlelight, she felt her shoulders relax and something loosen inside her.

Nobody knows I'm here. And I don't know anybody.

She had never been so anonymous. It felt both lonely and free.

She slid into a pew halfway up and, because it felt the right thing to do, knelt down, bowed her head and clasped her hands. Did she look like a Catholic? Wait, didn't they cover their heads? It didn't matter: the church was empty apart from two old ladies in the front row – she could only see their tweed-coated backs, but they did indeed have their heads shrouded in lace mantillas – and a man kneeling a few pews in front of her, across the aisle, clasping what she knew to be rosary beads. She half-closed her eyes, watching him from under her lids. She could only see his profile, his lips moving as he recited what she supposed was a prayer. *Idolatry and empty ritual*, she had heard her daddy and the Reverend McClure say. She tried not to stare but found herself mesmerised and lulled by the regular way the beads were threaded through his fingers. She didn't like to look at his face, so she focussed on his hands and the beads. Each prayer lasted exactly the same amount of time: she counted – eight seconds. She watched, counted, watched, counted, calmed by the cadence of it, caught up in this stranger's prayer, reassured by its regularity: eight seconds, new bead; eight seconds, new bead; eight – no! This one was shorter. And now – a longer one. By the time he had got back to the eight-second rhythm she felt cheated. She glanced back at his face, just as he looked up, crossed himself and sat back in the pew, smoothing the knees of his trousers.

It was Charlie Teal.

No! It couldn't be. It must be someone who looked like him. Since Friday night she had foolishly let herself dwell on this stranger and now she was conjuring him up everywhere. She'd see him a dozen times before she went home, and none of those men would be him either.

But it *was* Charlie.

He stood up, seemed to trip, and she had a ridiculous fleeting fantasy about him collapsing in the aisle and her rescuing him, until she realised he was deliberately doing a sort of curtsey – very strange in a man – and she stayed frozen in her pew, the kneeler digging into her knees. How did Catholics manage it for so long? Had they differently-shaped knees or did they just get used to it? Should she acknowledge him? Would he remember her? It had been April he noticed on Friday evening, not her. Well, he was wasting his time with that one! She immediately felt mean – what a thing to think in a church, even a Catholic one! – and then she found herself standing up just as he was passing her. She didn't try to do the curtsey thing: getting it wrong would look much sillier than not doing it at all. She looked ahead as if concentrating on holy thoughts. She wouldn't speak first. If it was meant to be he would—

'Hello again, Miss, er ...?'

She looked up, flooded with joy – no, that was silly. Worse than silly: *wrong*. All the same she didn't correct him by saying *Mrs*. And she was glad of the dim light because her cheeks felt hot. She placed her left hand into the pocket of her skirt and wriggled it about until she had teased off her wedding ring. She had lost so much weight that it slid off easily.

'Kenny,' she said. 'Evelyn Kenny. It's Mr Teal, isn't it?

95

I didn't recognise you without your horse. Is she parked outside?'

He smiled. 'I don't think Father Leonard would be best pleased. No, it's the bike today.'

They fell into step as they walked out. In the porch he said, 'I've never seen you at Mass, Miss Kenny.'

'I'm only visiting,' she said.

'From – is it Ireland?'

'Northern Ireland. I was just … you know. Calling in.'

'Aye. Me too. It's my mam's anniversary. I called in to ask Father Leonard to say a Mass for her and then I thought I should stop and say a few decades of the rosary.' He spoke without embarrassment, as if this were perfectly normal behaviour on a Wednesday evening.

'I'm sorry about your mother.'

'It's a while ago,' he said. 'But thank you.'

They were out in the street now where she was hit first by the brightness after the dim church, and then by the fact that, bright or not, the sky was shining with ominous intensity.

Mr Teal glanced up. 'I don't like the look of those clouds.' He gestured to the bicycle chained to the railings. 'I'm sorry I can't offer you a lift home, Miss Kenny. If I were you, I'd run before the rain starts. Have you far to go?'

'I … I don't really know. I mean, I sort of wandered into town, not really paying attention. I'm not actually sure *how* to get home – to where I'm staying, I mean.'

She could easily have worked it out. She need only have walked back in the direction she had come from. She could have asked someone in the street.

She did none of those things. She allowed Charlie Teal to look concerned, and when she said it was Riverside Road and he started to give her directions, she looked stupid and said she wasn't sure – she *thought* she would be all right – maybe she could ask someone …

He said that he could not think of her being lost in a strange town, and that he would walk beside her and set her on her way. As she had known he would.

But maybe because she'd been in a church, her conscience began to prickle. She was married! She was grieving. However delightful it might be to walk through the drizzling streets with this handsome English stranger, trying and failing not to notice his strong, supple fingers on the handlebars as he wheeled the bicycle, the curve of his cheekbone, the long legs in flannels keeping step with her, it was *wrong*. She stopped at the bridge and said, with regretful honesty, 'I know my way from here. It's just over the bridge and up Riverside Road.'

He frowned. 'Are you sure? It can be rough around the Queen's Head and up by Townsend Street. I don't mind—'

'No, honestly.' She placed a hand on his arm and then, shocked at herself, pulled it away. 'I'll be fine from here.'

And she was nervous enough about her reception at number eleven, without arriving with a more or less strange man in tow. Or maybe, she thought, setting off up the hill and allowing herself to turn back briefly (but it was too late; the bicycle had carried him away, as if she had imagined him), she just didn't want him to see April again. And at that thought, and at the memory of how she had left things with April, the enormity of having to walk back to that house and apologise, and worse, far worse, the prospect of going back home to Lisnacashan and Maurice – she felt her steps slow to a faltering shuffle. She was back at the spot where she had leaned on the railings more than an hour before. She breathed again the stale smell of the Queen's Head, noticed something on the wall that hadn't been there before: tattered strips of a poster, something about a meeting, but because it was half ripped off she couldn't read it. It looked torn and damp and sad.

The sky ahead blackened and the first big raindrops started to pit the dark river below the railings. Water snaked through her hair and down her neck, but she could not make herself walk on up the hill.

Twelve

When Felicity sat down to dinner, a dinner April had had little heart in making, she said, 'Did I hear some sort of vulgar brawl? I almost came down, but I needed to finish my article. I thought I heard shouting and a door slamming?'

'You did.'

April set a plate in front of her – potatoes, bacon and cabbage, traditional Irish fare as a nod to Evelyn's visit, and a novelty because they avoided pork when they had Jewish refugees staying. But April, with Evelyn's words nipping at her, had little appetite and Felicity, said, 'Gosh, I'm really not hungry. And I must get to the post before seven.'

'Do your best.' April gave a dejected laugh. 'I sound like my mammy.'

'What was the row about?'

'Och, something silly.' April slid into her own seat.

'It didn't sound silly.'

April sighed. 'She said … things about you.'

'*Things*? Me?'

'She called you my fancy woman.'

Felicity, to April's surprise, laughed. 'I've never been called that before!'

'It's not funny. She said desperate things. *Unnatural* and *disgusting* and – I can't even say them.'

Felicity was not laughing now. Her face flushed and then paled, and she set down her fork. 'She's been here for over a week. Why wait until now for the moral outrage?'

'She hadn't realised that we were, you know. Together.'

Felicity was quiet for a long time. Then, in a tight voice, she said, 'But you must have told her.'

April shook her head. 'I didn't exactly spell it out.'

'So what did you say? Pal? Chum? *Landlady*?'

'I don't remember. *Friend* probably. Does it matter?'

A pulse beat in Felicity's neck. After a long time she said, 'It matters to me.'

April came round the table and went to hug her, but Felicity stiffened so meaningfully that she walked to the window instead. The sky had blackened. She pulled down the blind. 'Felicity, we've had this conversation before. You know we have to be discreet. I can't run a marriage bureau if I'm parading round the town like Radclyffe Hall or—'

'Nobody's asking you to *parade*.' She had never heard Felicity so cold. 'But it would be nice to acknowledge who I am – who *we* are – to someone staying in our home.'

'I didn't *not* tell her. I thought she'd work it out. She wasn't born yesterday.'

'It appears she was.'

'Och, Felicity, don't be like that. Aren't we grand as we are? People who matter, like Martha and Fabian, accept us. It's nobody else's business.'

'So we stay below the parapet? Not drawing attention to ourselves? Making sure we don't offend anyone's sensibilities? Being grateful for their *acceptance*? Skulking in the shadows?' Her eyes sparked with passion as her voice rose and then cracked, as the speech ended in a burst of harsh coughing.

Normally April would have filled a glass of water, but now she stood back, leaning against the windowsill, until the fit passed and Felicity was wiping her eyes – April didn't know if they were sad tears, angry tears, or simply tears brought on by coughing. Felicity rarely cried.

'Felicity, you're the least skulky person I know,' she said. 'You're never done going on rallies and raising awareness and writing articles and I don't know what else.'

'And none of my friends care a jot that I'm a lesbian. *They* aren't small-minded and provincial.'

'Look, Felicity, this is Easterbridge. It's all right for you in your radical circles. Or in London or Paris or maybe even Manchester. But people aren't ready for a lesbian running a marriage bureau in a wee town in Yorkshire. And believe me, Easterbridge is sophisticated compared to Lisnacashan. Evelyn can't help being from there, any more than I can.'

'But you *can* help not being honest about our relationship. And letting her say those beastly things.'

'I told her to leave!' Her voice rose in indignation. 'What more can I do?'

'I don't know.' Felicity seemed to lose heart in the fight and slumped in her chair. 'But everywhere I look people are being kept down and deprived of their rights and forbidden to be who they are. I can't have it in my own home.' She pulled herself up from the table. 'I need to catch the post. There's a late collection from the post office.'

'Let me go,' April begged. 'It looks like rain and I could cycle there and back in ten minutes. You don't want to be dragging yourself into town and you coughing.'

'You're always saying I should get more air. No, I need to get away from here. For a while.'

'But are we ...?'

'What? *Friends*?' Felicity loaded the word with scorn. She sighed and rubbed her face, pushing back her heavy curls. 'I'll see you later.'

'I'll come with you.'

Felicity shook her head. 'I won't be long.' She gave a brief tight smile on her way out.

As April cleared up their largely untouched plates and poured hot water into the sink to wash up, she reflected that, counting Lily, that was three rows she had had today. Pretty impressive for someone whose vocation was bringing people together.

As the sky darkened further and then gave in to the sort of black shower that sped the tentative spring evening into night, April started to worry. About both of them. She had sat down with some work – grand plans for summer activities at Shaw's Mill that she wanted to discuss with Sybil – but found her mind jumping around in fretful bursts.

She hated fighting with Felicity. It happened very rarely, and when it did, April would rage and storm, but Felicity licked her wounds alone. She hadn't come straight back from the post office. Maybe she had walked to Fabian's – she had lately taken to appreciating his brotherly concern more than she used to, and she was fond of Martha. April could imagine her, cosied up in their elegant sitting room, in front of a roaring fire, drinking coffee and letting herself calm down. She would return in a better mood.

Oh, but she had been so hurt!

April's stomach squeezed with unease: *was* she guilty of putting the bureau, and her work, before Felicity? Should she be more open about their relationship? But why? It was nobody's business. And if they *all* reacted like Evelyn, once her best friend …

And Evelyn. Where could *she* be? She didn't know Easterbridge, and she had rushed out without coat or bag, so she would have no money to allow her to shelter in a café. She had always been quick to offend, but equally to forgive, so why hadn't she come back? Even if she had had a shock, she must surely accept that April had done nothing wrong.

April forced herself to remember Evelyn storming out – so angry and upset, out of all proportion, surely, to what April had told her. She *must* be expecting: that made women go funny, didn't it? Hanna had spent the first few months either crying or raging. April had mentioned, one sleeting December evening, when Hanna and Erich had come for dinner, that she had read in 'Nature Notes' in the *Easterbridge Recorder* that the winter weather was especially hard for hedgehogs, and Hanna had burst into heartbroken sobs. When Erich had gently passed her a handkerchief, she had turned on him and demanded that he breathe more quietly because the sound of his breathing made her want to scream. That wasn't too far away from how Evelyn was carrying on.

Well, the minute she got back, April would ask her straight out. No more pussyfooting around. But if she *was* expecting, and her so distressed, and grieving, well, she could do herself a mischief, or be taken bad or *anything*. April imagined the headlines in the *Easterbridge Recorder*: VISITOR DROWNED IN RIVER EASTER! *Irish woman's death occurred while the presence of her mind was disturbed.* You read stories like that all the time! What would she tell Maurice?

When the doorbell rang, her first thought was relief – *Thank God, one of them's back!* – but as soon as she went into the hall and switched on the light, for the passage was so dark, she could see that the shadowy head visible in the fanlight was too tall to be Evelyn or Felicity, and, besides, was wearing a policeman's helmet. Her hands shook so much she could hardly get the door open.

'Miss McVey?' It was Constable Armstrong. He cleared his throat and said, 'I'm afraid there's been a nasty incident in town. Your friend's been hurt. They've taken her to St John's.'

April gaped at him.

'The hospital,' he clarified.

Thirteen

The hospital bench was cold, hard and narrow, reminding Evelyn of the pew in St Anthony's – was that only an hour or so ago? There was nothing to read and very little to count – two doors: the one they had entered by, and another, with a sign saying *Private: Hospital Staff Only*; three tall thin windows, each with eight small panes; four plain green walls, enlivened only by the kind of poster not designed to bring cheer: *Diphtheria Kills! Your kiss of affection might spread infection: don't kiss babies!* The windows were set high, their sole purpose apparently to introduce a biting draught. Probably, during the day, they let in some light, but day, and light, and warmth, seemed very far away.

April, pacing the floor, also seemed out of reach, face frozen, shoulders rigid. Evelyn had known her since she was five, in every sort of mood, but she had never seen her so distant, or so worried. She didn't know what to say. 'I'm sure Felicity'll be all right' was clearly nonsense. Apologising for the row felt irrelevant now.

Beyond the waiting room, behind the scuffed dark-green door marked *Private*, was some inner sanctum, where something, presumably, was happening to Felicity. A fearsome nurse in a starched winged cap – how on earth did it stay on her head? – had refused to tell them anything except that she was Sister Metcalfe, that this was most irregular, and they should go home and let the hospital staff do their job.

'I live with her,' April had insisted. 'We share everything.'

Sister Metcalfe had looked her up and down and did not seem pleased with what she saw. 'You're not her next of kin, are you?'

April had looked disconcerted. 'Not strictly speaking I suppose. But for dear sake!'

'She has a brother,' Evelyn had said.

'Oh, a brother!' Sister Metcalfe looked mollified, demanded details, and swept out of the room.

'I'm sorry,' Evelyn said at once. 'Was that the wrong thing to say?'

April shook her head wearily. 'It doesn't matter. Fabian needs to know.'

But know what? They had been told only that Felicity had been brought in unconscious – *quite insensible*, the nurse had said, as if Felicity were doing this merely to vex.

The windowpanes, grey when they had first come in, gradually blackened. Evelyn put the time in by making anagrams out of the words in the posters. *Diphtheria kills* was the easiest: *Dish harelip kilt*, and then *Edith kill parish*, which made her smile – but she cut the smile off. *Hilda Hitler kips*.

The door they had entered by opened and Sister Metcalfe reappeared, leading a tall, smartly-dressed man in his forties, followed by—

'Martha! Thank God,' April burst out.

'My dear, you look *shattered*.' Martha sprang forward and put her arms round April. It was the most spontaneous of gestures but it jabbed at a cold spot in Evelyn's heart: *I should have done that*, she thought. And then: She wouldn't have wanted me to. Not after I said those terrible things.

'It's the not knowing,' April said. 'Maybe they'll tell *you*, Fabian?'

'I could try,' Fabian said. 'I'm not sure who I'd ask.'

He turned, but Sister Metcalfe had withdrawn. He looked as sick with worry as April, and Martha reached out a hand and placed it gently on his arm.

'Surely someone will tell us soon,' she said. 'We'll just have to be patient. Fabian, this is April's friend, Mrs Evelyn Kenny.'

They shook hands as if meeting at a dinner party – not that Evelyn went to dinner parties, though Fabian and Martha looked as though they might. Martha was in a fur coat which made Evelyn, still damp from the rain, feel very cold.

'So, what do you know?' Martha asked, settling down and placing her handbag beside her.

'Nothing!' April said. 'A policeman came – Constable Armstrong, Martha, remember?'

This meant nothing to Evelyn, but Martha nodded.

'He recognised her from the time he spoke at the mill. That's how he found out where she lived. But all he could tell me was there'd been an *incident*, and she was hurt. She's still unconscious. I put up a quare fight to make them let me see her, but they wouldn't.'

'How horrid of them,' Martha said.

April had been, Evelyn thought, quite frightening in her determination. It reminded her, uncomfortably, of when they had tried to keep her from Robbie's body, tried not to let her see—

But she had insisted, as fiercely as April. And unlike April, because she was his mother, because she had screamed like a banshee, she had prevailed. She sometimes wished she hadn't. She shook her head, as if to banish the memory, and focussed on the present.

'It doesn't sound like a *traffic* accident,' Martha said.

'*Incident* sounds more like an altercation,' Fabian said.

'Oh, Fabian! As if Felicity would be involved in an *altercation*.'

'Some of those rallies she goes to can be violent. Remember when she was hit by one of those ghastly Blackshirts in Olympia?'

'But this is Easterbridge. And if there had been any kind of demonstration or something, we'd have heard about it.'

'She only went out to post an article,' April said.

'Well then!'

But there was no doubt that *something* bad had happened. You didn't go out to the postbox and end up in hospital.

'You should have telephoned us at once,' Fabian said. 'We'd have driven you here.'

'Sure I wasn't thinking straight. Thank God I'd Evelyn. She arrived home just as Constable Armstrong was leaving.'

It wasn't much but it gave Evelyn a small glow.

'Did Constable Armstrong say *where* it happened?'

Before April could answer, the *Private* door opened to admit a short, bald doctor about Fabian's age.

Fabian stood up. 'Well?' he demanded. 'Can someone please tell us something?'

'Shall we all sit down?' the doctor said. 'I'm Dr Cuthbert.'

'Fabian Carr,' Fabian said. 'Felicity's brother.'

'Fabian Carr?' The doctor's forehead wrinkled. 'Peterdale?'

'Yes. Left in '14. Good lord – James Cuthbert? Jim?'

Dr Cuthbert rubbed a hand over his head. 'I know I've changed since my hair went west. But you look exactly the same!'

'Hardly.' If Fabian was trying to hide the fact he was flattered, he didn't succeed. 'But what are you doing here, old boy?'

April cleared her throat. 'This is a touching reunion, but d'you not think we've something more important to discuss?'

Both men looked abashed.

Cuthbert gave a gallant bow in April's direction. 'Forgive me. Carr and I were by way of being pals back in the dark ages. Lost touch after – well, the war and all that. Gosh, it really is splendid to see your old mug again. I heard you'd come through but ... anyway. To the matter in hand.'

'We aren't clear what happened,' Martha said.

'Neither are we. And Miss Carr is in no state to enlighten us.'

Martha and Fabian looked alarmed and April bit her lip. Evelyn reached across and took her hand and, after a brief hesitation, April squeezed it.

'She was found outside St Anthony's Church – someone saw her lying in the street, realised she was hurt rather than ... well, any of the other reasons why someone might collapse in the street, and called for an ambulance. She had no means of identification, and it was clear there had been violence, so we were obliged to inform the police. And, fortunately, the young constable recognised her.'

April's fingers dug into Evelyn's palm.

'As far as we can tell, she's been hit with something hard. She has bruising to the cheek which suggests—'

'Ah, God, no!' April pulled her hands away and cupped them over her eyes as if to banish this image.

'—but she's also hit her head, probably on the ground. She's coming round now, but chances are she won't remember.'

'Did it look as though she'd been robbed? Had her handbag stolen or anything of that sort?' Martha asked gently.

'She didn't have her bag,' April said. She screwed up

her face, trying to remember. 'No. She definitely didn't, because I saw it hanging in the hall, and I thought, *She won't have her keys*, but it didn't matter, because I was in.'

'She had a piece of paper in her hand.'

'A letter. She went out to post an article. She's a writer.'

'I believe it was more in the nature of a poster – a bill? Something of that sort? Sister Metcalfe said she was gripping it for dear life.'

They all looked at each other, puzzled.

'I have to see her,' April said.

'And you are …?'

'We live together.'

'*Five* minutes,' the doctor said, 'but don't excite her in any way. She needs to be kept very quiet. We're keeping her in for observation.'

He led April out of the room.

Left with Martha and Fabian, Evelyn felt awkward, though they were kind and polite.

'Wasn't it lucky you were here?' Martha said. 'And you can keep April company while Felicity's in hospital. I imagine they'll keep her in for a few days. Are you able to stay on, dear? I'm sure your husband is missing you.'

Her eyes slid towards Fabian with a look of such affection that Evelyn felt lonelier than ever. She and Maurice had never looked at each other like that, not even at first.

I assume you'll want to leave first thing tomorrow, April had said.

'I'm sure he'd understand if April wants me.' Evelyn crossed her fingers that April would.

Fabian and Martha drove them home. April had been very quiet after seeing Felicity, saying only that she seemed very drowsy.

'Need you go in early tomorrow?' Martha asked as the car made its way up a rain-slicked Riverside Road. 'Can't Lily hold the fort?'

April laughed mirthlessly. 'I've sacked her. No, I can't explain now.' She ran a hand over her face. 'What have I on tomorrow?' Her face fell. 'Oh lord – *four* new clients! Two in the morning, and two after lunch.'

'April! You can't possibly cope – you know how intense those interviews are. You'll be in no fit state.'

'I'll have to be. Oh, and that old bat Metcalfe said visiting was at three-thirty *exactly*, for half an hour. How'm I going to manage that?'

She sounded despairing and Evelyn wished she could help. But what did she know about interviewing clients in a marriage bureau?

'Maybe I could put Miss Merriman off until after four and rush back?'

'No.' Martha sounded very firm. 'I can't allow it. I'm sorry, April – you are, to all intents and purposes, your own boss, but True Minds is *my* bureau, and I can't risk you not being on top of things.'

'I think what Martha means,' Fabian said gently, 'is that she is very concerned about your wellbeing, and might pop into the office tomorrow to support you in any way she can – without interfering, of course. And to hold the fort while you go to see Felicity.'

'Thank you,' Martha said. 'That's exactly what I meant.'

They dropped them off, Fabian telling April not to worry too much, that Felicity was tough, had spent her whole childhood getting into scrapes and always came up smiling.

'This was hardly a scrape,' April said as she closed the door behind them. 'I'm gasping for a cuppa.'

'I'll make it.'

111

They sat facing each other in the kitchen where Evelyn had said those terrible things.

'I'm sorry,' she said now.

April nodded. 'I forgive you,' she said, 'but you need to understand ...' She ran her finger round the rim of her teacup. 'D'you remember when you were getting married, and I asked you if you were sure, if you really loved Maurice?'

Evelyn nodded slowly.

'D'you remember what you said?'

'Not really ...' She had never loved Maurice the way she knew now that April loved Felicity, the way Martha and Fabian clearly adored each other. Nor had she, even once, experienced the heart-quickening, stomach-plunging desire for him that – yes, she admitted guiltily – she had felt for Charlie Teal on those two brief meetings.

'You asked me why I couldn't be happy for you,' April reminded her. 'And why I couldn't just want *what normal people wanted*. I've never forgotten it.'

'Oh.'

'And I didn't understand. I knew I didn't feel romantic about men; I knew I'd never marry. But when I met Felicity I realised' – she looked up, her eyes bright with tears – 'I wanted *exactly* what so-called normal people want: love, companionship, someone to walk through life with.'

Evelyn bit her lip.

'That's what I have with Felicity. A partner. It's not our fault we can't get married, that the law doesn't let us be together the way you and Maurice are. But we are *not* unnatural, or-or disgusting. Any more than you and Maurice are. And you *have* to accept that if you want to keep being friends.' Her voice was stern.

'I can't believe I said those things. I suppose' – Evelyn stared into her cup – 'I was jealous.'

'Och, Evelyn!' April laughed, a sound that had once been as familiar to Evelyn as her own voice. 'Sure haven't you Maurice, and your lovely home and ...'

'Maurice ...' There was a moment when she could almost have said it. But she didn't. She shook her head. 'It doesn't matter.'

'Evelyn,' April said. 'Tell me this is none of my business, but I was wondering – I know you're grieving, but I wondered ... is there any chance you could be ... expecting?'

'Expecting what?' she asked stupidly, and then she grasped it. Miss Connaughton had wondered the same thing. 'Oh!' She shook her head. 'No. No chance at all.'

'Well, you'd know.' April stretched and yawned. 'Right, bedtime. Matchmaking stops for nobody, and it'll be no time till the morning.'

Fourteen

'Isn't this like old times?' Martha sounded like a contented cat, if cats talked rather than purred.

Both morning interviews had gone well, especially with Douglas Grant, a sandy-haired man in tweeds, who looked exactly as though he had just dismounted from his horse. He had come down from Kirkcudbrightshire to manage an estate north of Easterbridge and April warmed to him at once.

'It's partly the Scottish accent,' she told Martha after he left and they were enjoying a sandwich in the private office. 'It's not the same as mine but it's not a million miles away.' She yawned; she wouldn't have minded some fresh air, but last night's rain had persisted into an unrelenting wet day. 'I thought he'd be perfect for Miss Firth, and he will.'

'I'll make a note,' Martha said, reaching for the jotter pad.

April sipped her tea. 'I was grateful for you with wee Miss Catherwood,' she said. 'You're better than me with the shy ones.'

'I wouldn't say that. You're a natural, and you've a deeper understanding of people now. More empathy and maturity.'

'It's not being older. It's loving Felicity. That's why I understand better.'

'Well, yes.'

She and Martha had never discussed April's relationship with Felicity. But now she wanted to be more open.

'Martha,' she asked. 'Does it bother you – not personally, but as the owner of True Minds – that I live with Felicity? Do you worry that it doesn't set the right *tone*? I'm *so* discreet.'

'I know.' Martha set her cup down thoughtfully and April's stomach tensed.

Stupid to be so nervous, but she had had hardly any sleep, and she felt frayed and worn. Would Martha say that all her discretion had been pointless, and she could have declared her love for Felicity from the town hall steps if she'd had a mind to?

Or would she say that it was completely inappropriate for her precious marriage bureau to be run by someone so deviant? That people would be scared to consult them in case April encouraged them into unnatural passions and bohemian decadence? That she would prefer April to leave?

This being the real world, and the real Martha, she merely repeated, gently, 'I know you're discreet, April. I admit, I'd concerns at first – I always felt it lent the bureau a certain gravitas that I was myself a widow rather than a spinster.'

Martha's first marriage had ended at Passchendaele, after eleven days together; she and Gordon had both been in their early twenties; she had hardly been a wise old widow.

'But I soon stopped worrying,' Martha went on, and April's stomach relaxed. 'Most people who know you live with Felicity assume you are two spinsters sharing the housekeeping. That's hardly unusual. And if anyone thinks more ... well, it's none of their business.'

'That's what I've always thought.'

'In my experience,' Martha said, and now she did sound like that wise old widow, 'people take one at face value. People see *you*, April, as what you are – a jolly good sort, competent, busy, community-minded. If anyone is put off approaching the bureau because of your living arrangements, well' – Martha sounded brisk – 'they aren't the sort of clients we welcome, are they?'

'I suppose not.' Relief trembled through her.

'Don't give it another thought,' Martha said. 'The *tone* of the bureau is as healthy as ever. Though I'm glad you've given young Lily her marching orders.'

April had a brief mental image of Lily marching.

'Do you know where Miss Catherwood had come from?' Martha asked.

'Manchester.' April wondered what this had to do with anything. Miss Jane Catherwood had been a demure, good-living librarian with a passion for history. All her spare wages went on visiting stately homes and historic sites. She had grown quite animated about her recent trip to Whalley Abbey.

'Exactly!' Martha sounded triumphant. 'Not exactly round the corner. That *proves* you're doing well.'

April brightened. 'That's the third Mancunian this month. I wonder if it's Mammy?' Mammy hadn't been thrilled about April taking up matchmaking, but on a rare visit to Easterbridge she had been charmed by Martha (less so by Felicity) and completely won over. April suspected she was the talk of Mammy's missionary work class. Mammy would love to hear about the Honourable Augusta; she couldn't resist a title, not that she came across many in Eupatoria Street, where she helped her sister with her dressmaking business.

Then she sighed. 'It's grand to be doing so well, Martha,

but now I've got rid of Lily, I need a proper assistant. And you know yourself it's not everybody takes to the work. I don't need somebody as good as me,' she acknowledged modestly, 'but an awful lot better than Lily.'

The clock struck the three-quarter hour and both women started to tidy up their lunch. April opened the window to let out the smell of egg and onion. All morning she had thought of the day's appointments as a buffer between her and the hospital visit she longed for and dreaded. What if Felicity were worse? What if she had died and nobody had told April? What if Felicity, who last night had merely smiled groggily at her, had recovered her senses, remembered the row, and refused to see her? Her shopping basket sat in the corner, better prepared for the visit than she was. She hadn't known what to take, apart from a clean nightie and washing things. She had considered taking Felicity's current book from beside the bed, but surely even Felicity wouldn't feel like reading *Down and Out in Paris and London* after a head injury. Instead, she had packed *They Knew Mr Knight* by Dorothy Whipple, a birthday present from Martha which April had just finished. But with luck Felicity wouldn't be in for long. Surely she'd be better off recuperating at home in Riverside Road.

Their first client after lunch, Mr Cyril Henderson, was a history teacher from Leeds who spent his weekends visiting castles and battle sites.

'Of course I understand most women don't fancy traipsing over ruins,' he said apologetically, fingering his reddish beard.

'You never know.' April felt, for the first time in ages, the temptation to giggle.

'Now wasn't that the luck of God?' she said when he left. 'How often do you get a perfect match coming in the very same day?'

'Gosh, hardly ever,' Martha said. 'But are we getting ahead of ourselves? Just because he and Miss Catherwood both like history ...'

'Och, it's more than that. They're about the same age, both good-living – you heard him say he was Temperance – and much of a muchness in the looks department. Ah now, don't say that doesn't matter' – as Martha opened her mouth to object – 'you know yourself we can't match up a beauty queen to a fella with a face like a chewed chop.'

Martha laughed. 'Have you had many beauty queens in lately? No, you're right. They're both on the plainer side of *personable*.'

'Manchester and Leeds aren't next door to each other.'

'About an hour and half by train,' Martha said briskly. 'And *distance is nothing when one has a motive*, as Jane Austen reminds us.'

'Och, I've missed having someone with a titter of wit,' April said with a sigh. 'Lily was a wee bit light on Jane Austen quotations.'

'And I've missed hearing things like *a face like a chewed chop*.'

An unspoken thought hovered.

'Right,' April said, suddenly business-like because she found it hard to leave thoughts unspoken, but she had vowed never to voice that one. 'I'll send Miss Catherwood his details and see if she'd like to meet him. And I'll set up a meeting between Douglas Grant and Barbara Firth too, if Miss Firth's agreeable. And why wouldn't she be?'

And now there was no buffer between her and the hospital. April got her things together slowly, torn between longing to see Felicity, worry about how she would find her, and a weary reluctance to do battle with Sister Metcalfe and her like.

'Don't come back afterwards,' Martha said as she buttoned her coat. 'I'll see to everything. After Miss Merriman it's just a matter of filing, isn't it? I take it you haven't made any revolutionary changes to my excellent system?'

'Divil a one.'

'And I'm in no hurry. Prudence has a hockey match in Wetherby; she won't be home until late.'

'What about Fabian's dinner?'

Martha laughed. 'He won't starve. Mrs Perry will have left a casserole in the oven. So I shall enjoy playing at being Mrs Hart of the True Minds Marriage Bureau again. I'll come in again tomorrow – even when Felicity's home, she'll need looking after.'

Playing, April thought as she hurried down the stairs and out into St Margaret's Lane, putting up her umbrella in the doorway. Wouldn't it be grand to play at something while somebody else made your tea and cleaned your house? To come home to the smell of a casserole you hadn't cooked. She and Felicity did everything themselves, and they both worked *more* than full time.

In her two years in Easterbridge, April had never had cause to visit the hospital until last night. It was only a quarter of an hour's walk from the office, in a gracious treelined road which also housed the council offices. St John's was a misleadingly pleasant, triple-fronted redbrick building with a white door, an old cottage hospital rather than a former workhouse. Unlike last night, when the place had seemed deserted and eerie, a crowd waited in the black-and-white-tiled hallway, all, like April, grasping bags and umbrellas, some looking anxious, others resigned to tedious duty. At half past three precisely a bell rang, and they all made their way right or left. Last night had been so bewildering that April had worried about not being able to find Felicity, but she remembered that it was Ward 3, and she was relieved to see it signposted.

She saw Felicity as soon as a nurse, not Sister Metcalfe, opened the ward door and the half-dozen visitors streamed in. She was in the last bed on the right, and from a distance looked much as usual. Her face was turned expectantly towards the doorway, and she raised her hand in greeting when she spotted April. Thank God, April thought, flooded with relief and love, that Martha had made the visit possible. Imagine poor Felicity lying there waiting in vain. The closer she got, the less well Felicity looked: her right cheek, from cheekbone to jaw, was swollen and plum-coloured, and the rest of her face was very white.

But the hands that clasped April's felt as strong as ever. 'I didn't think you'd be able to get off work.'

'Amn't I the boss?' April set her bag on the floor and pulled out the clean handkerchiefs and the book, setting them neatly on the bedside locker. She needed these practical tasks to settle her, to help her get used to this battered, defeated Felicity. 'Och, love.' She kept her voice low as she sat on the narrow wooden chair at the bedside. 'You look like you've done ten rounds with Jack Peterson. Do you remember—?'

Felicity made to shake her head then winced. 'Ouch. I remember *some*. More than last night. Constable Armstrong spoke to me earlier which jogged my memory … but it's vague. I sort of remember the attack' – it was April's turn to wince – 'and I know I was posting an article, but I don't remember writing it.'

Did that mean she didn't remember their row? April wasn't going to ask. 'Can you bear to tell me?' she said instead.

'I *have* to tell you.' Felicity's voice was fierce and for a moment April wondered was she feverish, and if they hadn't been in such a public place, she would have placed her hand gently on Felicity's forehead. 'Because there's something very nasty going on in Easterbridge, and if we don't stop it—'

'Shh, love. Don't upset yourself. Thon nurse isn't missing a trick.'

She glanced at the round-faced nurse, who was apparently making notes at a small table halfway down the ward, but who looked as if she were presiding over a room full of naughty children and woe betide anyone who dared raise their voice or sit on a bed. April felt she should sit up straight and keep her elbows by her sides, when what she longed to do was snuggle in beside Felicity and comfort her.

Felicity needed no second bidding to tell her story, but the more she talked, the more horrified April became.

'I *think* I intended to post my letter then go for a walk,' Felicity said. 'I – did we have a row?' She frowned, winced, blinked.

'Not really.'

'Doesn't matter. I'd only got as far as the Queen's Head when I saw this frightful poster stuck to the wall. Advertising a fascist meeting in The Black Horse in June. Here in Easterbridge!' She coughed, waving away April's offer of water.

'That wasn't there when I cycled home earlier.' April screwed up her face with the effort of remembering. 'No, definitely not. I'd have remembered.'

'The paste was still damp. It had clearly just been put up.' Felicity's eyes burned. 'I tried to pull it off, but it only came away in strips and some of it stuck. Still, I'd made it illegible. But I knew the person who'd posted it must be still at large. And *I* had to stop him!'

'You make it sound like a penny dreadful.'

'Don't speak so disparagingly of the penny dreadful,' Felicity said with a tentative grin. 'It fixed the damp in the hall.'

'Aye, well.'

'I guessed if he – I was jolly sure it was a *he* – was posting his beastly filth on the Queen's Head, then he would be targeting other public houses and the like, so I carried on into town. I was running. I must have looked silly, but I didn't care.'

'Felicity! He was probably on a bike. You hadn't a mission of catching him up.'

'But he had to keep stopping to post his filthy bills. There was one on the noticeboard outside the Working Men's Club – quite fresh, so I knew I was on the right track. And then I had the most wonderful stroke of luck – when I turned into Queen Street, there he was! Slapping paste on the wall outside the Catholic church.'

April looked at Felicity's face. 'I'd hardly call it *luck*.'

'I didn't get a good look at the blighter's face. He was a big, dark-haired man, that's all I can say. With a satchel – full of posters I suppose. Anyway, I called out, "What do you think you're doing?" and he swung round and said, "There's no law against it." And I said there was a law about inciting unrest. And he shrugged and said he wasn't inciting anything, it was just a meeting and why didn't I come along? I said fascism *was* inciting hatred and there was no place for it in a civilised town.' She was breathing heavily through her nose, and though she was ashen apart from the bruising, she seemed to blaze with passion.

She loves this, April thought. She loves fighting – not being battered and knocked down in the street, nobody in their right mind could love that, but the cause. The certainty of being right.

'And he said they only wanted a fair deal and the chance

to work. He said we needed to ask ourselves what we could learn from Germany.'

'For dear sake.'

'So *I* said there was indeed a lesson to be learned from Germany, but that his lot weren't the ones to teach it. And then I grabbed the poster – it was still in his hand – and crumpled it up.' She ground to a halt, and breathed out shakily. 'It happened so fast, but he called me a commie bitch and I saw something flying towards me – it must have been his satchel – and it knocked me off my feet ... and then everything sort of ... stopped.' Her voice ran out of steam and she lay back against the pillow, coughing. 'And I woke up in here with some egg-headed doctor poking and prodding me and a headache the size of a continent.'

'Och Felicity! I can't believe you put yourself at risk like that. He could have killed you!'

'I didn't do anything wrong,' Felicity said quietly.

'You know what I mean.' April took a calming breath, remembering the time two years ago when a man had molested her. Nigel Johnson, a respectable schoolmaster, had posed as a bona fide client and lured her to his home. For weeks she had seen his face everywhere, been scared to walk the streets. Martha had blamed her for putting herself in a compromising position; April had blamed herself. It was Felicity who insisted that April had done nothing wrong. 'These are dangerous times, Felicity. There's a feeling of nastiness about. We must be careful.'

'No! We must challenge it!' Felicity's vehemence brought on an explosion of coughing and the nurse was beside them instantly, pushing April away as Felicity grappled for one of the new handkerchiefs.

'Now, Miss Carr,' she said, as if to an aggravating child. 'You mustn't let your visitor excite you.' She glared at April. 'Visiting time is over. I was just about to ring the bell.'

She was given no chance to say goodbye, the nurse rearranging Felicity's pillow with more dexterity but less gentleness than April would have done it. It was as though Felicity were her prisoner, trapped in the vast, inhuman machine of the hospital where April was admitted only on sufferance.

'I'll see you tomorrow,' she said.

Felicity couldn't speak for coughing, but she raised one hand in valediction and April marched out, trying to hide the ridiculous tears which had sprung to her eyes.

Tomorrow. Ages away. She turned back. Felicity was still hunched over, coughing in that terrible, harsh way.

Even from the doorway, April could see that her handkerchief was spattered with blood.

Fifteen

Outside in the street, April cursed herself. Why had she walked out so meekly? Why didn't she march back in, find that Dr Cuthbert, and demand to know what exactly was wrong with Felicity? It wasn't a bit like her.

But she knew why.

She was scared of what he might say. You didn't need to be Florence Nightingale to know what coughing up blood meant. Hadn't April grown up in a town where the quietest whispers and the most meaningful looks were reserved for those carted off, not to the lunatic asylum, but to the TB sanatorium? *She'll need looking after*, Martha had said, and April had pictured a few cosy days at home, with Felicity taking it easy for once.

Other visitors streamed past, many pausing at the hospital gates to light cigarettes. Some, like her, must have been consumed by silent terror, but to April they all seemed gay and light, as if their loved ones had no more to vex them than an ingrown toenail.

Loved ones. That's what Felicity was. Her loved one. And they shouldn't have to hide that.

The closed hospital door looked firmly forbidding. They'd send her away with a flea in her ear, tell her *she* wasn't next of kin. But what if that nurse hadn't even bothered the doctor? What if Felicity was abandoned there, coughing, bleeding, scared, and she, April, had crept out like a mouse and left her?

Could Fabian help? He loved Felicity too, and was unarguably related to her, not to speak of being a man, and a solicitor. And he knew Dr Cuthbert. If Fabian telephoned, they would listen to him.

Fabian would be at work right now, but surely he would drop everything and help. She closed her eyes, and that frightening scene played across her mind again – Felicity hunched and fighting for breath, and the blood-spattered handkerchief.

'April?' She jumped at her name.

'Evelyn!' She had forgotten all about her. 'What are you doing here?'

'I thought you'd need company. Maybe go for a cuppa? Hospital visiting's not the easiest.'

She spoke as if she knew what she was talking about, and April wondered if Robbie had been taken to hospital before he died. Yet another thing she didn't know and couldn't ask.

'How's Felicity?'

April shook her head. 'Not good,' was all she could manage, and then, very heartfelt, 'It's great to see you. I'd love a cuppa.'

'Have you time?'

'I do, aye. Martha's holding the fort. I've my club tonight so I could have something to keep me going and that would save having to cook tea.'

'I hope you don't mind,' Evelyn said, 'but I've actually got something in the oven. I did a wee bit of shopping. It's only mutton stew but it'd save you the bother – why are you laughing?'

'I'm just delighted. How long can you stay?'

Evelyn smiled and unselfconsciously tucked her arm into April's, and they chummed up the street as they had done as girls. As plenty of women did – but she and Felicity never had. Because ... Well, because. It was all right for Evelyn; she could do what she liked. Och, but it was grand to have the company. And the prospect of a cuppa, and a meal waiting, didn't dispel her terror, but made her think she might survive until tomorrow.

Later, when they were finishing the stew, which was delicious, Evelyn asked, 'Could I come with you to your girls' club? Would I be in the way?'

'It'll be like old times.' Evelyn had helped with the club April had run at Daddy's factory in Lisnacashan. 'It's just games and chat tonight, but they love a new face.'

'I'd like that. I enjoyed being useful today.' She had not only cooked but cleaned the house. 'I ... I appreciate that I haven't been the easiest guest.'

'Och, Evelyn!' Affection fizzed up in her. 'I understand.' More, she thought now, than she had at first. And she hoped, very much, that she wasn't about to understand even better.

She could hide the extent of her worry from Evelyn, and to the girls at the club last night she had probably seemed the usual, breezy Miss McVey. Lily wasn't there, but her next sister Daisy was, galumphing stolidly around. But when April entered the office on Friday – how lovely to see Martha in her old place! – she hadn't shrugged off her coat before Martha said, 'Oh, my dear! You look terrible.'

She sighed. 'Couldn't sleep.'

'Fabian phoned the hospital last night and they said Felicity was *comfortable*. Isn't she?'

April shook her head and tears sprang to her eyes. 'She-she ...'

She couldn't go on. She stood in the middle of the office, her coat half-on and half-off, and watched her hat fall to the floor where it lay crown-down on the parquet. The lining is a different colour, she thought, a brighter blue. I never noticed before. She clutched herself and shook with sobs.

'Oh my dear!' Martha was beside her at once. For a few moments she simply hugged her, her arms tight, her body solid and smelling comfortingly of rose cologne. 'You have a jolly good bawl,' she said, and then, once April had a hold on herself, she peeled off her coat as if she was a tired child and guided her to a chair. 'Now,' she said. 'What do you know that we don't?'

'N-nothing, exactly. But when I was there yesterday, she took this desperate coughing fit.' She told Martha, briefly, about the bloodied handkerchief and saw Martha's forehead crease with concern. 'Remember she'd that bad dose in February? She never really picked up. And she kept saying it was nothing, she was always wheezy in winter, but I knew it was more than that – only she's wild stubborn!' It felt disloyal to speak about Felicity like this, but a great relief too. 'And if she's got … what I think she must have' – she couldn't make herself say *tuberculosis* or *TB* aloud – 'then-then …' Her voice shuddered to a halt as it crashed into thoughts of sanitoria and consumptive Victorians. 'They'll take her away,' she wailed. 'To some desperate sanatorium in the mountains where I won't be allowed to see her. And she'll die alone on a veranda, with snow piling up on her bedspread!'

'April!'

April forced herself to take a deep breath. 'Martha, you used to be a nurse. What else could it be?'

Martha frowned and didn't respond.

'See? You know fine rightly.'

'I haven't been a nurse since 1918,' Martha said carefully. 'And it was mostly wounds. Towards the end there were plenty of patients with pulmonary haemorrhaging. But that wasn't TB – it was the Spanish flu.'

'That's not that comforting,' April said. 'Millions of people died.'

'I know. Including my father. But you're taking too much for granted. Like when you'd tell me to buy a new hat because two clients seemed to like the cut of each other's jib. Now, the first thing to do is to speak to the doctor today. You *must* insist on that. It's very possibly not what you fear. But if it is, we'll deal with it. We can help if it's a matter of finance ... I know Felicity's money goes as soon as it's earned—'

'On good causes!' April said, because this sounded like an accusation of profligacy. 'And on supporting refugees.'

She thought of some of the refugees who had turned up on their doorstep in the last couple of years – all suffering, all weakened by their privations in Nazi Germany. What if some of them had brought this *thing* with them? Had carried to eleven Riverside Road something more than their few possessions, their horrific memories and their gratitude? Was it Julius? Frieda? Even Hanna? Had the germs been lying in wait? She shook the thought off – Felicity could have picked it up anywhere. And she had always had a weak chest – that was what had first sent her to Germany, back in the twenties, for the healthy air of the Bavarian Alps. But she could hardly go back there now. April had a vague idea that if you'd money you went to Switzerland, or Austria – she remembered the TB San in the Chalet School books. But even in that cosy world, people *died*.

She took a deep quivery breath and reminded herself she was at work. The True Minds Marriage Bureau wouldn't run itself, nor could she hand everything over to Martha. And much as she wanted to run through the streets and hammer on the hospital door and *demand* to be told what was wrong, she had enough sense to know this would lead to nothing but a wee trip to St Vincent's, Easterbridge's mental asylum.

She became aware of three things: one, that Martha must somehow, in the middle of trying to comfort her, have put the kettle on and now a steaming cup of tea was sitting in front of her; two, that the room smelt of bluebells – she looked up to see that both desks and the mantelpiece sported big jugs of them; and three, that Martha had picked up the telephone receiver with her most determined expression and was asking to be put through to St John's Infirmary.

April hardly dared sip her tea. She looked on dumbly as Martha said, in what April thought of as her extra-posh voice, 'I'm her sister ... yes, she's Dr Cuthbert's patient ... yes, I'll wait.' She cupped her hand over the mouthpiece. 'Not a lie,' she said. 'I'm her sister-in-*law*.' She spoke into the telephone again: 'I see. The family are very concerned, naturally. Half past two? That will do nicely.' She replaced the receiver. 'Right,' she said in business-like tones, 'you have a meeting – well, I do but you're the one who'll turn up – with Dr Cuthbert at half past two. You can see Felicity immediately afterwards. How does that sound?'

'Thank you.'

Martha looked in the diary. 'You're free all afternoon, so if you'd like me to come with you—?'

'No.' April took a sustaining swallow of tea. 'Thanks, but I need to do it on my own. Mammy used to tell me to be a big girl. I'm thirty-one.'

'And I'm forty, but if it were Fabian, I'd be the same,' Martha said. 'You love her; you're worried.'

'Aye.' She drained her cup and set it down on the desk. 'Right, there's a rake of new forms in. It must be the spring – it makes them as frisky as mountain goats.'

Dr Cuthbert must have realised she was not Felicity's sister – after all, they had met the other night and she had an Irish accent – but he gave no sign of it. He was brisk and matter of fact.

'Miss Carr has healed well from the concussion,' he said. A shaft of light from the high window of his consulting room played on his shiny scalp. His face was round and benign. 'And the injury to her face, though unsightly, is superficial.'

'Doctor, that's not what I'm here about,' April said. 'It's her chest.'

'Ah yes.' He steepled his fingers.

April wanted to grab him by his collar and scream, 'Tell me, for God's sake!' But until he said the words, she could cling to that wee scrap of hope.

'I understand from Miss Carr that there has been a weakness for some time. Her mother, I believe, was similarly afflicted?'

'Hmm.' April knew little about Felicity's parents. She forced herself to concentrate, wishing now that she had accepted Martha's steady, sensible support.

'There is certainly damage to the lungs. Old scar tissue – I understand she has had one or two severe bouts of bronchitis.' He glanced down at some notes on his desk. 'She spent time in the Alps and has been much stronger since.'

Dr Cuthbert's voice was bland; he didn't *sound* as though he were about to impart a death sentence, but this was all in a day's work to him. Felicity was simply a patient, his old schoolmate's sister, someone who had got herself into a pickle by tackling a fascist in the street.

'I have examined her thoroughly.'

'And what have you found?'

'There is no sign of tubercular disease' – April's heart leapt – 'at present.' Her heart sank again. 'But there *is* a weakness.'

'She was coughing up blood,' April whispered. 'I thought that always meant …'

'It can mean a number of things,' he said. 'Tuberculosis, yes, but also cancer' – April's hands flew to her mouth; she thought she was going to scream – 'but it can simply be the aftermath of bronchial damage. I understand she had influenza recently?'

'Aye, it went to her chest. She wouldn't have the doctor.'

(*Nonsense*, Felicity had said. *I'm not paying some doctor to tell me to rest.*)

'And I don't suppose she rested enough,' Cuthbert said as though he could read her thoughts. A smile played at the corner of his lips. 'I imagine she is rather a stubborn patient.'

'So – she *doesn't* have TB?'

'No sign of it,' he said, but before April could burst into tears of relief he said, 'but there *is* a weakness I don't like. She's been taking her health for granted, the naughty girl.'

She's thirty-seven, April wanted to say. *Would you call a thirty-seven-year-old man a naughty boy?*

'So what's the treatment?' she asked instead, thinking worriedly of how small their savings were, how quickly any money was swallowed up. And Felicity would surely be unable to write for a while. She couldn't imagine her without inky fingers and a distracted expression, and the tat-tat-tat of the typewriter from the study which, when she was going all guns, seemed to rattle the whole house.

'She needs complete rest,' Cuthbert said. 'Bedrest initially, and then to take things very quietly. No excitement at all.'

April nodded slowly. 'We can manage that,' she said. It would be hard to keep Felicity quiet, but if she explained how terrified she had been of losing her ...

No excitement at all: she thought of how Felicity's eyes burned when she read about Hitler in the papers, or when she told April about the latest goings-on in fascist Italy. Of how she would come home from meetings and anti-fascist demonstrations shaking with feeling. Of how she had blazed with passion recounting how she had tackled the thug who had had beaten her and knocked her down. How could April keep her from all that?

'And of course,' the doctor went on, as if this were a mere detail, 'she *must* have a change of air.'

'Wh-what do you mean?'

'She must leave town. Easterbridge isn't Leeds or Bradford, but she would do much better in clearer, purer air. The Alps would be best. I understand that helped her before?'

'Aye.' April's voice was very small. 'But, Doctor, surely she wouldn't need to go all the way to the Alps? It's not like she *has* TB.'

'Not yet. Well, if it can't be managed, I suppose ...' He clasped his fingers, looking regretful. 'Perhaps the seaside? Or the Scottish Highlands are very health-giving? It need only be for a month or so.'

April had an unlikely vision of Felicity reclining on a deck chair in front of some crashing waves, and then, even more incongruously, striding up a mountain in a kilt. April wasn't in either picture. She would have to stay in Easterbridge and run the bureau. She cursed herself for her own arrogance: if she had had someone efficient like Clara to leave in charge, she could have taken a leave of

133

absence. She couldn't employ a temporary person: it was delicate, expert work, and much of it involved getting to know clients, building their trust, developing an instinct. No, the only person she could possibly trust was Martha, and while Martha had enjoyed helping out for a couple of days, she wasn't going to step in and take charge for ... how long had he said? A month or so?

And then there was the mill – she couldn't just disappear for a month.

'What would happen,' she asked, 'if she stayed in Easterbridge?'

Doctor Cuthbert shook his head. 'In my professional opinion, to carry on as she's doing would be most detrimental to her health. Really quite dangerous. I shouldn't like to answer for the consequences.'

Sixteen

From the moment Charlie parked the Colonel's shooting brake outside the cottage and fetched Tansy for her big race at Elland Road, he had a good feeling about the night.

The dogs weren't used to being disturbed at this time and they crowded to the front of their pens, ears pricked, tails up, front legs flailing goofily. Tansy, every inch a champion, four-square and alert, her black-and-white coat shining, knew she was going racing the minute he changed her kennel coat for her travelling one. She had more coats than he did. Tippy, aware she was being left behind, drooped her ears and gazed up at him with huge reproachful eyes.

'See you later, lass,' he said, turning out the lamp and leading Tansy to the brake, where she jumped into the back and lay down at once on the old Newmarket stable rug he had folded there for a bed. Good. If she settled now she would have more energy for the race. Some dogs fretted and fussed until they were past their best – Tippy, more highly-strung than her sister, had been one of those – but Tansy had a dour, purposeful approach to racing, and she wouldn't exert herself until she had to.

Charlie didn't drive enough for it to be second nature, so he needed all his attention for the winding country roads, the narrow streets and awkward bridges of Easterbridge, and then the main road and the busy approach into Leeds, where he had to stop and start at traffic lights. It distracted him from nerves about the race. Tansy was in great form, but she had only raced at the flapper track on the outskirts of Easterbridge. She had beaten all comers there, but at Elland Road she would be competing against a better class of dog. She mightn't be as good as he hoped, or she might, for all her stolidity, be intimidated by the noise and fuss, the bright lights and the thousands of people.

And driving distracted him from something much less familiar than the possible outcome of a greyhound race. And much more unsettling.

Evelyn Kenny. He had no idea why, suddenly, he should find himself so entranced by a woman. He was content as a bachelor, sometimes lonely, aye, but that was life. He certainly hadn't been looking to change it.

And Evelyn was only visiting. It would be daft to fall for her and then have her return home. No. Better stay alone than risk that kind of upset. If she were local it might be different, but if she were local he mightn't have noticed her: maybe it was something about her being Irish, and a bit exotic with her silky red hair and those big green eyes and that air of delicacy that made him want to look after her. And then, for her to be a Catholic, to share something so central to his life! Most of the women at St Anthony's were old enough to be his mam – there wasn't a thriving Catholic population locally, just a few posh old families, some Irish emigrants who'd dispersed from the big cities, and a few odds-and-sods like himself. Mam's family were Irish, and she had always kept the faith, Da not being bothered one way or the other.

He arrived at Elland Road and was glad to be busy with the dog, as Tansy was weighed, checked and kennelled. After that it was a long wait until her race, fourth on the card. She was drawn number two, wearing the blue sheet. As she was paraded round she trembled with anticipation. 'Save it for the track,' he whispered. He recognised a couple of trainers from Easterbridge, as well as Eddie Blythe, the man he had sold Ted to, and he nodded at them.

'How do,' Eddie said. 'That Ted's sister?'

'Aye. Ted running tonight?' He hadn't looked at the whole card, only at Tansy's race.

'Nine o'clock. Should do the business all right.' He nodded at his dog, a brindle bitch wearing the orange sheet of number five. 'This little lass knows her job.'

'So does mine.' He hoped he was right.

As Tansy was put into the traps, she took on the determined look that had served her well up until now. It was up to her. He had trained her, fed and groomed her better than he had ever looked after himself, and now he could only stand and watch and hope.

All six trainers took up positions at the front of the stand, clutching their programmes and squinting at the track, ready for the exact moment the mechanised hare whirred past. Most, like Eddie, looked nonchalant, but Charlie knew they weren't as cool as they seemed. He had snakes writhing inside him, and his heart seemed to have outgrown his chest, but like everyone else he leaned on the rail with narrowed professional eyes and a neutral expression.

The hare flashed by, the traps flew open and the six dogs hurtled out. Tansy got a good start and passed the number one dog to hug the rail. For a few seconds it looked like nothing would get near her, and then, coming from wide, the number five dog, with an uncanny burst of speed, approached her, drew level, stretched out its legs in a powerful arc – but Tansy plunged forward and stuck her nose in front. The crowd roared.

She'd done it! The little beauty! Eddie Blythe, give him his due, shook his hand and said, 'Well done, lad. That's a right good bitch.'

'Good luck with Ted. I'm sorry I can't stay to see him but it's a long run home.'

It was all as he had imagined. He collected Tansy in the pick-up, where she whipped her tail against his legs and, despite her heaving flanks and lolling tongue, looked like she would happily run another five hundred yards. *Do they know they've won?* Margaret used to ask, and he couldn't say for certain, but Tansy, eyes bright and tail wagging, certainly enjoyed the fuss. He led her on to the podium where they had their photo taken with the sponsor and his wife. The sponsor was a big carpet manufacturer who looked askance at Tansy's frothing jaws, but his wife, in a pink hat with the brim turned up at a strange angle, patted her head and said she was a clever doggie and did she need a lot of feeding?

Charlie said she was better fed than he was, and smiled at the camera. It was much fancier than winning at the flapper track, where it was just a matter of a few *well done*s or some ribaldry from other trainers. The stands were full – there must have been thousands there. Not all men either, but women, and groups of young people, and even families. He saw the glint of the stadium light on red hair and caught his breath. Evelyn? She was bending down, he couldn't see her face, only the bright red hair under a little green cap … and then she stood up. She had a child in her arms and she was lifting him on to the rail so he could see the dogs already parading round for the next race. She pointed at the parade ring and the child clapped its hands. Of course it wasn't Evelyn. She was probably home in Northern Ireland by now, and he'd never see her again.

It was daft of him to feel depressed at that thought.

Daft, once the tired dog was packed into the boot of the Bentley and he had cranked up the starting handle, to wish that there was someone in the passenger seat beside him, to talk over the triumph on the long road home.

St Anthony's only had one Sunday Mass, at nine o'clock. Which, the morning after a race meeting, with dogs to see to first and Easterbridge an hour's cycle away on an empty stomach, felt earlier than he'd like. The Colonel had told him not to worry about bringing the Bentley home last night, but using it to go to Mass was a liberty he couldn't take. He looked at it longingly as he pulled his bike out of the shed, but he had no sooner swung his leg over the frame and pushed off down the lane than he realised he had a flat tyre. He checked his watch: already past eight. By the time he pumped up the tyre he'd be late. Surely missing Mass was a worse sin than taking his boss's car? He could drive it straight up to the Colonel's afterwards. A sharp little gust of wind decided him. It was only fifteen minutes by car, and as he pulled up in the street near the church, he couldn't help feeling a bit of a swell.

He slipped into a back pew and had time for a few decades of the rosary before Father Leonard appeared, accompanied by two altar boys. Charlie breathed in the sweet familiar smell of incense, waiting for that comforting sense of being where God expected him to be, where he was meant to be, where he stopped for an hour and took stock of everything. But today that peace eluded him. He tried as usual to follow the Mass in his head – unlike most of the congregation he understood the Latin words Father Leonard was intoning – but his brain kept tripping itself up.

You're tired, he told himself. Greyhound racing on a Saturday night probably isn't what Our Lord wants of his servants. He closed his eyes, so as not to be distracted, but that felt like cheating – it was so lovely and restful! – so he forced them open to find himself looking straight ahead at a shining roll of red hair under a smart navy hat, and he knew, even from the back, that it was Evelyn. His heart jumped and all feelings of lethargy fled. She was still here! He struggled to concentrate on his responses, feeling his heart beat so loudly that she must be able to detect it through the solid oak of the pew. When they all sat, he rested his hands on the back of the pew in front, inches from her hair. Forgive me, Father, he prayed. Here I am at your holy Mass, thinking lewd thoughts. Well, not *lewd*: his thoughts went no further than stroking her hair, but inappropriate for Sunday morning.

Mass seemed to last for hours. He looked forward to Holy Communion, hoping to time his exit from the pew at exactly the right time to walk up the aisle behind her; in fact, he deliberately waited for her to move, hovering half-standing at the end of the pew with his knees locked uncomfortably – and then, after all that, she didn't get up, but sat on, head bowed, face shadowed by her navy hat. So all the while he should have been preparing to receive the Host, he was distracted. Why would she not take Communion? Was she not in a state of grace? His thoughts raced so hard that he could hardly concentrate on taking the Host himself, and it felt huge and dry in his mouth so that he had to mash it up with a lot of saliva in order not to choke. His stomach rumbled as he walked back down the aisle to his seat, and along with embarrassment came relief – of course! She probably hadn't fasted for some reason. Margaret used to faint regularly at Mass until one morning she said that she wasn't going to make herself ill because of a man-made rule.

'If God expected me to fast, he wouldn't have cursed

me with such debilitating monthlies,' she had said, cutting herself a slice of bread and spreading it with dripping.

Mam had been horrified. 'You should offer it up for the souls in Purgatory,' she had said, '*and* you should know better than to talk of such things in front of your brother.'

'Don't worry, I'm used to horses and dogs coming into season,' Charlie had said, in a clumsy effort to pretend he wasn't mortified.

It had misfired: Margaret screamed that he was disgusting and it was none of his business and Mam crossed herself and said he should wash out his mouth with soap. That had been one of the times when he thought he was as well not bothering with women; you couldn't do right for doing wrong. But he had admired Margaret's independence of spirit. Yet here she was preparing to take vows of obedience.

He didn't like thinking these thoughts with the Host melting (slowly) on his tongue, his eyes trying not to focus on Evelyn's demure downcast eyes and neat figure. He knelt and prayed hard, his own words this time, trying to send his thoughts heavenwards. He prayed for Mam, and his long-dead da, and for Margaret in her new life, which she seemed to be enjoying; and then he prayed for Tansy, that she would continue to do well and win races – *if it be your will*, he amended, though he couldn't see any reason why God wouldn't want Tansy to win. He carefully didn't pray about Evelyn, though he did allow himself to ask – through Our Lady, as he'd a feeling she might be more sympathetic – to be kept from loneliness. *And from sin*, he added.

He wasn't trying to catch Evelyn's eye on the way out – he would have said, rather, that she was trying to catch his, but however it came about, they fell into step much as they had done on Wednesday.

'I thought you mightn't still be here,' he said.

'Oh.' She bit her lip. 'The friend I'm staying with, her – well, *her* friend, the lady she shares with, is ill, so I couldn't just leave them. My friend has to work so I've been keeping the home fires burning.'

So she was charitable as well as beautiful! Charlie took a deep breath, feeling, even as he exhaled it to speak, that he was about to lose himself. 'Would you ... I mean ... There's a tearoom in the next road that's open on Sundays. If you don't need to rush home?'

'I don't,' she said.

'So is that a yes?'

She nodded. 'Where's your bike?' she asked as they passed out of the church gates and into the street.

'I'm in the car today,' he said, and was disappointed when she didn't seem that impressed, saying only, 'That's nice.' As if she was used to men with cars.

Was she a cut above him, not only in beauty but in her station in life?

If she'd been English he would have known from the way she spoke, but her Northern Irish accent gave him no clues. She could have been a housemaid or a duchess. To his eyes she seemed very well dressed; her navy hat and shoes were smart and the way her cherry-coloured coat swung as she walked along beside him seemed different somehow from Mam and Margaret's bunchy wool coats. But what would he know? The only woman he saw regularly was Thomasina Lucey, head-to-toe in tweed, and often mud.

Did Evelyn know he was a groom? He tried to remember any conversation the first time they'd met, but he could recall only that he had been on Scarlet, rushing to get her stabled before nightfall, and that he had been dumbstruck by the sudden appearance of three women. Would Florrie Yeadon have said anything about him? But why would she? He didn't imagine he was so very fascinating. And right now, walking along Queen Street, desperate to think of something to say, he felt the very opposite of fascinating. Everything he thought of – *Why didn't you take Communion? How long are you in Easterbridge? Are you a single lady?* – seemed much too loaded.

One hopeful thing did reveal itself: when they reached the Copper Kettle and sat down, and she removed her gloves, he saw that her hands were bare of rings.

They ordered tea and buttered toast, and though he felt shy about eating in front of her, hunger overcame self-consciousness.

'I'm always starving after Mass,' he said, 'for obvious reasons.'

She looked at him with wide eyes and he wondered if that was a blasphemous thing to say. She was clearly pretty devout.

'I mean,' he rushed on, 'of course I'm full of the Holy Spirit, but I can't help feeling hungry on a more earthly level.' Now he sounded like a big greedy lump of a man, bound up in the pleasures of the flesh, when that's not what he'd meant at all.

Good lord, he was hopeless at this! No wonder Margaret wanted to sign him up to a marriage bureau. And then he remembered, because Joseph had told him, that Evelyn's friend April actually ran the bureau. So was this sort of *meant*? *What's for you won't go by you*, Mam always said, but Charlie had let quite a lot go by him, one way or another. Our Lady, on the other hand, had wasted no time in answering his prayers.

'Your friend's the lass runs the marriage bureau, is that right?' he asked.

'Aye,' she said. 'Mrs Carr owns it – you know, the older lady who was with us at the farm? But April's in charge.

That's why things are difficult right now,' she went on in confiding tones. The tearoom was not busy, and they were in a little corner booth which felt quite private.

'Oh?' He gave the tea a stir to help it brew. (Margaret said this was common, but Evelyn pushed her cup towards him with a smile.)

'Her friend is in hospital,' Evelyn explained, 'and she's meant to go away to recuperate.'

'What's up with her?' Oh God, had he really said that, when it was bound to be some delicate female thing?

But Evelyn said, much to his relief, that Felicity had a bad chest. 'And then last week she was attacked in the street.'

'*Attacked?*' He stopped buttering his toast.

'She tackled some fella putting up posters, and he hit her and knocked her down.'

'In Easterbridge?' He shivered.

'Aye. She'd a bang on the head which is why they took her to the hospital, but then it all came out about her chest. I think she'd been hiding how bad it was, not going to the doctor.' Evelyn shook her head. 'She's one of those *new* women, you know what I mean?'

Charlie shook his head: he hadn't got to grips with old-style women; he definitely wasn't up to new ones.

Evelyn waved her teaspoon. 'Into politics and that. She's a writer,' she said, as if this explained a good deal.

Charlie wasn't interested in Felicity. 'And what about you?' he asked. 'Are you a ... a new woman?' He hoped not, though if she did have radical ideas, it might encourage her to overlook the fact that he was a servant.

She looked suddenly deflated. 'I don't know what I am,' she said.

Something seemed to have drained from her – some energy, a light in those big green eyes – so he said, desperate to bring it back, 'Well, you're a right good friend, staying to help your pal.'

'It's the least I can do. They've no help, so I've been trying to keep house. I've nothing to rush back to, really.'

Charlie chewed slowly on his toast, and wondered if he should order another pot of tea.

'And how long will the lady be in hospital?' he asked.

'Another few days. The problem is' – she leaned forwards, lowering her voice, though the neighbouring tables were empty – 'they want her to go abroad. Or at least somewhere bracing – the seaside maybe. For a month.'

'That sounds expensive.'

'Her brother's offered to pay, but I think she's too proud. And she can't go on her own. Or April doesn't want her to.'

'Couldn't she bring a nurse?' He had no idea how these things worked.

'Mr Carr's a solicitor, not Rockefeller. And she's not exactly *ill* – I mean, she doesn't need nursing. But April thinks she'd be lonely, and she worries that Felicity wouldn't rest without someone to keep an eye on her.'

'And April can't go because ...?'

'The bureau,' Evelyn explained. 'Mrs Carr could pop in for a day or so every week, but not full-time. I suppose her husband doesn't want her working; it looks bad, doesn't it? As if he can't keep her.'

'Could *you* go with her?' He hoped not.

Evelyn wrinkled her face. 'She wouldn't want me. She finds me boring.'

'*I* don't find you boring.'

They were both intensely embarrassed by this, and Charlie became very occupied in trying to get the waitress's attention to order more tea.

'You're lucky to have a car,' Evelyn said.

Charlie looked at her quizzically.

'If April had a car, she could go with Felicity to – how far away's the seaside?'

'About sixty miles.'

'I always forget how big England is. Well, that wouldn't work. I mean, even if she had a car, it would be too far to drive back to Easterbridge five days a week.'

'The car's not mine,' he admitted. 'It's my employer's; he lends it to me sometimes.'

'Must be a good employer.'

'Aye, he's not a bad old buffer.'

Something nudged at his memory. How the Colonel had given them the cottage after Da died, saying how healthy the moorland air would be for the frail widow and her baby. When Mam died, the doctor had told him that if she'd stayed in the city she wouldn't have lasted as long as she did. And the Colonel, last week, full of enthusiasm about the newly renovated gate lodge. *There's no healthier air in the whole of England,* he had said. And then, *You wouldn't want just anyone on your land.* But the Colonel thought April McVey was the bee's knees; he had often told Charlie so. Shippardsholme was only six miles from Easterbridge by road, about half that over the fields, and there was, albeit infrequently, a bus.

'Must it be the seaside?' he asked.

'I don't think so. Just somewhere bracing, April said.' She shivered. 'I always think that means cold.'

He started to tell her about the gate lodge and her face lit up. 'That sounds perfect! And April has a bike.'

'It'd be pretty tough to cycle every day,' he said, 'but even if she did it a couple of times a week, she'd be able to keep an eye on her friend.'

'And I could help. Between the two of us, we'd make sure Felicity wasn't overdoing things.' She clapped her hand to her mouth. 'Oh, Mr Teal! D'you think your boss would really let them have it? Let's go and ask him this second!' The light was back in her eyes now. She drained her cup.

'You mean, you'll come too? I can drive you back afterwards, obviously.'

He hoped this wasn't making too free with the Bentley. And was it rude to ask the Colonel for a favour on a Sunday? But he knew the old chap's routine, and Sunday mornings, when Charlie was at Mass, he liked to potter about his stables himself, flinging straw around with more enthusiasm than skill, and stuffing the hay nets so full that the horses could never believe their luck. But the thought of being with Evelyn in the car, so close to her, of walking with her on the tops – would he even show her his own home? His thoughts slowed. No, of course not! For a start, he hadn't tidied up in a few days, and apart from that, even he knew a man didn't invite a nice girl back to his house on her own.

And though he didn't know much about Evelyn, the one thing he knew for sure – apart from her unsettling effect on him – was that she was a nice girl. A nice Catholic girl.

Seventeen

The Bentley, smelling of dog, listed as Charlie negotiated a sharp bend on the steep moorland road, and Evelyn grabbed the door handle to keep her balance.

'Sorry,' Charlie said.

He looked older, more serious when he was driving. Evelyn tried not to notice his strong, lean fingers on the steering wheel, and the way his close-cropped brown hair curved into the back of his neck. She imagined how her fingers might cup the back of his head, what that hair might feel like. Shocked at herself, she looked down at her shoes. The wrong shoes! She remembered buying them in McConnell's in Cookstown: the dainty navy peep toes were perfect for churchgoing and sitting in a tearoom; hopeless for the country. She should have asked Charlie to stop at Riverside Road for her to fetch the brogues she had worn last Friday evening. But that would have been presumptuous – as if she *expected* him to spend the day with her. After all, she was the one who had invited herself along.

Though compared to what she had done already, that was nothing. She bit her lip, itemising her transgressions: taking off her wedding ring; pretending to be a Catholic – well, she hadn't exactly *pretended*, but obviously attending Mass was allowing Charlie to believe she was.

Her dad, an elder of the Presbyterian church, would be spinning in his grave. Her mammy used to murder her for sneaking into St Brigid's in Lisnacashan and that was only curiosity and divilment. The Mass had been in Latin, so goodness knows what it was all about, but she was sure that attending simply to see a man she had a notion of was a desperate thing to do.

And she was a married woman: she had no business having a notion of anyone.

Which led to her final transgression: she seemed to have abandoned her husband. *I'm sure you understand that I must stay on,* she had written to Maurice, *as long as April needs me.* She had exaggerated how indispensable she was in eleven Riverside Road. She couldn't expect his reply for another day or so, and she had no idea how he would react. Angry? Relieved? Worried her absence would kindle gossip in Lisnacashan? She could imagine what the old bitch would say – *I always knew she was no better than she should be; who does she think she is, swanning off to England; her first duty is to her husband,* etc, etc. But Mona would be glad to fuss round her son, feeding him up and buttering him up, telling him he was better off without *her.* She always pronounced *her* as though it had an o in it – *hor.* Which sounded uncomfortably like something else.

But Mona didn't know her precious son as well as she imagined.

And then a wave of guilt bigger than all the others swept over Evelyn. All of that was bad, but it was nothing compared to the fact that she had allowed herself to have these … feelings for Charlie, when *her* precious son lay over the sea in a graveyard. Would Maurice remember to visit his grave? How could she have left him?

She sighed, and Charlie said, 'Are you all right? You don't mind these roads? We're almost there.'

Evelyn shook her head. 'I'm used to country roads.'

His face sparked with an interest she had no intention of encouraging, so she talked instead about the scenery, how wild it was, how beautiful, how you wouldn't think you were only a few miles away from town.

'Aye,' Charlie said. 'It's grand. I grew up in Leeds, but I wouldn't go back to the city now. All this' – he gestured with his right hand towards some rolling, stout-walled paddocks, lusher than the rough moorland beyond – 'is the Colonel's land. See the horses?' His face softened. 'There's Scarlet – look, by the gate yonder. And Carnelian; they're great pals, those two. Old Mousie, who's been here longer than I have – she's doing too well on the spring grass. And that big brute is Hadrian, the Colonel's favourite.' He frowned. 'Looks light on that off hind. I wonder if he's cast a shoe. Hope that's all. Any road, I'll have a look later. And this' – he slowed down to take a sharp right-hand turn into a wide gateway – 'is the gate lodge.'

'It looks like it's waiting for someone to come and play with it,' Evelyn said as they passed it.

The lodge had a dolls-house look, all shining and fresh. It was in the same honey-coloured stone as most of the local architecture but much cleaner than the buildings in town, which were mostly various shades of smoke-streaked grey. It was tiny, all on one level, with leaded glass windows at which checked curtains hung.

The avenue was about a quarter of a mile long. She had expected a mansion, but it was a solid, square, unpretentious house. Charlie drove round to the stable yard, where several stalls had been converted to garages. The whole place looked old and cobbly; she wouldn't be able to walk far in her navy shoes. They parked, and he came round to hand her out of the passenger side, which meant she touched his hand briefly. Nice manners, she thought, and then felt ashamed: why wouldn't a groom have nice manners?

She stood awkwardly while Charlie looked into a few of the buildings, calling, 'Colonel Lucey? Colonel – oh, there you are, sir.' He disappeared into the darkness of a stable, and she couldn't hear, through the thick stone walls, what they were saying, only the rise and fall of their voices. She said hello to a white cat which blinked her at her from an old horse trough, and admired a tub full of overblown yellow tulips, flopping with drunken abandon.

Charlie emerged, accompanied by a stout, red-faced man in his sixties, who looked exactly as Evelyn imagined an English colonel, except that he had straw in his sparse white hair and was pushing a wheelbarrow piled high with more. The sweet dry smell hit her with a sudden pang of nostalgia for the days when Robbie was running around a yard not unlike this. Often in the evenings she would pick straw seeds out of his fluffy ginger hair and ask him what he was doing to get so covered in it and he would shrug and say, 'Only playing, Mammy.' That had been his life, *only playing*. He'd been *only playing* the day he died.

She forced her mind back to the present, where Charlie was introducing her as 'Miss McVey's friend from Ireland'.

'It would be capital to have Miss McVey about the place,' the Colonel said. 'And it would buy me a little time. Thomsy's keen to sell, but as you know I'm wary of its going to idiots who might leave gates open or throw grass cuttings into the horses' field. But Miss McVey is a thoroughly sensible gel and I expect her pal is too.'

Evelyn relished this description of April and wondered idly how the Colonel would feel about Felicity's political activities. Still, there wasn't much she could get up to out here on the moors, was there? And – her thoughts sobered again – from what April had said last night, Felicity was very low in health and spirits. April had cried, she was so worried. 'She has to get better,' she had said. 'If she needs to go away, we'll have to manage it. But I don't want her to be on her own.'

Evelyn had wished for a way to help. And now she had found one.

'Could we see the lodge?' she asked. 'Then I can tell April what it's like.'

The Colonel looked at his watch. 'I must go,' he said. 'Thomsy's invited the vicar for lunch. He's a decent enough chap but he'll only jaw at me for not being a churchgoer. I tell him I do my own prayers mucking out on Sunday mornings – *laborare est orare*, eh?' With which theological dictum he trundled off with his wheelbarrow, inviting them to look about the lodge as much as they liked.

The gate lodge was perfect inside, as well as out. It was on a miniature scale, though Evelyn felt this was more obvious to her than to Charlie, so she tried not to keep exclaiming how wee the rooms were, how low the ceilings and how tiny the windows. But it was spotless and cosy, furnished in well-worn but good furniture which must have been there for several generations, donated, probably, by a Victorian forbear of the Colonel. She had expected conditions to be primitive, but the Colonel had renovated properly, installing electricity and building on a tiny, white-tiled bathroom.

It felt strangely intimate to be looking into rooms with Charlie, talking about the cast-iron fireplaces and the wonderful view of the moors from the sitting room window. She remembered Maurice showing her round the new bungalow which had been Robert and Mona's wedding present. How proud he had been of its modern bathroom and kitchen, and the big windows which let in so much light. They had stood in the master bedroom, which even had a built-in washbasin, and he had hugged her and said they would be happy there. And she had leaned into his big, solid body and said they would surely. Even at the time, she had wondered who was trying to convince whom.

They hadn't been happy.

Apart from when she was carrying Robbie: they had both been overjoyed then, and Maurice seemed fonder of her, though he had stopped coming near her, which she hadn't minded. He had moved into the spare room and stayed there, even after Robbie was born.

At Lucey Lodge there were two smallish bedrooms, one with a high, wide double bed and one with two singles separated only by a shared nightstand. She blushed at the double bed and hoped that Charlie hadn't noticed.

'How will they – we – manage for messages?' she asked, and then, seeing his blank face, laughed and said, 'Shopping, I mean.'

'The village is only a mile away,' Charlie said, 'and I'm practically next door. I could call in from time to time – see if any help was needed.'

'That would be grand.' She turned away from the bed to look out the little window at the moors; yellow and green in the foreground, dotted with heaps of stone from tumbled old walls, purplish in the distance where they met the sky in a blurred horizon. She unlatched the window, pushed it open and breathed in the cool air. It was soft, that late spring Sunday, but with a sharpness that spoke of bracing winds never far away.

'It feels very healthy,' she said. 'I think Felicity could really recover here.'

She was not only thinking of Felicity.

Eighteen

It sounded, to April, too perfect to be true: a neat gate lodge on the moors, fresh clean air and within easy reach of Easterbridge. Free for as long as they wanted, with the Colonel's compliments. She was silent for a long time, imagining how it would work, trying not to get too excited. Lucey Lodge. It even sounded like a doll's house.

Evelyn said, half-shyly, 'There's two bedrooms. I understand if yous want to be on your own, but if you could do with a hand to clean and cook and keep Felicity company when you're at work, I'll stay as long as you need me.'

April would certainly need to go into the office, and she could not leave Felicity alone for long hours in the middle of nowhere. Felicity was very self-contained, but left to her own devices, April knew she would not rest and take gentle walks in the healthy moorland air, and eat nourishing meals and do everything Dr Cuthbert had ordered to regain her strength and give her lungs a chance. Loneliness and idleness would push her into either work or, worse, depression. April had never seen Felicity so low. Now that she remembered more about the attack, she fretted constantly about this new fascist group in Easterbridge. She had clutched the poster that had caused all the bother so tightly that for days her cramped fingers were almost as stiff and sore as her face. There had been a scene when she discovered that Sister Metcalfe had taken it upon herself, once the poster had been prised from Felicity's resisting hands, to dispose of it.

'It doesn't matter,' April had said wearily.

Felicity had struggled upright in the bed, her eyes blazing. 'How can you say that? Of course it matters! Rumours of fascist sympathisers gathering in a pub is one thing, but this is an organised public meeting! We must find out when it is and stop it.'

'I mean,' April said, with a worried glance at the nurse's station, 'that there's plenty of posters around the town.' Felicity looked indignant, as though April should have made it her personal mission to remove them all. (*When*? thought April.) 'It won't be hard to find out.' She knew already, in fact, that it was on the fifteenth of June, six weeks away, but thought it better to leave things vague. Who knew where they might all be in six weeks?

'Felicity – you have to be realistic. You can't just stop a meeting. It's not illegal.'

'Well, it should be. At the very least we must organise a protest. Oh, if only the others were closer. But I can speak to—'

'Felicity. You're in hospital. Could you maybe leave this to someone else for once?'

Felicity's face relaxed slightly. 'Oh, April, will *you* take charge and organise something? Things are so bad right now. Mussolini has invaded Abyssinia – I heard a couple of the doctors talking. He's as power-hungry as Hitler, and if we let these groups flourish ... I've thought for a while we need to start a local anti-fascist group.'

April bit her lip. Of course she was against the fascists – they were desperate so they were – but she could not take on one more worry, one more commitment. As it was, between the bureau, the mill, hospital visiting and home, all accompanied by the nagging fear about Felicity, she felt ready to snap. 'I'll see what I can find out,' she promised, and for once was glad when the bell clanged for the end of visiting.

So when Evelyn told her about the gate lodge, and even offered to keep house, she nearly cried with relief. She wasn't sure how it had all come about – something to do with Evelyn running into Charlie Teal in town – but she was too exhausted to care, grateful simply to accept. But she did find time to think that this purposeful Evelyn, who was determined to stay and help, seemed very different from the grieving, broken woman she had collected from Leeds station. She hoped that was nothing to do with Charlie Teal. Because no matter how understanding Maurice Kenny might be, how willing to let his wife stay away for as long as she wanted, no husband could be expected to be that indulgent. Then she thought – and it was a heartening thought, like the realisation after illness that you could fancy some buttered toast and maybe an egg – that if they were now in some way beholden to Charlie, it might be a good time to offer him a free consultation with the bureau. Which could solve all manner of problems.

Lucey Lodge was everything Evelyn had promised. Once April reassured herself that Felicity was not in imminent danger of galloping consumption, she enjoyed the convalescence. On the moors they fell into a routine that felt holidayish even though April was working five days a week. The house was tiny, but well appointed; its garden was separated from the road by a thick drystone wall at the front, and bordered the Colonel's grazing paddocks at the back, so that it was both sheltered and sunny. They were lucky with the weather, which was warm and dry, with lengthening days and mild evenings when they sat together in the garden after dinner, feeling the soft, clean moorland air settle around them. Often, they didn't retire inside until it was too dark to see each other's faces and the pages of their books.

They didn't talk much, but read. The lodge had had no books apart from an 1897 edition of *Enquire Within*, a shabby book called *The Sweet Story of Jesus*, and *Modern Dog Breeding* which, since it was published in 1906, wasn't that modern, even if any of them had been interested. But the Colonel was happy for them to bring a bookcase and had sent Charlie in his own Bentley to fetch it, along with the rest of their luggage. He himself had insisted on conveying *the gels*, as he called them, in his big Crossley, which he drove as if it were a temperamental horse, sounding the horn loudly on bends and saying, 'Come on, lad, you can do it!' on particularly steep slopes. *By Jove*, he kept telling them, he was *jolly glad to help them out; couldn't think of anyone better suited to look after the bally old lodge.*

Things were good at the bureau too. The meeting between Barbara Firth and Douglas Grant was one of the best April had ever overseen. She had to stop herself from grinning as their instant mutual attraction filled the downstairs office with a fizzing promise. Barbara, who said she was a friend of Jenny Dunn, one of April's first clients, was tall, dark and self-possessed. It was immediately obvious that they were delighted with each other, especially when Grant said that he had fallen in love with the moors around the estate he worked on and looked forward to exploring them further.

'It's the best scenery in the kingdom,' Barbara said.

'In England, maybe,' he said with a grin. 'But you should see our Scottish moors.'

The April of two years ago, Martha's enthusiastic but

green assistant, might have interjected that her own native Ulster was also a place of great beauty. She might even have joked that she had helped Jenny Dunn by finding her a job, not a husband, but that Barbara wasn't to be put off by that. But the mature and professional Miss McVey sat back and kept her own counsel, and simply enjoyed the feeling of what seemed likely to be a match very well made.

Grant was saying that the best way to see the countryside was on horseback, and, on learning that Barbara didn't have a mount of her own, said that he had the very horse he could lend her.

'If it's not being too presumptuous,' he said hurriedly.

Barbara Firth's dark eyes widened. 'Oh ... wonderful,' she breathed – and bless her, she was clearly so overcome by his perfection that she could scarcely get the words out.

It was *all* wonderful, April thought as, leaving them to chat alone – her standard practice when a couple had taken to each other and might welcome the chance to chat without a chaperone – she went back upstairs to her own office. After a very trying few weeks, it really did feel as though things were settling down very nicely indeed.

There was only one problem with the lodge: April soon realised that she would never manage to commute to Easterbridge every weekday – the buses were infrequent, and the steep roads made for tough cycling.

Colonel Lucey, keen to help, offered her the use of one of his horses.

'Couldn't be simpler,' he boomed. 'It's no more than three miles across the fields – decent tracks most of the way, and you can leave him at the riding stables while you're in the office. My niece runs the stables – she'd be glad to help.'

'But I can't ride,' April protested.

The Colonel gaped at her as though she came from another planet. 'Old Mousie doesn't need much riding,' he said. 'Point her towards town and she'll take you there. Thirty if she's a day. My old mother rode her well into her eighties. Bit of exercise would do her the world of good; she's much too fat.'

Vivid as her imagination was, April could not see herself galloping into Easterbridge every weekday, and she turned down the kind offer of old Mousie, much to the Colonel's evident disappointment. Instead, on Wednesdays and Thursdays she stayed in Riverside Road. That meant she could still run her club at the mill and she found, a little guiltily, that she enjoyed the nights alone, though Friday afternoons found her eager to push back up Shippards Hill to Felicity and Evelyn.

At first she worried about them, left to their own devices with little in common but her. But they put their days in well enough. At Lucey Lodge, Evelyn became less like a guest and more like a fierce nanny. She insisted that Felicity stay in bed every morning until Evelyn returned from her walk to the village shop; then, after a late breakfast for Felicity and a mid-morning cuppa for Evelyn, they would take a gentle walk together, following a sheep path over the moors or taking the bluebell-lined path through Shippards Wood. After lunch the invalid was expected to rest again while Evelyn did the housework and prepared the dinner.

'And to be honest,' Felicity admitted to April, 'I usually fall asleep. I've never been so lazy in my life. I've brought *Down and Out in Paris and London* with me but all I can concentrate on is *They Knew Mr Knight* – it's awfully good.'

'Told you so.' April looked at her with affection.

Felicity was still thin, though her bruises were fading.

Exertion brought on her cough, and though the meals Evelyn cooked were tasty, she struggled to have much appetite. But she coughed much less at night, and, as far as April knew, there had been no more of that terrifying blood. Best of all, at least for the present, she had stopped agitating about the local fascist cell and had, at April's suggestion, written to her activist friends and various editors to explain that she would be out of action for a while. A month, she suggested, and April, not wanting to disturb this unwonted peace, said, well, they could play it by ear. Behind her back she crossed her fingers that the idyll could last much longer.

'Maybe she'll forget about this fascist meeting,' Martha suggested when April told her. She had taken to coming in at least three half days a week, which worked so well that April was in no hurry to employ anyone else. Martha called it 'lending a hand' and as she did not draw a salary – except that the whole enterprise was her business – April hoped she would come to see it rather like Sybil Barrett at the mill: less a job than a voluntary, almost charitable role, eminently suitable for the wife of a successful solicitor.

'Felicity's like an elephant; she never forgets,' April said. 'But I'm hoping the change of scene helps her to focus on things closer to home.' She frowned. 'Mind you, she did ask me to bring a paper home today.' She gestured at the *Easterbridge Recorder*, which was sitting on her desk. 'She said she mustn't lose touch with the world and she needs to know more about the fall of Addis Ababa.'

'She'll see precious little of the world in the *Recorder*,' Martha said. 'It's mostly fat lamb prices and what the lady mayoress wore to Wetherby Races. They don't pay much heed to Addis Ababa.'

'That's why I'm not bringing what she'd call a *real* paper. I don't want her getting too upset about those craturs in

Abyssinia and Germany and I don't know where else. The world will have to jog along without her for a wee while – sure she's no good to her various causes if she's an invalid.'

'Well exactly.' Martha put on her spectacles and peered at the diary on what was fast becoming re-established as 'her' desk. 'Now, my dear, you've got a Miss Dalrymple coming in at two to meet – is it Mr Hadley?'

'Yes.' April sighed. 'I've been trying to suit Daphne Dalrymple for a while – she's awful picky, but Hadley's new on the books. They both like country walks, so fingers crossed.'

'Have you ever met anyone who *doesn't* like country walks?' Martha asked doubtfully.

'Felicity hates them,' April said. 'At least she used to. She only saw the point of walking *to* somewhere – or with a banner in her hand. But now Evelyn has her walking every day – part of her cure.'

'Good for Evelyn.'

'We couldn't manage without her. Or you. People have been so kind.'

'People *like* you, April. They're glad to be kind.'

'God love the Colonel, he keeps stopping by with game he's shot – rabbits, and on Sunday a pheasant. Felicity and I hadn't a clue what to do with it, but Evelyn was fit to pluck away at thon boy like a good'un. All those years of being a farmer's wife I suppose.'

'And her husband doesn't mind her staying so long?' Martha, who fretted if Fabian was away for more than a night, looked puzzled.

'Between you and me, Martha, there's something queer going on there. She barely mentions him. They were never love's young dream – she settled for him because she was near dead to get off the shelf – but I always thought they tholed each other rightly.'

'I have, as so often, my dear, no idea what *tholing* might be.'

'It means they rub along together. Like you and Prudence, maybe?'

'I've become quietly fond of Prudence,' Martha said.

'Well, I reckon that's all there was between Evelyn and the bold Maurice.'

'But the child must have been a powerful bond.' Martha spoke, April thought, wistfully, and she wondered, not for the first time, if Martha regretted not having a baby with Fabian.

Yet, she amended: sure look at Florrie Yeadon. But if Martha had a baby, that was the last they'd see of her at True Minds: a married lady might amuse herself by dabbling with work; a mother, never. Unless, she thought soberly, remembering her visit to Lily's home, you were poor. If you were poor you worked in *and* out. As she did herself, of course. And there was no denying she could get used to having someone to keep house, as Evelyn was doing. The trouble with an arrangement like hers and Felicity's was that they both had to work *and* keep the home fires burning. Maybe, when things settled down, they would think about getting a char. It would be better than nothing.

Martha was still musing about Evelyn and Maurice. 'I suppose without the child, there's not so much between them,' she suggested. 'They may need to learn a different way to be together.'

'They'll hardly learn it in different countries.'

And they would never learn it if Charlie Teal kept sniffing around. He had called once or twice, replacing a washer on a leaking tap and shaving a little off the back door, which was inclined to stick. They were grateful for both services and he had said it was all part of his job.

'I thought you were a groom,' April had said suspiciously.

'This time of year, I do whatever needs doing. The horses are out at grass.' He had smiled his slow, rather shy smile. 'The Colonel asked me to keep an eye on the place, make sure you had what you needed.'

The evening after April introduced Miss Dalrymple and Mr Hadley, Charlie appeared at the garden gate looking very clean and spruce, clutching a large bunch of rhubarb in one hand and two greyhounds – or at least their leads – in the other.

They were all sitting around a rough little table Evelyn had found in the shed and covered with a cloth. She had placed a jug of cow parsley, some late cherry blossom and a couple of early roses in the centre. Fabian had sent a case of wine for the invalid – a label Felicity loathed but not enough to refuse the gift – and a bottle sat open, while they all had glasses at various stages of emptiness. For a moment, April saw the scene as Charlie might: bohemian, even slightly romantic. Felicity was brushing April's hair, which had grown tangled on her long cycle back from Easterbridge. Evelyn had washed her own hair just before dinner, and it was spread over her shoulders, a silken sheet gleaming red and gold and chestnut in the dappled evening sunlight. They had all laid their books down while April told them about Miss Dalrymple and Mr Hadley, how they had obviously loathed each other on sight and were both much too polite to let on. She never disclosed anything revealing about her clients, but sometimes the lovelorn were asking to be made sport of. But she shut up as soon as she saw Charlie: the last thing she wanted to do was to put him off signing up himself. She made herself look at him objectively. He was very presentable. He might be just the ticket for that fussy Daphne Dalrymple.

Evelyn jumped up to welcome Charlie.

'I thought you could use some rhubarb,' he said as she came forward and took the bunch from him.

'Oh, how wonderful!' She buried her nose in it, as if it were a bouquet of flowers, and then looked confused and self-conscious.

'Thanks,' Felicity said. 'Will you take a glass of wine?' She didn't pause in brushing April's hair, not being afflicted by self-consciousness.

He shook his head. 'No. I've to take these two for a walk.' He glanced down at the dogs at his heels and then at Evelyn. 'It's a lovely evening. I wondered … if you'd like …'

'Oh yes!' Evelyn beamed.

'Your hair's wet,' April said. 'You could catch your death on the moors.'

'You sound like Nelly Dean,' said Evelyn, who was rereading *Wuthering Heights* because of being in Yorkshire. 'I'm outside anyway, and it's as warm as can be. But if it makes you feel better, I'll fetch a hat. Oh – and stouter shoes.'

Evelyn managed, in the few minutes she was away, not only to dig out a very pretty straw hat with a blue scarf tied round it, but to change her old skirt and blouse for a gingham frock in soft lemon and a pale blue cardigan. Though she was obediently wearing the hat, her hair still hung loose, catching beams of sunlight. She looked like a milkmaid, and standing beside Charlie Teal, so obviously a countryman in his fawn corduroys and tweed cap, they looked like the illustration on True Minds' publicity brochure – two attractive people who belonged together.

'I'll come too, if you don't mind,' April said.

She felt the pressure of Felicity's hand on her shoulder. *Don't be daft,* it clearly meant. *Let's enjoy some rare time alone.* She also saw Evelyn struggle, not wholly successfully, to hide her dismay. Charlie she couldn't read, she barely knew him, but she imagined he was disappointed too.

'Aren't you tired?' Felicity asked.

'I've been cooped up in town for two days; I could do with the exercise,' April said, and hoped nobody would point out that she had just cycled six miles, mostly uphill.

She knew Evelyn and Charlie didn't want her; she knew Felicity wanted her to stay. And Evelyn was a grownup and what she did and with whom was none of April's business. But if she was a matchmaker to her core, she was also blessed, or cursed, with a strong sense of justice: even if Evelyn and Maurice only did just thole each other, Evelyn was a married woman and though April couldn't stop her from gallivanting over the moors with a man, still, she needn't make it easy for her. And if Charlie was trying to seduce her old friend, and her still vulnerable with grief – never mind married – she wasn't going to be a party to that either.

For the first mile, with the two greyhounds lolloping at their sides, she wasn't sure whom she most wanted to protect, Evelyn, Maurice or Charlie.

Evelyn seemed as happy as Larry, chatting away to Charlie about how much she loved the lodge, and asking questions about the dogs, which he answered in such detail that April remembered Margaret saying they were all he lived for. And Evelyn surely couldn't be as riveted as she appeared by his explanation of why they thrived on tripe.

Poor old Maurice had done nothing to warrant being cuckolded, but he was too far out of sight and mind in Lisnacashan for April to worry much about.

No, as the sheep path over the moor grew steeper, and the dogs' ears shot up like antennae at the thump of a rabbit's hind legs, it was Charlie Teal she felt for.

That he was besotted with Evelyn was obvious. Every

remark was for her, even though, with scrupulous politeness, he addressed both women. When they came to a rough stile over a high drystone wall, he handed April over with brotherly casualness, then turned to take Evelyn's hand as though it were made of spun sugar. April noticed, as Evelyn stretched out her hand, that she wasn't wearing her wedding ring. And now she remembered Evelyn plucking the pheasant, her fingers flying deftly; Evelyn pinning sheets out on the line; Evelyn rubbing down the old garden table with sandpaper – no ring. When had she removed it? And why?

What are you playing at, my girl? she wondered. Charlie was, Margaret had told her, inexperienced with women. He *couldn't* know Evelyn was married. It would only take April to say something, to ask Evelyn if she'd heard from Maurice, to reveal the truth. Which would be fairest for everyone. Charlie wouldn't get false hopes and Evelyn couldn't carry on with foolishness which could only lead to heartbreak. Heartbreak was the last thing she needed after losing her child.

But ...

There was taking care of your friends, and there was trying to take charge like an interfering old trout. She thought about her own longing to live in privacy and peace. That was different, though: she and Felicity weren't *betraying* anyone. They hadn't made any vows. Ha! Chance would be a fine thing.

In her musings, she had dropped behind. They were heading west, and Charlie and Evelyn, with the two elegant dogs, were almost silhouetted against the reddening sky. It was a still evening and she could hear the lilt of their conversation, and occasional little bursts of laughter from Evelyn – clearly the conversation had moved on from tripe – but not actual words. But they looked happy. And who was she to burst that? She owed nothing to Maurice Kenny. Evelyn was a woman of thirty; she didn't need April interfering in her life.

Though she's staying in our house, she thought. If there's any talk about her carrying on with Charlie, it won't do the bureau any good. She remembered her conversation with Martha – how hard they strove to keep the good name of True Minds.

But nobody in Easterbridge knew Evelyn. Would it matter if she and Charlie had a wee flirtation? For that was all it could ever be. Once Felicity was better, Evelyn would go home to her own life in Lisnacashan. How much damage could be done between now and then? Charlie looked a robust, sensible fella: he wouldn't be broken-hearted, and the dalliance might wake him up to what he was missing. After all, that's what had happened two years ago, when Fabian had misguidedly asked April to marry him. He'd only been practising, he'd no real notion of her, as April knew rightly, and there had been no hard feelings and everything had worked out perfectly. Charlie was probably practising with Evelyn, learning not to be shy with women. Och, he'd miss her when she left, but he'd pine for a few days and then he'd hotfoot it down Shippards Hill like a lilty to consult her at True Minds. So everybody would be a winner, and no hearts would be broken.

And could you even call it a dalliance? Had two years in a marriage bureau made her fanciful? They were walking side by side, but there was no touching, no accidental bumping of hips or twitching of fingers that longed to reach out towards each other. They were just neighbours enjoying a lovely spring evening.

April felt much better as she quickened her steps and cried, 'Wait for me!'

Nineteen

Charlie tried not to go to Lucey Lodge too often. There were only so many times you could turn up with a lettuce, a bunch of rhubarb or, when May gave way to June, and the gels, as the Colonel called them, showed no signs of shifting, some early potatoes, without looking like you'd come courting. He resisted the temptation to bring flowers, even when his garden sprang into a riot of pink and yellow roses. And though at times he felt that Evelyn might be glad for him to come courting, at others she was distracted and remote, even sad, and at those times she seemed unreachable.

Which made him all the more enraptured.

Colonel Lucey agreed that Mousie was doing too well on the lush spring grass and she was ensconced in Charlie's rough paddock instead.

'Take the gels out riding! She's so quiet you could put a baby on her.'

Charlie loved the idea but when he suggested it, Felicity said horses made her sneeze and April said she didn't have time. Evelyn hesitated, as though about to agree – and of course Evelyn was the one he wanted to take out! – but then she shook her head. And he was too shy to ask again.

Colonel Lucey put the Bentley more or less at his disposal.

'Treat it as your own, my boy,' he said. 'Does it no good to sit mouldering in the yard. Motorcars are like men. Need to be kept at it, eh?' And then the sly old dog said, 'After all, with the gels in the lodge you never know when you might need to be a knight in shining armour.' He didn't wink, but he might as well have done.

So it would have been no bother to collect Evelyn for Mass on Sundays, but she always insisted on setting off on foot and meeting him along the road.

'I don't want the engine to disturb them so early in the morning,' she said. 'Felicity needs her sleep, and April works long hours. Sunday's her chance for a wee lie-in.'

It wasn't a surprise that her friends weren't churchgoers: there was something very modern and bohemian about them, especially Felicity. Charlie had never met a writer before. She always looked at him as though he were very stupid, with the result that he became clumsy and tongue-tied. But April was a grand lass. He knew that she and Evelyn were lifelong friends: that was about all he knew about Evelyn's background, except that her father was dead, and her mother in Canada. At first he had wondered if a broken engagement or even a dead sweetheart brought that fleeting sadness to her green eyes and that pink to her cheeks, but she seemed too shy to be experienced with men. Which was strange, as she was so beautiful.

Not that Charlie ever told her she was beautiful. He'd sound daft, and he didn't want to frighten her off. She was like a nervous pup. Sometimes a dog couldn't take to the crowds and the noise and the lights. Tippy and Tansy's dam, Tiptoe, could fly up a field like lightning after a rabbit, but when he had taken her for a time trial she had jumped a mile when the mechanical hare whizzed past, and stood shivering with her tail between her legs. She never ran a race. Maybe Evelyn was like that. Untried. Like him.

Well … almost: there had been Jeannie. He found himself thinking about her for the first time in years. Busy with some mundane task, creosoting stable doors or weeding lettuces, his mind would fly back to those furtive meetings; her plump shoulders; the way her top lip curled; the sweaty warmth of her heavy dark hair when he pushed it off her neck to kiss it; the swell of her white breasts under her shift. Knowing, night after night, that it was wrong. Praying – oh God, he'd prayed! But never confessed. He couldn't have said it aloud, let alone to a priest. Even now, half a lifetime later, he couldn't imagine telling anyone. At the time he had been bombarded with such a rush of feelings – guilt, mortification and then, finally, relief at being forced away from her when Da died. And then his new life here on the moors, with the horses and the dogs, and, for a long time, Mam and Margaret. And nobody who knew about Jeannie. He'd never told them. Even when Mam had said how bad she felt about him giving up his vocation for her, he had never made her feel better by admitting that he might have had to give it up anyway; he wasn't cut out for the life after all. He could have spared her a lot of guilt – and he hadn't.

No wonder he had never let himself look at another woman. No wonder he thought Evelyn was too good for him.

And no wonder being with her stirred up such feelings and memories that he had to pray hard, and exercise a lot of self-control when he lay in bed those warm nights, trying not to think of how Evelyn's red-gold hair caught the light, and the tiny freckles that were coming out in the sun. Not only on her face but on her arms. The way she said his name, pronouncing the 'r' in the middle, *ChaRRRlie*.

It was in Mass that she disturbed him most. Three or four times now they had gone together, and people in the congregation were bound to think they were courting. He couldn't pretend he didn't love walking in with her at his side. During the service she seemed almost painfully focussed, as if her faith meant a great deal to her. When they were kneeling side by side at prayer or during the preparation of the Eucharist, she would bury her face in her hands, as if to block out the world and commune more deeply with God. He tried to follow her example, but every so often he would yield to the temptation to open his eyes and loosen his clasped fingers to see little slices of her: the straightness of her spine; the soft tendrils of hair on her neck beneath her hat; the way that hair slightly, delightfully, clashed with her red coat.

One Sunday there was a bigger than usual crowd – it was a Month's Mind Mass, and the deceased relatives had turned out in force – so instead of having the pew to themselves, they were bunched up closely. She was so near that when they went to kneel their sleeves brushed. Every time he breathed in he inhaled her rose soap, or maybe it was scent – he wouldn't know, but it was delicious. But damning. Not *here*! He tried to force himself to meditate on the Blessed Sacrament, on the sacrifice of Our Lord, tried to let the familiar Latin words work their magic, taking him to that place deep inside where he met God, but for once the magic didn't work; the door was barred. And the awful thing was, he wasn't so bothered about meeting God: he wanted to reach out and prise Evelyn's hands away from her face and kiss her lips and then run with her, out of the church, up to the moors, and to lie down close to her in the springy heather, or to bring her home to his cottage, which would not feel empty if she were in it. He imagined leading her to his bed—

He buried his face in his hands and bit the insides of his cheeks hard, wanting to distract himself with pain, grateful for the sudden nip as his teeth broke flesh, for the rush of salty, metallic blood that flooded his mouth. He swallowed it as unobtrusively as he could, and tried to think himself back into the Mass.

Please God, he prayed, keep me from these mucky thoughts.

Father Leonard was intoning over the Blessed Host – the body of Christ! What sort of man was he, to be so distracted by a woman?

A normal one?

Evelyn was so still – he envied that serenity. Thank God she couldn't know what he was thinking!

And yet, as always, she did not go to Communion, but sat back in the pew to let everyone else past, looking down at her clasped hands, her face hidden.

He couldn't ask why. It was too private, too intimate. He had realised early on that she wasn't comfortable talking of spiritual matters; clearly her faith ran too deep to discuss. Well, nobody respected that more than him. She would tell him, or not, when the time was right.

As they came out of the dark church into the bright morning, a stocky dark-haired man he didn't recognise stepped forward and pressed a flyer into his hand.

'Tomorrow,' the man said. 'All welcome.'

Charlie took it without thinking: it wasn't unusual to be given something by the St Vincent de Paul Society or a mission charity.

Evelyn looked over his shoulder. 'What is it?' she asked. She half-turned to look back at the man. 'He didn't give me one.'

'I expect he thought one would do between us.' *Because he assumes we're together.* 'He won't have realised we're only – well, temporary neighbours, would you say?' He glanced down at the flyer. 'Have it if you want. Some sort of political meeting in the Black Horse tomorrow. Not my cup of tea.'

She wrinkled her nose. 'Nor mine. I get enough of that at home – I mean, not *home* home. With Felicity. She's always fretting to change the world. April thinks that's what made her health break down – she was never done going to meetings about this and rallies about that and protests about the other.'

He was less interested in Felicity than in the rare mention of what she called '*home* home.'

'You must miss your home?'

She shrugged. 'I needed a change. I'd never been anywhere till now. Only London once.'

'I've never been further than Durham, and that was only to see a man about a dog.' He laughed. 'I mean – it really was. I got Tippy served there.' Oh heck, what a thing to say, and on the way out of Mass! 'I mean, er ...'

'Don't be daft. Didn't I live on a farm?'

So she was a farmer's daughter? He tucked that away with the other small revelations about her life. There were so few of them.

In the car he stuffed the flyer down beside his seat and forgot about it. He had something more important to think about. He had been trying to work out the best way to get round to it.

'Talking of Durham,' he said over the sound of the engine, 'I've to take a pup there on Saturday. The sire's owner got the pick of the litter, but he's not been able to take him till now – had to sell a dog to have space. I wondered if you'd like to come for the run? It'd be a shame not to see more of the country.'

'Durham?' she asked. 'Wouldn't that take all day?

'By car,' he said, 'but only a couple of hours by train. I thought it might be a day out for you. It's a beautiful city.

Anyway' – he tried to sound casual, though it was the first time he had ever asked a woman to go anywhere – 'it's just if you fancied the day out.'

It seemed an age – he had time to change gear for the hump-backed bridge over the River Easter, which had to be taken very slowly, and then shift up again on the other side – before she said, 'That sounds lovely.'

He nodded, and once again had to bite the insides of his cheeks, this time to stop the idiot grin threatening to take over his whole face.

Before that, on Thursday, he had a less enjoyable duty to perform: conveying the fearsome Felicity to a medical appointment.

'I wouldn't ask,' April said, 'only I don't want her trailing on and off buses. I'll leave work and meet her at the hospital, but I can't take the whole day off and I need to stay in town for my girls' club. Martha and Fabian are visiting her brother in Devon, and you're the only other person we know with a car.'

'It's not actually mine.'

'Och, the Colonel won't mind, will he?'

'No,' Charlie admitted. 'He thinks you're the bee's knees.'

April grinned. 'Sure, d'you blame him?'

She had a way of being able to say things like that, and you knew she wasn't flirting. It was sort of sisterly. You knew where you were with April.

He half-hoped to see Evelyn, but when he pulled up outside Lucey Lodge, Felicity was waiting alone, wearing a smart patterned frock, her curly hair pinned up under a rose-pink hat.

'This is very kind of you,' she said as they set off down the hill. 'I'd have taken the bus, only April fusses.'

'I've to call at the saddler's any road.' He jerked his head towards the back of the car, where a saddle and a couple of bridles were stacked. 'Scarlet's saddle needs restuffing, and there's a cheek piece needs stitching – that's Hadrian's, it got caught in a thorn bush last time the Colonel had him out – and ...' He caught sight of her face. 'Sorry,' he said. 'My sister says I'm the most boring person in Yorkshire.'

She laughed. 'You should hear my brother talking about the law. Or April and Martha going on about matchmaking.' She paused and looked thoughtful. 'I can probably be *slightly* boring myself, occasionally.'

'Surely not?'

She laughed again. 'Touché,' she said, and though he wasn't sure what that meant, he detected amusement and started to relax.

You see, he thought, you *can* talk to women! It's only Evelyn, and *that's* because she's got under your skin so much.

'If the doctor says you're better, will you leave the lodge?' he asked.

'I don't know.' She sounded cautious. 'I feel much better in the country. But I've neglected things I ought to be doing.'

'Your writing?'

'And activism.' She frowned, a line deepening between her brows.

He didn't ask what she meant, because he suspected she would reply in great detail. He never bothered with politics himself apart from voting Labour. He chose a newspaper, on the occasions he bought one, according to its coverage of the dogs.

St John's Hospital was in a leafy road, and as he slowed the car he could see April already on the pavement outside. Even from twenty feet away he saw the concern on her face, the relief to see Felicity safely delivered, the anxiety about what the doctor might say, and he thought how nice it must be, to have someone care so much.

Business at the saddler's didn't take long and when he called back for the women they looked cheerful, especially April who, he had learned from relatively slight acquaintance, showed her emotions clearly. If only Evelyn did! But he was grateful, he thought, springing forward to open the car door, that his own feelings didn't show so openly – at least, he hoped not.

He wondered if he should enquire about the appointment. Mam had loved people asking about her health, but some women wouldn't like it.

Fortunately April said, 'Good news from Doctor Cuthbert; she's doing the best.'

Felicity smiled briefly.

'Will you move back to town?' Charlie tried to keep his voice neutral.

'He thinks I should stay on the moors for now,' Felicity said. 'But I can start work again.' She sounded very satisfied.

'A *wee* bit,' April stressed from the back seat. 'And you're not to excite yourself.' She leaned forward. 'Charlie – you know the Colonel better than we do. D'you think he'll let us stay? We should pay rent, at least.'

'That's between you and him,' Charlie said, 'but if you ask me, he's happy to see it lived in.' He hesitated. 'It's nice in the evenings, seeing a light on. I always thought the lodge looked lonely.'

'The lonely lodge,' Felicity said in a thoughtful tone. 'That might make a good story. Ghosts maybe? It's time I started a new juvenile; I've wrung every last drop from that blasted Forest Fay. But perhaps I should concentrate on what April calls my penny dreadfuls, which are the only things that bring in *more* than pennies, ironically. I write terribly sensational stories for vulgar story papers,' she explained to Charlie, who was bewildered by this torrent of words.

'And articles for *Time and Tide*,' April said, which did nothing to enlighten him. '*And* serious political stuff.'

'Which bring in precisely no pennies at all,' Felicity said. 'I suppose if I'm only to do a *little* work I should concentrate on the lucrative stuff. It just feels wrong.'

'Not wrong – sensible,' April said.

He dropped April at their terraced house in Riverside Road, a long, shabby road that hugged the riverbank.

'That's where I help out when I'm not at True Minds,' she said, pointing out a big complex of industrial buildings a few doors down.

'What is it?'

'For dear sake, Charlie, you'd think you lived a hundred miles from town,' April said as she fished in her bag for her latchkey. 'Have you never heard of Shaw's Mill? There's a carpentry works, but there's more to it.' She started talking about clubs and sports and dancing. 'Maybe you'd come and talk to the lads about your dogs? They'd love that.'

'Maybe.' He couldn't imagine talking in front of strangers.

With April gone, waving from the doorstep as they carried on up the road, Felicity, for all her brave talk, looked tired as she settled back for the last leg of the journey.

'I'm sure the lodge is quiet when April's away,' Charlie said. 'Of course you have Evelyn,' he went on, just to say her name. He hoped he didn't blush.

'Oh yes. She's frightfully bossy – always making me rest, or eat, or go for a walk – she's worse than April. Perhaps it's a Northern Irish trait.'

Before he could respond, Felicity gave a shriek.

'What's wrong?' he said, scared she had taken ill.

'This!' She waved something in his face, so that he almost had them in the ditch.

'Hold on.' He checked there was nothing behind and pulled into a gateway. 'What's up?'

Her face was stiff with anger. 'How dare you have this *filth*—'

'*What?*'

She thrust a piece of paper at him. It took him a moment to recognise the flyer he had been given after Mass and stuffed down the seat.

'I don't even know what it is. A meeting?' He looked at the flyer and read aloud, '*The Easterbridge branch of the British Union of Fascists*.' He shrugged. 'Any road, it's over. So what of it?'

'You didn't *go*?'

'Course not. I'm not interested in that kind of thing.'

'You should be. You should be doing everything in your power to stop it. We all should. Oh!' She clenched her hands, her face whitening.

'I'm sorry, but I don't know what you're on about. It's nowt to do with me. I'm not bothered.'

'Not *bothered*?' Her blue eyes blazed. 'Not bothered that fascism is on the rise? That Hitler's making life hell for the Jews and anyone else he doesn't like? That Mussolini has marched into Abyssinia as if he owns it? That in Spain—'

'Aye, I know.' He interrupted what was obviously going to be a long lecture. 'But over here—'

'Yes! Over here – here in *England,* Charlie, here in *Easterbridge*' – she waved the flyer again – 'that bastard Mosley and his British Union of Fascists are still recruiting. Still spreading bigotry and hatred. Still scapegoating the Jews and the workers and the unemployed and ...' She was seized by a fit of coughing that forced her to a spluttering standstill.

'It's only something someone handed to me in the street,' he said. 'I'd have thrown it out if I'd known it would upset you.'

'I'm glad you didn't!' She had recovered the power of speech. 'It reminds me how slack I've been. I *did* know about it, you see – I challenged someone putting up a poster—'

'April told me. That was terrible. What sort of man—'

'Well, precisely. But I forgot – at least, I knew vaguely that there was to be a meeting, but I did nothing about it.'

'You've been ill.' And in the aftermath of the coughing fit she looked far from well, red-faced, sweating and trembling. 'You can't keep up with everything.'

'No.' She sighed. 'Mosley's been spreading his poison all over the north for years, but I thought things had slowed down. I didn't expect a branch here in Easterbridge. I'll have to find out more. I don't know why people haven't been keeping me informed.'

'I suppose they're trying to protect you,' he said, 'because you've been ill.'

She frowned, and then she seemed to cheer up. 'Charlie, you don't seem terribly well informed about the current political situation. Let me explain a few things.'

It was a great deal more than a few things. The remaining miles felt like a hundred as Felicity proved to Charlie that he was, in fact, far from being the most boring person in Yorkshire.

Twenty

When Charlie had said *pup*, Evelyn imagined a tiny wriggling thing cuddled into his coat. But Tommy, leggy and strong, trotted confidently along the platform at Durham railway station, though the trundling of trolleys and shrieking of trains must have been a shock after his quiet life. Charlie said this augured well for his future.

'They must get used to the lights and the crowd – even the mechanical hare makes a noise,' he explained. 'But this lad'll take it in his stride. Now' – he pulled a piece of paper out of his jacket pocket and scanned it – 'I've been here before, when I brought Tippy to be served. It's not far.'

They went down a steep path, crossed a road and went under the biggest viaduct Evelyn had ever seen. She had gasped at the sudden sight of the castle and cathedral as the train had pulled into the station, at their immense ancient grandeur. But these narrow, cobbled streets under the viaduct were modest and homely. How could anyone train greyhounds here? Surely they needed space? She had walked past Charlie's cottage on her daily walks and had seen the long, sloped paddock where he galloped his dogs. And of course there was vast moorland all around. They were taking Tommy to a world of stone terraces and narrow streets and brief glimpses of sky. Yet Charlie had said Jacky Raine was a good trainer.

Charlie laughed when she voiced her uncertainty. 'Most greyhounds are exercised in towns. They get a run round a schooling track once in a while. Here we are – number sixteen.'

Jacky, a balding man with a drum-like belly slung over short legs, looked with satisfaction at the pup. 'Chip off the old block, all right,' he said. 'Let's see what his da makes of him.' He led them through a dark hallway, a tiny kitchen smelling of fresh baking, and out into the back yard, which was dominated by a brick shed, out of which ambled the longest dog Evelyn had ever seen, brindled dark and light brown like Tommy. His ears pricked when he saw the pup and they touched noses briefly before having a good sniff at each other's nether regions.

A small girl flew out of the back door. 'He's come!' She dropped on to her knees and crooned at Tommy, and he lolloped over, happy to be fussed over.

Evelyn stiffened. The child was about five, the age Robbie would have been now, and her joy reminded Evelyn of Robbie's delight in calves and kittens and even baby chicks.

'Now he's not a pet, Annie,' Jacky warned. 'He'll live in the shed with Nobby here and earn his keep. Make us our fortune one day, eh, Charlie, man?'

'Aye, you never know,' Charlie said, smiling down at Annie. 'It's what keeps us going, isn't it?'

'You'll have a cup of tea?' Jacky said. 'Sarah's gone through to Framwellgate Moor to see her mam, but she left some nice fresh scones.'

'I wouldn't go to my gran's.' Annie looked up, her eyes shining, her arm round Tommy. 'I couldn't wait to see Tommy.'

Jacky ushered them into the parlour, and showed her and Charlie to what was clearly the best seat, a highbacked, hard settee, where they had to sit quite close together. The men talked about dogs and races and betting and Annie sat on a homemade hooky rug in front of the empty fireplace with the pup on her knee. A shaft of sun coming in the front window haloed her dark curls. Her legs, in drooping socks, had the same solid plumpness as Robbie's.

Keep her safe, she wanted to warn Jacky.

'Tommy'll need to go outside before your mam comes back, or she'll have something to say,' Jacky warned, but Annie clearly thought she need not concern herself with this just yet, and carried on with her single-minded puppy-worship.

Charlie and Jacky were discussing every aspect of Tommy's anatomy, parentage and prospects, and Evelyn, partly to take her attention away from Annie, and partly because she couldn't help herself, focussed on Charlie. He was dressed smartly, as he always was for Mass, but because the day was warm he had removed his jacket and set it between them on the settee, its light tweed almost touching the polka-dot green cotton of her own best summer frock. His shirtsleeves, though he had turned them up, looked neatly laundered and ironed, the shirt a very nice pale blue, and she wondered who did his housekeeping. She couldn't imagine that a groom could afford to send his laundry away, yet he did not have the neglected look of a bachelor of modest means. Maurice was hard on his clothes – she was never done sewing on buttons and darning the elbows of jerseys.

But she mustn't bring Maurice into this place. She took a last sip of her tea and concentrated on cataloguing the stripes on the fireside rug to keep him safely at bay: orange, brown, cream, black, red, brown, cream ... She frowned. Why were they not in order? She had a sudden memory of Miss Connaughton, back in Lisnacashan, telling her about

Robbie's delight at the coloured wools in her shop. Oh, Robbie! A little breath shivered in her throat and she made herself focus on the rug again. Black, red, orange. Why had Sarah – if Sarah had made it – put red and orange beside each other? *She* wouldn't have done that.

No, and Sarah, baker of scones and visitor of her mother, probably wouldn't have done what Evelyn was doing right now.

What exactly was she doing?

Charlie reached out to accept another scone from the plate Jacky was offering him, and she noted the muscles in his forearm; the strength of his hand, long-fingered, work-roughened but clean. She imagined him washing in the early morning light, stripped to the waist perhaps. Oh God! She choked on a crumb and had to wash it down with a mouthful of tea.

Someday, maybe soon, she would have to face reality – that she had more or less run away from home, and was keeping company with a man who knew nothing about her, who believed her to be all sorts of things she wasn't.

You're not *keeping company*, she argued. He's being friendly because you're a visitor, showing you about a bit, taking you to Mass because—

Because he thinks you're a Catholic.

How had she let that happen? What sort of a woman was she?

She thought again of her conversation with Miss Connaughton, encouraging her to go to England for a break. But nobody had encouraged her in *this* – she had only herself to blame. What was she doing here, in this strange city, in a stranger's house, watching a stranger's child, when her own child lay forgotten in a grave ...

No. Never forgotten.

It was a relief when Charlie started to make leave-taking

noises, and soon they were back out in the street, with Annie making Tommy wave a paw and Jacky promising to keep Charlie informed about his progress.

'Sorry,' Charlie said as they fell into step along the cobbled street. 'When greyhound men get together—'

She made her voice breezy. 'You promised me a day in Durham. Now, how do we get to this famous cathedral?'

She would tell him the truth. But not yet. Surely they could have this one day? One day away from reality, and then, before things could develop any more, she would tell him ...

She wasn't sure what she would tell him, but she would not worry about that today.

They walked down a dullish shopping road, and then crossed the river, which was much wider than the Easter or the Blackwater at home. The huge stone castle loomed over the river, and beyond it, apparently rising out of clumps of trees, the towers of the cathedral. She stopped on the bridge, leaning on the parapet.

'It's grand, isn't it?' Charlie said.

'It's wonderful.'

The street wound uphill to a busy market square. Charlie made nothing of the exertion, while she tried not to huff and puff too unbecomingly – her daily walks with Felicity were gentle. Another steep, narrow street, and another, busy with shoppers and trippers and smooth young students. A couple of times they had to step into the road to let people past, and once, when a couple of young lads barged past, Charlie took her elbow to guide her. It was a relief to reach the green where castle and cathedral faced each other across an expanse of close-cut grass. The early afternoon sun seemed to infuse the cathedral with light so that it glowed almost golden.

Evelyn caught her breath. 'I've never seen anything so beautiful,' she said.

'I know. It's …' Like her he seemed to be struggling for the right words.

'It's a very fine example of a Norman cathedral,' said a voice behind them, with such projection that they assumed the speaker was addressing them and turned round. Ignoring them, the red-bearded man continued to lecture his companion. 'You'll know, Jane, that the towers would originally have been topped with spires.'

'Of course I know that, Cyril,' said his companion, a young woman. 'And did *you* know that the stained glass, though it looks older, actually dates from only …'

By tacit consent, exchanging brief grins, they left Cyril and Jane to it and walked quickly on to look at the cathedral. Evelyn, glancing back, couldn't help comparing the dusty-looking Cyril unfavourably to Charlie, but Jane looked delighted with him.

And Jane most likely wasn't married to someone else. If only Evelyn had a – what was the word Felicity had used? – a doppelganger, who could live with Maurice in Lisnacashan – he wouldn't notice the difference – and leave her here to start a new life with Charlie.

They stopped at the castle and peered down the short pathway, through an arched gateway topped by a turreted gate lodge. A stream of young men in cricket whites jostled past.

'It's a college,' Charlie said. 'Part of the university.'

'Imagine going to college in a castle!'

'Do you want to look round? I think they do tours.'

'I'm happy looking in from here.' She didn't want to waste precious hours trailing along after a guide. 'I'd like to see the cathedral. And then can we take a wee walk by the river?'

'Oh aye. That sounds grand.'

The cathedral seemed even bigger inside than out,

almost too much to take in. Afterwards, when she tried to describe it to April, Evelyn could say only that it was huge and echoey, and that there had been a lot of pale stone pillars with zig-zag edgings, and that the sun had come through the rose window and made patterns of coloured light dance on the stone-flagged floor. 'And you just couldn't believe that people could make something that big and that beautiful all those centuries ago.'

She didn't tell April that being with Charlie distracted her from her surroundings, that she was more aware of him than of the splendours of ecclesiastical architecture. That every time he moved close to her, or caught her eye, she felt something stir deep inside her which was both unsettling and comforting. Both old and new. Both wrong and right.

And she certainly didn't tell her what happened on the bridge.

'It feels,' Charlie had said as they walked along beside the Wear, its banks densely wooded and smelling of wild garlic, 'like you're on an island. Cut off from the rest of the world.'

'You don't feel like you're in a city at all.' Just as she didn't feel she was in her real life.

They came to a pale stone bridge, its three arches magicked into perfect circles by the stillness of the reflecting water.

'This is the best view,' Charlie said. 'Don't look up until I tell you.'

They crossed halfway, then he put his hand on her arm and told her to turn round and look up.

The cathedral reared above her, plunging out of the greenery as if not rooted in the earth at all. Cream towers against blue sky, massive and intricate at the same time. From the banks a blackbird trilled and another answered.

They sang back and forth filling the stillness. A fish bubbled at the surface of the water. Charlie, standing slightly behind her, still had his hand on her arm and as she leaned against the bridge, the stone's warmth seeping into her fingertips, she could feel his breath soft on the back of her neck.

'Evelyn,' he said, his voice hoarse with feeling. His fingers played on her arm, stroking the fine wool of her cardigan sleeve. She closed her eyes, forced herself not to lean back against him as she longed to do.

She knew that if she turned round, he would kiss her. And if she did not, he would not. He would not spin her round to face him; he would never force his attentions. If she did not encourage him, he would drop his hand and they would walk back through the town as if they had touched by accident, would leave the enchantment of river and stone and sky for the ordinariness of the North Road shops, tea in a tearoom perhaps, and then the climb back to the station. And the train would speed them south to Easterbridge in the fading evening light, and she would thank him for a nice day and then she would distance herself. She would stop going to Mass. She would be out when he called. She needn't say anything. He was an intelligent and sensitive man; he would get the message.

All these thoughts crashed into her head while the blackbirds called and answered, and then she turned and looked into Charlie's face. Into his dark, questioning eyes.

It was a very gentle kiss, almost uncertain, but her arms closed round his neck and she reached up to kiss him again, and they stood on the bridge, holding each other tight, while the sun glinted off the water and the blackbirds kept singing.

Twenty-one

The knock on the bureau's door on Monday morning was so uncertain that April wondered if it was the wind, or youngsters acting the lig. But she went downstairs to find a tall, nervous-looking man, fidgeting with his hat and clearing his throat. It was only when he spoke in a Geordie accent that she recognised him.

'Constable Armstrong! I hardly knew you out of uniform.'

He looked at the floor and shuffled his feet.

'I assume this isn't official police business?'

'Aye, I mean no. It's – er …'

'Marriage Bureau business?'

'Aye, well, I was thinking maybe I should be thinking about … er …'

She beckoned him in, and up to the first-floor office, where interviews took place. 'Let's get you thinking less, Constable, and talking more.' She checked the clock. 'I've nearly an hour before my next appointment. Normally people write or telephone for a registration form first.'

He looked mortified, as if caught breaking the law. 'Ee, I shouldn't have just walked in off the street. Should I go away again?'

'Divil the bit,' April said cheerfully. 'Sure don't I half-know you already? We'll fill in the form together and take it from there. I've tea made – would you take a wee cup?'

'Aye, thanks.'

Sitting, he seemed no less nervous, setting his hat down beside him, lifting it up again, then setting it down. His teacup presented further issues, until he realised he could set it on the low table in front of him.

Careful handling, April categorised him. Some clients needed more than others. And they always had more women than men, and of the men who did sign up, only a fraction were as personable as Constable Armstrong. April might not be romantically interested in men, but she had eyes in her head.

As Constable Armstrong – Sidney – relaxed enough to sip his tea and tell her where he had come from and how he was getting on in Easterbridge, she was already sorting through the files in her mind. Miss Merriman was the right age. He might even suit the hard-to-please Daphne Dalrymple. Sidney Armstrong was thirty, likely to stay in Easterbridge now and thought it made sense to seek a local wife. He had been back home on his weekend off and had noticed how all his old mates were courting, or already married, or even about to be fathers, and he felt left behind.

'It used to be all beer and football and now it's all bairns and furniture,' he complained.

April nodded and *hmmed* as if she had never heard this before, jotting down the details.

'We get a lot of enquiries on Mondays,' she said. 'Weekends make people notice that their life is – well, that there's space in it for someone special.'

'Aye, that's it,' he said eagerly. 'I'm sick of living in rooms. I'd like my home comforts.'

'Which is perfectly natural,' April said, 'but *not* how I'd advise you to phrase it to a potential match – it sounds like you're looking for a housekeeper.'

'Oh Miss McVey, I didn't mean that!' He looked horrified again, and she wondered how he coped with such a demanding job. He seemed to have removed, with his uniform, the kind confidence he had shown the last time she saw him – that terrible night when he had knocked her door to tell her that Felicity had been struck down in the street. But then, look how self-assured *she* was, here in her own little queendom: she wasn't like that everywhere.

When she had completed all she could, she handed him the form. 'Fill in the rest when you've had time to think,' she said, 'and post it back. And then the next stage is to set up a meeting with someone.'

'And d'you think you'll find me a lass?' He spoke as if this were but a slim hope and April laughed.

'You're a grand fella, with a good job and your own hair and teeth. I mean' – since he looked alarmed – 'you're in fine fettle.' Oh dear, now she'd made him sound like a prize bull. 'Yes. I'm confident we'll be introducing you to someone very soon.'

As he stood up, folding the registration form into a wad and trying in vain to force it into his breast pocket, she said, 'I hope you don't mind me asking, but do you know anything about this?'

She handed him the flyer Felicity had flung at her when she'd got back on Friday. April had been ready for a quiet evening, pottering in the garden, reading after dinner, listening to the wireless, but Felicity was bursting to discuss this new local fascist group. Evelyn was pressing her frock for a trip to Durham the next day with Charlie Teal – another complication April could have done without, but she'd decided not to get involved. The only way she could calm Felicity down was to promise to investigate. Otherwise, she knew from the glint in Felicity's eyes that she would move back into town herself, and undo all the good of the weeks on the moors. So now she had this on her To-Do list as well as everything else.

Sidney frowned at the flyer. 'I've seen these about. That the crowd your friend got into bother with?'

'If you mean, one of them attacked her in the street—'

'Aye.' He cleared his throat. 'Well, this meeting was last week. There can't have been trouble or we'd have known at the station.'

'What do you think of fascism?'

Sidney shrugged. 'My job's to keep the peace.'

'But you've seen newsreels of Mosley's Blackshirts? Felicity was at Olympia in 1934; you should have seen the bruises she came home with. They're thugs.'

'Aye, but that'll not happen here in Easterbridge.' He waved the flyer. 'This'll just be a few crackpots.'

'It only takes a few crackpots.'

'They get young lads joining,' Sidney said. 'Lads on the dole looking for a lark. Something to do.'

'Exactly! They tell them the Jews or the Communists, or even women are to blame for them having no jobs. And then they turn them into thugs.' Flip me, she thought, I sound like Felicity! 'Look at what's happening in Germany. How things are getting worse and worse for the Jews – for anyone who disagrees with Hitler, but especially the Jews. It all started *somewhere* – and it started with this kind of thing.' She nodded at the flyer still in Sidney's hand. 'It started with people dismissing it as *a few crackpots.*'

'But it's not illegal,' he said. 'We can't barge in and tell them to stop unless they're breaching the peace or hurting someone.'

'They *are* hurting someone. And sooner or later they will breach the peace.'

They were already breaching the peace of Lucey Lodge.

'But in the meantime—'

In the meantime she could kill two birds with one stone. 'Sidney – you know what you said about this kind of thing appealing to bored young fellas?'

He nodded.

'And you like football?'

'I'd a trial once for Newcastle United.'

'Brilliant,' said April, who had no idea if it was or not. 'Well, you know I also work at Shaw's Mill – where you did the road safety talk?' She rushed on. 'We're always trying to get young lads involved, but they drift off at fourteen or so. Exactly the age when they're vulnerable to gangs and' – she gestured towards the flyer – 'this kind of thing. Would you think about running a wee football team, for the older lads? Henry Barrett, who owns the mill with his wife, coaches the younger ones, but he doesn't always have time.'

'*I* don't have time.'

'Och, away of that! Aren't you here looking a wife? If you've time to court, you've time to help with a wee bit of football. You'd be keeping lads off the streets. And how about,' she pressed on, seeing that he was weakening, 'if I say you've my blessing to stop it once I've found you a wife?'

Sidney considered this. 'What if you put off finding me someone just to keep me at the football?' he asked.

'Sidney! Compromise my professional integrity? That wouldn't do my reputation any good.' She went on slyly, 'Of course there's some lovely women help out at the mill. You never know …'

He laughed. 'Aye, all right,' he said. 'I'll give it a go.'

They arranged for him to call at the mill on Thursday evening – 'I might even have news for you by then,' April said – and off he went, with a swagger that made her grin. It would be a good story for Martha, who was due in this afternoon. Though she'd need to be careful – she couldn't have Martha thinking she was using the mill to undermine the bureau.

Her noon appointment was exactly the sort of client she loved to help: a capable, cheerful woman in her forties, whose husband had died in India some years ago and who had come home to be closer to her family. 'But they've all moved on,' she said. 'And I'd like to as well. If you don't think it's daft at my age.'

'Divil the bit,' April assured her. She enjoyed the chat with Alice Hewitt, and as it happened, they had several nice middle-aged men on their books. Since she had got so great with the Colonel, there had been a steady stream of retired military bachelors seeking True Minds' services in the last few weeks. Some of them were impossible, all breeches and bluster, but one or two might suit. Last week there had been a very nice Major Hardaker, who had spent most of his career in India. She made a note to check his details after lunch. So she was feeling what Martha called *very jolly* as she bounded downstairs at lunchtime, ready to treat herself at the Copper Kettle.

She almost collided with the young man coming out of the jeweller's shop beneath the bureau.

'Sorry!' they both said at once.

April stepped back and only then saw that it was Charlie Teal.

'I was just ... I was picking up the saddle and bridles,' he said.

'In the jeweller's?'

'The saddler's. They're in the car.' He pushed something down into his inside breast pocket.

She *couldn't* ask him what it was. It would be the height of rudeness and nosiness. And none of her business. And it was *ridiculous* to imagine it was an engagement ring for

Evelyn. Evelyn *must* have made it clear by now that they could only ever be friends. Probably he'd been in having his watch mended. No – there it was, on his wrist.

'Were you buying something nice?' she asked innocently.

'Oh! Er, well, I think so.'

'Is it for anyone I know?'

He hesitated. Looked, suddenly, haunted and desperate.

'Sorry,' she said. 'I'm a nosy article. I always was. Evelyn used to say I was asking for a slap on the bake.'

At Evelyn's name, colour flooded his cheeks. April's heart plummeted.

Lunch in the Copper Kettle, a rare treat, might as well have been a bowl of gruel.

'You're overreacting,' Martha insisted when she came into the office after lunch. 'Talk about putting two and two together and making twenty! As far as we know they've had a few walks together, and one trip to Durham to deliver a dog. It's rather premature to think he's bought the ring!'

'How soon did Fabian buy the ring?' April demanded.

'That was different. We were mature. Widowed. We both knew what we wanted.'

'They're not youngsters. Charlie's older than me.'

'But Evelyn's *married*. She can't possibly …'

'I know. But I'm almost certain Charlie doesn't.'

She thought of how he had blushed. How urgently he had stuffed whatever it was into his pocket. She must tackle Evelyn. It was all very well not interfering; it was all very well Evelyn being an adult. It was all very well saying Charlie could look after himself. She thought of how earnestly his sister had begged her to find him a wife, and of how she, April, had imagined that a harmless flirtation with Evelyn might put him in the notion.

She hadn't reckoned on real feelings being involved.

And whatever feelings had made Charlie blush and stammer outside the jeweller's, they were obviously very real.

Which left Evelyn. What did *she* feel? For Charlie, and for Maurice? Had her grief over Robbie driven her slightly mad? Well, the time had come to ask. There had been too much pussyfooting around, and April wasn't normally a pussyfooter.

But she decided, as she cycled home, to consult Felicity first. All those walks she and Evelyn took while April was at work: maybe Evelyn had confided something. The thought gave her the push she needed up Shippards Hill, and when she stopped for breath halfway up, she took a moment to enjoy the tangled froth of the hedgerows, the rolling green fields and beyond them the stone-dotted moorland and the big sky, wispy blue and white in the soft June evening.

Lucey Lodge felt like home now. It was smaller than Riverside Road, but because of the garden and the soft moorland air drifting in through the windows, it never felt cramped, and as she wheeled her bike up the cobbled path she hoped Felicity would agree to stay all summer. The Colonel had pooh-poohed any suggestion of paying rent; with Martha's approval she was giving a special rate to his marriage-seeking military pals, but she must find a way to thank him personally. She mentally added that to her To-Do list, set her bike against the cottage wall, and went into the back garden to seek Felicity.

But Felicity wasn't there. A pram was parked in the shade of the cottage gable, and Evelyn and Florrie Yeadon were bent over the table, shelling peas, chatting nineteen to the dozen so that they didn't notice April's approach. April took a moment to look at Evelyn: her red hair glowed in the sun and she had put on weight. Both women looked up and smiled.

'We're shelling these for dinner,' Evelyn said. 'Rabbit pie and new potatoes and peas.'

'Lovely.'

'Joseph sent the rabbit,' Evelyn said, and when April started to thank Florrie, she waved it away.

'The fields are teeming with them. I dropped three at Charlie's place yesterday – he can always use them for the dogs.'

Evelyn did not blush at Charlie's name, but then, if April's suspicions were right, she was more practised at hiding her feelings than he was. *Sleekit*, Mammy would have said.

'Where's Felicity?' she asked. 'She's the one meant to be benefitting from the fresh air. She'd better not be frowsting indoors.'

Evelyn gestured to the bottom of the garden, and there was Felicity, sitting on the stone wall, hands clasped round her knees, and talking seriously. Her audience was young Sally, clutching the latest Forest Fay book and gazing up at Felicity with rapt adoration.

'Sally insisted on wearing her best frock because she'd never met a famous author before,' Florrie said.

April smiled. 'God love her.'

'Felicity signed that book for her and they've been chatting for ages. She's very kind.'

It struck April that Evelyn and Felicity had lives up here of which she, at work all day, knew little. Felicity didn't make friends easily – comrades and political allies, yes, but she was often too impatient and preoccupied for ordinary friendships. She hated discussing her work and said she couldn't bear children. Yet there she was, looking relaxed and well and happily engrossed. Lucey Lodge was helping more than her lungs.

There would be no chance, now, of talking to her

privately about Evelyn and Charlie. But the opportunity to tackle Evelyn herself presented itself so neatly that April couldn't pass it up. Baby Dorothy woke fussing and Florrie said she would have to take her home to change her nappy. 'I didn't expect to stay so long,' she said, 'or I'd have brought a spare. But I must get home to do the dinner anyway.'

When Evelyn offered to set the Yeadons on their way, April said she would tag along. Felicity said she would set the table and cook the peas. As Sally, bursting with importance, pushed the pram and the three women followed, April reflected that, without True Minds, Florrie would likely have no husband now, and no baby, and Sally might still be motherless. There was no doubt that many people were happier than they would otherwise have been.

They took their leave at the crossroads, from where Charlie's small cottage was clearly visible, its weathered grey stone and old slates looking almost as natural on the moor as the tumbled stones and brackish streams.

Right, April, thought, here goes.

'I bumped into Charlie in town,' she said as they turned to walk home.

'Oh?' Evelyn's tone gave nothing away.

April could have slapped her.

'He'd been at the jeweller's.' She paused meaningfully.

Evelyn shrugged. 'Maybe getting a present for his sister.'

'She's a nun.'

Evelyn said nothing and they walked on in a silence punctuated only by the bleating of some half-grown lambs who had ventured through a hole in the hedge of their field and couldn't find their way back in. Their mothers stood bellowing on the other side.

'Poor wee craturs,' April said. She tried to shoo the lambs

back in, but they gawked at her in horror and skedaddled all over the road.

'Here.' Evelyn stepped forward, grabbed a lamb round its chest and plonked it through the gap in the hedge. The others followed, tails waggling, and dashed straight to their respective dams, where they all began at once to feed, and the field settled back into contentment.

'Look at you, Little Bo Peep,' April said.

'Och, I'm well used to sheep.'

It was the perfect opening.

'Maurice must miss you,' April said. 'Have you any thoughts about going home?'

'Are you saying you want me to leave?' Evelyn pulled at a bramble flower.

'I'm *saying* I'm worried about what's going on between you and Charlie.'

'Oh.' She began to shred the pale pink petals.

'I know you'll tell me it's none of my business.'

Evelyn's voice was defensive. 'You don't know anything about it.'

'Are you just friends?'

'Yes.' Then Evelyn shook her head. 'No. I don't know. I mean, we *are* friends, but ...'

'Something happened?'

'In Durham. We ... well, he kissed me.' She let a few petals free and a sudden breeze skittered them up the road.

'I take it he doesn't know you're married?'

'Of course not.'

'Evelyn! D'you not think that's unfair? On him *and* on Maurice?'

'Of course it's bloody unfair!' she burst out, her cheeks flaming. 'And it's unfair that my Robbie was killed and it's unfair that I've left Maurice on his own and it's unfair that I've fallen in love with a man I can't have. It's *all* unfair.

I *know* that. I don't need you to tell me. God, April, just because you run a marriage bureau it doesn't give you the right to judge everybody's lives!'

'It's got nothing to do with that! I'm *judging* as you call it because you're my friend, and I'm worried about you. You're a married woman carrying on like—'

She shouldn't have said *carrying on*.

Evelyn flared up. 'How can you possibly understand? You're not married.'

'As good as. *I* wouldn't kiss someone else.' It was her turn to blush. Never, ever, did she talk about herself and Felicity that way.

'But if you did,' Evelyn said. '*If* you fell for someone else, or Felicity did, you could just move on, couldn't you? You're free. You're not bound by wedlock. You could walk away and start again. Nobody would judge you. Nobody would even know.'

'*Free?*' April thought of how society viewed women like her and Felicity; the need to keep so much secret; the way she had been treated at the hospital. Oh, she was free all right. Free to be dismissed. 'I love Felicity,' she said calmly. 'I'm as bound to her as anyone could be. And we would never just *walk away and start again*. You're talking as if our feelings are *less*.'

'I didn't say that.' Evelyn sounded sulky.

'You didn't have to.' April's mind looped back to something Evelyn had said earlier. 'You said you'd *fallen in love* with Charlie. Do you mean that?'

'Oh God. Yes. *Yes*. I'm so confused – and I feel so guilty, you've no idea how much – but I'm not confused about that. What am I going to do?' Evelyn burst into ugly sobs.

'Evelyn. You're not a wee girl. If you've fallen for Charlie, you need to be honest with him. Does he not deserve that?'

Evelyn's sobs subsided, and she was quiet for so long that April started to worry. Then she said, 'Aye. Maybe I do.'

And without another word, scattering the last petals, she set off back up the path they had come.

Twenty-two

All his life Charlie had let things happen to him. Even the biggest decision he had ever made, when he was no more than a boy, had felt more like something he was called to than a choice he had worked out for himself. Called by God? He used to believe so, but now he knew he had been swept along by the romance and grandeur and by people's approval. Especially Mam's – a son a priest! Only he never got that far.

But he didn't even take responsibility for changing his mind: everyone assumed it was because Da died, and Mam needed him. He was the dutiful son who abandoned his lofty dreams to care for his mam and his baby sister. Nobody knew the relief he had felt. Nobody knew the guilt. Nobody knew the truth. Nobody knew about Jeannie, whom he'd met out walking on the moors above the seminary and become so hopelessly, illicitly entangled with.

He had never forgiven himself for his dishonesty. Sometimes he thought he wasn't much of a man, shirking real life and hiding out with horses and dogs. He hadn't been lonely. He was too busy; he had always made sure of that. He wasn't looking for a woman.

But he had found one.

When he kissed Evelyn on the bridge in Durham, and

she kissed him back, shyly at first and then with more confidence, and they had travelled back on the train almost in silence, not speaking about it, but with everything shifted between them, he knew that he couldn't pass up *this* chance.

He had let Jeannie go. He had let his so-called vocation go. He had had to let Margaret go and she was happy; her vocation, unlike his, seemed genuine.

But he could not let Evelyn go.

It's too soon, he told himself. You've kissed her once! You've never said a word about love or a future or even asked her to walk out with you officially! She might want to go home to Northern Ireland. She wasn't going to stay in Easterbridge forever, a guest in April and Felicity's home. She would want her own life.

Aye, but couldn't he be part of it?

If Margaret had been here, she would have told him on no account to buy the ring. She would have said it was daft, he would scare Evelyn off, he should bide his time and get to know her properly. But Margaret was far away in Dublin. He had a few mates, lads at the dogs, or in the Blacksmith's, but it was all beer and banter; if he mentioned keeping company with a girl, they'd call him a sly old goat and make a dirty joke. The Colonel would approve – *damn fine gel*, he'd say – but the Colonel was his boss; he couldn't *talk* to him. Joseph? They often saw each other on the moor, and fell into conversation while Joseph mended a wall or checked on sheep, but every time Charlie tried to mention Evelyn, shyness stole the words, and they talked instead about Tansy's next race, or the rabbits overwhelming the bottom meadow or how well this year's lambs were growing.

He was thirty-seven years of age. He should be able to take action himself.

So today he'd bought the ring. Had taken himself into town, withdrawn some of his modest savings from the National Provincial and gone straight to the jeweller's before he lost courage. The young assistant had been very helpful, reassuring him the ring could be altered, advising him that a solitaire diamond was not, as he feared, cheap-looking, but classic. It had cost more than three times what he'd imagined. He handed over the notes, thinking that he could have exchanged them for a really top-class dog, the type he'd always dreamed of.

The ring in its cushioned box looked insignificant, a mere trinket you could drop and lose. But then he imagined it sparkling on Evelyn's slim finger, and himself lying beside her every night, breathing in her skin, feeling her hands reach for him, coming home in the evenings to find her in the kitchen; imagined, even, someday, being blessed with children ... He remembered how she had looked at Jacky Raine's bairn that day in Durham: there had been a softness in her eyes, a kind of yearning. It was easy to picture her with her own children. *Our* children, he let himself think. What was the best greyhound in the world beside that? Then, on the way out of the shop, he had run into April, and though he'd been mortified that she might guess what he was up to, he decided to see the meeting as a Sign.

As a Catholic, he was a great man for Signs.

He planned to stop by Lucey Lodge later this evening and ask Evelyn to go for a walk. He had the ring waiting, and his best blue shirt airing; he was just going to clean out the kennels and then he'd get himself ready. For what could be the most significant night in his life. His heart pounded all afternoon, and he couldn't face the rabbit stew he'd put into the haybox that morning; he just brought it straight out to the delighted dogs. He'd never planned anything so carefully: they'd take the path over the tops to the back of Shippards Hill; there was a tumbledown wall there, with the most wonderful view down to Easterbridge and across to the higher moors beyond. It had been a grand day; it would be daylight until after nine, but for the walk home there would be the glow of the setting sun. They would hold hands, and he would look down and see the glitter of her new ring, and he would know a happiness he had never expected. They would want to draw the walk out, to keep the engagement private and sacred for just a short time until they told people. Until they started their life together. He imagined taking her racing; her excitement when the dogs won, her reassurance when they didn't. He imagined walking into Elland Road, and everyone turning to see this lovely woman on his arm. He imagined them talking all the way home, reliving the race. The Evelyn of his imagination was perhaps more knowledgeable about greyhound racing than the real one, but no matter.

He had planned the very words he would use, and to stop himself getting too nervous, all the time he was mucking out the kennels he tried to pray the rosary, the words so familiar that he didn't need to think about them, but his own words kept interrupting: *Oh, please God, let her say yes.*

But of course Evelyn would say yes. She was serious and deep. She had kissed him and then been too overcome to speak.

As he spread clean straw over the dogs' beds, he checked his watch. In an hour it would be time to set off. In two hours – two and a half if they walked slowly – he would have asked her, and both their lives would have changed forever.

Twenty-three

Evelyn was throbbing with indignation by the time she reached Charlie's cottage, heart juddering, mind jamming with half-formed thoughts and justifications. On the one hand, how dare April – she'd always been far too interested in other people's business, but dear help anyone who dared to say a word about *hers*! On the other – well, she wasn't proud of how she was carrying on.

Carrying on. The words stung.

She would have to tell Charlie the truth – that she was sorry she hadn't been honest; she wasn't actually free to get involved with anyone; she was in fact – she smarted at the word – married. He would be hurt, probably angry. But then she would explain that she was estranged from her husband. She needn't go into details, but surely he would see that she was not really to blame. She would underline, above all, that her feelings for him were genuine. And then …

She wasn't sure what would happen then, but it would be all right. It would have to be.

Nobody answered her knock at the white-painted cottage door, though a plump grey pony lifted its head from grazing in the back field and looked at her with benign interest. Old Mousie, she supposed. She remembered Charlie offering to take them riding. She had longed to say yes, but she had resisted. She hadn't *carried on*, whatever

April said! She was about to turn away when Charlie stepped out of a shed, carrying a bucket. He set it down when he saw her, eyes widened in surprise and dismay. He was in old working clothes she had never seen before, a grubby shirt and breeches covered in dog hairs.

'Evelyn?

'Sorry.' She stepped back. 'I shouldn't have ...'

'Don't be daft! I was cleaning out the dogs. But don't come too close; I don't smell great.'

It's all right, I'm a farmer's wife.

'Go on into the house,' he said. 'Make yourself comfortable and I'll be in when I've cleaned myself up.'

She should have said no. She should have gone back to Lucey Lodge and apologised to April. And then, later, she might have been able to tell Charlie *something* that wouldn't hurt him too much, and maybe they would have had a chance after all, despite Maurice, despite her lies.

I haven't told any lies, Evelyn thought, but she knew that wasn't true.

Instead, she let him show her into the dim, cool kitchen, while he busied himself in the yard – she heard the clank and swing of the pump handle and then the splash of water, and she realised that he was washing. She felt terrible: she should have realised that he would not want to be caught on the hop, with dirty straw stuck to his breeches, carrying a bucket full of dog faeces. She tried her usual trick of looking round for distraction: a Sacred Heart picture above the mantelpiece, a little statuette of the Virgin Mary on the windowsill and, on a clothes horse by the open window – the fire wasn't lit – a clean blue shirt was airing. None of which made her feel better. The walls were whitewashed and plain, so there were no helpful floral sprigs or stripes to count. She counted the roses on the faded chintz covers of the armchairs on either side of the fire, and then she saw, with a squeeze of her heart, a little navy-blue velvet box sitting on the scrubbed wooden table.

April had met him coming out of the jeweller's.

Oh, please God, let it not be a ring, she prayed, and then felt even worse: praying, or the pretence of it, had helped get her into this mess.

She jumped up and slipped out the front door.

'Evelyn! Wait up!'

Don't turn round, she told herself. Keep walking. He'll think it's weird, it *is* weird, but it's easier than trying to explain. She quickened her step. Then something nudged the back of her skirt and a wet nose was thrust into her hand.

'Tippy!' Tippy wagged her whippish tail, delighted, and, like Evelyn, ignored Charlie's shout to come back.

Evelyn stopped and turned.

He looked bemused. 'I thought you were in the house …?'

She shrugged. 'I needed air.' Her hand reached out for Tippy, the dog's soft warmth reassuring under her fingers.

'Are you all right?'

'Fine.' She made herself smile brightly. She could see that he had come after her in a hurry; his blue shirt was hastily tucked into his trousers, one of his braces wasn't properly done up, and he was carrying his jacket, as if he hadn't wanted to waste time putting it on. His hair was still damp.

'I thought you were running away!'

She forced herself to laugh. 'Och, Charlie, why would I do that?'

And then she thought, *I am running away*. But she wasn't sure what she was running from: Maurice? Or Robbie? Or herself?

'Will we go for a walk?'

'All right.'

She would tell him properly. Not everything, but enough to help him to understand that she never meant to lead him on, she had intended no harm. And it would be fine. It had to be, because Charlie was a lovely, serious, well-intentioned man, who clearly liked her every bit as much as she liked him.

They fell into step, heading over the dry sheep-beaten path to the high moor. She let herself be lulled by the soft evening light, the patter of the dogs' light tread, the calming bulk of the man at her side. She matched her step to his, and her breathing to her steps, so that she was almost in a trance, keeping everything at bay. It was like they walked in a spell, and she would not be the one to break it. If neither spoke, but just kept walking, then somehow it would all be all right.

Charlie spoke. She was so deep in her reverie that it took her a moment to register that he had said her name. And he stopped walking, so she had to stop too. He turned to face her. She looked past his left shoulder at the purpling moor, at the wispy sky, at the tumble of boulders from what had once been a wall, but then she felt his hand, warm and hard, on her shoulder, and she had to turn and look at him.

'Evelyn.' He cleared his throat. 'I – well, I think a lot of you.'

She didn't know what to say, but she found her own hand, without her bidding, reach for his. Maybe she meant to push his off her shoulder, but instead her fingers laced round his.

'I've not known you long,' he went on, 'but ...' He tightened his fingers round hers.

Her heart throbbed. She looked into his face. She had

never seen him so serious, his dark eyes fixed on hers, his mouth working to find words, every muscle tense.

'I've never felt like this before,' he managed.

She found herself saying, 'Me neither.' It was the truth. She had dreamed, since she was a girl, of a man who would make the world feel different and full of possibility, a man who made her heart pound and her legs wobble. But no such man had ever come along, and suddenly she wasn't that silly, romantic girl; she was a woman who'd need to get a move on, and, when nothing else offered itself, she had got a move on to Maurice Kenny. Maurice, with a farm and a good name, and the promise of their own bungalow and, above all, the chance to be, *not* a despised spinster, but a wife and a mother. Maurice wasn't a bad man.

She had fulfilled a need for him, as he had done for her. A marriage of mutual convenience. She became fond of him, and even proud to be his wife. But he had never made her feel like this. He had never looked at her like he could hardly believe she was real. Why, oh why, had she been so impatient? Why hadn't she had the courage, like April, to leave home and seek independence? Imagine if she had left Lisnacashan to visit April, and met Charlie just the same, only without the encumbrance of a husband? Maybe she had always been meant to meet him. She imagined a parallel life, where a free Evelyn had met Charlie and was now, like this Evelyn, walking on the moors with him, but with everything honest and free between them. The image was so intoxicating that she could almost see the other Evelyn and Charlie, walking slightly ahead, hand in hand, easy and happy.

But what she really saw was her own face reflected in Charlie's serious dark eyes, and it was the face of a woman who had no idea what to say or do.

The face of a woman who could not possibly wish for a life where she had never given birth to the child she had loved so much.

She tried. 'Charlie,' she said. 'I … I like you too. I didn't expect—'

A high scream split the moor and they both froze.

'Tansy! Tippy! Leave it!' Charlie shouted. 'Bugger them. Sorry, Evelyn – it's only a rabbit.'

She had heard the expression *limb from limb* but never seen it: the blood and the bits of skin and the frenzied bloodied mouths of the snarling dogs, and the blood spattering the grass …

The blood.

Another scream, from her own mouth, and she was collapsing, her hands scrabbling at the air, then no breath to scream, heart bursting, throat choking, gasping, then the hard ground slammed into her knees, grass in her nostrils, blood in the grass—

'Evelyn!' Hands on her shoulders, a brusque shake. 'It's only a rabbit! Don't be daft, love.'

'Not – daft,' she choked out. *Love.*

'All right. Come on then. Shhh.' He gentled her as if she were a frightened horse.

She struggled to come back to herself. Knees on the earth, breathe in the grass and flowers. Sweet. Not blood, the blood is somewhere over there. Charlie is here, holding you. Oh God, he must think you're crazy.

'I – the blood,' she managed to choke out. She shuddered, retched, took a deep breath. 'It reminded me …'

'What, love?' He stroked her hair back from her forehead. His hand was dry and gentle and she couldn't help the words from pouring out.

'My – my wee boy. He was killed. Like that.' She looked up and saw the shock in his face. 'Not by dogs, I don't mean. He …' She had never said it aloud. 'He fell – he …' She gulped, swallowed. 'There was – blood. They tried to keep me from seeing but I-I did see.'

Charlie's face was working in disbelief. 'Your *wee boy*? Your child?'

She nodded. Forced herself to say his name. 'Robbie. He was four.'

'So are you a widow?'

'No.'

He looked almost stupid as he tried to make sense of it. 'Were you – *unmarried*?'

Oh God, she thought, it's like Tess of the bloody d'Urbervilles. And look what happened to her. She shook her head. 'No, of course not. What sort of woman d'you think I am?'

An unfortunate question.

'You're married?' His voice was a rough whisper. 'You're *still* married?'

'It's not that simple.'

He held up his hands as if to defend himself. 'But you let me think …'

'I've left him.' She had said it, so it must be true. She reached for Charlie's hand, but he snatched it away. 'Charlie – I've *left* him. It wasn't much of a marriage. When Robbie died … long before that really, I knew we'd made a mistake. Maybe I could – *we* could still …'

'What?' he said. His eyes glittered with an emotion she couldn't read. 'Have you forgotten you're a Catholic?'

Oh God. She had, in fact, forgotten this aspect of the mess. She looked down at her hands. What was the least worst thing she could say? The truth?

'I'm not – exactly.' When she saw his face she raced on. 'I didn't *say* I was. You saw me in the Catholic church … you *assumed*—'

'It was a pretty bloody reasonable thing to assume!' He was shaking.

'I'm sorry. I wanted to keep on seeing you. I didn't tell any lies. Not really. I just ... I let you think ... because I so *wanted* to be free, Charlie. Can you not understand that? I'm in love with you.' Again she tried to reach for his hand.

'Don't!' He jerked away. 'You lying bitch.' His face was ugly with hurt and disgust. 'Oh God, I can't—'

And he was running from her, back down the path over the moor, the dogs loping at his heels, loving the unexpected sport, their barks harsh in the empty landscape. He didn't look back.

Twenty-four

July was always slow at True Minds; April didn't need Martha's regular help, but, though the workload was manageable, she had never been more grateful for her quiet good sense, especially as the rest of the world seemed to be going mad.

The morning after that horrible row, Evelyn had sneaked off at dawn, leaving a note thanking them for their hospitality, but not saying where she was going or why. And divil a word since. April wrote once, to Lisnacashan, to tell her Hanna had had twin boys, and wishing her well, but there was no answer. She didn't even know if the letter had reached her.

Without Evelyn, Lucey Lodge was lonely for Felicity and tricky for April. Though she was friendly with Florrie Yeadon, Felicity did not have April's need for companionship. Left to her own devices, she was likely to write all day and forget to go out and benefit from the air. April didn't like leaving her overnight, but cycling back after the club wasn't feasible, so for the past two Thursdays Martha had run her home in the car.

'I can't keep expecting you to do this,' April had protested, but Martha said she was glad of the driving practice and she didn't have anything else to do.

As for the clients, what a contrary lot! Were people

getting harder to please? Daphne Dalrymple refused even to meet Sidney Armstrong. A *policeman*? She wrinkled her pretty nose. Oh no, she didn't think so. It wouldn't be quite *nice*. Getting involved with murders and suchlike.

'I don't think Constable Armstrong's work involves much murder,' April explained. 'It's more lost dogs and burglaries.'

Daphne shuddered. 'You never know. Easterbridge isn't the town it was.'

April graduated Daphne from *Hard to Place* to *Too Damn Fussy for Her Own Good*. In theory, those who ended up there should be matched to each other, but it never worked out that way.

She introduced Armstrong to a lively, pretty girl called Fanny Smith, with short fair hair and a wide smile. She was fascinated by his job, but her breeziness made Sidney so nervous that he spilt his tea on his trousers, and his voice, when he found it, squeaked up an octave, so Fanny was understandably underwhelmed and said she would prefer someone *jollier*. And Sidney said that what he had really hoped for was a nice, quiet, old-fashioned girl. 'Like my mam,' he said helpfully, and April, who had spent two years trying to make True Minds thoroughly modern, had sighed.

Not everyone, thankfully, was so perverse.

Ada Thompson, who had baulked at the sickly missionary, had instead bought a fluffy golden Pomeranian bitch, and, walking her in the park, had struck up an acquaintance with, of all people, Doctor Jim Cuthbert, who had got a fox terrier to help him take more exercise. April saw them often, walking on the riverbanks with the two dogs. If not exactly a win for True Minds, it gave her great satisfaction.

Alice Hewitt proved willing to give the Reverend Waters

a try, and met him on a day when his bowels were not playing up, with the result that he made a much better impression and they were keeping company. April prayed that his bowels would hold out at least long enough for Alice to become fond of him, after which they could be tolerated with resignation if not affection. They too were often seen taking the air along the banks of the Easter, which was doing wonders for his constitution.

One damp Wednesday towards the end of the month, when there were no clients to see, and she and Martha had tidied the office and updated all the files, they were reading the papers and drinking tea, looking up from time to time to share a story.

'Things look bad in Spain.' Martha had *The Times* while April was reading the 'Out and About' column of the *Easterbridge Recorder*. 'The government are asking for foreign help.'

'Hmm?' April looked up. 'Oh aye. It's desperate so it is. Some of Felicity's pals are going over there to fight.'

'Gosh.' Martha looked serious.

'On a happier note.' April passed Martha the paper, open at a photo of the Honourable Agatha Wyndham-Howard arm in arm with Clarence Taylor-Scott at the Great Yorkshire Show, and as she had hoped, Martha looked impressed and said that was a jolly good *coup* for True Minds.

She turned the page. 'Isn't that your friend Mr Teal?'

'Oh?' April did not say that they had not seen him since Evelyn left – no more potatoes or lettuces, only a brief – possibly even curt? – nod when they had passed on the road one day.

'He seems,' Martha went on, skimming the story, 'to have won rather a big greyhound race.'

'Let's see.'

Charlie, flanked by two important-looking big-bellied men, smiled out of a grainy photo, one of his dogs – Tansy, according to the caption – wearing a sash round its neck, standing on a podium. 'Fair play to him,' April said. 'His sister said he lived for those dogs.' She had never seen him look so happy and proud. 'This might be a good time to ask him to talk to the boys at the mill. The wee football club's going well with Constable Armstrong, but this would be something different.'

And asking Charlie would give her an excuse to call. Maybe *he* had heard from Evelyn?

That very afternoon, after Martha left, something happened to give her an even better excuse.

In the two years that April had worked at True Minds, she had seen clients in all sorts of moods, but never before had someone flown in, collapsed into a chair and burst into tears. And what made it even stranger was that it was Barbara Firth, last seen looking adoringly into Douglas Grant's nice blue eyes.

April sprang up. 'Miss Firth!' she cried. 'Whatever's the matter?' Surely the lovely Douglas hadn't turned out to be a rotter? Not all their matches worked out, but if ever she had imagined two people to be mutually attracted, it was these two. Was she losing her touch? 'Has Mr Grant, er, wronged you in some way?' This sounded awful dramatic but Barbara wasn't sitting here breaking her heart for no reason.

'Oh, Miss McVey.' Barbara raised tragic dark eyes. 'I'm in a terrible pickle. You have to help me.'

April's mind flew to Lily's predicament. But surely not – good lord, this wouldn't do the bureau's reputation any good! It was a relief, therefore, albeit a surreal one, when Barbara burst out, 'It's the horses!'

April wrinkled her brow. 'Horses?'

'I haven't ridden since I was eleven! Jenny and I had a brief pony phase, but that was all. But *he* seems to think I'm some kind of hard woman to hounds. He keeps asking me out on a ride and I can't keep putting him off. I like him *so* much! He's just perfect, but – oh, what can I do!' She burst into fresh sobbing. 'I don't know *how* he got the idea I liked horses …'

Unease crept through April and lodged in the pit of her stomach. 'But you said on your form …' She closed her eyes and saw again Barbara's messy writing. 'You said *old* horses – I thought maybe you looked after retired pit ponies or – or something …' Her voice trailed away as she realised Barbara was staring at her in disbelief.

And then Barbara's face cleared.

'Old *houses*. I like old *houses*.'

April gasped. 'Oh dear lord! How careless of me.'

But if she had not misread it she might have matched Barbara to Cyril Henderson, and she couldn't imagine her having fallen for his dusty charms as readily as she had become smitten with Douglas Grant's.

'Could you not just tell him?' April said. 'You can blame me. Sure, yous'll maybe have a wee laugh about it. Yous are obviously getting on well and—'

'I've *lied* to him! That's no basis for – well, for a future.' She blushed.

'It was my fault. I made the mistake.'

Barbara wailed, 'But I've gone along with it! He said he met lots of horsey girls but they were always weather-beaten and hearty. He keeps asking when we can go for a long ride over the moors. I've told him I've strained my knee and have to rest it for a while, but I can't say that forever. Especially as I keep forgetting which leg to limp with. Besides I … well, I'd *love* to ride over the moors with him.' Her face grew dreamy. 'It sounds *so* romantic. But I don't want to make a fool of myself.' She covered her face with her hands. 'Oh, what can I do?'

April watched her, horrified and bemused. She couldn't see why Barbara didn't simply confess, but then she remembered the first few weeks after she and Felicity had declared their feelings. How desperate she had been for Felicity not to think she was ignorant, how she had pored over newspapers and old copies of *Time and Tide*. Maybe everyone tried to impress the people they were falling in love with.

But *old horses* reminded her of the Colonel's offer of old Mousie for commuting to work on: he had said she could leave the pony at the riding stables.

'There's a riding school just outside town,' she said. 'Surely they could teach you?'

Barbara shook her head. 'Douglas knows Miss Lucey who owns it. What if he found out? No, it would need to be a private arrangement. In books people are always taught by their old grooms, but in real life ...'

That gave April another idea. She said she had a neighbour who might be able to help, and Barbara's face lit up with relief.

'Oh, that would be marvellous! Only it must be secret – I couldn't bear Douglas to get wind of it.'

'Colonel Lucey's groom is very discreet,' April assured her. 'You leave it with me.' She hoped she wasn't being overconfident.

It would have to be after dinner because she had promised to visit Lily on her way home. Lily's house was in a bedraggled row at the far end of Townsend Street, behind the toffee factory. The cloying sweetness in the air gave way to the smell of fried food and damp clothes indoors. Lily was six months pregnant now, her skirt pinned awkwardly to accommodate her belly, but she was very cheerful.

'I'm getting married,' she said, 'soon as I'm sixteen.'

April failed to hide her surprise. 'That's wonderful. To – er …?'

'To the daddy,' Lily said triumphantly.

'I haven't seen you at the club lately,' April said, this being another reason for calling. 'I don't want you to think you aren't welcome.'

Lily looked important. 'Now that I'm engaged, I can't be wasting my time with little girls.'

'They're starting housecraft lessons next week – that might be useful when you set up home with …?'

'Reginald Binn. Reg. We'll live with his mam, so I won't need house-whatever you call it.'

'Why not bring Reg? Oh, not to housecraft' – Shaw's Mill was not *that* modern – 'but he might like to play football.'

Lily pondered. 'He's not got time.'

That sounded promising. 'Does he work?' An apprentice serving his time at a trade, even a factory worker with a regular wage, could be the very thing.

She shook her head. 'How can he? The foreigners take all the jobs.'

'That's not true, Lily.'

'It is then. Reg says. He goes to meetings.' Her head bobbed with self-importance.

Leave it! April told herself. Don't get involved. But she had lived too long with Felicity for that. 'I've heard that nonsense too,' she said, and Lily gaped at her, open-mouthed. 'Saying refugees are taking jobs. It's not true.'

Lily shook her head. 'That's not what my Reg says.'

'Where are these meetings, Lily?'

Lily shrugged. 'I don't know. Reg doesn't bring me. He doesn't want other men gawping.'

The visit demoralised April profoundly. As she cycled

home in the rain she wondered how she had ever considered Lily a suitable employee for True Minds. What did that say about her judgement?

'You can't blame yourself,' Felicity said later as they sat by the glowing fire – April had arrived home soaked and shivery, delighted that Felicity had lit a fire in the sitting room and cooked one of her hearty stews. 'You can't help every lame duck.'

'But she's no better off now than if she'd never worked for me or set foot in the mill. She'll have a life like her mammy's: a child every year till her body breaks down, and a man in and out of casual work at best. And *he's* obviously no brighter than her, given that he's been sucked into this fascist nonsense, so the children will be slow-witted too, and so it goes on – an endless depressing cycle.'

Felicity poured them both some cocoa – it was that sort of evening – and said, with more of her old manner than April had seen for months, 'First, you can't assume he's *stupid* to have been taken in by that beastly rhetoric – that's how it works. People like Mosley deliberately appeal to people who feel hard done by and are looking for a scapegoat – the Jews, the Polish miners, women. But it's dangerous to dismiss them as stupid. And second, the mill does wonderful work, but you have to see it for what it is.'

'What do you mean?'

'Well, it's hardly an agent of radical social change.'

'I – sort of thought it was.' She thought of her bright-faced girls, dancing and laughing, learning new skills and making friends, of the boys in the football teams, of people like Miss Dawson who had found a new focus, a community.

'Oh April!' It wasn't often, these days, that Felicity made her feel ignorant, but she was doing so now. 'It's one step up from Victorian do-gooding. No, that's not fair' – as she saw April's face – 'it's more than that. But it's a rich woman's pet project.'

'And what's wrong with that?' April would never forget the excitement of Sybil and Henry Barrett asking for her help with their scheme, of her satisfaction in knowing that, in matching this unlikely couple – the richest girl in town and the clever tradesman – she had brought about a true marriage of minds which benefitted the whole community.

'Look, I respect the mill,' Felicity said. 'It's been a lifeline for Hanna and countless others.'

'But?'

'But people shouldn't have to rely on individual philanthropy. We need a society where the kind of support the mill gives is available to *everyone* – not only those within the sphere of a Lady Bountiful.'

'Don't let Sybil hear you call her that.'

'But as long as there *are* people like Sybil, governments get away with not taking responsibility.'

April took another sip of cocoa. 'I understand,' she said. 'But in the meantime, *before* the revolution, we have to be pragmatic. You're worried about this fascist group – I am too. But the mill's a defence *against* that kind of thing. People are looking for *something* – and we can give them something better. And talking of the mill' – she drained her cup and yawned and stretched – 'I'm going to ask Charlie Teal to bring his champion greyhound in.' She didn't mention the other favour; she didn't really want to admit, even to Felicity, to having made such a heedless mistake as to misread a client's registration form. 'I won't be long.'

Charlie was clearly surprised to see her, and a little wary. He showed her into a kitchen which instantly reminded her of somewhere, though she couldn't think where. Not Lucey Lodge, which was brighter and more modern. It was as small as Lily's house, but much cleaner and neater, almost austere, and she guessed Charlie spent little time indoors. The Sacred Heart picture over the mantelpiece reminded her of Margaret: hard to imagine her going off to boarding school from such a simple place. Like them, he had lit an unseasonal fire, in front of which sat a wooden clothes horse, with some undershirts and socks steaming gently. He moved it into the scullery with a word of apology. 'There's no drying outdoors today.' He didn't sit down, but stood, obviously waiting to know why she had called.

'I saw your photo in the *Easterbridge Recorder*,' April said.

His face relaxed. 'Aye,' he said. 'I knew old Tansy had it in her. That was a great night.'

'The only greyhound I've ever heard of is Mick the Miller,' April admitted. 'And Master McGrath of course – sure he was a good Ulster dog.' And then she had no more to say about greyhounds or anything else and they stood awkwardly until she came up with, 'I'm sure you wonder what I'm doing here. I've something to ask you.'

He said nothing but she saw, so fleetingly that she might have imagined it, a spark of anxiety in his eyes.

'It's a professional matter,' she said, and the anxiety changed to curiosity. 'Could you teach someone to ride?' She explained about Barbara and his face relaxed into a grin when she admitted her mistake. 'It was my fault in the first instance,' she said, 'so I'd like to put it right. She'd pay you of course.'

'I've never taught anyone to ride.'

'I think she knows the basics. She just wants to feel confident. And the Colonel's old pony – you've both said she was very quiet.'

Charlie laughed. 'Dead slow and stop. But yes, it'll do her good to work for her keep. The Colonel won't mind – he said I could do what I liked with her, and he's always keen to help you.'

April didn't think she had seen him laugh before and she thought how attractive he was, and what an irony that she was introducing him to an equally attractive young woman who definitely wouldn't be interested. Still, perhaps Barbara would have a friend … It wouldn't be an *official* True Minds match, but April would still claim it. And then she realised that, as usual, she had let her imagination run wild, and remembered that she had another favour to ask Charlie.

'It's about your dogs,' she said. 'I once asked if you'd come and talk about them at Shaw's Mill.' She rushed on in her most entreating tones. 'I'd be so grateful – we're worried about some of the other influences in the town – fascist groups and the like – so anything wholesome like dogs would be a great sort of antidote.'

'There's plenty don't think dog racing's wholesome. A lot think it's cruel. And then there's the gambling. Winston Churchill calls it animated roulette.'

'Och, who listens to that eejit? No, the kids'd love it. There's a field behind the mill – I thought you could give the dog a wee sprint there? And answer a few questions? Och, please, Charlie! She's a celebrity – they'll have seen her in the paper. You could bring that lovely trophy to show them.' She had just caught sight of it on top of a chest of drawers, shining in the low-ceilinged gloom.

'I'm not one for public speaking. I'd be tongue-tied.'

'Don't be daft.' April tended to dismiss qualms she didn't share. 'You'd only have to answer a few questions. It would be an act of' – she tried to think what Felicity would say – 'civic responsibility.'

'You sound like you've swallowed a dictionary.'

'Well, that's a nice change. Normally yous English haven't a clue what I'm on about.'

Charlie smiled and the tension eased. 'Would you take a cup of tea?' he asked. 'It'd not take long to boil a kettle.'

She was about to refuse when she remembered, during her very first week in Easterbridge two years ago, taking tea with Fabian Carr in his sitting room. *That* was what this room reminded her of: Fabian's house was grand and comfortable but, before Martha, it had had the same look as Charlie's – a sense of absence and the space not healed around it. A house without a woman. A lonely house.

'Thanks,' she said and, without being asked, sat down in one of the old-fashioned chintz armchairs. Had Evelyn ever sat here? Was hers the absence she sensed, or his mother's and sister's? Well, there was only one way to find out, and the kindest time to do it was now, while Charlie was busy spooning tea into a pot and fetching a jug of milk from the scullery.

And then she caught herself on. For dear sake, hadn't the visit gone well? Hadn't he agreed to both her requests, either of which *might* lead to him meeting a nice wee woman who'd be free to love him as Evelyn wasn't? Why under God would she mention Evelyn at all?

Evelyn was back home where she belonged and that was that.

Twenty-five

As Charlie turned the Colonel's Bentley through the iron gates of Shaw's Mill, he wished he'd never agreed. Some lads were kicking a ball around a patch of grass, and the thought of talking to them made him want to turn round and not stop driving until he was safely home. But Tansy whined, thinking she was going racing, puzzled by the short trip, and he pulled himself together.

He had been anxious about teaching Miss Firth to ride, had regretted saying yes almost at once, but it had been grand. She had been terrified even to sit on Mousie at first, but Mousie was exceptionally patient and by the end of the first half-hour lesson Miss Firth was begging to be allowed to trot. 'It's all coming back to me,' she said, her cheeks pink with enjoyment. She told him he was a born teacher and insisted on paying him half a crown. She wanted three lessons a week, which also had the benefit of using up much of his spare time, so the half-crowns would soon mount up, and once she overcame her nerves, she proved to be a chatty, easy-going girl, and he enjoyed the work. So if he could do that, he could talk to a few lads.

April came to meet him, accompanied by a younger woman, dressed in what even Charlie recognised as high fashion, her hair elaborately waved. But she greeted him with the same easy warmth as April, and immediately made a fuss of Tansy.

'I'm Sybil Barrett,' she said. 'It's frightfully good of you to give up your time. Colonel Lucey tells me you're a genius with his hunters.'

'I do my best,' Charlie said. 'It's quiet this time of year – end of next month we'll bring them in and start fittening them up.'

'I suppose it's not unlike training dogs?' Sybil had a long, expressive face. 'Henry and I went to the races at Belle Vue last year. It's an awfully jolly night out; I won seventeen and six on a dog called Perendar.'

'Oh aye? That would have been the Northern Flat.'

'It was indeed.' Sybil looked impressed. 'I say, can you tell me—?'

'Can we leave it for the talk?' April said. 'We don't want Charlie to run out of steam.'

'I'm not sure I've got much steam to start with.'

But he enjoyed the talk more than he'd expected. The boys were shy at first, but soon crowded round with questions.

'Does she bite, Mister? Is that why she's got a muzzle?'

'Does she kill things, Mister?'

They seemed disappointed that the answer to both questions was no. (Not, in the latter case, that it was absolutely true, but he had placed everything that happened the night the dogs killed the rabbit into a very strong box, and locked it, and thrown the key down a very deep well.)

'D'you starve her? Is that why she's so skinny?' asked a podgy little buck-toothed lad, and everyone laughed.

'Don't be daft, Albert; they're meant to be like that.'

'Aye, they couldn't run if they were as fat as you.'

'That's enough, Freddie Hick,' April said at once. 'I've your mammy's permission to box your ears.'

Some older boys slouched over to see what was happening. One of them had a whippet at home; one had a grandad in Leeds who trained dogs – when he said his name Charlie knew him for the biggest crook this side of the Pennines, but he said only that he'd met him and he'd had a lovely big fawn bitch. Some boys tittered at the word *bitch* but April said firmly, with a hard look at Freddie Hick, that a bitch was a lady dog and there was no need to be an eejit about it.

The highlight, of course, was seeing Tansy run. Charlie got a volunteer – a burstingly important Albert – to stand at the far end of the field, with a rag of rabbit skin on a stick. Charlie took Tansy about a hundred yards away and held her firmly, legs arranged ready for action. Bored with standing around, missing the lights and the noise and the crowd, she trembled with pent-up energy, and when he said, 'Now then!' and Albert waved the rabbit skin, she flew up the field, her lean, muscled body bunching and plunging, ears flat. The lads cheered her on, and when she reached Albert he rewarded her, as Charlie had shown him, with a scrap of mutton.

The boys were as excited as if they'd witnessed the Derby.

'Can she go again, Mister? Can I hold the rabbit this time?'

He gave her three runs, then said that was enough. Tansy was panting, her tongue hanging out and her flanks heaving.

'She's not a machine,' he said. 'She needs a drink and a rest.'

There was a lot of grumbling until April called out, 'Right, let's see who can run as fast as Tansy – once round the field; first one home gets a lollipop.'

Off they tore, Albert clearly determined not to be last.

April and Sybil fell into step with Charlie and Tansy as they walked back to the yard. They were joined by a tall, fair man a little younger than himself; April introduced him as Constable Sidney Armstrong, the boys' football coach.

'That was canny,' Armstrong said.

'I told you the wee fellas would love it,' April said. 'Now, let's get you a cuppa. What about Tansy?'

'She'd love a cuppa,' Charlie said.

Sitting in a downstairs room that seemed to be a café-cum-meeting place, watching people dash here and there, listening to folk songs from somewhere above, he reflected that, for the first time since Evelyn had gone, he had enjoyed himself.

No, not the first time – there had been that wonderful night at Elland Road, seeing Tansy, in the red jacket of Trap One, peel away from the others to win by a clear seven lengths. It was the most prestigious race she'd ever qualified for, the biggest he'd entered, and as he'd collected the thirty pounds prize money, he'd thought, well that would help make up for the money he'd spent on the ring. But then, smiling for the photographer, the familiar heft of Tansy's leather lead in his hand, her warm flanks against his legs, he'd blinked out at the crowd – thousands of faces, and not one of them gave a damn about him. He had acquaintances, men he chatted with and chaffed, but no more. And driving home, Tansy's snores whiffling from the back of the Bentley, and the road stretching dark and long ahead, he felt lonelier than he ever remembered. It was daft; he should have been over the moon, and he *was*; it was just—

If I'd never met her, and *hoped*, he thought, nothing would be different now.

But that thought belonged in the box, at the very bottom

of the well, so he gave himself a shake and accepted another cup of tea and a lemon biscuit.

He had arranged to take April back to Lucey Lodge and was glad of her company. He was grand going through his usual routine – horses, and dogs, and chores at home and at work, keeping the house decent and making sure he had clean clothes and enough to eat – it was when something different happened that Evelyn's absence bit. Like that night at Elland Road. And then the lurch of loneliness would be compounded by embarrassment: How can you be so daft? You only knew her five minutes. It was all in your head. Anyway, she was a – he thought of how April had chastised the boys – a lying bitch.

But he shouldn't be thinking about any of this with April sitting beside him, all warm and chatty, delighted with how the evening had gone.

They met no traffic on the steep moorland road, until they were approaching the village, when Charlie had to pull out past a big black taxi parked outside the vicarage. A burly taxi-driver was pulling a large suitcase from the boot.

'Oh!' April said, turning back in her seat to look. 'Jenny's home!' She turned back to Charlie. 'You know Jenny Dunn?'

'Only to see.'

But he remembered the shock of the whole village when the vicar's daughter had been badly injured in a motor accident some years before. She had been a bright young thing, rambling the lanes with a long, easy stride on the rare occasions when she was home from college or her teaching job. She always looked as if she was about to break into laughter or dance, or both. Until the time she had come home in an ambulance, and was not seen for months, and then only hobbling on crutches, her face drawn with pain, and people had said what a shame it was. And then, out of the blue, she had taken a job as some kind of governess. She came home from time to time, and walked round the lanes with a stick, slowly, but with something of her old lightness. She was spoken of no longer with pity, but with respect.

'She's been working in London,' April went on. Her face sobered. 'She's home because her father's ill.'

'Oh aye. Mrs Lucey mentioned the vicar had taken badly.'

'Jenny's going to help her mother. But we're hoping she'll have time to teach some dancing at the mill.'

Charlie made a non-committal noise, unsure what this had to do with him, and an awkward silence grew until April blurted out, as if she'd been building up to it, 'Look, Charlie, I wasn't going to mention Evelyn …'

He kept his eyes steadily on the road. 'Best not, then.'

'But I need to say – well, obviously I knew she was married.'

'Obviously.'

'And I did wonder – more than once – if I should have told you.'

'I wish you had.'

'I wish I had too, but it wasn't my business.'

He couldn't see her face, but he could guess the expression. 'That doesn't usually bother you.'

'That's not fair. I didn't know if yous were just friends or … She didn't make it easy for me.'

'She didn't make it easy for me either.'

'I don't know what happened between yous,' April said. 'I know she went to see you the night before she left. That day I met you outside the jeweller's?'

He didn't want to be reminded of that ludicrous purchase, all that ridiculous *hope*.

'I told her she wasn't being fair to you. She went off to – well, talk to you I suppose. But next morning she bolted. And not a word since.'

He sighed. 'I might as well tell you. I'd planned to ask her to marry me. I know it sounds daft.'

'It doesn't,' she said gently. 'You acted in good faith. And is that when she told you?'

'Bit more dramatic than that.' He found himself telling her about the rabbit, Evelyn's collapse and then those terrible revelations about her child's death, about her being married, the heart-stopping realisation of how foolish he had been. Something about April made him say more than he'd imagined he could, pouring out the whole terrible story as the moors flashed by.

By the time he had finished they were parked outside Lucey Lodge.

'She's never told me the details. Dear bless us, it must have been absolutely horrific.' April shivered. 'Och, Charlie – surely you can forgive her? She must have been so unhappy. I don't think you or I can even begin to understand that kind of grief.'

Deep down he knew that. Deep down he knew he was letting his own pain blind him to hers. But he couldn't forget that image he had dared to have – of Evelyn with a child, his child, when all the time …

A fox screamed, making them both jump, and though he wanted to say something kind and understanding, his feelings seemed to have tangled into a horrible, jagged muddle and he couldn't help lashing out: 'But she's married! All those weeks she let me … when she *must* have known how I felt.'

April was silent for what felt like a long time, before saying, 'I'm not sure how things are between her and Maurice – her husband. She barely mentioned him.'

Maurice. He made himself ask, 'What's he like?'

'Quiet big fella. I paid him no heed until Evelyn started walking out with him, and then the next thing they were married. I think she panicked. She was heart-scared of being an old maid. Like me.' She grinned. 'She's not the first woman who married for the wrong reasons.' She played with the clasp on her bag. 'Look, Charlie, I don't know if this makes you feel any better, but I've never thought she loved him.'

'How could it make me feel better?'

'Because whatever she felt about you – it was *real*. And she never set out to hurt you.'

'But she was married. She'd no business to lead me on!'

'Things aren't that black and white, Charlie.'

'They are to me. Anyway' – he made his voice as dismissive as possible because the conversation was growing unbearable – 'she's gone back to him and that's that.'

'We don't *know* she's gone back to him,' April said slowly. 'I've no idea where she's gone.'

'It's no odds to me. She's married. She can never be not-married, so ...' He leaned forward to indicate that he intended to drive on.

Before she got out of the car April said, 'Charlie, I'm sorry Evelyn hurt you. But if the whole affair—'

'It was hardly an affair!'

'If the whole *experience* made you think you might, sometime, like to meet someone ... well, you've only got to ask me.'

'*What?*'

For a moment he thought she was propositioning him, but she jumped in.

'No! *I* don't fancy you. I mean' – in some confusion – 'you're a fine figure of a man. But I do run a marriage bureau. If you ever decided—'

'I won't,' he said. 'I've no interest in – in all that. And I can't believe you'd tout for business like that. Goodnight, Miss McVey.'

He thought, as he drove away, that he saw her lips form an apology, but he couldn't be sure, and it didn't matter. The last place on earth he would go was to April McVey's marriage bureau.

Twenty-six

When you ran a marriage bureau, wedding invitations were an occupational hazard. It was always a secret relief if the wedding was too far away, or to hear afterwards that it *took place quietly*. But in early August two invitations arrived on the same day, and April could ignore neither of them.

The first, on stiff white card, was from Sir Granville and Lady Sophia Wyndham-Howard inviting *Miss April McVey to the wedding of their daughter, the Hon. Augusta Louise, to Clarence George Taylor-Scott, elder son of, etc. etc.* on Saturday the seventeenth of October.

Oh lord, thought April in dismay, how can I get out of that?

'You can't,' Martha said when she rang her up for advice. 'Think of all those lovesick debutantes. All that potential top-drawer business.'

'I'm not an advertisement!' April wailed. (*I can't believe you'd tout for business like that.* It still stung.) 'And they'll hardly introduce me as Miss April McVey, purveyor of husbands and wives, will they? They'll want to be discreet.'

'Not necessarily. The rich can be eccentric. They probably think' – she affected a voice not unlike the Hon. Augusta's – 'it's a frightful jape. But seriously, April, a society wedding might be fun.'

April wondered if the Wyndham-Howards and the Taylor-Scotts would think it a *frightful jape* if she accepted the invitation on behalf of herself and her partner, Miss Felicity Carr, writer, left-wing political activist, and, of course, lesbian. She sighed as she replaced the receiver. In the old days she and Martha would have been invited together, and it might indeed have been fun. The Yeadons' wedding had been a grand day out, the small congregation bursting with goodwill, and a tea party in St Luke's church hall afterwards. But a posh wedding on her own, in tight shoes, knowing nobody, and anxious about using the wrong fork or mixing up her sirs and her lords, or accidentally drinking too much champagne, would be a tedious reminder of something she and Felicity would never be allowed.

I don't want orange blossom and a veil, April thought, setting the invitation on the mantelpiece in the interview room, beside a jug of pinks and zinnias from the garden. Or a white frock and speeches; I would just like to be *recognised*. Even if marriage was, as Felicity said, bourgeois and conventional.

The second invitation was delivered personally, announced by a familiar stomping on the stairs. April arranged her face carefully to welcome Lily, with a sudden guilty fear, as she crossed the office to open the door, that she had lost the baby and was seeking reinstatement. But Lily was unmistakeably still pregnant.

'Wedding's next week,' she said with no preamble beyond a sniff. 'You'll come, won't you?'

'I ... er ...' April, rarely lost for words, was lost for words. 'I assumed it would be a quiet ceremony.'

'Why? It's not like me and Reg are ashamed,' Lily said. 'We'll have a right do.' She fingered the browning leaves of an aspidistra on top of the filing cabinet. 'You never did remember to water that.'

'When's the wedding?' She added hopefully, 'It's hard to get away, being on my own …'

'Not been able to replace me, then?' Lily asked smugly.

'Not exactly.'

'I thought not. I said to Mam, she'll not get another me that easy! But when you're going to be a wife and mother …' She stroked her belly. 'Saturday week. The fifteenth. St Margaret's and then the Black Horse.' She said the latter with as much as pride as if it had been the Ritz. 'Reg has a connection there. We'll have the back room. Back lounge I should say.'

'I don't know if I can …'

'Oh, Miss McVey, you must!' Lily's lip trembled. 'You'll lend it a bit of class. I don't want my side looking poor beside Reg's.'

Later, recounting this to Felicity, April said, 'God love the cratur if I'm the classiest person she knows. And then I'll be the commonest person at the posh wedding.'

Felicity laughed. 'This is much more important than the society wedding. You can't snub her *because* she's a pregnant working-class girl from Townsend Street.'

'Good.' April grinned. 'Because you're invited too.'

'*What?*'

'She was in your writing class, remember? Apparently you told her she had great potential and gave her the confidence to try an office job.'

Felicity groaned. 'I only wanted to give her some self-respect.'

'Sadly it worked. Up to a point. So you can flipping well put on your best frock and come too.'

'The only wedding we've ever been to together was Fabian and Martha's.'

Fabian and Martha's wedding was a day April always saw as bathed in happiness, she and Felicity bridesmaids with Prudence, in bluebell-coloured frocks. The choir sang 'Love Divine, All Loves Excelling', and Erich played 'Jesu, Joy of Man's Desiring' on the violin. Everyone cried at Fabian's speech, and at the wedding breakfast in the Royal Oak, Prudence and her friend Susan had too much champagne and had to be sobered up with strong coffee.

'It won't be that good,' April warned. 'But as you say, we can't snub her.'

Felicity groaned good-naturedly. 'All right. I'll dig out my best bib and tucker and we'll take the Black Horse by storm. We might even enjoy it.'

On the fifteenth, as they stood at the bus stop outside the village shop, both in best frocks and hats, April felt an unaccustomed ripple of contentment. Felicity rarely coughed, and was eating and sleeping well. She wrote every day, but was obediently taking the air as well, even without Evelyn. She wheeled Dorothy out most afternoons so Florrie could put her feet up for an hour. 'And then we have a cup of tea afterwards,' Felicity explained. 'Florrie's become quite a pal: a fascinating case study of a woman who's experienced life as a spinster, and now as a wife, stepmother and mother. I'd like to interview her for *Time and Tide* – you know, how society's changing view of her as a woman has impacted on her view of herself.'

'Hmm.' April smiled at Miss Batley, who was sweeping the pavement outside her shop. 'Maybe don't tell her she's a *fascinating case study*. I'd stick to *quite a pal*.'

Miss Batley paused. 'Look at you bobby-dazzlers,' she said. 'Off somewhere nice?' She looked them up and down, stocky and plain in her floral shop coat, and April saw herself and Felicity as Miss Batley must – young and pretty, Felicity in soft pink with a little green cape, herself in spotted mauve with fashionable big buttons down the yoke.

'A wedding,' she said.

Miss Batley's muddy complexion flushed. 'Ooh, I love a wedding.' She looked up at the hazy grey sky. 'It's to brighten up later. Fancy do, is it?'

'Oh, no, quite modest,' Felicity said. 'They're very young.'

'Young, are they?' Miss Batley looked wistful.

April was quick to say, 'Too young. I much prefer the weddings of older people.'

'Oh aye?' Miss Batley leaned on her broom and looked shy. 'I've heard that you, er, work in that ...'

'Marriage bureau?' April supplied. 'I'm in charge of it. We help all sorts of people. All ages.' Her mind started running through the older men on their books. Perhaps one of the Colonel's pals ...

The green-and-cream bus trundled into view and Felicity stuck out her arm as it wheezed to a stop. They waved goodbye to Miss Batley as they settled down between an old man with a smelly pipe and a woman with a basket of clucking hens.

'Honestly, you're impossible!' Felicity slipped her return ticket into her bag and clicked it shut. She imitated April's accent. '*Och aye, we even help old people like you. Come and give us a try.* I'm surprised you don't hand out brochures.'

April laughed. 'What about you? – *a fascinating case study.*'

'I suppose we're never off duty.' A feather from the hen basket floated past Felicity and she wrinkled her nose, but did not, as she would have done a month ago, start to cough.

Wellbeing stole over April like the midday sun starting

to break through the grey sky, as Miss Batley had foreseen. 'We are today.'

They relaxed into the seat, chatting about Erich and Hanna's twins, watching hedgerows of ripening brambles and elderberries speed past the windows, until the rough moorland gave way to gentler fields, lone cottages made way for straggling stone terraces. Finally the bus clattered over the cobbles of the bridge and came to rest in the town square beside the Crimean War memorial, from which it was a short walk to St Margaret's.

Lily and Reg's families only filled the first few rows. Everyone was in Sunday best, but there was no disguising the air of poverty and compromise. The women looked tired, the men awkward, and the children goggle-eyed and restless. April and Felicity were indeed the best-dressed there, apart from a broad man near the front: his heavy brown tweed suit was of good quality, and even from the back there was an assurance about him that nobody else had.

Except Lily. Twice the width of her father, she beamed down the aisle with a brashness April couldn't help admiring, her equally bold bouquet failing to cover her belly. The hymn was 'Lead Us, Heavenly Father, Lead Us', but April seemed to be the only one confident enough to sing out, her bravery deserting her when she realised she was getting no support apart from the bass voice of the man in brown tweed. The vicar was trying so hard to avoid staring at Lily's belly that he appeared cross-eyed. Reg was a spindly youth sweating into an ill-fitting suit, and both mumbled their responses inaudibly. But in twenty minutes it was done, and Lily Lumley was Lily Binn, flashing her wedding ring and clutching Reg with her other hand. Her gaudy bouquet was being carried by her sister Daisy, wearing a yellow bridesmaid's dress which had been made for someone shorter and thinner.

'We needn't stay long,' April whispered as they trickled out of the church. 'We can catch the four o'clock bus. I said I'd call on Jenny this evening. Her father's quite a bit better. Hello there, Mrs Lumley' – Lily's mother had appeared at her elbow – 'Aye, she was a wee picture, right enough.'

The Black Horse was an establishment neither April nor Felicity had ever entered before. It had the usual stale beery pub smell, but the landlord ushered them to a back room, where plates of sandwiches and sausage rolls sat on a long trestle table, with an urn of tea and an iced fruit cake with a white bow tied round it.

'See?' Lily said. 'Doesn't it all look proper?'

'Very proper. Congratulations.'

'Get us a port and lemon, love,' Lily wheedled. 'I'm that weak after all the excitement.'

Reg trotted off to do her bidding but was waylaid by the stocky man in brown tweed.

'Allow me, Reginald, my good fellow,' he said with great bonhomie, smiling behind a heavy moustache. 'And a pint for the blushing bridegroom, eh?' He looked with curiosity at April and Felicity.

'This is my former employer, Miss McVey,' Lily said importantly. 'And Miss Carr. And *this* is Mr Johnson.'

But April's body had recognised Nigel Johnson, the man who had assaulted her two years ago, even before she heard the name. Acid scalded her throat, icy fingers crept down her skin and her legs seemed to have vanished.

She felt Felicity grab her arm, heard a voice say, 'Are you all right?' and then she was blessedly outside, gasping for breath, shuddering, with Felicity beside her, saying, 'What on earth's up?'

'It's him,' she said.

Felicity stared. '*Him?*' Then her face cleared. 'You mean that bastard who—?'

April nodded. There was no need to say more.

'Right.' Felicity stood up and for the first time in months she was the fearsome Amazon that April had fallen in love with. 'I'll kill him.'

'You can't! It's Lily's wedding! Felicity!'

But Felicity was already storming back into the Black Horse.

She can't tackle someone at a wedding! It's crazy! I have to stop her.

But she couldn't make herself move from the wall outside the Black Horse, listening to the laughter and chatter of the wedding party, powerless to do anything but sit and wait for the inevitable roar of Felicity as avenging angel. What would she say? And what would Johnson do? What could he do, in front of everyone?

But there was no roar. No break in the muted merrymaking. Instead, Felicity came out, looking – looking terrible. As bad as April had ever seen her.

'It's him,' she said.

'I know. I told you. Nigel Johnson.'

'No. I mean …' Felicity rubbed her hands over her face, pulling at a stray curl the way she did when she was upset. She took a deep, steadying breath. 'That's the man who attacked *me*. The one who knocked me down in the street.'

Twenty-seven

Lisnacashan on the fifteenth of August. It was the same every year.

'It's the marching I don't hold with,' Mona said.

Evelyn reckoned that if her mother-in-law pursed her lips any tighter, she would swallow them.

'You didn't say that when the Orangemen marched last month.'

'That's completely different,' snapped Mona. 'Don't you agree, Maurice?'

Maurice looked up from his dinner. 'Och, Mammy. They do no harm. We have the twelfth of July and they have the fifteenth of August. All they do is march up to the Hibernians' Hall and play a few tunes. Sure they're bothering nobody.'

Mona humphed. 'Lisnacashan was always such a nice town. So quiet.'

'You mean so Protestant?' Evelyn asked.

'Let's not talk about religion.' Maurice looked helplessly from mother to wife and back again.

I bet he wishes I'd never come home, Evelyn thought.

But that wasn't fair. Maurice hadn't reproached her. He hadn't asked questions or said she had a quare cheek. On that day two months ago when she had walked back up the lane and across the farmyard, he had glanced up from hosing the tractor and said, 'Och, it's yourself,' as if she had been to Cookstown for the day. He had crossed the yard and stood in front of her, and made a clumsy gesture to take her in his arms. She had stiffened and then allowed him to hug her. It was the first time he had touched her since long before Robbie died. She tried not to think how different he felt from Charlie.

'Are you feeling more like yourself?' he had asked.

She said yes, because that was what he wanted to hear. And because she no longer had much sense of what *yourself* meant. Had she been herself in Easterbridge? With Charlie?

She had had one short letter from April, telling her that Felicity was much better, that Prudence had won the school tennis tournament, that Hanna had had twin boys, Daniel and David, but she had not replied. She would never see these people again. What did she care that Hanna and Erich had chosen names that wouldn't make the boys stand out as German and Jewish should they grow up in England? Her own child would grow up nowhere. Did April think she was going to skip along to Miss Connaughton's and buy a skein of white wool to knit matching matinée coats?

When Mona had tried to interrogate her – how on earth could she have left poor Maurice for so long, why did she write so seldom, how could she possibly have thought her friends needed her more than her own husband? – Maurice said, 'Leave her be, Mammy. Evelyn's home now and that's all that matters.'

All summer they lived peaceably in the bungalow. Maurice was gentle and conciliatory. He was busier than ever because poor Jamesie was having one of his bad times. Evelyn cleaned and cooked and tried not to be irritated when Mona insisted on helping. ('I got used to doing it when poor Maurice was all alone.') She went without argument to First Lisnacashan Presbyterian every Sunday morning and let the Reverend McClure's words wash over her. It was so different from St Anthony's in Easterbridge that it was easy enough not to imagine Charlie kneeling beside her. Easy enough, as she cleaned the picture windows of the bungalow and ran the Ewbank over the sitting room carpet, not to imagine the polished wooden floors and tiny casement windows of Lucey Lodge. Easy enough, as she walked further and further into the gentle hills and dark woods around Lisnacashan, and along the green rushy banks of the Blackwater, not to fancy that a quiet Yorkshireman kept step with her, his greyhounds at his heels.

It was all easy enough because she had left the real Evelyn – the Evelyn who felt and remembered and cried and laughed and hurt – somewhere else. On Shippards Hill, maybe, above Lucey Lodge, where the sheep paths meandered across the moor, and the dark peaty streams trickled over the stones. But she never let her imagination go there, or to Easterbridge, so she didn't know exactly *where* she had left that other self.

And it didn't matter, because the shadow Evelyn who stood in the queue in the butcher's, and sat between Maurice and Mona in church, and kept the bungalow like a wee palace, was a perfectly acceptable substitute. A doppelganger. Certainly nobody in Lisnacashan noticed anything. 'You look better, Mrs Kenny,' they said. 'Nice to see you back again.'

Mona was the only one who looked at her sideways, but the new shadow Evelyn was immune to anything Mona said or did, which was very convenient. Even today, when Mona was complaining about the Hibernians having their annual fifteenth of August parade, she was only going through the motions of arguing with her, there was no sting in it. Her doppelganger didn't care about Hibernians, or Mona, or anything.

The only time the doppelganger couldn't help her was when she visited Robbie's grave, which she did early in the mornings, when there was nobody around, and never after Sunday service when the churchyard was busier. When she had left Lisnacashan, the daffodils had been nodding their sunny heads in front of the stark grey headstone; now it was brightened with pinks, dahlias and zinnias. She wondered if Maurice had planted those too, but she didn't ask him, in case he said it was Mona. She hadn't cried much before she went away, and she didn't know if it was better or worse that the tears came so easily now. She always made sure to blow her nose and dry her eyes before she went back to the bungalow, and she was always back in time to make Maurice his breakfast.

There seemed no reason why she shouldn't keep on like this for ever.

Twenty-eight

Martha reached out a hand to April and one to Felicity. 'Oh, my dears, how ghastly! I'm glad you came to us.'

'But, Fee, you can't be *sure* ...?' Fabian, reliably lawyerlike, asked. 'You couldn't stand up in a court and *swear* it was him?'

Felicity shook her head. 'No. I mean, I *am* certain, but I know how easily I'd be discredited – bang on the head, lost my memory. I'd no idea what he looked like until today. Not even when I first saw him. It was only when I went back inside after him that I recognised him. I'd remembered his voice' – she shuddered – 'but I couldn't have *described* him.'

'I could.' April pressed her hands tighter round the cup of tea Martha had given her. 'Every detail. I used to be scared to look up in the street in case I saw him. Once or twice I thought I did – I'd see some big man with a moustache, or I'd hear someone's voice in the post office queue. But it was never him. I'd nearly forgotten – and then there he was.'

'Utterly reprehensible,' Fabian said. 'To hit a woman – to, er, molest a woman—'

'And he's clearly the leader of this local fascist group,' Felicity said. 'Which is how that pathetic Reg knows him.' Something of her old spirit crept into her voice. '*That*'s how we get him. I can't swear as to what he did to me. What he did to April was over two years ago—'

'Realistically, neither of us can get him for attacking us,' April said. 'It'd be a waste of time to try, wouldn't it, Fabian?'

'I'm afraid so.'

'Never mind.' Felicity sounded business-like. 'Where we *can* get him – bring him to justice, whatever you want to call it – is through his beastly fascist group. I wonder if it's officially affiliated to Mosley's lot?'

Fabian sighed. 'I'm almost sure it's not illegal,' he said. 'Yes' – as Felicity opened her mouth to protest – 'I agree it should be, but we must deal with the law – and the world – as they are, not as we'd like them to be.'

'I disagree,' Felicity said. 'We must fight for change. Otherwise everything stays the same.'

'Actually,' Martha said, 'I'd say things have got worse.' Her dark eyes were very serious. 'People are ... unsettled. It's not just the unemployment and worry about the cost of living. There's a kind of *nastiness* in the air. At home and abroad.'

'That's why we need to fight the fascists,' Felicity cried.

'You've been fighting fascism for years,' her brother said.

'And you thought I was mad – a bunch of Commies and radicals, you called my friends.'

'I worried about you getting hurt! And I wasn't wrong, was I?'

'Fabian, you have to stand up for what's right. Especially when there are people who *can't*. Look at Germany, and Italy, and now Spain ...'

'And now Easterbridge,' Martha said quietly.

Felicity rounded on her. 'Exactly, Martha! It's not enough to say it's somewhere else, it's someone else's problem. It's *here*. Those kids at the wedding today, Reg and his pals, do you suppose they understand the tenets of fascism? The so-called ideology?' Her face twisted in disgust. 'They only understand that they don't have jobs, and that some man in a nice suit with a loud voice and fancy words is telling them who to blame. Getting them riled. Making them feel no end of smart fellows. Making them feel part of something.' Felicity ran out of breath. She leaned back, took a sip of coffee and grimaced.

'Cold?' Martha asked. 'I'll make fresh.'

'I'll come with you.' April followed Martha into the clean, bright kitchen.

'You seem worried,' Martha said as they waited for the kettle to come back to the boil.

'You know Felicity when she gets a bee in her bonnet. And this is a quare big bee. I don't want her putting herself at risk.'

Martha spooned coffee into the pot. 'But she's so much better now – even after today's shock. She looks well. You both do.'

'It's the country air,' April said. 'Part of me wishes we could stay there, but it's awkward to be so far from town. The ideal would be to go for weekends – but it's not ours! The Colonel's been wonderful, but we can't expect to just use the lodge whenever we like.'

'Would he sell?'

April laughed. '*We* couldn't buy it unless we sold Riverside Road, and, like I said, we can't live there all the time, no matter how healthy it is.' She looked at her old friend closely. 'Actually, Martha, you're looking peaky. Maybe you're the one needs country air.'

'I'm fine!' Martha waved this away. 'Just rather fed up.' She lifted the kettle off the hob and poured water carefully into the coffee pot. 'Hello, Prue!'

Prudence, all long legs and short gym tunic, her plaits wound round her head, glanced into the kitchen. 'I'm off to the mill now, Mar,' she said. 'Let's hope those idiotic girls have learned left from right since last week.' She grinned at April. 'Gosh, you look fancy!' She grabbed an apple from the bowl on the table and dashed off.

'She calls you *Ma*?' April said.

Martha smiled. '*Mar*. Short for Martha. But yes – it does sound like Ma. I don't mind.' It was clear that she liked it.

'But …?' April returned to the conversation Prudence had interrupted.

'Why should there be a *but*?' Martha spoke lightly.

'You said you were fed up.'

'Oh – sometimes, with Fabian and Prue out all day, things can be a little dull.'

'For dear sake, Martha, you're used to running a business. A business you built up from nothing. Of course being at home all day's dull!' April had been so careful not to pressurise Martha into coming back to work, but now she was admitting she was fed up, that life could be dull – surely the solution was simple? 'Why not come back properly? All this talk of *helping out* until I recruit a new assistant. I don't want an assistant. I want *you*. And it needn't be every day. I could manage with, say, three days a week.'

Martha sighed. 'Don't think I haven't thought about it. But Fabian—'

'Don't tell me Fabian would forbid it?'

'Not *forbid*. But it's not done, is it? For a solicitor's wife to go out to work. People would think it odd.'

'So?'

'It would hurt Fabian if he thought this' – she waved a hand round the tidy kitchen – 'wasn't enough for me.'

'Well, it's not!' April laughed. 'Och, Martha: there's you

wishing for more to do, and me wishing for less.'

They brought the coffee pot back to the sitting room, where Fabian and Felicity were deep in conversation.

'Can you talk to her, April?' Fabian appealed. 'She won't listen to me.'

'I listen to my conscience,' Felicity said.

'Well, I'm hoping your conscience tells you to be careful,' Fabian said, 'because we don't want you getting hurt again.'

'I've no intention of getting hurt, but—'

'Promise you won't take direct action against this group,' Fabian said. 'Or at least' – as Felicity opened her mouth, clearly to protest – 'not without telling us.'

'Discretion is the better part of valour,' Martha said. 'There are more strategic ways to beat those thugs.'

'Such as?' Felicity demanded.

'Your writing?'

'Don't think I don't try! But Reginald Binn or that cad Johnson aren't going to read *Time and Tide* or *Labour Monthly*.'

'Well, write something that reaches the people who need it. Instead of preaching to the converted.'

'And at least promise not to do anything without discussing it with me,' April said.

'Oh, all right,' Felicity said. 'I promise.'

'I have a horrible feeling,' Martha said, 'that that simply means she's going to drag you with her, April.'

'I'm not easy to drag,' April said. And at the time she meant it.

Twenty-nine

In late August Charlie brought the horses in from grass to start the slow process of fittening them up – steady hacking round the roads and over the moors, nudging Hadrian out of his default indolent dawdle, while checking Scarlet's desire, on feeling the springy moorland turf under her hooves, to break into a canter.

'Soon,' he promised her one Monday morning, smoothing her red mane. 'Need to get this grass belly off you first.' The moor stretched as far as he could see, and Scarlet fretted to be off the sheep-beaten track. 'We'll head up by Yeadons',' he decided. That would take the fizz out of her. Chances were he'd meet Joseph around the fields.

But there was no sign of Joseph on the approach to the farm, and as he drew rein at the top of the track he saw, below in the farmyard, Joseph, Florrie with the baby in her arms, and the two children, clutching a large picnic hamper between them, climbing up into the old cart with Bobby in the shafts. Little bursts of laughter floated up the hill towards him. He should have remembered it was August Bank Holiday. Miss Firth and Mr Grant were going for the long-awaited picnic ride today; she had made wonderful progress and was trotting and cantering Mousie as though born to the saddle. And there were the Yeadons off on an outing too. At least he hadn't wasted time riding all the way down to the yard before finding them gone. He raised a hand in greeting, but they hadn't noticed him, so he rode back across the moor, looking ahead to Saturday night and the final of the Autumn Cup.

Tansy had got through her qualifying heats. Other trainers were starting to regard him with respect, to ask if he'd any more like her at home. Soon he would start training the pups, see if any of them showed anything of their aunt's speed and attitude. At the last heat, Tansy had been impeded at the second bend by a dog cutting across her and for a few yards she'd been last of all. But the dour fighting spirit he so loved had kicked in and she came from behind to finish second to Ted, her old littermate. Charlie and Eddie Blythe had shared wry grins. Second place was enough to get her into the final. All six dogs on Saturday night would be good ones, but someone had to win the Autumn Cup. Why not Tansy? Why not him?

'Why not, eh?' he asked Scarlet, and she responded with a flick of her ears. A rush of optimism flooded him and, figuring a short canter wouldn't do any harm, he gave her her head, crouching over her withers like a jockey as her reaching stride ate up the moorland turf.

She was sweating and blown when they clattered into the stable yard half an hour later, and he crossed his fingers that the Colonel wasn't about. A rustle in Carnelian's box suggested that he was, but it was two freckled setters who emerged, tongues lolling and tails flailing, followed by Mrs Lucey, in voluminous breeches and a patched tweed jacket, banging a soft body brush against a steel curry comb to clean it. Puffs of reddish horsehair lifted in the air.

'Good show!' she said. 'We're going for a jolly picnic ride.'

Charlie ran his hands over Scarlet's damp neck, hoping her mistress wouldn't notice she was sweatier than she should be. The setters snuffed hopefully round Scarlet who laid back her ears.

'I could have had Carnelian ready for you, Madam.'

She waved a hand. 'Tosh! The day I can't groom my own horse is the day I hang up my boots.' She raised her voice. 'Walter! We're losing the best of the day!' She went back into the stable, emerging with Carnelian tacked up and ready. The Colonel appeared with two spaniels and Hadrian, who was wearing a Boer War-vintage saddlebag.

'Good show!' he said. 'Tally-ho!'

Charlie smiled as he watched them go, Mrs Lucey's breeches like elephant ears on either side of her solid figure, the Colonel as upright as he must have been as a young man riding into battle, the four dogs loping behind. And, not for the first time lately, he felt the need to turn and share the smile, only there was nobody there but Scarlet. And then, as the companionable little group disappeared over the moor, he found the smile had faded anyway.

All week he devoted himself to Tansy's every need. She was walked just enough to keep her fit and happy, without taking the edge off her energy. He made up bran mashes and eggs with a care he wouldn't have taken for himself. And every evening after work he spent an hour grooming her, massaging liniment into her lean, strong limbs, checking that every inch, to the last tooth, was in the best fettle it could possibly be.

A couple of times, walking the lanes, he met Jenny Dunn, her fair curls ruffled by the moorland breeze and her cheeks pink.

'What a magnificent dog,' she said, her bright eyes running over Tansy's lithe muscular body. 'She'd give those Olympic athletes a run for their money.'

Charlie laughed. 'She'd leave them standing. Aye, she's a big night on Saturday – she's qualified for the Autumn Cup.'

'Gosh.' Jenny fondled Tansy's soft black ears and seemed in no hurry to go on.

For a crazy moment Charlie thought of asking if she would like to come and watch, but he stopped himself. The vicar's daughter at a dog track! And anyway, he thought as he watched her walk on up the lane, without a stick, her limp discernible but not holding her back, he had learned his lesson about getting involved with women. He would stick to horses and dogs. They didn't break your heart.

On Saturday evening, Tansy hopped up into the Bentley as if she couldn't wait to get to Elland Road and perform. And as she paraded round, Charlie's heart swelled with pride: not only had she qualified for the biggest race of her career, and his, but he had worked so hard to make her look every inch a champion. Even if she didn't win, her presence in this final was enough to add value to any pups she would have. But he would race her for at least another season before he bred from her: she was only three.

She was drawn number five, and was like a bullet out of the traps, plunging ahead until the first bend. Charlie tried to suppress the excitement building in his chest. Too soon. Ted was at her heels, drawing level – and then a big blue dog, Candlestick Boy, started to make ground and the three of them slogged to the second bend. Tansy pulled away and swerved to hug the hare rail. Maybe she was tiring; maybe she was feeling the pressure of better company; maybe she just misjudged things. He went over it time and time again without knowing any more than what happened.

Which was that one moment Tansy was at full pelt, the next somersaulting, dogs running round her, and then she was a crumpled heap against the rail.

The course vet destroyed her immediately. Her leg was smashed too badly for there to be any hope.

That was when Charlie found out that dogs could indeed break your heart. And that, although it was sad to have nobody to share your triumphs, it was much, much worse to have nobody to share your tragedies.

Thirty

April looked round the clean, swept rooms and sighed.

'We've been so happy here,' she said.

Felicity pulled the strap tight around her old suitcase and, with difficulty, buckled it. 'We have,' she agreed, 'but I'm ready to go home now. And you couldn't do that cycle in winter.' Her voice changed. 'Blast!'

'What's up?'

'That parcel you asked me to take to Florrie' – Miss Dawson had made Dorothy her first teddy – 'I meant to, but I got so involved with Moorland Molly. Who'd have thought living up here would have inspired my next juvenile series?'

'We could take it now and say goodbye,' April said. 'And you could tell Sally more about Moorland Molly – you know how excited she was when you said you'd dedicate it to her.'

Felicity surveyed the mess of books, paper, blotting paper and pens which surrounded her and sighed. 'I must sort this out before Fabian arrives.'

It was grand, April thought, setting off over the moorland track in the direction of Yeadons' farm, to have a final walk. Martha had been under the weather lately, so she had had no help in the bureau, and every evening had been spent either packing, or preparing Riverside Road for their return. The air seemed sweeter than ever, the moorland colours more vivid, the sky wider. No wonder this landscape had inspired Felicity's writing! If only they could afford to buy or even rent the lodge. Wouldn't it be great to have it to escape to, at the weekends, maybe, or any time they – especially Felicity – needed a top-up of moorland air? But even if the Colonel didn't sell, they couldn't expect him to keep lending it to them indefinitely.

The path to the farm took her past Charlie Teal's house, and she was glad it was Sunday morning, and him safely away to Mass. She still smarted at the memory of their last conversation – *I can't believe you'd tout for business like that.* Not for the first time, as she felt the breath of September on her cheek, she determined that her managing days were over: in future she wouldn't try to take charge of anybody. Unless they were paying good money to True Minds! She was cross with herself for blundering in and asking about Evelyn last time she saw him: Charlie had worked wonders with Barbara Firth, and his visit to the mill had gone beautifully; everything had been grand between them, until she had spoilt it. When was she ever going to learn to leave well alone?

She had been so confident Charlie would be out that she was nearly on top of him before she saw him. He was digging in his garden, bent over his spade, tossing earth into a neat pile. A quare big hole too; he must be planting a tree. She hoped he wouldn't look up and see her, but if he did, they could pass a civil remark about gardening, and the change of season, and by this afternoon she'd be back in Easterbridge, with no need for their paths to cross again.

Charlie didn't look up, he was entirely focussed on his task, but as she grew closer, she saw the object lying on the ground beside him, wrapped in a rug, and unmistakeably not a sapling shrub, but a dead greyhound.

April clapped her hand to her mouth. Oh God! She was about to call out, to offer sympathy, to ask what had happened—

And then she walked on quietly, before he could look up and see her.

I'm not intruding, she told herself. Not this time. I've learned my lesson. She could see the tree that marked the top of Yeadons' lane; she would mention to Joseph that Charlie had lost one of his dogs and might appreciate a neighbourly call. Only – not from her.

Unlike April, Felicity hadn't set foot in Riverside Road since May, and she kept exclaiming, 'Isn't this room dark! I never noticed before. *There's* the *Left Review*: no wonder I couldn't find it! Gosh, was it always so dusty in here?'

'It's not dusty!' April felt stung. 'Wasn't I here after work twice this week dusting away like a good'un? The last thing we need is you coughing all over the place again!'

Felicity looked guilty. 'Sorry,' she said. 'You're right. It's because the lodge was so fresh and shiny.'

'But it's home,' April said. 'You put the kettle on and I'll run down to Booth's for some jammy buns. You know we could never get anything like that in Shippardsholme.'

Tea with buns, in their own bright kitchen with their own familiar yellow jug and Felicity's beloved Bavarian pottery cups, made everything feel much homelier.

Felicity brought her typewriter up to the study, flung her favourite orange shawl round her shoulders, and pronounced herself ready for what she called *proper work* again.

'Not *too* proper,' April warned. 'You need to keep well.'

'There's a lot to do. The Easterbridge fascist group isn't going to go away on its own. I need to set up a local *anti-*

fascist group. And write an article for the *Easterbridge Recorder*, about the positive contribution Hanna and Erich and other refugees have made. And I've contacted some people in Leeds – the Jewish community there is very well established – oh, and my agent *loves* Moorland Molly! I'm going to spend the mornings on her and the afternoons on other work. You don't mind doing the dinner, do you?'

April sighed. They were back to porridge. Porridge cooked by her.

Thirty-one

Miss Connaughton saw through Evelyn's doppelganger.

One September afternoon, Evelyn dashed into her shop for darning wool, and she greeted her with warmth, though she had been about to turn the sign to *Closed*.

'I'm glad you'd a wee break,' she said, parcelling up the grey wool into a neat package. She looked closely at Evelyn. 'I hope you don't me saying – Caroline always told me I was pass-remarkable – but it doesn't seem to have done you much good. You don't look yourself.'

Evelyn did not know how to respond.

Miss Connaughton paused in the act of taking her money. 'You look *well*, but not' – she wrinkled her forehead – 'quite *with* us.'

Evelyn could have been furious, but instead she felt, for the first time in ages, *seen*. Or seen *through*?

'I was going to make tea,' Miss Connaughton said. 'Will you take a wee cup with me?' and Evelyn found herself sitting above the shop, in a high-ceilinged flat, being handed a green teacup and a soda farl with butter and homemade gooseberry jam.

A framed photograph of Caroline and Miss Connaughton sat on the mantelpiece. They must have been in their twenties, in the big sleeves, tight waists, and bouffant hair of the period, standing on a beach with their arms around each other. Their smiles were unselfconscious and hopeful.

'Where was that?' Evelyn asked.

'Portballintrae. We took a cottage for a fortnight. That was the only day it didn't rain. Such a happy time.'

She nodded at her teacup, and Evelyn realised that Miss Connaughton knew more about loss – and love – than Evelyn had given her credit for.

'April lives with a woman,' she said, deliberately not saying *pal* or *friend* as she might once have done.

'I hope they're happy,' Miss Connaughton said simply, 'and I hope they have peace to live their lives.'

Evelyn blushed at the memory of some of the things she herself had said: *Fancy woman. Unnatural.*

'April is anxious at times,' she said, 'because of her running the marriage bureau.'

'I can imagine.'

'I didn't realise at first,' Evelyn admitted. 'I felt a bit stupid.'

'People see what they want to see,' Miss Connaughton said. 'Caroline and I were fortunate – nobody passed any remarks about us setting up home together. And after the war it became common for spinsters to share.' She heated Evelyn's tea without asking, and said, very gently, 'Have you any idea what you'll do now, my dear?'

'*Do?* Stay here, I suppose.'

'With Maurice?'

'He's my husband.'

Miss Connaughton nodded. 'Of course. And if you're happy ...'

She didn't make it a question, but Evelyn knew it was. 'Oh,' she said. '*Happy.* How can I ever be happy when Robbie ...?' She looked into her cup.

'You will find a way,' Miss Connaughton said gently. 'You don't get over grief, but you learn to live with it. I know my loss isn't the same as yours, but I miss my dear Caroline every day. I wish we could have had twenty more years together – but we were happy. The sorrow doesn't spoil the memories.'

On the way out through the shop Evelyn said, surprising herself, 'Och, I'll maybe take a few ounces of that white baby wool.' And when Miss Connaughton raised her eyebrows, she said, 'One of April's friends had twins. They're refugees – she might appreciate a few wee vests.'

Walking home up the main street, noting the damp green smell of the river and the sign in McDaid's window: *Autumn Lines Now In!* she poked a hole in the paper parcel and stroked the soft white wool. She had knitted things like this for Robbie. So had Mona and her own mammy: tiny white and lemon and blue vests and matinée coats and, when he was older, warm jumpers in darker blues and greys. Once Evelyn had knitted him a red cardigan and Mona had said it wasn't very suitable for a boy, but Robbie had loved it. He had been wearing it the day he— that day ...

And he had worn it on lots of happy days, too, she made herself think. *The sorrow doesn't spoil the memories.*

Yes. She would knit for Daniel and David. She remembered the day she had met baby Dorothy. Her sweet baby smell. Probably the twins would be showered with knitted gifts from Miss Dawson, but it would give Evelyn something to do in the evenings.

Her spirits fell as she crossed the farmyard to the bungalow and Mona came to the back door, wiping her hands on a striped towel. She gave the towel a slight frown, though Evelyn had changed it that morning.

'I was hoping to catch you,' she said, without apologising for being in Evelyn's house. 'Oh, you've been to the shops.' As though Evelyn had been ordering a new autumn wardrobe from Madame Isobel in London.

Evelyn brandished her package. 'Wool for Maurice's socks. He's desperate hard on them.' She smiled, trying to make a pleasantry of it.

Mona sniffed. '*I* didn't find his darning too onerous, when you were' – a momentary pause – 'away. Of course, if you'd rather leave it to me – it's never too much bother ...'

Evelyn felt her lips tighten. 'No need, thank you, Mona,' she said.

'That's a quare big parcel of wool for darning socks.'

And that's a quare big nose for poking into my business.

She showed Mona the white wool. 'For some wee refugee babies in Easterbridge,' she said quickly, in case Mona should get the wrong idea.

'Indeed?'

'Was there anything else, Mona, or did you just want to examine my shopping?'

'No,' Mona said. 'There is something else. Something ... delicate.'

Oh lord. What had she done or not done now?

'Something I noticed when I was putting some of Maurice's shirts back in the press,' Mona said. 'The ones I ironed yesterday.'

'You'd no need. I was planning to iron later.'

'On a *Thursday*?' Mona shook her head. 'Dear bless us. It was always drummed into us: wash on Monday, iron on Tuesday, churn on Wednesday ...'

Evelyn, for something to do rather than because she wanted tea, went to the sink to fill the kettle. The tap spluttered and water splashed her frock.

'You should have put your apron on.' Mona took Evelyn's pink-and-green checked apron from the hook beside the towel and handed it to her. 'Bit late now, though I suppose it'll be time for you to peel the potatoes.'

'I don't feel like peeling potatoes tonight,' Evelyn said as she folded the apron round her and tied the string tightly. 'Maybe we'll have baked beans on toast. They're the whole go in England.'

'You can't give a working man baked beans on toast!' Mona exploded and then, when Evelyn laughed, she pursed her mouth and said, 'Don't be facetious, Evelyn.'

Evelyn put the kettle on to boil and her mother-in-law said, 'As I was saying, I couldn't help noticing when I was putting away the shirts that, well, that you seem to be occupying the spare room. Or am I ... mistaken?'

Evelyn's temper flared. The dozy, dull doppelganger seemed to have ganged off. 'You certainly are mistaken, Mona,' she said. 'You're mistaken in thinking you've the right to snoop round my bedrooms.' As Mona went to open her mouth, Evelyn went on, '*My* bedrooms. *My* business. And Maurice's,' she added.

'And Maurice's indeed.' Mona drew herself up and surveyed her daughter-in-law with evident dislike, though she forced her lips into a smile. 'I expected you'd be thinking of another child by now.'

'A – *what*?' She had not been expecting this.

'It's well over a year now since poor wee Robbie—'

'Oh, *I* see! My God, if I'd done my duty, I could have produced another one by now, couldn't I? Maybe even two.' She made a show of counting on her fingers. 'Aye – nineteen months. I could have managed two and a month off in between.'

Mona clapped her hand to her tightly buttoned chest. 'There's no need to be vulgar! I merely meant – the best thing—'

'And there's no need for you to be so bloody nosy. Where I sleep is no concern of yours.'

'But poor Maurice – it's hardly fair. What sort of wife—?'

Evelyn's brain formed the words *And what sort of a husband*, but her lips wouldn't say them, and her brain wouldn't finish the sentence. But as she held open the back door for Mona to leave, she knew that even the nascent thought had destroyed all possibility of her continuing with this half-life. *I hope they have peace to live their lives*, Miss Connaughton had said. *We were happy.* I'm not living *my* life, Evelyn thought, and is it really so unreasonable to want to be happy? Or at least as happy as I can be?

She tied her apron strings tighter and threw a load of new potatoes into the sink to wash for Maurice's tea.

Thirty-two

Guilt and loss lodged deep in Charlie's heart and would not be shifted. It wasn't only that he missed Tansy herself, her keenness and gaiety. It wasn't only the terrible knowledge that his vanity and ambition had destroyed her so swiftly and brutally – left to herself, she wouldn't have *chosen* to run round a racing track, no matter how she seemed to enjoy it. It was also losing everything she had brought to his life – the sense of purpose, the hoping and dreaming, the build-up to the Saturday nights of company and action and wild hopes.

He still had faithful Tippy, and the leggy pups who charged around the paddock like spring colts, all ears and flailing forelegs. One of them might be a star, but there would be months of waiting and working and it was just as likely they would turn out duds, or pedestrians at best. Or they could all get distemper and die. He painted the dogs' kennels, mended some loose bits of the paddock wall, and went over all their winter kennel coats to check for rips, but though he had always enjoyed caring for the dogs, without something to look forward to it was little more than routine. Because of Tippy's leg, he couldn't walk her far, and the pups were all still at the mooching about the paddock stage.

He hadn't known how much he lived for his nights at

the dogs until they were taken away. The first Saturday he forced himself to go to the Blacksmith's Arms, hoping Joseph might be there, but the men at the bar, though he half-knew most of them, were in their own groups, behind layers of smoke and bonhomie that he couldn't break through. He stood on the outside, letting their chat – Leeds United's piss-poor start to the season; the vicar's daughter and what they wouldn't mind doing to her – wash over him like the pints of ale he swallowed.

One day, riding over the moor, he saw Jenny Dunn. She looked as though she wanted to stop and pass the time of day, but he couldn't bear the thought of her asking about Tansy, so he merely nodded and sped on, pressing the surprised Carnelian into a canter.

He could have gone to Elland Road as a spectator, but it wouldn't have been the same. And how could he bear to look at the place where his lovely Tansy had smashed against the rail and never got up? He could have gone to the flapper track in Easterbridge, or hung around the waste ground at the end of Townsend Street where some greyhound men galloped their dogs for fun. At all those places there would have been men he knew, people he could talk to, but without a dog he didn't belong.

'Why not buy another one?' Joseph suggested. They were standing in the paddock, watching Sally and Sam take turns jumping logs on Mousie, who was enjoying a new lease of life.

'I don't have the money for a good dog.' He didn't say that he had spent more than he could afford on an engagement ring which was sitting in a drawer in his bedroom because he was too mortified to return it to the shop.

'Well, buy a bad'un,' Joseph said. 'If all you want's a bit of fun.'

'I might as well wait and see how the pups turn out.'

'Have it your own way.'

He didn't add, *you miserable sod*, but Charlie wouldn't have blamed him.

Joseph raised his voice. 'Oh, well done, Sam, lad!'

At Mass, the old sense of meeting God eluded him. He prayed but it was only words. His faith, always central to his life, proved to have been little more than habit. The second Sunday after Tansy's death, dodging the burly, moustached man who was once again handing out pro-fascist leaflets, he left the bike chained to the railings and wandered through the town. He walked for miles, round the riverbanks, up and down the steep cobbled streets, looking in shop windows at things he would never buy, passing the time of day with one or two acquaintances – an old friend of his mam's, a man walking two black greyhounds he remembered from the flapper track – and all the time staving off the inevitable homegoing. It was a bright day, still warm, and the town seemed bursting with couples walking hand-in-hand. He forced himself to walk past the café he had been to with Evelyn. He couldn't help his steps slowing, and then he realised someone was waving to him from within – the window was steamed up so he couldn't see clearly, but they were waving frantically and smiling. April, Felicity and another woman he couldn't quite see, her hair bright in the café's fug.

The door flew open and April said, 'Charlie Teal! I thought that was you! Come in and join us – och now, you will. There's someone here who'd love to see you again.'

His heart stammered. For just a moment.

It was Jenny Dunn. She stood up to greet him and he remembered what the men in the Blacksmith's Arms had been saying about her. His cheeks burned as he shook her hand.

'I used to see Mr Teal riding round the village,' Jenny

said to the other women. 'I was terribly jealous of your beautiful horses.'

'Oh, I'm only the groom.'

She would know this; everyone knew everything in a village, but he couldn't think what else to say. He hoped she wouldn't ask about Tansy.

April pulled out a chair. 'We're celebrating,' she said, indicating a table cluttered with sandwiches and little cakes. 'Join us, please.'

He felt awkward, remembering the hostility of their last parting, but she didn't give him the chance to refuse. He sat down obediently and within moments April had arranged an extra cup and Felicity was pressing a cheese sandwich on him. His stomach growled and he realised that it was after two – he had been walking round for hours.

'So what are you celebrating?' he asked.

'They've captured me,' Jenny said with a grin, and April gave her a playful shove. Jenny explained. 'Daddy's a good deal better, but I don't feel I can go too far from home. I can't bear to be idle so I'm going to work at the mill.'

'*Run* the mill,' April explained. 'Sybil's going to be extra-busy. And obviously I already have a job.'

'She's having a baby,' Felicity put in. 'April thinks it's indelicate to say so.'

'Sybil, not me,' April said. 'And it's hard to get the right person. You need someone—'

'Bossy,' Felicity said.

'Organised,' April said. 'With imagination and vision.'

'Notice,' Jenny said, 'how they talk about me as if I'm not here.' She poured Charlie some tea.

'Will you travel in every day, Miss Dunn?' he asked.

'I'm lodging in town.' Jenny grimaced. 'It's not *ideal* – but as you know the buses aren't reliable. I'll go home at weekends.'

'Pity you hadn't a car,' Felicity said.

'When we first moved up to Shippardsholme,' April said, 'the Colonel was all for me commuting to town every day on a pony.' They all laughed. To Jenny she said, 'I can't wait to have you. Sybil's never been able to give herself to the mill as much as she'd like.'

'Which means *you've* had to do far too much,' Felicity said.

'Pot, meet kettle,' April said.

'That's not fair; I'm better than I was,' Felicity said. 'Look at me now – out for tea on a Sunday afternoon when I could be writing. Or investigating,' she added darkly.

'Felicity's got a bee in her bonnet about this fascist group in Easterbridge,' April explained, her voice lowered.

'It's hardly a *bee in my bonnet*! It's a determination to counter its influence with positive action,' Felicity said.

'Positive but safe,' April added.

This was obviously not the first time they had had this conversation.

Jenny looked from one to the other and then at Charlie. 'Isn't it marvellous,' she said, 'being with people who *care*? My last job was with a family who thought of nothing except what the king was up to and what shape hats would be next season. I thought I'd die of boredom. Talking of which, I must look over those figures Sybil left me. I knew this job wouldn't be all folk dancing and fun, but I didn't think there'd be so much numberwork.'

'Sure you're well able,' April said. 'And you teaching arithmetic to all those girls.'

'I was often only a few pages ahead of them in the textbook,' Jenny admitted.

She limped to the door and turned back to wave. Charlie jumped up to open it for her.

'Och, it's grand to have Jenny back,' April said when he

had regained his seat. 'One of my first successes.'

It took him a while to understand her meaning. 'At the bureau? But she's not married.'

'Married to her career,' April said. 'And I wouldn't mention it, only Jenny tells everybody, she thinks it's a great joke – she came to True Minds *thinking* she wanted to meet someone, but I could tell fine rightly she was pining to get back to work. So I sort of … made it happen.' She grinned and poured out more tea all round. 'And now she's running the mill. Which will be more challenging for her than being a governess. Sure it couldn't be better. And talking of the mill, we'd love to see you again. Sidney could do with a hand with the football team.'

He didn't *hate* the idea: this past half hour had been the easiest since Tansy died. So he said, cautiously, 'I suppose I've more time these days.'

'On the subject of time,' Felicity said, 'I don't suppose you're free next Sunday morning?'

'Mass, obviously.'

Felicity waved that away. 'And could you get the car? Only to go to Leeds.'

'Felicity – you can't,' April said, but Felicity shook her head.

'Why not? You're the one said we needed a driver. And Fabian and Martha are going on that mysterious trip to Manchester so …'

'I'm sorry,' April said to a confused Charlie. 'This is what I meant about the bee in her bonnet.'

The café door opened and a crowd of young people burst in. Felicity frowned.

'Actually,' she said, in a lowered voice, 'this isn't a conversation we should be having in public. Can you walk with us?'

'I can, aye. I've left my bike outside St Anthony's.'

'Perfect. We'll walk you there and make sure we're not overheard. You can't be too careful.'

Feeling as if he were being recruited to a gang of spies, Charlie let them fall into step beside him.

'There's a fascist rally in Leeds next week,' Felicity explained. 'Mosley and his beastly Blackshirts plan to march through the Leylands – which I'm sure you know is a Jewish area.'

He nodded.

'Obviously there'll be local resistance,' Felicity went on, her blue eyes gleaming. 'Communists and socialists and trade unionists – and plenty of ordinary decent people who want to show Mosley that fascism isn't welcome in Yorkshire.'

'It could get nasty,' April said.

'But this isn't Germany or Italy,' Charlie said. 'The fascists didn't even win any seats last election, did they?'

'It hasn't stopped them spreading their lies and poison,' Felicity said.

'Anyway,' April said, 'we're going to go and join the protest against them' – she didn't sound as keen as her friend – 'but I've made Felicity promise to go by car.'

'Why?'

'April thinks that if we get the train we're bound to fall in with Johnson and his lot. She thinks I'll cause a row.' Felicity looked as though she relished the idea.

April said, 'I want us to be able to make a quick getaway if we have to. Felicity has a talent for getting herself injured.'

Felicity snorted. 'I have a talent for standing up for what's right.'

'Who's Johnson?' Charlie asked.

Both women looked troubled.

'He's in charge of this local fascist group,' April said.

'But he's …' She looked at Felicity. 'Will I say?'

'You might as well,' Felicity said. 'Charlie's an ally, aren't you?'

Was he? 'Aye,' he said. 'Course I am.'

'Well, he *appears* to be this very respectable fella,' April said. 'Teacher at the boys' grammar, ex-army, but we've both had run-ins with him. That's to say' – since Charlie looked blank – 'violent encounters.'

She clearly wasn't going to say any more.

'I don't mind giving you a lift,' Charlie said, 'but I'll need to check with Colonel Lucey.'

'Say it's for me,' April said. 'And maybe downplay the whole political demonstration side of things.'

'We'll be parking some distance away,' Felicity said, 'and marching with our comrades.'

April stopped walking. 'Och, for dear sake!' she cried.

'What's wrong?' Felicity asked.

April rummaged in her bag. 'Jenny's book – the one for the accounts. I forgot to give it to her.' She held a black notebook out to Charlie. 'Look, you'll pass her lodgings – it's two King's Lane. Would you mind? We're in the other direction.'

'No, I don't mind.'

Two King's Lane was a tall stone house with a bright red door, opened by a landlady who didn't have to say a word to show how much she disapproved of him.

She said, as Jenny answered her knock at a door on the ground floor, 'You needn't think you can make a habit of gentleman callers, Miss Dunn. I run a respectable house.'

'I'm so sorry.' Charlie handed out the book so they would both know he was only here on an errand.

'Don't worry,' Jenny said as he was admitted to a small, dank room and the landlady grudgingly took herself off. 'She won't turn me out because of one *gentleman caller.*

Come in properly, won't you? Might as well give the old bat something to flap about. And her house might be respectable, but you don't you think it *smells* very peculiar? Please sit there.' She cleared a pile of books from a chair. 'Actually,' she said. 'I'm very glad you've called. There's something – well, I've had an idea, only it might be the silliest thing ever. Could I ask you about it?'

Charlie nodded, feeling that, since leaving for Mass this morning, life had shifted somehow.

Her idea was unusual, but he didn't think it silly, and it was indeed something he could help with. As he bade her goodbye, clipped on his bicycle clips and set off up the road home, he found himself quite excited at the prospect.

Thirty-three

April had always felt, deep down in a place she rarely let herself go, that she came a poor second to Felicity's political activism. Their months on the moor had been the most relaxing and loving time they had ever spent together. But the summer was over and with Mosley and his Blackshirts poised to march on Leeds, she knew there was no holding Felicity back.

But this time, April wouldn't leave her side. Otherwise she would be stuck at home, waiting, wondering, worrying, while Felicity took God knows what risks. Her activist friends were principled people who stood up for decency and fair play. But in the heat of battle, they might not stand up for Felicity as April would.

The heat of battle! Would it really be like that? April had never been to a political demonstration, but she had grown up during the Troubles of the early twenties. Even in Lisnacashan there had been riots. One night some boys set fire to the courthouse and Daddy hadn't let her out to watch. She had told Evelyn she was raging to miss the excitement, but deep down she had been relieved. So she was not looking forward to Sunday morning in Leeds. At least they had enlisted Charlie, so there would be no chance of clashing with fascists on the train.

'There won't *be* trouble,' Felicity reassured her. 'It's a

peaceful protest to show Mosley that we don't tolerate fascism in Yorkshire. Erich's coming, and he hates crowds; that shows how strongly people feel.'

April thought that Hanna, left at home with two tiny babies, might have strong feelings of her own, but she said nothing.

News of the demonstration made all the local papers and even Easterbridge buzzed with gossip. Every time April passed a newsstand there was a fresh headline, and when she slipped into the Teaspoon Café for a bowl of soup on Thursday, she couldn't help overhearing two elderly ladies at the next table.

'I don't hold with that Mosley,' one said. 'Marching through Leylands! That's asking for trouble.'

'Drink your tea, Betty,' said her friend, 'and give over.'

The other woman snorted. 'I'll not give over, Lou. I've not forgotten the riots in 1917 if you have.'

'Nowt to do with us,' Lou said. 'Have a teacake.'

April shivered, and her soup – brown, the least appetising of the Teaspoon's three varieties – lost whatever appeal it had had. She returned early to the office and tried to distract herself by going through the files to see if there was anyone, anywhere, to suit Daphne Dalrymple. She did this every few days, expecting she didn't know what – a miracle, an eligible man hiding in the files. She knew there wasn't. Maybe now that Charlie had stopped being so hostile, he might reconsider. Though she hadn't forgotten how he had blushed when he had met Jenny in the tearoom.

Jenny always said she didn't want to marry. But she had also said she wanted to travel, and yet here she was, settling down in Easterbridge – so who knew?

That night April asked Felicity, 'What were the riots in 1917?'

Felicity considered. 'In Leeds? Antisemitic riots. I don't remember much; I was at school and we weren't encouraged to take an interest. There's a big Jewish community in Leeds – there's not usually any trouble. Otto and Frieda are in the Leylands with Frieda's aunt. Frieda says it's crowded, but they feel safe with people who understand. Lots of the older people were forced out of Russia in the pogroms. They know how it feels to be a refugee.' She sighed. 'It's horrible to think it's *still* happening. Thank goodness we've the chance to show them that decent British people won't tolerate fascism and bigotry. And surely the fascists won't be allowed to march through Leylands – they'd be asking for a bloodbath.'

April shivered at *bloodbath*, but the Leeds Watch Committee clearly agreed, because next day Felicity told her that the march would not be allowed to go through Leylands itself.

'They're planning a big rally on Holbeck Moor instead,' she said. 'But *we'll* be there to greet them.'

To April, *Holbeck Moor* sounded quite bucolic, somewhere you'd go for a picnic, and *greet* quite friendly, but she suspected the reality would be nothing of the sort.

The whole day seemed surreal, from the moment Colonel Lucey's Bentley drew up outside, Charlie at the wheel looking very smart. April wondered if this was because it was Sunday or if he, like her, wasn't sure what to wear to an anti-fascist demonstration.

'Your carriage awaits,' he said, which was such an un-Charlie-like thing to say that she guessed he felt strange too. They drove through streets still deserted before the rush to morning service.

'It's good of you to miss Mass,' she said.

Felicity said, 'He's doing something *much* more Christian – standing up for his fellow human, and for justice.'

April wished that Felicity didn't always sound as if she was making a speech.

'Well, we appreciate it,' she said. And then, to lighten the mood, and because it was true: 'Jenny was asking after you. I think she's taken a wee shine to you.'

'Honestly, April!' Felicity sounded disgusted. 'How can you think about matchmaking on a day like this!'

But April couldn't help smiling at the memory of Charlie's recent encounter with Jenny. And Jenny had done more than *ask* after him. She had confessed, when April saw her at the mill earlier that week, that she had had a pash on him when she was younger.

'Riding around the moors in his breeches,' she had said with an enthusiasm generally reserved for folk dancing. 'I told myself it was the horses, but honestly, those *legs*. Pity he never took up dancing. He'd be super at morris.'

Morris reminded her of Evelyn's husband. According to Mammy, who had it from the minister's wife in Lisnacashan, Evelyn was indeed back with Maurice. Which was the right thing, really, so wouldn't it be great if Jenny and Charlie took up with each other! For all Jenny's talk about being a career woman, she must wish for her own home. She smiled at the back of Charlie's neck, where the brown hair was cropped close. He was still tanned from the summer sun; Jenny was very fair – they'd have gorgeous children.

'Right here,' Felicity said.

April jerked herself back to reality as Charlie turned the car into the quiet street where Erich and Hanna lodged. They stood on the doorstep to wave Erich off, Hanna and their landlady, Primrose, with a baby each. Primrose made Daniel – or David, all babies looked the same to April and in fairness these wee fellas were actually identical – wave a tiny hand.

'Don't forget your sandwiches,' she said, as if Erich were a child on his first day at school.

Hanna, in a shabby tartan dressing gown, a baby nestling into her neck, did not smile. 'Sei vorsichtig, mein Liebling,' she said as Erich got into the front seat, and he raised the hand without the sandwiches – a gesture of promise, or valediction, or both.

April liked Erich, a quiet, intelligent man. He looked grave as he placed the packet of sandwiches in his jacket pocket.

'There has been trouble overnight in the city,' he said. 'Otto telephoned from the public telephone.'

'What sort of trouble?' Felicity demanded.

Erich sighed and ran a hand through his beard. 'The sort we became very much accustomed to at home – broken windows, slogans daubed on the walls of Jewish shops' – his face twisted – 'swastikas also.'

'That's bloody not on, Erich, lad,' Charlie said.

'That'll be the fascists,' Felicity said.

'Well, that's obvious, isn't it?' Even Charlie knew that much.

'Mosley's lot,' Felicity clarified. 'Not locals. They'll have come up last night to stir up trouble. Well, we'll stir *them* up.'

Erich sighed. 'We all know that some of these people *are* local,' he said. 'It is not as in Germany, Gottze dank, but Hanna and I ... we have noticed a change. People are not so welcoming as before. I have heard them in the shops – they hear of more Jews coming; they talk now of refugees from Spain. They say England is a small country, and there are not jobs for all.'

There was silence apart from the thrum of the engine.

April looked out the window. An elderly woman in a spotted headscarf turned the corner and was gone. A fluffy brown dog barked at the car as it slowed at a junction.

Felicity reached forward and squeezed Erich's shoulder. 'England might be small,' she said, 'but its people aren't: they're big-hearted, and fair-minded, and nowhere more so than here.' She waved her other hand expansively at the outskirts through which they were now speeding, the green gardens and neat hedges in front of squat, comfy-looking stone terraces. She raised her voice. 'And that's what today is all about. To show those bastards we don't tolerate fascism in Yorkshire, or in the north, or in England, or anywhere.'

She smiled round them all, and April's spirits rose, and then fell. Because for all Felicity's grand talk, the fascists they were fighting today hadn't *all* been bussed in by Mosley from Somewhere Else. Among them were Nigel Johnson and Reginald Binn, and other people from Easterbridge. People who had served her in shops, lads she had walked past in the street, maybe even couples she had introduced. As they approached their destination, April fancied that even from the cocoon of the car, she could hear boots ring on the pavements. She had heard there were to be a thousand fascists! What if the resistance was only a few dozen? What hope would they have?

And what sort of fallout would April have to live with if Felicity was disheartened by the local response?

Far from being windswept and wuthering, Holbeck Moor was only about a mile from the city centre. Charlie drove them through an industrial area surrounded by tight-packed terraced streets that reminded April of her few visits to Belfast. They began to be surrounded on all sides by people, closing in, gathering together, ready to meet the invaders. These men and women came from terraced houses and working men's clubs; they walked from the east and north and south of the city; they cycled from outlying villages. Some carried red flags, some trade union banners.

'You'll never find your pals,' she said to Felicity as they parked the car in a side street and walked four abreast past red-bricked terraced houses.

'They're all comrades,' Felicity said loudly, and a couple of men in cloth caps and working clothes cheered. '*We're* all comrades,' she said, encouraged.

'Maybe so, but I'm heart-scared of losing you,' April said.

'We'll link arms.'

April felt herself firmly taken up by Felicity at one side and Charlie on the other side. She wasn't used to holding a man's arm; it felt hard and strong. As the four of them – Erich linked Felicity's other arm – fell into step, more and more people streamed from side streets to join what had become a march.

'If we are separated,' Erich said, raising his voice above the noise of the crowd, 'we go back and wait at the car. Yes?'

'We won't get separated.' April clutched Felicity's arm even tighter.

They reached the end of the street and there in front of them, held back by policemen on horses, were more people than April had seen in her life, a solid mass. On either side, she felt both Felicity and Charlie stiffen, and Erich let out a long breath. Maybe there would indeed be a thousand fascists. But here to greet them there might have been twenty or thirty times that. She wanted to stay back but Felicity pulled her on and on, closer to the front, and she simply kept hold of her arm, and Charlie's, until, bashed by a hundred elbows, stepped on by a thousand feet, they were near the front and could see everything.

Someone called out, 'Here they are, the bastards!' and the fascists marched into view. April had seen the Blackshirts on newsreels, aping the Nazis with their stiff-armed salutes, but to see them pass in front of her, Mosley himself leading, a tall, arrogant figure, physically impressive, in long black boots, smiling about him like the king on a walkabout, made her shiver. The followers waved union flags. When she saw Johnson, even though she had expected him to be there, her stomach roiled and she gripped Felicity harder.

The anti-fascist crowd surged forward. Some of the police horses neighed and pranced. There were yells of *Shame!* and *¡No pasarán!* and snatches of 'The Red Flag'. Noise and scuffle broke out at the front and the police seemed to be manoeuvring the fascists to one side.

'What's Mosley doing?' Felicity stood on tiptoe to try to see.

'Looks like he's getting on top of a van,' Charlie said.

He was using the van as a stage. His voice rang out, shrill, chilling, thrilling – but not for long. Someone struck up 'The Red Flag' again and this time it took hold, drowning out his speech. April felt self-conscious, though she loved singing. Felicity was belting it out from lungs that sounded perfectly healthy. Every time Mosley started to speak the people sang louder. And now the crowd was surging forward, on and on, and the singing was deafening, and she was being pulled with them, her one thought not to let go of Felicity, not to let Felicity get hurt. She lost contact with Charlie, and Erich was somewhere in the crowd, but she clutched Felicity grimly. The locals were surrounding the van now, one jostling, shouting, singing, defiant crowd. And then the stones started, fired from those at the front, pelting the fascists. The police rounded on the stone-throwers, but there were always more to take their place.

It was all a raucous blur of faces and shouting and once or twice she had to duck. Mounted police rode at them, trying to force them back.

Over the barrage of noise, she heard Felicity's clear, husky voice: 'Take that, you fascist bully.' A stone flew from Felicity's hand and hit Johnson on the head.

And then she felt Felicity pulled away from her, and the crowd swallowed her up.

'Felicity!' she screamed, but it was like a nightmare where you try to scream and nothing comes out, so loud were the shouts around her. She was jostled from all sides. Someone cried 'April!' and grabbed her other hand – Charlie, she thought, but she needed Felicity, she had to look after Felicity! She tried to pull away and then there was a pounding of hooves and the crowd parted and she caught the glint of iron—

And then Charlie yanked her sharply away and she stumbled. It took her seconds to realise the hooves had just missed her, and she scrambled up, in time to see the horse gallop on, over Charlie's flailing body.

'Charlie!' she screamed, and this time she could hear herself.

But Charlie, face down in the dirt, was still.

Thirty-four

For the last few days Evelyn had avoided Mona, but on Sunday morning her mother-in-law was waiting by the car, bible clasped in her kid-gloved hand, her hat fearsome, her mouth grim, though when she saw her beloved Maurice her lips stretched into a gracious smile. It was drizzling and her hat and coat were misted.

'Och, Mammy, you should have let yourself into the car,' Maurice said. 'It's not locked.'

'Indeed and I would not,' Mona said. 'I'm not one to take liberties.'

'Only with my bedroom,' Evelyn said, not quite under her breath.

When church was over, Mona decreed, 'You'll come for your lunch.'

Maurice said something about never missing his mammy's Sunday roast. So seen on him, the great lump.

'You please yourself, Maurice,' Evelyn said clearly. 'But I won't be joining you.' Maurice looked at wife and then mammy. 'I have something to discuss with you. I *could* say it in front of your mother, but I'm sure you'd rather I didn't.'

His face registered surprise, then shock, then – fear? He fumbled with his tie; his Sunday shirt was tight round his neck.

'I'll maybe come in for a wee beef sandwich later, Mammy,' he said.

He followed Evelyn into the bungalow, pulling his tie off and setting it on the kitchen table. 'Will we not go in for lunch?' he said. 'Sure the old cratur's on her own.'

'I had a very interesting conversation the other day with the old cratur, as you call her. Personally I'd use something like interfering old bitch—'

'Evelyn! And you only out of church.'

She said, very pleasantly. 'Indeed we are just out of church, Maurice. Did you pray?'

'What? Of course I prayed.'

'And what did you pray for?' She kept her tone light, conversational. The tap dripped, each tiny blob of water hitting the ceramic of the sink with a little *plup* ... *plup* ... *plup* ... He kept forgetting to change the washer.

'Well ... the usual ...'

'God bless Mammy and God bless Evelyn?'

She did not let her mind conjure up the memory of Charlie, on his knees at Mass, praying the rosary, his lips moving as he intoned the strange words. She especially did not let herself think about his lips.

'Did you pray for another child?'

Maurice made a glug of shock in his throat and she pressed on. 'Because that's what your mammy expects. She asked me the other day was it not time?'

She picked up his tie from the table and started to roll it neatly, smoothing out the wrinkles where it had been knotted. It was not the black tie he had taken to after Robbie's death, but one in the blue and white stripes of the local rugby club, though he had not played since he was a young man. Another uncomfortable thought assailed her – Maurice might have had his own reasons for enjoying rugby.

'And – what did you say?'

She smiled. 'What would you *like* me to have said, Maurice?'

'I don't know, Evelyn. You're being very strange.'

'Am I?' This cool, enigmatic self felt both strange and familiar. She was glad to meet her, wished she had known sooner that she was as much part of her as the Evelyn who had been half-dead all summer and the Evelyn she had left behind in England. Maybe this Evelyn could find a way to live with the memories of Robbie. She thought of Miss Connaughton and Caroline, their puffed sleeves on the beach, the seashells in their hands.

We were very happy, Miss Connaughton said. *The sorrow doesn't spoil the memories.*

Maybe I do deserve to be happy one day. I don't know how, but it can't be here.

'What would you like me to have said?' she repeated. She rolled and unrolled the tie. Behind her, the tap kept on its *plup ... plup ... plup ...*

'Do you want another child?' Maurice asked, as though Robbie, with his fluffy ginger hair and his *Why, Mammy?* and his plump determined legs in their small wellington boots, could simply be replaced.

'Do you?'

He looked down at the table and sighed. 'I don't know. I don't understand why you're carrying on like this.'

'And I don't know why you were carrying on with Michael Donovan when you were married to me.' The air around them crackled with her audacity. The tap still dripped. It would never stop dripping unless he did something about it. 'Well, maybe I do know. I understand better now than I did then.'

'Evvie! Please.'

'April's that way inclined, you know,' she said in a

conversational tone. 'A ho-mo-sex-u-al.' She said the word slowly, giving weight to all five syllables. 'A lesbian, strictly speaking.'

He sat opposite her, his face drained apart from the red farmer cheeks that never paled, a pulse beating in his throat.

'It's not the same, though, is it?' she went on.

'I don't know.' He looked down at the table.

'No, it's not. Because *she* didn't lie. She didn't *pretend* she wanted one thing when she wanted the other. And she and Felicity, her friend, don't hide in barns and' – she didn't have the words – '*do* things. They're not cheating on anyone.'

'Evelyn – I'm sorry, you weren't meant to—'

'I wasn't meant to know. I was meant to stay in the kitchen and ask no questions. I was meant to be grateful for a husband and a child and a nice bungalow.' Tears squeezed her throat but she forced the words past. 'Were you doing it all along, Maurice? Since we got married? Did you know then you were' – again she didn't have the words – 'that way?'

'Please.' He was gripping the table with both hands, his big frame shaking. 'I tried not to – I didn't *want* to be' – he swallowed – 'that way. I resisted it for years. Honestly.' He raised his head and looked her in the face.

'So why did you marry me?'

'I wanted a family, a normal life ...'

Same as her.

'But you wanted to do those things more?'

He was silent for a long time. She saw his face working as he fumbled for the words. 'It's not about *wanting* or – or *choosing*. It felt like who I *was*. When I let myself, you know, *with* someone. A man.' He swallowed, looked ashamed. 'I felt *right*.'

She was about to say, *Oh well, as long as you got to*

feel right, *that's all that matters, isn't it?* but into her mind flitted the memory of Charlie's arms around her on the bridge in Durham, the soft firmness of his lips, the feeling of everything being *right*, even though it was wrong. And if Charlie, instead of walking chastely back to the train, had led her to a convenient barn and—

She squeezed her eyes shut with the intensity of the longing that swept over her. I led him on, she admitted. I didn't mean to, but I did. Not because I *wanted* to, but because it felt – *I* felt – *right*.

She looked at her husband, this familiar stranger whose home she had shared for six years, whose bed she had shared for some of those years, the man with whom she had had, and lost, a child, and for the first time, a gentler response stirred in her. Not pity – pity would have diminished them both, but fellow feeling.

When she found her voice it was kinder, less accusing. 'Tell me, then. No' – as his eyes met hers in disbelief – 'I want to understand.' She stood up. 'I'm going to make a pot of tea,' she said. 'I think this is going to take some time.'

It didn't take that much time, but it was so different from their usual conversations, so outside ordinary life, and yet, for both of them, the first time they had been completely honest, that time seemed to slow, to add weight to every word and pause.

Growing up, Maurice said, he had always felt *something* for other boys. He thought he'd grow out of it; he thought it was because he didn't know any girls. He had heard of men like that – the bits in the bible about Sodom and Gomorrah, but he didn't understand it, didn't find any connection between ancient bible people and the feelings that stirred him.

'I didn't *do* anything,' he said, looking, for a moment,

not the big farmer he was now, with hands like hams and ruddy, weather-worn cheeks, but the confused boy he must once have been. 'I just – thought – and – well, you know.'

He looked down at the table and she guessed he meant *self-abuse*.

'And then – when I was older, playing rugby, taking a drink, there would have been the odd ...'

She nodded.

'Just lads being – och, you know.' His face became desperate. 'But Evvie, I *fought* it – I knew it was against the law and ...' He looked down again, and she saw his chest heave with the effort. 'I didn't *want* it,' he repeated. 'I was getting the farm, I'd always known that. And I wanted a son.' His voice broke.

'Which meant getting a wife.'

'Aye.'

Charlie says *aye*, she thought painfully. It sounds different in his accent – longer, slower, but it's the same word.

'I didn't want to be arrested,' he said. 'I didn't want secrets and hiding and feeling disgusted with myself. I thought if we got married everything would be all right. And it wasn't *bad*, was it?'

She thought about their marriage. The awkward couplings she had endured rather than enjoyed, never experiencing anything like the passion that one kiss from Charlie, one touch of his hand as he helped her over a stile, had awakened. Her relief at being pregnant, and Maurice's subsequent move into the spare room. She had thought he was being considerate only of *her* feelings, and was grateful when Robbie's birth had not brought him back to her bed. She had never once thought about Maurice's feelings, not even that day in the barn.

They would have to talk about that day.

But not yet.

'I thought it was me,' she said. 'I thought I was doing something wrong.' When she forced herself to think back to those clumsy, frustrating, sometimes painful nights, she had worried about him guessing at her lack of passion for him. When all the time …! A choked giggle burst out from her and he narrowed his eyes in surprise. 'It's just' – she struggled to explain – 'I was blaming myself for not feeling – for not *desiring* you' – what the hell; two could play at uncomfortable honesty – 'when all along you didn't … you couldn't … it wouldn't have mattered what I did. Unless I'd been a man.'

He looked at his hands. 'I'm sorry,' he said. 'It wasn't your fault. And Evvie' – he looked up again and his blue eyes, very like Robbie's, were anxious and frank – 'I was fond of you. I *am* fond of you. You're a good woman. And when Robbie was born I hoped it might be enough, for both of us. I was happy, in a way. And you were.' He said it half-questioningly, and she was forced to agree.

'Happy enough. I wanted the same things as you – a home, a family.'

'We had that.'

'But not properly.' She teased at this, needing to get it right. 'It wasn't enough. I pretended it was. But I never loved you either.'

Two years ago, when she'd first discovered him and Michael, even six months ago, before she had fallen, however hopelessly, for Charlie, she would have said this to hurt him. But she said it now without spite, maybe even to make him feel better.

'I wanted a family too, and to be a wife, but I should have waited. Or been brave enough to go away and spread my wings, like April. But you asked me and' – she shrugged – 'I thought I might as well. I didn't *not* like you.'

This honesty felt so bleak that she went on, 'You were a good father. A good provider.' And then she couldn't stop a note of bitterness creeping in. 'But I didn't know what was really going on.'

'It wasn't,' he muttered. 'I promise you. Not until Michael.'

Michael Donovan. He had appeared a couple of years ago, when the work started to get too much for poor Jamesie. A quiet man her own age with a southern accent. Nothing about him, any more than there was about Maurice, to suggest he was – she thought of the words for homosexual men – a fairy, a queer. Nothing fairylike about Michael Donovan. Good enough worker, kept to himself, lodged in the town and cycled out to the farm six days a week. Mona hadn't approved because he was *the other*, but when she found out he never went to Mass, she was confused about whether this should make her disapproval greater or less. She would have reason to disapprove, Evelyn thought now, if she had come upon them that day in the barn, as Evelyn had done.

To think about the barn was to think about Robbie, to open wounds that would never heal, but she made herself do it now, this strange Sunday, the last she would ever spend in this house, with her husband.

Made herself say, 'When I saw yous that day …'

His big red – honest, she used to think – face turned puce. 'Don't.'

She ignored him. 'I'd run into the barn, looking for Robbie; he hadn't come in for his tea. Remember the trike?'

He nodded. The tricycle had been a Christmas present, passionately loved.

'I thought he might have cycled it into the barn. It was a wet old day – well, you don't need me to tell you, I imagine that's why you and Michael—'

'Evvie. Do we have to?'

She nodded. 'I'm sorry, but we do.' Nausea twisted in her belly as the memory played out – a spiteful December dusk, the cobwebby dimness inside the barn, the drumming of rain on the tin roof, a thousand times the intensity of the dripping tap at the edge of her hearing now. She had run in, nearly skidding on the wet cobbles at the door, cursing Robbie for making her go out and get him. There was a cow in the barn with a sickly calf. She had told him not to power into the barn on his trike and upset her, but he was adventurous. Thinking, at first, she had found him, because there was noise and movement – but a deep groaning, not the high babble of a child, more like the noise Maurice used to make on those rare occasions when he had reached climax with her. She had had that thought even as she told herself off for being so daft – most likely it was the cow. A sudden fear that Robbie was trapped by an angry cow propelled her to the dim corner where the movement came from. It took her a moment to realise what she was looking at. Her eyes had never seen the like of it, and though they were doing their best to tell her brain faithfully what they registered, her brain, her heart, everything in her resisted. No! These writhing, grunting men were not, as she first believed, fighting, but coupling, unaware of her, unaware of anything except their pleasure, their need for each other. Part of her knew that her husband was enjoying this abomination as he had never enjoyed being with her.

Maurice saw her first, at the moment of his climax, and for weeks the sight of his open mouth, the groans that ended in a cry, haunted her: at night, waiting for the fretful dozing that was all she ever found, and by day, dragging round her chores, trying and failing to forget that awful, bestial noise.

She had run from the barn before his cry had subsided, had half-collapsed, her legs suddenly useless, over the old horse trough in the yard, sobbing – or maybe just thinking, she was never sure, *OhmyGodOhmyGodOhmyGodOhmyGod*. Then Robbie had trundled round from the back of the house, his short legs pistoning, his hair in wet spikes, and said, 'What's wrong, Mammy?' and then, 'I'm going in the barn to see the wee calf.'

'You. Are. Not.' She grabbed his handlebars, jolting him so that he nearly fell off. 'You're not allowed in the barn,' she stated. '*Ever.*'

His mouth opened in outraged protest. 'Why?'

'Just *why*.' She had hated being told this as a child. But it was all she had. She propelled Robbie into the house. 'You're late for your tea,' she said.

'Why are you cross, Mammy?'

Just *why*.

She had poured herself a wee nip of Bushmills while the child was drinking his milk. For the shock. To stop the trembling in her hands and to silence the constant roar in her mind. And then, when the sleeplessness became too much to bear, she kept on with it. Wee nips of whiskey, just enough to blur the edges of her horror, to make the sight of Maurice about the house bearable, to help her tolerate Robbie's endless prattle and bounce.

Oh God, she thought now. How could she ever have found Robbie annoying for a single moment? How had she let him out of her sight?

Michael moved on, back down south. She and Maurice never talked about it. They circled each other like territorial cats. Like sleepwalkers.

She had been, she realised now, sleepwalking *not* since Robbie died, but since that day. If she hadn't been, if she'd been more alert, she might have been watching him the day of the accident, and it might never have happened.

She became aware that Maurice was talking.

'I'd give anything,' he said, 'for you not to have seen—'

'Don't.'

She had taken against the barn, had stopped her usual practice of going in to check that poor Jamesie had fed the calf or stacked the rakes and brushes and pitchforks safely. And yes, she told Robbie he wasn't allowed in, but Robbie was a wee boy. He didn't always do what his mammy said. If he did, he mightn't have run in to see the calf that day, mightn't have climbed up into the hayloft to find the nest of kittens and then – jumped or fallen, they would never know. The pitchfork might not have been left carelessly on the ground and he might not have been impaled on it and bled to death before Maurice had found him, the blood soaking the strewn straw around his body.

She had thought life was over. Now, on this late September Sunday, with a pale grey sky outside the kitchen window, and a blackbird calling from the hawthorn tree in the field behind the house, she knew she had only been sleeping, letting a doppelganger walk around in her body.

And now she was awake, and she wanted to stay that way.

No matter how much it hurt.

Charlie woke me, she thought – and that did hurt, a sharp stab that pierced her heart and lodged somewhere in her belly. But it wasn't only, or even mostly Charlie. It was Miss Connaughton, and April and Easterbridge and Lucey Lodge. It was Mona daring to insinuate that she should have another child.

It was Maurice, sitting opposite her, his face working in distress, one big hand rubbing the handle of his untouched teacup.

'We have to get a divorce,' she heard herself say.

'A – och, Evelyn, you're joking! That's for – for people like Mrs Simpson. Racy people. Not people like us. Farmers in Lisnacashan. Can you imagine what Mammy – and the minister ...'

She kept her voice very level. 'There's worse disgraces than divorce,' she said. 'If your mammy and the minister knew— No!' – as his eyes widened in horror – 'of course I wouldn't tell them. I want to divorce you, Maurice – or you can divorce me, I've no idea how it works – but not to punish you. I just want to live my life and let you live yours.'

'But I can't ...'

There were tears in his eyes, and she had never seen that, not even when he had carried Robbie's body out of the barn, a trail of blood in his wake.

'Have you – did you meet somebody?' he asked.

And somehow it was easy then to say, 'I did, aye. But nothing happened – not really.'

'Will you go to him?'

She shook her head. 'He wouldn't have me. I hurt him too badly. I don't think he'd forgive me. And he's a Catholic – he'd never have anything to do with a divorced woman. I won't go to him. But I will go back to England. Not Easterbridge. Maybe Liverpool to start with. Say I deserted you – say what you like, I don't care. I won't be back here. I'll leave this week.'

And then – it felt odd, but right – she reached across the table and shook her husband's hand.

Thirty-five

If we get separated, we'll meet at the car, had been the arrangement, and April had insisted that they would *not* get separated.

That seemed a long time ago now. The agonising half mile back to the car might as well have been ten, with Charlie having to stop every few yards. Every time it seemed harder to get going again.

And, oh God, where was Felicity?

'They're showing the injured over to that school,' April said, watching a stream of people mostly holding handkerchiefs up to bleeding faces. She saw the burly figure of Johnson, clutching a bloodied handkerchief to the side of his head, supported by a younger man. Felicity hit him, she remembered. It didn't seem to matter much now. 'Maybe we should—'

'I'm fine,' Charlie insisted.

'Charlie, you were out for the count. I thought you were dead.' She shuddered at the memory of him insensible on the ground, and then, when his eyes opened, that terrifying fight for breath, and her with no idea what to do, and nobody stopping to help. The battle was behind them now, Mosley's voice silenced, but the air still rang with shouts and shrieks. The streets were full, as they had been on the way, but this time with the bemused, the angry and the walking wounded.

'Only – winded,' he coughed out.

There were hoofmarks on his coat, and she was scared to imagine what damage lay beneath.

'Not – my first time – under a horse.' He tried to smile, winced, and clutched his side.

'You could be hurt inside.'

'I want to go home,' he said, and she felt, under the nagging worry about Felicity, a twist of guilt. Charlie had only come to help them, and this is how it had ended up!

She took his arm and he didn't protest.

'Just round this corner,' she said, praying they would make it. His ragged breathing reminded her of Felicity when her lungs had been so bad. She saw again that horse trample him down, the big iron-shod hooves grinding him into the ground. Maybe he'd punctured a lung!

Clearly Charlie wasn't fit to drive, but at least when they reached the car – if they ever did – they could wait inside it for Felicity and Erich. And if Charlie got worse? She supposed she would stop someone in the street and beg for help.

But worst of all, so bad she could hardly let herself think it – Felicity! All those injured, bleeding people they had passed, that angry crowd, the crushing hooves – how could Felicity *possibly* be safe?

'Nearly there,' she made herself say in jollying tones, when everything inside her was screaming *Felicity! My love, where are you? Please, please be safe!* It seemed impossible.

When they rounded the corner and she saw Felicity and Erich standing safely by the Bentley she thought she was dreaming. One more oddity in this nightmarish day. But Felicity started to run towards her, and seemed, as they got close, to be perfectly real. Her hair streeled in tangled curls over her shoulders, and her sleeve was torn, but otherwise she was perfectly, wonderfully, undamaged. April pulled away from Charlie, forgetting him, forgetting they were in the street, forgetting everything except that her love was safe.

She flung her arms round her. Buried her face in Felicity's neck. Held her so tightly that she felt Felicity's heart thump through her jacket and Felicity's hair tickle her cheek.

'I love you,' she said, not caring that they were in the middle of Leeds; she wouldn't have been bothered if the entire population of Easterbridge had been watching.

She felt Felicity stroke her hair. 'I love you too, my darling,' she said, her voice thick with tears. 'I'd die if anything had happened to you. Those bloody policemen—'

Suddenly April remembered. 'Charlie!'

But Erich was already helping Charlie to the car.

'Good God, what happened?' Felicity asked.

'He was trampled by one of the mounted police.' April saw it again in her head: she thought she'd never stop seeing it. 'He pushed me out of the way – otherwise it would've been me.'

Felicity shivered and clasped her hand tightly as they followed the men to the car. Charlie, slumped against the Bentley, white and sweating, fumbled in his pocket and handed Erich the keys.

'See how he assumes the *man* will drive,' Felicity said as Erich opened the car and helped Charlie into the back seat where he slumped back, his eyes closed.

'Well, neither of us can,' April said.

'*Charlie* doesn't know that,' Felicity said. 'He just assumes—'

'Can you drive, Erich?' April asked.

Erich made a slightly helpless gesture. 'I have driven,' he said. 'But in Germany we drive on the right.'

'Can you manage?'

'There is no alternative,' Erich said, going round to the front of the car and starting to crank up the starting handle.

Felicity looked in at Charlie. 'I'm sorry,' she said, over the noise of the engine spluttering into life. 'It all got rather nasty, didn't it? I know the way,' she went on, getting into the front passenger seat. 'I'll navigate.'

April got in the back beside Charlie, and they set off cautiously down the street.

'Did you *see* the crowds?' Felicity said. 'Those Blackshirts won't show their faces up north again. And I hit that bastard Johnson right on his smug face. That was personal, I can't pretend otherwise.'

'Felicity – I must concentrate,' Erich said, and she subsided, except to give directions.

Beside April, Charlie seemed barely conscious, though he winced when the car shuddered and stalled, which it did a fair bit until Erich got used to it. April looked at him with growing unease.

'Should we go straight to a hospital?' she said.

Charlie's eyes flickered open. 'They'll do nowt in hospital except tell me to rest. I can do that at home.'

Felicity said, 'Florrie could take a look,' and April, with a rush of relief, remembered that Florrie Yeadon had once been a nurse.

Erich relaxed slightly as they left the busy streets of Leeds behind. The country roads were quiet, and if Erich did tend to drift to the right, there was rarely anything coming. All the same, even though she wasn't the praying kind, April sent up more than one petition.

When they finally reached Shippardsholme, it was obvious that Charlie was in no state to be left alone. Erich needed to get home to Hanna and the twins, and he didn't know the way to Easterbridge without Felicity's guidance. April would have to stay.

'We'll call at the farm,' Felicity promised as they drove off, 'and send Florrie over.'

Charlie insisted he was grand, and wouldn't let April help him in, but once he made it to an armchair, he sank into it with a groan – of pain, or relief or both, she wasn't sure. She felt alone and scared. Capable as she was, she was no nurse. Then she gave herself a shake. For dear sake! Hadn't she said *all* she wanted today was for Felicity to be safe? And she was – not a bother on her! Despite everything, she couldn't help a glow at the memory of Felicity's heartfelt declaration of the love April had sometimes been unsure of.

And Charlie was tough. Didn't he say himself he'd done this kind of damage before? April went without permission into his bedroom – an austere room with a single iron bed and no pictures – to fetch some pillows to prop him up.

'Does that help?' she asked as he sank back into their softness with evident relief.

'Aye. I'm sorry to give you all this bother.'

'For dear sake! *You've* nothing to be sorry for! If you hadn't pushed me out of the way—'

'Could you see to my dogs? They'll want emptying. Just let them into the paddock. And check on Mousie.'

Mousie, the old grey pony, was dozing in the corner of the paddock, resting a hoof, her bottom lip hanging open. The long-legged pups frisked and danced, and the older dog looked up at her with anxious brown eyes, as if asking where her master was.

'He'll be back with you soon,' she promised, with no idea if this would be true.

How hard life was for people on their own. Could a postulant nun get leave for a family emergency? But even if Margaret could come, it must be at least a day's journey from Dublin. If Evelyn hadn't left, *she* could have looked after him, though that would have excited gossip.

But Evelyn had gone home to her husband. Which was how things should be, but April couldn't help thinking, as she went back into the cottage to make tea, that it would have been quare and handy to have had her here now. Respectable or not.

By the time Florrie arrived, April had lit the fire and the room felt cosier. Charlie was quiet, refusing food though he drank two cups of tea.

'Sorry it took me so long,' Florrie apologised. 'Joseph was up the back field with a calf that'd got stuck in a ditch. I can leave Dot with Sally for a short time but I didn't know how long I'd be.' She was taking off her coat as she spoke, looking at Charlie with a professional eye. 'You don't look so clever, my lad,' she said.

'Bust my ribs,' he said. 'That's how it feels, any road.'

'Let's have a look.'

Florrie helped Charlie to unbutton his shirt and pull up his vest. His torso was lean and muscled – April had never seen so much of a man's body before – but the right side was mottled and swollen with angry red bruising, just starting to purple. Florrie touched it and he winced.

'Sorry,' she said. She made him cough, listened to his chest, and again ran her fingers over the bruising, with Charlie biting his lips hard. Finally, she stood back and frowned. 'Well, I'm no doctor, Charlie, but I'd say you've cracked a few ribs. Have you anything for the pain?'

'I've something I gave Tippy when she broke her leg.'

Florrie's face showed exactly what she thought of that.

'I think there's some phenacetin powders in the cupboard over the sink,' he said.

Florrie went into the scullery and returned with some little white packets. 'Take one every four hours,' she said, 'but no more.'

'I'll take some now.'

301

Florrie and April went back out to the scullery and April looked for a glass to fill with water.

'Will he be all right?' she asked quietly. 'I feel so responsible.'

Florrie hesitated. 'I don't *think* there's anything worse than the ribs but ...'

'What sort of something worse?'

'There's always a risk of internal injury.' Florrie started to say alarming things about spleens and lungs and organs that April wasn't sure she'd heard of, let alone be able to locate, and then to list an even more alarming set of symptoms to look out for. 'But it's unlikely,' she finished. 'And I don't want to put ideas in his mind by mentioning the risk. You know what men are.'

How funny that Florrie, April's very first client at the marriage bureau, should have changed from a confirmed spinster into someone who said 'You know what men are' in that knowledgeable tone.

'Stay here tonight,' she said, 'and keep an eye on him.' She made it sound easy. 'If he seems fine, he probably is. If not – send for a doctor.'

'He's not on the phone!'

'We are – just run up to the farm if you need me. Chances are, a good night's sleep and he'll be right as rain, only a bit sore. I'll send you down a bit of dinner with Sally.'

It was dawning on April that she had no choice but to spend the night here, alone with a man. That wouldn't look good for the manager of True Minds Marriage Bureau, no matter how incapacitated he was!

But it was Monday tomorrow and Martha was away. She had hardly been in to the office at all lately, once or twice letting April down at the last minute, which was very unlike her. April ran her mind over her diary. No appointments in the morning, thank God, but she would have to be there by the afternoon to see a Miss Herriot. There was a bus at midday. She remembered catching it with Felicity to go to Lily's wedding. The day they found out about Johnson. Who was looking after Johnson now? His wife, she supposed.

Charlie gave a start and April looked up in panic.

'What's wrong?'

'I'm meant to meet somebody. This evening at six.'

'You'll be meeting nobody,' Florrie said.

'No, but I need to let them know. I suppose St Luke's vicarage is on the phone?'

Florrie and April exchanged glances.

'Can you speak to Jenny – Miss Dunn – and tell her what's happened?' Charlie said. 'And tell her same time and place next week. She'll know what I mean.' A little colour touched his face for the first time since he had been dragged under those thundering hooves.

Well, well, April thought. Did that mean what she thought it meant? And would it be very unethical to spend this enforced evening with Charlie trying to find out?

In the end, though it almost killed both her professional interest and her personal nosiness, she decided it would be. Charlie, despite the painkillers, was in no state for conversation, let alone revelation. Sally appeared with stew, but neither of them had much appetite.

After the meal, Charlie dragged himself out to the shed and supervised her feeding and bedding down the dogs, but the effort made him shaky, and when she suggested he might be better off in bed, he didn't argue. She was struck anew by the lack of comforts in his bedroom, and though the late September evening wasn't cold, she was glad to locate a hot water bottle in the cupboard under the sink. It was a modern rubber one, rather to her surprise, as the cottage was so otherwise lacking in conveniences, with oil lamps and a tiny lean-to lavatory. She brought it to him, and found that she wasn't, after all, particularly embarrassed to see a man in bed.

He clutched the bottle gratefully. 'I'd forgotten that,' he said. 'It's Margaret's – I didn't know she hadn't taken it.'

'Maybe nuns aren't allowed hot water bottles.'

'I don't know, now you mention it.'

April bedded down in Margaret's room, though she must at one time have shared with her mother, because there was only one big bed, sagging in the middle. It wasn't aired, and as she kicked the sheets to warm them, she would have given a great deal for that hot water bottle. Sleep eluded her: every time she drifted off, she dreamed about the flashing metalled hooves and the shouting and the stones whirring through the crowd, and then she fell into a deeper sleep and dreamed that Charlie was dead. When she woke from that, heart thudding, she went to check on him, scarcely daring to push open the bedroom door.

Oh God, *was* he dead? He looked it, in that awkward half-sitting position, head slumped to the right. She thought of all the alarming things Florrie had mentioned – burst lungs and ruptured spleens and she didn't know what all. Then a whistle of breath huffed from his lips, and she relaxed and crept away again.

But she didn't know the ways of the old cottage and as she pulled the door to, it gave an alarming creak and Charlie started.

'Shh, Charlie,' she said in what she hoped were reassuring but authoritative tones. 'Go back to sleep.'

'Evelyn?'

Well, that's what she thought she heard, but she must have been mistaken.

It was a long, tense night, but in the morning as she was raking out the ashes and relighting the fire, Charlie appeared, white, unshaven and somehow older looking, but apparently no closer to dying than she was.

'Did you sleep all right?' he asked conventionally, and she said, 'Grand.' Because the truth, in the clear light of day, was too ridiculous to share.

Charlie's prospects seemed less bleak than last night. Though clearly sore, he could hobble about slowly and see to his dogs. He worried about not turning up for work, but village gossip – Sally and Sam meeting the Colonel in the village on their way to school – saw to that. April was washing up after their breakfast porridge when she heard the roar of an engine outside and Colonel Lucey himself showed in the back doorway.

'Dashed bad business,' he said, shaking his head. 'Busted ribs myself in South Africa in 1902. Fell off a veranda. Damned silly.'

April wasn't sure if it was himself or Charlie who was damned silly.

'Still feel them in damp weather.' He clapped his stout tweed sides. 'Think you'll be ready for the season, eh, lad?' He wrinkled his heavy brows.

It took April a moment or two to realise he was talking about hunting.

'Oh yes, sir, I should think so,' Charlie said. 'I'll be right as rain in a day or so. I'm sorry to let you down.'

Colonel Lucey made the sound generally rendered *harrumph*. 'Don't want to see you till you're fit,' he said. 'I remember a stable boy we had. Horse stood on his back. Lad seemed right as rain, went about his business and – poof! Dead the next day. Punctured lung.' He shook his head.

'Thanks, sir, that's very reassuring,' Charlie said.

'I'll send Thomsy round to check on you – she can walk the setters this way. Too fat the lot of them; do 'em all good.'

April showed him out.

'Teal's a dashed good worker,' the Colonel said. 'I'd be lost without him.'

'Will he, er, be paid if he can't work?' April asked. 'I don't know if he's in an insurance scheme and I don't like to ask.'

'Don't you worry your pretty head; we look after our own,' the Colonel said.

Which was comforting in its way, though not to be shared with Felicity unless she wanted a lecture about patronage and serfdom and lords of the manor.

She left in good time for the midday bus. Matchmaking might not be life or death, but it was her livelihood and wee Miss Herriot would be expecting her.

'I'll telephone Florrie this evening,' she promised Charlie. 'Hopefully she'll tell me you're fine.'

He waved away any other possibility. 'I'll be grand,' he said. 'Tough as old boots, me.'

Which, April thought, dashing for the bus, always struck her as a strange thing to say: didn't old boots give up the ghost, with holes and flapping soles and frayed laces? Wouldn't it be better to be as tough as a nice strong new boot?

Her last sight of Charlie, who insisted on seeing her to the gate, was of him trying to wave, and then wincing, and clutching the gate for support. He looked very far from grand, and terribly alone.

Thirty-six

Once the decision was made, Maurice was surprisingly compliant, reminding Evelyn why she had married him. They had been unable to love each other, or to keep their child safe, or to live honestly together, but he was not a bad man.

The day after the conversation he came in from his day's work to find her packing.

'Only clothes and a few bits my mammy gave me,' she said.

'What's that—? Oh.'

'Yes.' She indicated a neat pile of children's clothes sitting on the table. 'I think – if you're in agreement – we should let these go to someone who needs them. There must be poor children in the town – maybe you could ask the minister. I've kept a few special things – you can too, of course.'

Maurice nodded. 'Aye,' he said. 'There's no sense in them being wasted.' One large hand reached out and stroked the top garment, a striped jumper. 'Aye,' he said again, and then, in a different tone, 'How'll you manage?'

'I'll get a job.'

The country was full of women who had to work. Maurice had already said he would give her some money to keep her going, and though she would rather not have taken it, she had very little of her own.

'You're not going to that – that man?'

She shook her head. 'I told you – he doesn't believe in divorce. He won't have me.'

It felt very racy to say the word *divorce* out loud. She could only imagine what her mammy in Canada would say, let alone Mona. Charlie wouldn't be the only one to think she should have honoured her vows and stayed married for better or worse. But she couldn't help that. Nobody knew how bad the *worse* had been. And without Robbie, there was nothing for her in Lisnacashan but more lies, more surreptitious glances at her belly, more unhappiness – for her and for Maurice.

'I'll shift for myself,' she said, and though she was terrified, a spark of excitement flared. April had set out alone from Lisnacashan nearly three years ago. And she had found work, and a home, love and fulfilment. Evelyn might not manage all of those, but she could try.

'But what will you do?'

She sighed. 'Realistically, all I'm suited for is to be someone's lady-companion. Or nursemaid.' Life had equipped her only for marriage and motherhood. 'I can't type, or take shorthand, or anything. I thought of Liverpool – there's bound to be jobs going in a big city.'

'You can't go into *service*.'

'I'd have a roof over my head. And *don't* tell me your mammy won't like it.'

She knew Mona would never live down the shame. But then, she would never live down the shame of divorce anyway, even if Evelyn had left her son to marry King Edward himself!

Gosh, she thought, I'm like that Mrs Simpson. No better than she should be.

* * *

The temperance hotel near Lime Street Station was quiet and respectable, but Evelyn had never stayed somewhere alone before. Maybe people weren't staring at her, but she felt as though they were. She was glad to seek sanctuary in her room.

It was clean but soulless, overlooking a yard full of bins and, beyond that, a sea of damp rooves and grubby brick. She had taken it for a week, hoping to have found work and lodgings before then – preferably a live-in job. She couldn't help remembering her previous arrival in England: April's welcoming attic, with flowers on the table and a hot water bottle in the bed. Her pretty little room at Lucey Lodge overlooking the green and purple moor. She felt, as she sat on the hard bed – there was no chair – that she would even have preferred her room in Lisnacashan.

She must not look back.

The only thing that had been hard to leave was Robbie's grave. But it had always felt a cold place, little to do with the real child. Strangely, Maurice seemed to have an inkling of how she felt. He had, without saying anything, dug up some of the daffodil bulbs from Robbie's grave, and given them to her in a paper bag.

'When you're settled somewhere you can plant them,' he said. 'It might help you.'

She had been touched, and had packed the bag very carefully in her suitcase along with the few photos she had, Robbie's first bootees, and the worn teddy he pretended to have outgrown but still slept with. He had never really got the chance to outgrow anything.

Now, she gave herself a shake. She would go out and buy a newspaper. She had never lived in a city; the novelty might be just what she needed. And though the future was terrifying, she felt, for the first time in months, properly alive. Awake. Evelyn again: no doppelganger, no shadow –

but one complete person. Scared of the future, grieving for Robbie, guilty about Charlie and how she had left April – but *real*. Herself.

Feeling modern, independent, and fired with determination, she put on her hat and jacket – it was the last day of September and the evening was cool – and called into a corner shop for the *Liverpool Echo*, which seemed the sensible place to look for a job. She found a Lyons Corner House, ordered a Welsh rarebit and a pot of tea, and opened the paper with a sense of anticipation. She didn't know what she expected – a list of inviting-sounding jobs for a woman with no experience, no references and no skills beyond the domestic. Oh, and no home. There was no such list. Even the more depressing-sounding jobs for maids-of-all-work asked for a character reference. What did women like her *do*? Her position was unusual, but there *must* be other single women and widows who needed to support themselves and had no particular skills.

The waitress, a young girl with dark plaits coiled neatly under her cap, smiled as she set down her meal. Maybe waitressing was something Evelyn could manage – she'd had plenty of experience waiting on Maurice – but all the girls here looked very young. They reminded her of the girls in Shaw's Mill, with their bright faces.

Shaw's Mill. Now there was somewhere full of people with good advice. People whose lives were dedicated to giving people opportunities. April—

No. Whatever she did, and wherever she went, she was *not* crawling back to Easterbridge, where she had behaved so badly. She would sort herself out, and *then* contact April, when she could hold her head up.

But thinking of April reminded her of the marriage bureau. There were similar bureaux for finding employment. She wasn't qualified to answer any of these advertisements, but to a real person, someone sympathetic like Martha or April, could she explain her situation more easily? They might not accept divorced women, but she wasn't a divorced woman *yet*. She could say truthfully that her husband was in Ireland, imply perhaps that she had been abandoned.

Emboldened, she asked the waitress, as she paid her bill, 'Do you know of any employment bureaux in the area? I'm looking for work.'

'Oh, I wouldn't know,' the girl said in the accent that Evelyn supposed would become familiar. She called over her colleague. 'Jean, d'you know of any – what did you call them? Employment bureaux?'

'If that's the right term,' Evelyn said, feeling very much stupider than these competent young women.

'Irish, are you?' Jean asked.

'There's loads of Irish here,' the first waitress said, before Evelyn could say she was from *Northern* Ireland. 'Why don't you go up to St Peter's and speak to the priest? They stick together, your lot.'

Evelyn had a sudden memory of St Anthony's in Easterbridge. Walking in with Charlie. Living a particularly horrible lie. No, she would not be seeking out St Peter's.

'I thought the Irish came here for the *un*employment,' said a man at a nearby table and his companion guffawed. 'Benefit, that is,' he added.

'I didn't ask you.' Evelyn wouldn't have said that at home; she would have pretended not to hear. She left the café with no further information about finding work, but with the feeling that she might be braver than she thought.

And she was in the city centre: why not simply walk about and look for an employment bureau? It would be closed, but it would save time tomorrow to have a definite destination. She walked along quite briskly, the heels of her good navy shoes tapping on the pavements. She checked out the buildings as she passed: café; tobacconist; high-class ladies' fashions; Martins Bank – no, the offices she needed would be in less commercial streets, with lawyers and dentists and house agents.

But it was growing dusky, and she felt less brave as she turned into a long straight road of tall Georgian houses. It was deserted and the tapping of her heels was not so much friendly and comforting as eerie, emphasising her solitude.

And now she only wanted to be back in the hotel. She made a few wrong turns – so many streets, so many tall brick houses – and ended up walking almost as far as the university until, realising she was completely lost, she had to turn back. She would ask the first respectable-looking person she saw. *Not* that man – he was looking at her with a little too much interest; she walked past haughtily, avoiding eye contact, hoping he couldn't hear the thump of her heart. But here was an elderly couple, arm in arm. She asked them and, with one interrupting the other, and with much good-natured banter – Liverpudlians seemed more *immediately* friendly than people in Easterbridge – they set her on the right road. By the time she saw the black front door of her hotel she was so tired she could have wept.

She ordered a cup of cocoa and tried to settle to sleep. But, though she was exhausted from the journey, and everything that had preceded it, she couldn't rest. Her thoughts skittered hither and yon – Maurice, the farm, Mona, Robbie, the barn, Easterbridge, April, Charlie, divorce, finding a job – would she be a maid? Work in a factory? Don't you know there's three million unemployed? *The Irish come over for the* un*employment*. What had she done? How would she live?

She hadn't even packed a book, apart from *The A.B.C. Murders*, which she had finished on the journey. She had imagined herself walking into a big municipal library, with a local address, and signing up for a library card. She had imagined everything being much easier. Why, oh why, had she gone so far from home? Couldn't she have tried Belfast, where she understood the accent, where she would not be lumped into the despised category of *the Irish*? *Your lot.*

She stretched out her arm and switched on the light. A mean little light it was, but enough to plough on a bit with the *Liverpool Echo*. It was all fairly boring and might send her to sleep. Something about football, a row about streetlights, some trouble between Irish and local youths – good lord, there was no getting away from it. Violent clashes at an anti-fascist rally in Leeds; she skimmed over that one.

And then something small, buried in a corner, caught her attention – not a headline, or a photograph, not an advertisement, but a name she recognised: *Felicity Carr.* Her heart fluttered; she knew Felicity wrote for various newspapers, she had seen her articles in the *Yorkshire Post* and even the *Manchester Guardian*. This was a letter, and she read it with growing horror.

I take exception to how the battle against fascism which played out on the streets of Leeds on Sunday has been reported in both local and national newspapers. The events at Holbeck Moor on Sunday past should not be dismissed as a 'riot', but celebrated as a clear sign to Mosley and his acolytes that their vile doctrine has no place in a decent society. The crowd which met at Holbeck Moor to oppose the Blackshirts did not, as some of the reporting suggests, consist mostly of Communists – though they were represented. The majority of the 30,000-strong crowd, of which I was one, were ordinary Yorkshire folk who wanted to send a clear message to Mosley, and indeed to Hitler, Franco and Mussolini, that we – Yorkshire, the north, England, Britain as a whole – reject their message of hatred. Sadly, I speak with authority on this matter because I was supported at the rally by a number of friends, none of whom is what the papers call 'a political agitator'. A dear friend was badly injured and now lies fighting for life after being knocked down and trampled by a mounted policeman.

There was more, but Evelyn stopped here, her heart hammering.

A dear friend.

Who could that be only April?

April, who had been so good to her. April who had been her own best friend for years and who had taken her in when she was so low. Who had asked so little, and given so much. April who was always working, always helping people, always on the go. April who loved Felicity so much, and worried so deeply about her. April who must have gone with her to that anti-fascist rally, just to protect her. April trampled by a horse and fighting for her life!

All thoughts of jobs, and Liverpool, fled from her mind.

There was only one place Evelyn should be, and that was Easterbridge, with her oldest friend.

If she wasn't too late.

Thirty-seven

Charlie had known dark times before. When Mam died. When Margaret left. When Evelyn – well, whatever she did. And when Tansy was killed, less than four weeks ago. But through all these trials he had had his work, and his strength. With no work to occupy him, and the relentless, unfamiliar nag of pain, he dragged himself through long, hard days and endless, tossing, sweating nights.

The simplest tasks were gruelling; by the time he had got himself up and dressed, and given the dogs the rudiments of care, he was drained. It bothered him to see the dogs' coats rough and ungroomed and their beds given the most cursory of cleanings, though the pups didn't mind, and were happy to gambol about the paddock, watched by a disapproving Mousie. Tippy would always detach herself from the pups and slink to his side, pressing against him in such a comforting way that he was tempted to bring her indoors. She'd never race again, she was a pet really, so why not have her in the house for company? But common sense got the better of him: Tippy had never lived inside. She would find everything strange, she wasn't house trained, and he wasn't fit to be constantly letting her out to empty, or to bend down and clean up if she soiled the floor.

The Luceys called every day but after they left he would sit very still, somewhere between awake and dozing – the pain kept him awake at night and he was trying not to take too much phenacetin – until the need to see to the dogs forced him out of his chair again. They were kind but he felt the pressure to keep up appearances. He didn't want Colonel Lucey giving his job away, or Mrs Lucey gossiping about his accident around the village or in the vicarage – she was very thick with the Reverend Dunn. The last thing he wanted was people fussing round like he was a charity case.

Florrie, pushing baby Dorothy in her pram, and bringing fresh bread that filled the kitchen with a homely smell, was an easier visitor. She would make a brew and sit down to drink it with him, but he guessed from how she'd blow on her cup to cool it that she needed to get back to her own chores.

On one of her visits the baby set up a low grizzling. Florrie took something from her pocket and slipped it into the pram. 'Teething ring,' she explained. But soon Dorothy's grizzling became a wail.

I know how you feel, lass, Charlie thought. It must be nice to be a baby and just let all your woes out.

'She's maybe coming down with a cold,' Florrie said as she took her leave. 'Joseph's harvesting, but Sam'll come down after school to clean the kennels. And April phones every day to ask after you. Hush, Dot, my love.' She jiggled the pram. 'She says she'll call at the weekend if that's all right.'

'Grand,' he said. 'I'll look forward to it.'

He worked out that it was Wednesday. The last day of September. The weekend felt years away. Everything had slowed down; every task took an age; every day lasted weeks. He felt like an old man.

Then he told himself not to be daft. He had a couple of cracked ribs, that was all! It wasn't the first time and it probably, in his line of work, wouldn't be the last. The weekend was only a few days away, and it was time he gave himself a shake. Because the weekend would bring Jenny. He felt himself smile. Jenny had been hit by a van in a street accident which had killed people: she had known pain and despair on a level that he couldn't even imagine – she had told him, during that unexpectedly intimate talk in her rooms, that there had been fear of her losing her leg. He had had to let her down on Sunday, but he had promised to meet her next week, and by God he would. This mooching about feeling sorry for himself was ridiculous.

He gritted his teeth and stood up with a sudden sense of purpose, lifted the cups he and Florrie had used, placed them in the sink and reached over to turn on the tap. But he stretched too far and too quickly. The pain caught him off guard, robbing him of breath and pitching him backwards, water spraying over the floor, so that, as soon as he was recovered enough, he had to stagger forward to turn off the tap again. He collapsed over the sink, wheezing, feeling the icy sweat creep down his back and the hard cold porcelain dig into his stomach. He heard himself groan.

Outside, something disturbed the dogs and they set up a frantic howling and barking. Instinct made him shout, 'Give over!' but the effort made him cough and he could do nothing but let the sink hold him up, waiting for a breath, waiting for relief.

He waited a long time, but the relief didn't come.

Thirty-eight

On Thursday morning April tore the September sheet off the office calendar and breathed a wordless prayer that October might be easier.

All week, life had assaulted her from every direction.

At home, Felicity burned with agitation, writing letters to all the papers to complain about their reporting of Sunday's events.

'Tell me *exactly* what happened to Charlie,' Felicity had begged her, pencil and shorthand notebook at the ready, before April had even got her coat off after work on Monday evening.

'Felicity! It was horrible. Can you not let me forget about it?' All she wanted was to have her dinner, and maybe tell Felicity about her new client, Miss Herriot, who would be perfect for Sidney Armstrong.

'Absolutely not! Because it says here' – Felicity indicated the *Yorkshire Post* – 'that the only violence was locals throwing stones at the fascists, but that's not true, is it? Those policemen mowed Charlie down like—'

'They didn't exactly mow him down – not deliberately. Everything was so confused.' She closed her eyes wearily. 'I don't want to go over it.' She sighed. 'Have you thought about dinner?' she asked without much hope.

'I've *thought* about it ...' Felicity frowned at her notes.

'What would be a better word than *riot*? I don't want to repeat myself. *Battle*? *Affray*? And you know that bastard is planning another rally next weekend – in the East End of London? Another Jewish area – they've clearly learned nothing from Holbeck! I'm hosting a meeting about it on Thursday. What d'you think sounds better – Easterbridge Against Fascism or Easterbridge Action Against Fascism?'

April thought she should go into the kitchen to make the dinner herself.

On Tuesday Martha had appeared unexpectedly in the office. 'Are you busy?' she asked.

'I'm always busy. I'm behind with the filing and the accounts.' April tried not to sound accusing, but the truth was she was as far from being on top of things at True Minds as she had ever been.

Martha frowned.

'Och, it's not that bad,' April rushed on. 'I don't want you thinking I'm running your business into the ground. It's just been busy.'

She had hoped Martha might take the hint and offer to come in more, but instead she said, 'April, you need an assistant – a proper one. Not some silly girl like Lily and not … well, not me.'

'I thought you were going to ask – *tell* – Fabian that you wanted to come in regularly.'

Martha set her bag down on the other desk and said, without looking up. 'I planned to, but then I started to feel unwell.'

April gasped. 'Och, Martha, no!' She looked carefully at her friend and colleague, who was now sitting at the other desk. For dear sake, how could she not have noticed how pale she was? No wonder she hadn't been in!

'I thought it was' – Martha looked embarrassed – 'the *change*. But I started being awfully sick, and I started to

319

wonder – to *hope* – though I knew at my age it was *much* more likely to be something else. But we went to see a specialist in Manchester last week and' – she bit her lip – 'it seems that I'm expecting a baby.'

'Martha! Oh my goodness! I thought you were going to tell me something terrible!'

'I'm sorry. I couldn't help fearing the doctor might tell *us* something terrible. And Fabian's been down that road before, with his first wife. But no, I'm not ill. However,' she went on, 'I am forty, and this is my first, er, pregnancy. We aren't telling anyone but you and Felicity – not even Prudence for another month or two. So please—'

'I won't breathe a word,' April promised.

Martha left, refusing a cup of tea, and April added to her To-Do list: *Advertise for new assistant*. It was too late to put anything in the *Easterbridge Recorder*: it would have to wait until next week. And she should place one in the *Yorkshire Post* as well. Another baby! Dear lord, they were all at it! If all went well, Martha and Fabian's baby would be just a wee bit younger than Dorothy Yeadon, and of course Sybil and Henry's child. And Hanna and Erich's twins. Not to mention poor Lily's wee baby – though *that* wouldn't be a frequent visitor in the Carr nursery.

On Wednesday, she had popped into the mill on her way home to see how Jenny was getting on. She found her in the middle of a crowd of excited children and looking unusually harassed, her bright curls standing on end and ink on her cheek.

'I didn't realise the after-school club would be so busy,' she said.

'Bring in a couple of bigger girls,' April suggested. 'Prudence's pals would love to help.'

'Good idea,' Jenny said. 'Mabel! Leave Bertie alone. I don't suppose you've half an hour to stay and help, do you?' she begged April. 'Just this once.'

'*If* you come back to our house for dinner afterwards,' April said. 'Otherwise you'll stay here till all hours and then go home and eat an egg.'

'How d'you know?'

'I remember living in rooms.' And she had visited Jenny's room and found it pretty bleak. 'At least you'll get your home comforts at the weekend.'

'It's funny,' Jenny said. 'I'm used to living away, but being *near* home but not *at* home – especially with Daddy so seedy – doesn't suit me. I'm so looking forward to seeing Mummy and Daddy on Friday.'

And to what else? April wondered, but she asked, very discreetly, 'You heard about poor Charlie?'

Did Jenny blush? Or was that April's imagination?

'Oh yes,' she said. 'How dreadful. I hope he'll be all right.'

'Florrie Yeadon's keeping a wee eye on him.' She wondered how to fish without making it obvious. 'He was very anxious to get in touch with you on Sunday. Was he meant to meet you or – or something?'

'Hmmm.' Jenny was non-committal. 'I won't come to dinner if you don't mind. I've letters to write and I want them to catch the last post. Perhaps another day.'

Interesting, April thought as she walked the short distance home. Did Jenny really have letters to write or was she wary of April trying to pump her for information about Charlie? As if she would!

And now it was Thursday, and October, and the week seemed to have gone on for a very long time. But she had drafted her advertisement for an assistant and sent it to the Leeds papers as well as the *Recorder*. She had her girls' club that evening, and Felicity was hosting her new women's anti-fascist meeting. April would have something to eat in town and go straight to the club. But before that, at three o'clock this afternoon, she was going to introduce Sidney Armstrong to Miss Herriot.

Miss Rosemary Herriot had wafted into the office on Monday afternoon, bringing with her an aura of church flowers and bone china. Her soft fair curls and floral-sprigged frock reminded April of the kind of girl Mammy had always wanted her to play with. Or be. She had been living – 'very quietly' – with her mother until recently, 'but Mummy's going to stay with my sister in Madeira. For the climate,' she explained, 'and to be with her grandchildren. It'll be awfully lonely when she leaves. She'd love me to find a chap to look after me.'

And Sidney Armstrong might be just that chap! Protective, old-fashioned, chivalrous – now, if only they would take to each other! Despite all the worry of this week, she was looking forward to their meeting.

Sidney telephoned, all of a dither, to say he had mixed up his work shifts. He *could* make the meeting at three, but he would have to come straight from the station.

'Och, never worry about that,' April reassured him.

She hadn't quite realised that this meant he would turn up in uniform, but suddenly there he was, cheeks reddened with his efforts not to be late, in his close-fitting, dark-blue tunic and trousers. He took off his helmet when he saw Miss Herriot, and smoothed his sandy-fair hair.

'I'm sorry about the uniform,' he said.

'Oh, please, don't be.' Miss Herriot took one look at him and her pale, slightly anxious face relaxed into a broad smile as she held out a soft white hand and murmured how delighted she was to meet him.

And from then on, it all went swimmingly.

If Martha were here, she would have quoted, after they had finally left, still casting appreciative glances at each other, '*I remember the time when I liked a red coat myself very well.*' April said it now to the hatstand, but it wasn't the same. She was delighted for Martha, of course, but dear God she would miss her! But her advert would be in the paper next week; maybe she'd find another kindred spirit. Kindred spirits were what matchmaking was all about.

Her mood restored, she decided to lock up early and celebrate with a decent tea, instead of something rushed and cheap at the Teaspoon. She grabbed her hat and woollen jacket – it wasn't quite cool enough for a winter coat – and ran lightly down the stairs to the street door. She locked it behind her, walked down St Margaret's Lane, and hesitated on the corner – should she turn down towards the station, and *really* treat herself at the Royal Oak, or try the Copper Kettle?

And then she heard a voice she knew very well, but hadn't heard in three months.

'April?'

She spun round, making an elderly gentleman tut and swerve.

'Evelyn! What on earth—?'

But Evelyn didn't seem able to speak. She grabbed April's arms and choked out, 'April! You're alive. I can't believe it. Oh, thank God!' And she fell into her arms, sobbing her heart out.

April had been wrong. October clearly wasn't going to be any quieter at all.

Thirty-nine

Evelyn felt herself pulled into a doorway and plonked firmly down at a table. The solidness of a chair under her, a table in front of her and all around the aroma of grease and stewing tea. Voices rose and fell. Her heart, which had been in the icy grip of dread since last night, trembled. April. Alive and well.

'Here.' A steaming cup and a sticky bun were thrust in front of her. 'Beat that into you,' April said in her bossiest voice. 'I thought you were going to keel over on me.'

'I thought you were – were dead.' Evelyn took a mouthful of tea and picked a bit from the bun, which was slightly stale but surprisingly moreish. She hadn't eaten since tea in Lyons last night.

'Why under God would I be dead?' April asked. 'I'm grand.' She looked the same as ever, in one of her smart office costumes in soft green. She gave Evelyn a warm but confused smile. 'It's lovely to see you but I haven't a notion why you're here and why you thought I was dead.'

Evelyn dug the page from the *Liverpool Echo* out of her pocket, crumpled and smudged by now, and thrust it at her. 'Look! *Dear friend – fighting for life*. Written by *Felicity. You're* her dear friend.'

April tried to say something but once Evelyn had started, she couldn't stop the words from gushing out.

'I went to your house and – and it was full of people! Cars outside and I don't know how many bicycles and' – she clutched the warm handle of the heavy cup – 'the blinds were shut. So I thought ...'

'It was a wake?'

Evelyn nodded.

April burst into laughter. 'For dear sake! I thought I was the one who let my imagination run away with me! First, the English don't *do* wakes like us. And second – I'm not dead.'

'But you were hurt? In that riot or whatever it was? Look – *fighting for life*! It's here in black and white.'

April let out a long sigh. '*I* wasn't hurt. Felicity was just making a better story. It was—'

'But the people – and the blinds?' Even though April was sitting opposite her, alive and well, she couldn't bear to relive that moment when eleven Riverside Road had looked for all the world like a house in mourning, like her own home nineteen months ago.

April lowered her voice. 'Felicity's holding an anti-fascist meeting. I suppose she pulled the blinds so everybody felt safer. That's all. But why didn't you just knock the door and find out?'

'I couldn't bear to. I felt so guilty about running out on you, and not even writing. How could I have faced Felicity?'

'So you came all the way from Lisnacashan, and you were just going to slink home again, without seeing *anyone*? Without even checking?'

'No. I only came from Liverpool.'

April, who had been taking a sip of tea, choked and spluttered. '*Liverpool*? Mammy told me you were back home.'

'I was.' But what did *home* mean? 'Only – now I'm not.' She drained her cup. 'It's a long story.'

April glanced at her watch. 'I've an hour and a half before I've to be at the mill. Will that do it?'

Evelyn nodded. 'It will, aye. Only we might need more tea.'

It took several pots of tea, two portions of chips and some jam roly-poly of astounding solidity for Evelyn to get through her story, but April was the best kind of audience. She asked enough questions to show she was really listening, and commented with surprise at Maurice's secret. 'Away of that! There was a man came to the bureau when I just started. I'm pretty sure he was that way, but his mammy wanted him married. A pity of him, really.'

'A pity of the girl he married,' Evelyn said drily.

She smiled at the conversation with Miss Connaughton – 'och aye, she was always a decent cratur' – and reached a comforting hand across the table when Evelyn told, for the first time, the full story of Robbie's death.

When Evelyn said she and Maurice would get divorced, she looked very serious. 'Divorce! Well, I suppose you have grounds enough.'

'I don't even know if I do, but I think he can divorce me for desertion. It's easier for the man.'

'Isn't it always. I never knew anybody divorced before.' April looked impressed. 'Well, fair play to you, Evelyn. It'll be hard, and people will talk but you couldn't live like that.'

'Society—'

'Och, never mind society. Nobody knows better than me how judgemental people can be.' She drained the teapot. 'Will I order another pot?'

Evelyn shook her head. 'I'm tea-ed out,' she said.

'And you'll stay? Your old room's there.' She looked down at the small bag at Evelyn's side. 'Is that all your luggage?'

'Most of it's in the hotel in Liverpool. I packed an overnight bag. All I could think of was getting to you before – before …'

'Before I shuffled off this mortal coil,' April said drily. 'And here I am, not a bother on me.'

'So … were you just a wee bit hurt, then? You said Felicity was making a better story?'

'Oh. Well. Yes.' April looked uncomfortable. 'Actually, it wasn't *me* got hurt at all. It was Charlie Teal.'

The cold hand which had only lately relaxed its grip on Evelyn's heart squeezed tighter than ever.

'*Charlie?*' His name sounded strange in her mouth. 'What was he doing there? And is he – is he …?' *Fighting for life.*

'He's all right as far as I know,' April said, but a wariness had crept into her voice, as if she wasn't telling the whole truth. 'He broke some ribs—'

'It says here, *trampled by a horse.*' Evelyn couldn't keep the fear out of her own voice. 'Is that true?'

'Well, more or less. But he'd be the first to tell you he's well used to that kind of thing in his line of work.' Her voice was light, but strained.

Evelyn, whose spirits had risen on learning that Charlie wasn't dead or dying, felt them sink again. Because he wouldn't be the first to tell her anything. He wouldn't want to speak to her ever again.

'Why was he there? He's not political, is he?' But how much had she ever really known about him?

I only know I loved him.

April shook her head. 'He gave us a lift.' She sighed. 'I feel awful about it.' Then her face cleared. 'I'm going to see him on Saturday. I thought I could clean the cottage, bring him some shopping, that kind of thing. Florrie and the Luceys are keeping an eye on him, but he must get lonely. He won't be able to work for a while. 'Why don't you come?'

Evelyn shook her head vehemently.

You bitch. You lying—

'He won't want to see me again.'

April traced a spilt dribble of tea on the tabletop with her finger. 'So you didn't come here hoping, now that you're free …?'

Evelyn looked down at her empty pudding bowl and heaved a deep sigh. 'I'm not exactly *free*, am I? And he's a Catholic, so even if – *when* Maurice and I are finally divorced' – it still felt such a strange thing to say – 'he'd never accept it.' She rubbed at a mark on the end of her spoon. 'Easterbridge was the *last* place I wanted to come. I didn't want to be reminded … I treated everybody so badly.'

'Especially Charlie,' April said.

It was the truth, but Evelyn was annoyed to feel tears spring to her eyes. She blinked them away.

'Look,' April went on slowly, 'I don't know if this will make you feel better or worse, but I've a wee feeling Charlie's moved on.'

'You mean—?'

'I don't want to jump to conclusions.'

'You're talking to the woman who jumped on a train from Liverpool because she thought you were dead.'

April smiled but wouldn't be distracted. 'I *could* be wrong,' she said, as if this was a very outside chance, 'but I think he's keeping company with Jenny Dunn.'

The name meant nothing to Evelyn, but she immediately detested it. *Jenny* – so fresh and innocent, like a little wren. And *Dunn*. Done. Finished. *Fait accompli*. No hope for her then.

'She's been working in London but she's home now,

running the mill – did I tell you Sybil's expecting? Jenny and Charlie have run into each other a few times and I've a wee notion *they've* a wee notion – of each other.'

'Oh.'

April looked at her keenly. 'I'm sorry,' she said. 'Maybe I shouldn't have said.'

'No. He's a good man and he deserves—'

'I might be wrong. But she gets awful coy when you mention him. Blushes and that.'

'Maybe she's just got a pash on him.'

'He was supposed to meet her last Sunday – he had to send a message that he couldn't make it. And she *definitely* had a pash on him when she was younger. She said' – April screwed up her face to remember – 'well, she mentioned his legs in his riding breeches.'

A memory of those very limbs flashed into Evelyn's mind before she could stop it, and she found herself squeezing her own thighs tightly together under her skirt.

'Mind you,' April went on. 'She's a trained dancing teacher. Maybe she's teaching him to dance? It *could* be something like that.' She sounded unconvinced.

Evelyn couldn't imagine Charlie learning to dance. And if it was only that, well, *why* learn to dance if not to meet a woman? So even if he wasn't keeping company with this Jenny Dunn ...

Well. She had known there was no hope for her. The least she could do was be glad for him.

April looked at her watch and gave a squeak. 'I need to get to the mill. Why don't you come too? You could meet Jenny and—'

Evelyn shook her head. 'I should get back to Liverpool,' she said slowly. 'I'd planned to stay there and get a job.' It sounded, when she said the words aloud, improbable, but April took her seriously.

'I understand,' she said. 'And I can see why you wouldn't want to stick around somewhere where you might run into Charlie, but at least stay for the weekend? We missed you. You're an eejit, disappearing like that. Sure, I could help you find work. You wouldn't be the first.' She grinned. 'It was me got Jenny a job. She came looking for a husband but I knew fine rightly she'd no more notion of one than I had.'

'*That*'s changed, if what you say's true.'

'Ah, come on, Evelyn – stay the weekend and then start the week fair in Liverpool on Monday. Or *somewhere*. Between us all we're bound to have some contacts for you.'

Evelyn liked the way April didn't dismiss the idea of her earning her own living.

'Now,' April went on, 'I'll chum you the length of the mill and then you can go and surprise Felicity.'

April kept up a bright chatter while they walked through the town, over the bridge and up the steep pull of Riverside Road. She told Evelyn about Erich and Hanna's twins, about Felicity being much stronger but still inclined to put work and politics before health.

And before April, no doubt, Evelyn thought.

She told her about Constable Armstrong running a football team for the younger boys at the club. 'Oh, and I shouldn't tell you this, but I *think*' – she crossed her fingers – 'I've matched him up with a grand wee girl. The sort he can take home to meet his mammy.'

'I'll never again be the sort of girl a man could take home to meet his mammy,' Evelyn said ruefully. 'Not when I'm divorced.'

April shot her a sharp glance. 'Don't you go feeling sorry for yourself, Evelyn Brady,' she said, using Evelyn's maiden name, and, as if to discourage such self-pity, told her about Miss Dawson, whose feet were so painful now she rarely made it to the mill. 'I'll need to call with her when I've a moment,' she said.

Evelyn had a mental image of April's 'To-Do' list, which never seemed to get any shorter.

'I could ...' She started to say, 'I could visit her.' She had liked Miss Dawson. But then she remembered that she wasn't staying in Easterbridge. She was only here for the weekend and then she was going back to Liverpool. Somewhere she had no friends or contacts, right enough, but also where the streets didn't offer up constant reminders of the man she had to forget. Here was the spot they had parted that night when she had first run into him in St Anthony's, and he had walked her partway home. If only she had been honest with him from the start! They could have been friends without her leading him on, and maybe now there would be a chance for that friendship to deepen. And then her mind bumped hard against the immutable fact: she was going to be a divorced woman. He was a devout Catholic. It was never to be.

'I don't see why not,' Felicity argued, half an hour later.

Evelyn had parted from April at the mill, and carried on alone to number eleven, where Felicity was surprised, but by no means displeased, to see her. Her meeting was over, and she was dealing with a mountain of washing up in the bright, shabby kitchen which, like everything else in Easterbridge, was familiar in a way that was partly comforting and partly disconcerting. Her curls were bundled up in a scarf and there were stray soap suds on one cheek. Evelyn, glad of a mindless task, started drying up and found herself telling Felicity the whole story.

'Well,' Felicity said, 'Jenny's a vicar's daughter. She's no more Catholic than you are.'

'A vicar's daughter's hardly the same as a divorcée.'

Felicity stacked the last cups on the drainer and plunged one hand into the sink to pull out the stopper. 'Heaven knows, it's iniquitous that people aren't free to love whom they choose. *I* know that,' she said, 'but the fact is, however difficult it was for him, Maurice deceived you, *and* he was unfaithful. So don't berate yourself too much. But *talk* to Charlie. Tell him what you've told me; tell him what you feel. All right, maybe he's fallen for Jenny and they're courting, and you've got no chance. Maybe he *hasn't* fallen for Jenny and you've still got no chance. But at least you'd know. After all, knowledge is power,' she said grimly.

She wiped round the sink, wrung out the cloth and put the kettle on the hob. 'For ages I sort of knew there must be a fascist cell in Easterbridge – the signs were everywhere. And it was horrible, wondering who might be in it, who you could trust. Was it someone in my writing class? Someone I bought my newspaper from, or one of April's clients? Or was I imagining things? Had I become so caught up in politics that I was seeing fascism everywhere? And now … well, we know for sure there's a group; we know who leads it' – her mouth curled in distaste – 'and some of the people in it, and we know how they target those people. And that's *horrible*, but at least now we understand what we're dealing with. Guess how many women came to my meeting this afternoon? Twenty-seven. For a small town, on a Thursday afternoon, that's fantastic. I think people were disgusted by Holbeck Moor.' Her face darkened and then brightened as she said, 'So go and *talk* to Charlie; find out the truth, where you stand. I promise you'll feel better.'

Evelyn bit her lip. Felicity made it sound easy.

The kettle started to whistle urgently and Felicity said, 'Take your bag upstairs, and a hot water bottle to air the bed. It's not been slept in for months. Time we had another refugee, really.'

The white attic assaulted Evelyn with another rush of bittersweet nostalgia. But she would not be staying long, so she unpacked the sponge bag and nightie, which were all she had brought, and slipped the hot water bottle between the cold white sheets.

When she got back downstairs, April was home, bearing a huge bunch of chrysanthemums in shades of rust, yellow and orange, and Felicity was rooting in a cupboard for a vase.

'We'll need a couple,' April said. 'There's a quare rake of them.' She set the flowers carefully on the draining board. 'From the garden at the mill,' she said. 'My girls are delighted. Some of them, from the old tenements on Townsend Street, had never grown anything before. They've all gone home with big bunches for their mammies. We've far too many here. I should take some to wee Miss Dawson tomorrow.'

'I will,' Evelyn said, 'if you tell me how to get there. I might as well do something useful.'

Miss Dawson lived in a boarding house that smelt of long-ago fried bread. She remembered Evelyn and greeted her with candid delight, clapping her hands at the sight of the flowers. 'How lovely! Oh, and what a joke!'

'A joke?'

'Come in – you'll see!'

She ushered her in and Evelyn saw, on the mantelpiece of a room that seemed, at first glance, to be fashioned entirely from wool, a china jug brimming with chrysanthemums, identical to the ones Evelyn was clutching.

'See!' Miss Dawson said. 'How wonderful to have *two*

lots.' She bustled stiffly about, filled another jug from the little sink in the corner, and placed it, full of flowers, on the table beside her bed.

The room was, no doubt, as clean as she could manage, and bright with homemade rugs and cushions, but there was no disguising the fustiness of a one-room home lived in twenty-four hours most days. Evelyn longed to yank up the peeling sash window to let in some fresh air, but she suspected Miss Dawson, more or less chair-bound, felt the cold. Nevertheless, her hostess made a pot of tea and beamed at the tin of biscuits Evelyn had also brought. Evelyn guessed she had few callers.

'So where did the other flowers come from?' she asked.

'Jenny Dunn brought them,' Miss Dawson said. 'She often calls. Isn't it good of her when she's so busy? *You're an angel, Jenny*, I always tell her. *An angel!*'

Was there no escape from this paragon? This capable paragon who was – she remembered the casual way April had said it – running the mill.

And then – it was like picking a scab, but she couldn't ask April or Felicity without embarrassing herself – she said casually, 'I haven't met Jenny. What's she like? Is she – is she pretty?'

She longed to be told that handsome was as handsome did, which would reassure her that Jenny was as plain as a toad, but of course Miss Dawson went into raptures.

'Oh, she's bonny,' she said. 'Very fair, with lovely curls. And so *good*. She was doing a grand job in London but when her poor father took ill she didn't hesitate to come home. You know how some people are just beautiful, inside and out?'

Evelyn raked her fingers through her straight, red, in-need-of-a-wash hair, thought of her own very unbeautiful feelings, and forced her features into a bright smile. She

334

had only herself to blame for asking. Miss Dawson waxed lyrical about Jenny until Evelyn changed the subject by asking about her woolcraft.

Miss Dawson's face lit up. 'I'm lucky that my hands haven't gone the same way as my silly old feet,' she said. 'I've always plenty to be getting on with. The only problem is the price of wool.' She picked up a scrap of blue knitting. 'We've started making blankets for Spanish refugees. Isn't the world in a terrible state? I'm glad I'm not young.'

The visit clearly gave Miss Dawson more pleasure than it gave Evelyn. I wonder, she thought, walking back to Riverside Road, using the map April had sketched for her, if that will be me in fifty years' time – alone in one room. Miss Dawson had worked hard all her life, and now she was dependent on the kindness of acquaintances making time for her in the odd moments of busy lives. And she regarded herself as fortunate. Evelyn shivered. I can't let that happen to me, she thought, but how do I stop it? And for a moment the old life with Maurice – the modern bungalow, the respectability of being Mrs Maurice Kenny, the town where she knew every shopkeeper and every family – shimmered enticingly. It hadn't been *so* bad, and now she knew the truth about Maurice, maybe they could find a way to rub along together. The thought of the Lisnacashan shopkeepers reminded her of Miss Connaughton. *As long as you're happy.*

If I could have even a chance of happiness one day, Evelyn thought, I'd work so hard, I'd put up with living in rooms and the shame of being divorced. If I just had that hope. As she crossed the bridge and started up Riverside Road, she had a more practical thought: Miss Connaughton owned a haberdashery! She must have oddments of wool she wouldn't mind sending to Miss Dawson. The thought pleased Evelyn: it was the kind of thing April thought of, the impulse to order and help and bring together that made her a matchmaker. Maybe April could indeed give her some good careers advice.

Felicity's advice, to talk to Charlie and find out the truth, flashed back into her mind. She was terrified of seeing him, but she knew now that she couldn't move forward until she did.

April came home from work full of chatter about her plan to visit Charlie the next day.

'I spoke to Florrie this morning,' she said. 'She hasn't called for a couple of days because the baby's sick. So he'll be glad to see us.'

He won't be glad to see *me,* Evelyn thought, and then, mindful of her newfound resolve, told herself not to be so feeble. At the very least she could apologise.

As for her decision that evening to take advantage of April and Felicity's big bath and soak in April's nicest bath salts; to wash her hair and plait it loosely so that it would dry in waves; to sponge and press the frock she had travelled in – they were only about giving herself confidence for a difficult situation. They didn't mean she was trying to compete with the perfect Jenny Dunn, and they certainly didn't mean she had any hopes of Charlie being swept away by her beauty. It was only a matter of what the magazines called self-esteem.

Forty

For all her efforts, Evelyn was uncomfortably aware next morning of looking pale and puffy-eyed. Despite the relaxing qualities of April's lavender bath salts, she had slept fitfully, dreaming of Charlie's cottage being overrun by children, all answering Miss Dawson's description of the sainted Jenny. Beastly little cherubs, she thought viciously, and woke to find that it was not yet dawn but that she was as wide awake as she had ever been.

'You're quiet,' April said as the bus trundled along the once-familiar road to Shippardsholme, stone walls stark against the green fields and just-yellowing trees.

'I know.' She didn't try to explain, but April patted her arm affectionately.

It was a good walk from the village to the cottage and they took turns carrying April's basket, which contained a cherry cake baked by Martha and a bag of apples from her garden; a packet of tea; a fresh loaf and a few tins.

'I thought of bringing him some of the chrysanthemums,' she said, 'but I didn't want them to get squashed in the basket.'

The closer they got to the cottage the faster Evelyn's heart pounded and her stomach began to cramp. How embarrassing to have to use Charlie's lavatory the moment she arrived! She concentrated on deep slow breathing so that April looked at her in alarm.

'You sound like you're going to take a turn,' she said.

The only *turn* I want to take is to turn round and walk away, Evelyn thought, but she gave a tight smile. You will face him, and then you will know, and then it will be over, she told herself.

And after all that, Charlie was nowhere to be found!

They weren't surprised that their knock wasn't immediately answered. Someone with broken ribs wouldn't be running to answer the door. But when a minute passed and the door remained stubbornly shut with no noise coming from inside, April frowned.

'He'd hardly be out,' she said, 'and him hurt.'

'Should we try the back door?' Evelyn suggested. 'He probably never uses the front.'

'It's a tiny cottage,' April argued. 'It's not like he won't hear us, whatever door we use.'

From the shed, the greyhounds set up a frenzied barking.

'Maybe he's made a miraculous recovery,' Evelyn said, trying to ignore the imaginary greyhounds now sprinting around her tummy.

'I hope so.' April peered through the window. 'I can't see much,' she complained. 'D'you think we should go in? In case he's …'

She didn't finish the sentence, but the Charlie of Evelyn's imagination, stern and unforgiving – even, in some of her wilder fancies, barring her entrance with a shotgun – was immediately replaced by a Charlie lying helpless on the stone floor, dying perhaps. Alone. Maybe it was already too late.

She started to stammer some of this to April.

'For dear sake, Evelyn, you need to stop thinking people are dead! Sure hadn't you me in my coffin being waked by half the town?'

April tried the door and it opened easily into a tiny dark hall. 'Right,' she said. 'In we go. I'm sure he won't mind, and at the very least we can leave the food. Oh – what's this?' She bent down and picked up a white envelope from the doormat. 'Well, he hasn't picked up his post.'

Evelyn steeled herself, partly for the horror of finding a dead or dying Charlie, and partly for the pain of simply being in his home.

'It doesn't feel right to barge in,' April said, 'but then again ...'

She opened the door to the kitchen. It wasn't quite as tidy and swept as it had been when Evelyn had been there before. Two blue-and-white cups sat on the draining board.

'Charlie!' April called. 'Hello?' Nothing stirred. 'I'll go and check the rest of the place. I suppose he could be in bed?' Even she was starting to sound anxious.

'I'll stay here,' Evelyn said.

Swallowing nameless dread, she found herself doing her old trick of itemising the objects in view to calm herself. She listed the colours: two blue-and-white cups; one yellow-and-white checked tablecloth, in need of a wash; one stripey hooked rug in front of the range, too many colours to list; orange chrysanthemums in a chipped cream jug—

Oh.

She looked again.

A chrysanthemum was a chrysanthemum, but these looked very familiar: orange, rust and yellow, fat and cheerful, exactly like the ones from the mill. Exactly like the ones in Miss Dawson's room. The ones from Jenny.

She dashed outside, with no clear thought of where she was going, except that she had to leave. Flowers from Jenny! You didn't bring a man flowers, surely, unless ...? And *two* cups! How stupid she had been, imagining him lying hurt while all the time – oh my goodness! April was going to check the rest of the cottage! What if she found him, indeed, in bed, but not asleep, and not alone? No! She mustn't let that memory of Maurice and Michael in the barn tarnish her thoughts of all men. And Jenny a vicar's daughter!

She had taken the path that led on to the moor. It would fork shortly, with the main path heading past Yeadons' farm on up to Shippards Hill, and a narrower sheep-pad meandering over towards Lucey Lodge. She hesitated, not wanting either direction. The moors, which she had last seen in midsummer, were still golden and purple-hazed with heather, but faded now, and the air on her cheeks was cooler, with a hint of bleakness. She closed her eyes and tried to calm herself, leaning against the drystone wall that bounded the lane, listening for the tiny sounds of the moor – a faint rustle of grass, the distant cry of a bird, further away the indignant bleat of a sheep. That wall's been there for hundreds of years, she thought. The moors for thousands. They'll be here when I'm gone, and Charlie's gone. None of it really matters. *I* don't matter, except to myself.

Then into her consciousness crept, or rather thudded, a new sound. Hoofbeats. She snapped open her eyes in case it was Colonel or Mrs Lucey. She'd never have to see those people again, but she didn't want to look like an eejit, standing about on the moor with her eyes closed.

The horse was below her, near enough for her to see clearly. It was a stocky grey pony. Just strangers, she thought: a girl riding, and a man walking close beside her – was it Joseph Yeadon and Sally? And then the pony came a little nearer and she saw that the girl had bright fair curls and was not a girl but a woman of about her own age, and that the man walking beside her, with his hand on her leg – on her thigh! – was Charlie.

So there was no doubt now, and the tiny crumb of hope she only now admitted she had allowed herself dried up into a hard speck of disappointment. The only positive thing – apart from the fact that Charlie was clearly neither dead nor dying – was that they clearly hadn't seen her.

They were much too absorbed in each other.

Forty-one

April thought the fresh air hadn't done Evelyn much good. She had dashed straight to the little lean-to lavatory and emerged pale and distracted.

'I'm fine,' she said. 'I just need to get away from here.'

It didn't feel right to April, to leave the cottage with only a note for Charlie, but if they missed the midday bus there wasn't another until evening.

Evelyn didn't speak on the walk to the village, or in the bus, until April said, 'Well, there was no sign of Charlie, was there? Which I suppose we can take as a good sign that he's better.'

'Oh, he's better all right,' Evelyn said.

'How d'you— Oh! You saw him? Was it— You didn't have a row, did you?' She remembered her conversation with Charlie after Evelyn had left in June. How angry he had been. Surely he wasn't still bitter after all this time?

Evelyn shook her head. She was staring down into her lap, tracing the checks on the pleated skirt of her blue frock. April remembered her pressing those pleats yesterday evening, working hard to get them perfect.

'He never saw me,' she muttered. 'He was too busy with Jenny Dunn. At least I assume it was her.'

'Fair? Pretty? Walks with a limp?'

'Oh.' Evelyn's hands stopped moving. She frowned. 'I

thought she was a dancer?'

'Och, in her day she'd have danced to the rattle of a bucket, from what I hear. But she hurt her leg in an accident, so she can't dance now.'

'She was on a horse.'

April wrinkled her forehead in surprise and then started to laugh. 'Oh, *that* wasn't Jenny. That'll have been Barbara.'

'Barbara? How many women is he keeping company with?'

'Barbara's one of my clients,' April said. 'Charlie's been teaching her to ride because she's very much smitten with a horsey fella called Douglas.'

'Are you sure?'

'I arranged it,' April said. But to reassure Evelyn, she added, 'Tall? Oh, I suppose it's hard to tell on horseback? Very dark hair.'

Evelyn's face, which had been briefly hopeful, looked dejected again. 'This girl was short with fair curls. It sounded *exactly* like Jenny – not that I've met her, but I keep hearing about her.'

'Oh.' April tried to imagine Jenny on horseback. Was this all to woo Charlie? Honestly, the things people did for love! But she wasn't going to leap to conclusions. Look where that had got her in the past! 'Just because she was riding a horse with him doesn't mean—'

'He had his hand on her leg.'

'Oh.' April was torn. On the one hand, there was no doubt that whatever she said, Evelyn had been holding out a wee candle of hope about the bold Charlie. On the other – it *was* grand to be right.

But wasn't Jenny the dark horse! Saying she'd no notion of getting married, and here she was, riding a horse over the moors with a man she had admitted to once having a pash on! She wondered what the Dunns would think of Charlie being a Catholic, and so far below them socially. But April couldn't help hoping it would be a long engagement: she didn't relish having to help find yet another person to run the mill. Though, as the wife of a groom, Jenny might well have to work even after she married – at least until children came. And come they would if she was anything like April's other friends. For dear sake, they were all at it like rabbits! The mill should start its own crèche. She was thinking seriously about this – who could run it? – when the bus juddered to a halt and it was time to get off.

As soon as they got home, Evelyn disappeared to the attic. April sat down at the kitchen table and wearily pulled out some of the bureau's paperwork from her old leather satchel. She was just opening the first letter when Felicity came down, carrying four coffee-stained cups, expressing delight to see her home so soon, and asking how they had got on.

April told her the whole story.

'Well, he's clearly better,' Felicity said, looking relieved. 'But I somehow don't see him and Jenny together.'

'You never know,' April said, conscious that, in this matter at least, she was more expert than Felicity. 'Sometimes it's the unlikely ones. You get an instinct for it in my line of business.'

Felicity indicated the papers on the table. 'Talking of business, I thought you tried not to bring work home?'

April sighed. 'It's only clerical stuff. If I do a few hours now, it'll take the pressure off next week. I've some difficult meetings planned. Including one where I tell Daphne Dalrymple I'll have to take her off the books once and for all. I hate giving up on a client, but some people are just impossible.'

'I'm the last person to lecture you about working too

hard' – Felicity sounded unusually humble – 'but I was hoping …'

'What?' April slit an envelope open and frowned. 'Oh dear, I really don't think— Sorry, what?'

Felicity set her cups in the sink. 'I thought we could go for a walk. Since you're unexpectedly free.'

'Are you not busy working on your new anti-fascist group? And you haven't been for a walk since—'

'Since Lucey Lodge. I know. Well, I'd like to go for one now. With you. I thought we could go to the park and then call on Fabian and Martha.'

'But your group?'

'I'm not going to be in charge.'

'What?' April set the letter down.

'I know I assumed I'd run it. But *so* many people came, April – it was marvellous! And some of them are terribly well qualified: Miss Ingleby, who's just retired from the Girls' High School, is willing to take the chair, and Rosanne from my very first writing class said she'd be secretary. And there are others. It made me realise … it needn't always be me taking charge. It *shouldn't* always be me. As long as there *is* a group, that's what matters.' She bit her lip, and went on, sounding uncomfortable, 'I know I take on too much. All week I was wondering how I could get down to London to try to stop Mosley in the East End—'

'That's tomorrow, isn't it?' April tried to keep her voice neutral, as if she had not been worrying all week about Felicity doing that very thing.

'I'm not going. I don't want to be part of a mob. Hitting Johnson with that stone … I can't deny it was satisfying for a moment, but when I thought about it afterwards I felt sickened. There are things I'm so much better at. Things that won't hurt *you*.'

'D'you think it'll be as bad as last week?'

'I'm fairly sure it'll be worse,' Felicity said simply. 'I mean – it's wonderful that so many people are standing up against the fascists. But last week, when I couldn't find you, when I thought you'd been hurt …' She shuddered. 'It helped me understand how hard it's been for you, worrying about me. I've taken you for granted.' She sounded very serious. 'I never will again. I promise.' She came behind April and leaned over her, clasping her arms.

April pulled her into a tight embrace. 'Och, love,' she said. 'You will surely. But that's what people do when they love someone.'

'I'm probably not the easiest person to love,' Felicity said.

April made an incoherent all-purpose noise.

'Leave the work till later,' Felicity implored. 'I'll help – or let Evelyn. It might take her mind off things, and if she's serious about getting a job she might as well put in some practice.'

'That's a good idea.'

She could scarcely remember the last time she and Felicity had walked together in Easterbridge. It was a stiff pull up the hill to the park, but Felicity managed it with no wheezing or catching her breath. Please God this winter wouldn't see her bad with her chest. The park was busy with families and couples, and bright with late roses and rows of chrysanthemums that reminded April of the ones at the mill.

'Another few weeks,' she said, 'and the leaves will have turned.' She hung back to smell a deep red rose, and when she caught Felicity up, she took her arm. 'You're really quite easy to love,' she said.

Felicity looked down at their two arms and said nothing, but she smiled, and they walked very close together, their hips brushing from time to time, and April wondered why she had ever been so self-conscious about something so natural.

'Come on,' she said. 'Let's see if Fabian and Martha will give us tea.'

Forty-two

Charlie inhaled the soft, cool air, thankful it no longer hurt to breathe. October had sneaked in while he was housebound. The scents of heather, fleece, and something intangible that he thought of simply as 'moor' mingled with the closer smell of Mousie's thick, oily mane and the leather of her saddle. Another familiar smell that he had missed during this long week of pain, boredom and isolation. Even the lead rope in his hand made him feel he was getting back to normal.

'Glad you let me persuade you?' Jenny asked.

He looked round at her, sitting in the saddle, and smiled. 'I was worried I wouldn't be fit for it, but I'm grand.'

'*You* were worried? I've been terrified all week,' Jenny admitted. She didn't look terrified, sitting tall on the pony, her back straight. He supposed her years of dancing had helped her balance.

'You don't look it.'

'Not of Mousie.' She reached a hand forward and stroked the grey neck. 'She's a darling. And not of you.'

'Pleased to hear it.'

She laughed and said, more seriously, 'It was my silly leg. I'd no idea if it would co-operate. At first I didn't think it would. When you had to hold it in place for me, I could have cried.'

'The trick is not to let it stiffen. Don't be afraid to give it a good stretch if you need to. Try it now.'

Jenny did what he suggested, beaming the bright smile that made her look much younger than the thirty-odd he knew her to be.

'That makes all the difference,' she said, bending her leg back into position. 'At first I thought I was daft even to try – I can't walk properly, so what made me think I could ride a horse, let alone commute to work on one?'

'There's an old pal of the Colonel's, needs a Bath chair to get around in, but stick him on a horse and he's a new man. Jumps hedges the Colonel would baulk at.'

Jenny laughed. 'If I can walk and trot and steer and stay on, I'll be happy.'

'Shall I unclip the lead rope? Mousie's as quiet as a sheep.' He had been going to say 'lamb' but there was nothing skippy about the mare's sedate plod.

'Promise she won't bolt?'

He laughed. 'She won't even notice. And I'm right beside you.'

Mousie mooched placidly across the sheep-grazed path, white ears flicking at their voices.

Jenny gave a contented sigh. 'It's starting to feel real now, instead of a crazy plan. It was April who put the idea into my mind.'

'That doesn't surprise me.'

'Not in so many words. But when she mentioned the Colonel's offer to let her commute on Mousie I wondered if *I* could.' She grinned. 'I am rather a *where there's a will, there's a way* sort of person. And when I asked the Colonel, he said it would be a jolly good show for the old mare to have a job to do and his niece would give her a dry billet while I was at work.' She imitated the Colonel's voice, and Charlie smiled.

'And we're moving to Lucey Lodge when the new vicar starts,' Jenny went on, 'so he said she can go back to her old home and I can pick her up every morning.'

'You're going to live at the lodge?'

Jenny nodded. 'It's just been arranged. Daddy's had to retire, and of course the vicarage belongs to the church. So we'll be neighbours. I can't wait to tell April – she knows I'm not settled in town and I think she's worried I'm going to give up the mill. But I'll be able to put her mind at rest now.' She flashed him one of her luminous smiles. 'I shall go and tell her in person on Monday. I can't wait to see her face! It's really going to happen, isn't it?'

'Looks like it. I'll have Mousie ready for you every morning,' Charlie promised. 'And in the meantime, you need to practise as much as possible.'

'Every weekend. You're sure you didn't mind me changing to Saturday? Only my parents weren't awfully happy with Sunday. They think I'm just doing it for exercise – I don't want to get their hopes up about me living at home if I can't manage.'

He shrugged. 'I've not got much else on. I've no dogs in training.'

'I'll pay, of course. The same as Barbara.'

He shook his head. 'Don't be daft. It was a business arrangement with Miss Firth. This is just friendly like, between neighbours.' He hoped that wasn't too forward. 'Right, that's enough for your first time. Let's turn for home.'

Mousie, released into her paddock, buckled her legs down for a roll with an exhausted grunt as if she'd been twice round Aintree, before she set to grazing with great concentration.

Charlie emptied the dogs and gave them a run round. A squirrel darted along the top of the back wall and one of the pups tore up the paddock with a turn of speed that made Charlie hold his breath. It lolloped back to him, exhausted, and he rubbed its ears.

He was relieved to be indoors – the exercise and fresh air had taken more out of him than he expected – but the house felt particularly cold and empty, especially after Jenny's easy company. The kitchen was tidier than he had left it and when he opened the larder, there were some unfamiliar items. A note on the kitchen table explained it: he had missed April. There was also a letter from Margaret.

Typical, he thought, to be more or less alone all week and then to have missed one visitor because he had been busy with another. *Lady* visitors, no less.

Imagine telling Margaret that! *Charming lady visitors.* He wouldn't, of course. But, oh dear, he'd have to write *something*, or she'd worry. He'd put off answering her last one; sometimes, especially lately, it was hard to know what to write. Her own letters were as lively and chatty as those she'd sent from school, full of anecdotes about Sister This and Mother That and how happy she was. But now there were no dog racing triumphs to recount, Charlie had little to tell her in reply except that the leaves were turning and the odd snippet about the village. Miss Batley from the shop had had a perm and her hair turned yellow. The butcher's cat had had thirteen kittens. *Tell me how YOU are*, Margaret would beg. But *charming lady visitors* would give her the wrong idea. Neither April nor Jenny was *that* kind of lady visitor.

Thank God he had never mentioned Evelyn.

He tightened his lips. That ache in his chest was his damaged ribs protesting. It was nothing to do with the fact that he'd let himself think about her. He never thought about her.

He opened Margaret's letter while he waited for the

kettle to boil for tea. It was shorter than usual, in her familiar neat hand in the bright blue ink she always used: *You haven't written for AGES! I don't know whether to scold you or worry about you!!! This week we've been talking about renouncing things of the world. You know all about renunciation of course. I sometimes think I have more fun in a convent than you do out in the world! Did you go back to Shaw's Mill? Have you seen Constable Armstrong again? He sounds a good chap. Why don't you invite him for a drink at the Blacksmith's Arms? (Is that what men do? I wouldn't know.)*

And then, something she hadn't mentioned for months: *Did you keep that brochure I got for you? About the marriage bureau? Chastity isn't for everyone and you sound lonely even though you say you're not. Why not give it a try?*

Why not indeed?

To stop the thought, and to give himself something to do, and also out of guilt – he shouldn't have neglected her so long – as soon as he had drunk his tea, he rummaged through Mam's old bureau for the writing pad and envelopes that were always kept there. There were stamps too – the new ones with the boyish profile of Edward VIII. They still looked odd, but he supposed they would soon become familiar. If he set himself the task of walking to the village postbox next day, that would give him a reason to leave the house. He could bring Tippy; she would enjoy the change of scene and it wasn't too far for her. So there was nothing to stop him writing to Margaret.

Nothing except that he had little to say, and couldn't tell the truth. *I've been trampled by a police horse and broken some ribs so I've been stuck at home all week in agony and it's made me realise how bloody lonely I am. You were right.* She'd only worry. The nib of his pen dried up several times as he sat and wondered what to say.

Mousie the old pony is enjoying a new lease of life. As if she'd care.

One of the pups had a corn on its pad but it's grand now.

Why not the truth, then? He sucked the pen, tasting the ink, and found himself writing about Holbeck Moor – not about getting hurt, what would be the point in that? – but the event itself.

You never saw such a crowd, Maggie. It felt grand to be with so many people, all wanting the same thing – to show fascism it wasn't welcome in Yorkshire. I can't pretend to know much about it, but there's something sinister about all those black shirts and aping Herr Hitler.

So far, so good. But she would write back, *What about you?*

He looked back at her letter and a word jumped out at him: *Renunciation.*

At first he chose his words as carefully as if he were encouraging a young dog into the starting trap for the first time, but then, possibly because he hadn't been to confession for some weeks, his pen fairly raced across the page. He hadn't always been a groom, after all; he had been at school until he was seventeen, and then studied briefly at a seminary. He knew – or had once known – Latin and divinity and how to express himself in an essay.

I don't think I do know much about renunciation, he wrote. *Mam used to say I'd given up the priesthood for her, but to be honest, Maggie, it wasn't the life for me, and deep down I was relieved. I didn't have a true vocation, not like you.* That was enough; she didn't need to know about Jeannie. *I wouldn't want you to think I was sad about giving up the priesthood and I'm sorry if I let Mam think that. I really love my life here, with the horses and the dogs.*

And he did, he realised, as he blotted the page. He remembered the way that pup had raced up the field, with the promise of something special. He thought of riding out on crisp autumn mornings on a fit hunter, their breath frosting the clear moorland air. All he needed was to get his strength back.

All?

But maybe I will consider your marriage bureau idea, he scrawled at the end. He wouldn't, but it would please her.

He gathered the sheets together and stuffed them into an envelope. He stamped it and set it on the mantelpiece, ready to take to the post next day.

It felt as though he had been writing for hours, his hand cramping with the unfamiliar action, but it was only mid-afternoon. Hours of the day left, and then a long Sunday. He was nowhere near fit enough to cycle to Mass; all he could hope was that someone might call.

He felt unsettled and couldn't work out why. After all, this was the best day he had had since that damned police horse had galloped over him, and he had the prospect of Jenny's company for the next few Saturdays. He had had no more crippling attacks of pain like the one that had poleaxed him on Wednesday. He felt stronger every day, and hoped to get back to work soon, even if only light duties. He'd written the letter that had been hanging over him. So why did he feel so low? Lower even than when he had been struggling from dose to dose of phenacetin, every endless day and night a blur of pain.

He poured out more tea, but it was lukewarm and stewed, so he left it on the side and went out to see the dogs. Tired after their romp, the pups were curled up in a tangle of gangly legs and skinny tails, and barely acknowledged him, but Tippy thrust her pointed fawn head into his hand and looked up at him with her golden-brown eyes.

'Come on then, lass,' he said, taking down her lead from the hook on the wall. Might as well have a turn over the moor. He could take it slow and Tippy was always happy to amble, her gait stiff because of her wonky leg.

'Look at us, lass; couple of crocks, aren't we?'

Tippy wagged her tail.

They went further than he had intended, to the spot where on a clear day you could see for miles, across the purpling moor in one direction and down the valley in the other, towards the town. His ribs pinching, he sat down on a tumble of boulders from what had once been a wall, and breathed in the cool sweet air. Some sheep looked up from grazing, but seeing he was no threat, Tippy lying at his feet, they soon lost interest. On the horizon he saw the silhouette of what he thought was a horse, but which revealed itself presently to be two people walking together, their heads bent in conversation.

And now he admitted what was unsettling him. It was the loneliness. Being with Jenny, and with Barbara before her, had wakened a need in him, a recognition that he didn't want to live alone forever. Not Jenny and Barbara themselves – they were grand girls but there had been nothing romantic in it for anyone – but what they reminded him of.

Evelyn.

He made himself think her name.

Well, Evelyn wasn't for him; he'd made a right fool of himself over her and no mistake. But there were other women. Women who weren't married.

I can't.

The thought of making that kind of mistake again – letting himself stumble into something so shattering – stabbed in a place he couldn't kid himself was the cracked ribs. It was his heart. Well, maybe that was cracked too, but it could mend after a fashion – like Tippy's wonky leg.

I wouldn't know where to start, he thought, and then, of course I do!

He thought of what Jenny had said: *I am rather a* where there's a will there's way *sort of person.* And he wasn't. Or at least he hadn't been. But he could be.

All right, Maggie. This is what you wanted. Maybe I should have listened to you all along. Oh aye, and you, April. All these bloody women, taking charge, knowing what's best for me, when I can't see it myself.

Maybe he said it aloud because Tippy perked up as if she had heard something and then unfolded her legs with a sigh, ready for home.

They set off together.

Monday morning: he'd make himself do it. He'd take the bus into Easterbridge and consult the True Minds Marriage Bureau.

Forty-three

It was satisfying to spend Sunday afternoon helping April tackle her unruly pile of paperwork, while Felicity chopped things for dinner before disappearing to her study.

When they were done, April grinned at Evelyn. 'Great job.'

'It wasn't hard,' Evelyn pointed out. 'Lily managed it.'

April got up and went over to the cooker. She opened the oven door. 'Aye, that's done. I'll turn it down low and give Felicity a shout.' She turned back to Evelyn. 'Lily *didn't* manage most of it. But you're a natural. It's mostly common sense. And the shorthand and typing you could learn in evening classes. There's a wee commercial college in—'

'April. Stop it.'

April was looking at her with innocent blue eyes. 'What? I only said—'

'I can't stay in Easterbridge to be your assistant.'

'Why not?'

Evelyn threw up her hands. 'A million reasons! I'm not qualified. We'd gossip all day and get no work done.'

'Och, you don't know me at my work. I'm Miss Professional.' April sounded smug and Evelyn was sure she was right.

But of course those weren't the real reasons.

'You don't want to stay in Easterbridge because of Charlie,' April stated.

Evelyn, glad of an excuse to hide her face, started to remove the piles from the table and stack them neatly on the broad windowsill.

'But he's hardly ever in town. And wouldn't you rather stay with us than in some dreary room in Liverpool? Queues for the bathroom and stains on the mattress? Jenny hates living in lodgings – she's putting a brave face on it, but I can tell. Though I suppose—'

'Of course,' Evelyn interrupted before April said something about Jenny not needing to live in lodgings for much longer. 'But I can't see myself in a marriage bureau. All those happy endings.' She shuddered. 'Anyway, Martha wouldn't want a *divorcée* working for True Minds, would she?'

'Sure who'd know? And hasn't she me, and me living with my fancy woman?'

Evelyn blushed. 'I wish I'd never said that.'

'Och, you were hurt and grieving.' April took cutlery from the drawer and started to set the table.

True, but it wasn't even the worst thing she had said or done during her months in Easterbridge, and tempting though it might be to snuggle down indefinitely in the attic in number eleven, she couldn't. Too many reminders. Too many reproaches. And, no matter how April dismissed it, the constant fear of running into Charlie – and the lovely Jenny.

'At least,' April said, as if she could read her mind, 'you don't need to feel guilty about Charlie. I mean' – as Evelyn opened her mouth to protest – 'it does seem as though he's happily courting Jenny. It's not like you've scared him off women.'

'I suppose.' To change the subject, she said, 'That smells good.'

'Aye. It's getting to the time of year for a bit of stodge, isn't it?'

A bit of stodge was not how Evelyn would have described the delicious sausage casserole they sat down to presently. Its herby aroma triggered a wave of nostalgia – had Felicity remembered that this was her favourite when she had stayed before?

Maybe it was the prospect of leaving for that solitary room April predicted, or maybe, newly alone, she was sensitive to the happily coupled, but Evelyn felt something different between April and Felicity. A new contentment, an easy affection and solicitousness that she didn't remember from the spring. At least ... she tried to remember ... yes, April had always been concerned for Felicity's wellbeing, but now it seemed more reciprocal. As if Felicity had suddenly realised what a treasure she had in April.

'You look tired, my love,' Felicity said, helping April to more casserole.

'Och, you know me – just busy. And I've got the curse. Attacking on all fronts.'

It took Evelyn a moment to realise April was talking about her monthlies: imagine having a partner you could share that with! She had never mentioned hers to Maurice, except as an excuse to dodge his attentions, but once Robbie was born his attentions ... well, they weren't being turned on her.

'The sooner you get your assistant the better,' Felicity said.

Evelyn bit her lip, but April changed the subject. 'No word from your contacts in London?'

'It's too soon.' Felicity set down her fork, looking worried. 'But I don't have a good feeling, given what happened at Holbeck.'

'Is this the march in the East End?' Evelyn asked. 'Mosley and his crowd?'

Felicity's face darkened further. 'I don't know what's going to stop him, but surely to God this will. They were predicting thousands would turn out in protest.'

'Sure it's madness to let him go through a Jewish area. It's just provocation,' April said.

Evelyn was whooshed back to Mona's kitchen, on the fifteenth of August, and their row about the Hibernians and the Orangemen. The first time she had ever stood up to Mona. And thinking of Mona stiffened her resolve: no matter how hard it would be to manage on her own, it had to be better than the half-life she had left.

April yawned.

'Early nights all round,' Felicity said. 'I've a bundle of stories ready for the post in the morning – ones that pay well, thankfully.' She turned to Evelyn. 'The sillier the story, the better the pay. It's maddening.'

'Some day you'll write your masterpiece,' April said.

'I expect so,' Felicity said, 'and nobody will buy it. Now – if everyone's had enough, may I suggest that you, April, take a long, relaxing bath, while Evelyn and I do the washing up?'

At the sink, Felicity said to Evelyn, 'Why don't you stay for a week? No, listen' – as Evelyn started to protest – 'I literally mean one week. To help April get straight in the office while she appoints her new assistant.'

Evelyn thought of how tired April seemed, how busy. How she was always taking charge, not because she was bossy – though she could be – but because she cared so much about people. How she had welcomed Evelyn back with hardly a word of reproach. How she had forgiven Evelyn's hateful remarks with an understanding *you were hurt and grieving*. And she was clearly under the weather – Evelyn remembered, when they were young, that April had occasionally been laid low with her monthlies. Surely

Evelyn could help her for a week? She could easily send for her luggage from the hotel.

'And you can do a few things for me,' Felicity continued. 'I need to sort out some old papers. And then both of us, separately, will give you glowing references. We needn't say you only worked for one week, or that we're your pals. Otherwise, you could end up being a lady companion or something ghastly like that.' She poured coffee into one of her Bavarian pottery mugs. 'Not going to nag. But it's a jolly good idea and you'd be all sorts of an idiot not to agree. Now, I'm going to take my coffee into the sitting room and listen to the news on the wireless. I want to hear what's happened in the East End. You're very welcome to join me.' She turned at the kitchen doorway. 'And if you're mostly worried about running into a certain person, then you couldn't have chosen a better week. He'll be lying low after his argument with a police horse.' She lifted her coffee cup in valediction. 'Easterbridge is the very last place he'll be.'

Forty-four

'Och, isn't this lovely!' April said for what Evelyn reckoned was the tenth time that morning. 'You and me working together.'

'For one week,' Evelyn stated firmly, handing her a manila folder.

'Don't worry, I'll get a quare load of work out of you in a week.'

So far it had mostly been updating files and moving the older ones to another filing cabinet.

'There's a wee bit of cleaning,' April said, 'if that's all right. The blinds need dusted and the window cleaned.'

'I thought you'd a char?'

'She won't do anything window-related. A fortune teller told her to beware of glass.'

'I don't mind. I might have to take a domestic job.'

'Not with the references we'll give you. But I could give you a separate one for cleaning. Then you'd be ready for all eventualities.'

They both laughed, and April said, 'Och, Evelyn. Don't go *too* far away, will you? I missed you.'

Evelyn knew she didn't only mean the past three months. And it was fun, working here – doing something useful, if menial: the novelty of an office environment, with its sense of order and purpose. She let herself imagine staying. For the winter maybe. Easterbridge was a great wee town, and she wouldn't be completely on her own. She might make new friends at the mill …

They were taking tea at eleven when the phone rang.

April grinned. 'Now wait till you hear my phone voice,' she said. She swallowed the last of her bun, lifted the receiver, and said, immensely properly, 'Good morning, True Minds Marriage Bureau. Miss McVey speaking. How may I help you?' Then her voice switched back to normal as she said, 'Jenny!' and Evelyn's bun stuck in her throat. 'That sounds intriguing,' April went on. 'Today? About twelve? You'll have to come here – I've a client at half past. Aye, all right, see you then.'

She replaced the receiver and said, unnecessarily, 'That was Jenny.'

Evelyn nodded.

'She wants to talk to me – something important. She wouldn't tell me over the phone.'

'She's leaving the mill to' – she made herself say it – 'marry Charlie?'

'Och, Evelyn, you're worse than me! It could be anything.'

'I'll get out of your way.'

'No need. There's a downstairs office where we interview clients. You didn't think we brought people in here, did you? No – you get those windows and blinds sparkling. I told you, I'm going to get my money's worth out of you.' She spoke lightly, but for Evelyn the joy had leaked out of the morning.

It was silly of her. It was only making official something she had been sure of since that moment on the moor when she had seen Charlie place his hand on Jenny's thigh. They finished their tea and carried on filing, but without the easy chatter which had made the morning so pleasant.

Just before twelve, April said, 'I'd better go down and make sure the interview room's ready. I've a tricky meeting at half twelve with the fussiest girl in Yorkshire.'

The office felt much less friendly when she had left. Evelyn went, as instructed, to the little broom cupboard and took out what she would need for cleaning. As she was still wearing her good blue frock, she also took a voluminous floral pinny which she supposed belonged to the char. It wrapped around her twice, but would keep her frock clean. A lurid purple and orange spotted headscarf was in the pocket and, after giving it a cautious sniff, she tied it over her hair. She was used to cleaning windows: Maurice was in a fair enough way of going, but she had never had domestic help, and she found it satisfying, though unlike the bungalow, she couldn't do anything about the outside which was streaky with grime.

St Margaret's Lane was a quiet, cobbled street, mostly offices and a few shops. There was hardly any through traffic. As Evelyn polished the window, she saw two older men coming out of the country outfitters and a delivery boy lean his bicycle against the butcher's wall. She could read the headline on the newspaper poster in the mesh-covered board outside the newsagent's: 84 ARRESTS AS THOUSANDS STAMPEDE IN LONDON RIOTS.

She wasn't exactly looking out for Jenny Dunn, but neither could she avoid seeing her. And she was easy to spot. Despite the limp, her lithe figure gave the impression of grace and merriment. *She'd have danced to the rattle of a bucket*, April had said, and you could tell that even now. Her turquoise hat was modishly small, and the October sun glinted off her bright yellow hair. Evelyn would have described it as *golden* if it had been anyone else's hair. She leaned against the window, confident that if Jenny looked up, she would see only a charlady, wrapped in pinny and headscarf. Jenny walked straight to the office and Evelyn heard the ring of the doorbell, and then the clatter of April's feet on the stairs as she dashed down to let her in.

For some time, trying not to think of the conversation downstairs, Evelyn scrubbed viciously at a stubborn sticky mark on the glass. Or was it on the outside? She peered more closely, and then her breath shuddered and her hand stopped rubbing.

It couldn't be …

Her breath had steamed up the window, so she wiped it clear with her cloth and peered out.

Charlie. Walking up the street in the good suit she remembered from Mass, and a grey tweed cap, walking slowly and stiffly, so that his gait wasn't unlike Jenny's. *Made for each other* said a sarcastic, bitter part of her, while another part – her heart? – ached to think of him in pain. They must be telling April together! Evelyn swallowed. If ever she had wanted to run, it was now – but there was nowhere she could go without actually running past him in the street! On Saturday she had recognised Charlie easily, but he had been quite far off and she hadn't seen his face. Today, she could see it clearly. It was serious and set, his cheekbones sharper than she remembered, his lips more determined.

Don't look at his lips!

He glanced up. He couldn't possibly have seen her, but she shrank back from the window. Her insides turned to liquid and she couldn't breathe. Her hand on the window was all that was keeping her upright.

Any possibility of staying in Easterbridge for a day, let alone a season, fled.

She sank on to the nearest chair, which was at April's desk, and waited, sickly, for the inevitable ring of the doorbell. April would let him in, and he would be just downstairs, so close, and so lost to her.

But no ring came. Even allowing for him walking slowly, he should have got here by now. Unless – of course! – he was expected, so April had simply left the door open for him.

Well, she might as well get back to her cleaning. There was no way she was going to let April catch her being so feeble. She dragged herself back to the window and looked down the street.

Charlie was walking away. Alone. And something about his demeanour had shifted: where he had seemed purposeful, now he seemed dejected. Where he had looked determined, now he looked defeated.

Everything inside her – jealousy, bitterness, regret, love – merged into one overriding impulse. She had to see him. She had to explain. She had to apologise. He deserved that at least. And maybe then she would be free to live some sort of life without him.

She dashed out of the office, down the narrow stairs two at a time and pushed open the door into the street.

'Charlie!' she yelled.

He stopped. Turned. Looked.

She ran towards him.

'I'm sorry,' she said.

'Evelyn?' He sounded incredulous. 'Is that really you?'

'Yes. I ... I saw you from the window. I'm sorry. I didn't mean to lead you on, or ... or lie, or pretend, or – any of it. If I could go back, I'd change it all.'

He was right in front of her. She could see the flecks in his dark eyes and a tiny, tiny razor cut on his cheek. She could see his heartbeat pumping in his neck. When she breathed in, she could smell his familiar scent – fresh air and soap and a hint of dog.

'All?'

She shook her head. 'No. I behaved terribly. But I did love you. I wouldn't change that. I just wish I'd been honest. I wish I hadn't hurt you so badly.'

He was staring at her as if he still couldn't believe his eyes. His lips parted as though he were going to speak but the words didn't come.

She rushed into the silence. 'I'm not staying in Easterbridge. I'm going away again. You don't have to worry about bumping into me, or that I'd try to make mischief between you and Jenny.'

'Jenny? There is no me and Jenny.'

'But I saw you. And she's here now – at the bureau I mean. I thought that's why you were here. I thought you were going to tell April you were engaged.'

He shook his head. 'I didn't know Jenny was here. But it's nothing to do with me. She's got no interest in me. Or me in her – not in that way.'

'So, you're *not* in love with her?'

'Not at all.'

'So why are you here?'

For a wild, hopeful, ridiculous moment, she thought he was going to say, *For you. I heard you'd come back.*

But of course he didn't. Instead, he looked embarrassed and said, 'I was coming to ask April if ... um, my sister thought I should ... but then when I got here, I, er ...'

Slowly it dawned on her. 'You were coming to the bureau?' Her voice rose and a smart girl in a beautifully cut mauve tweed costume looked at them with interest as she passed. Evelyn lowered her tone. 'As a client?'

'I *was*.'

'So ...?'

He looked down at the cobbled street and thrust his hands into his jacket pockets. 'Look – there's nowt going on with Jenny. There never was. But she's a grand lass, and being with her made me realise I needed ... and I thought April could find me a nice woman who, well, wouldn't waste my time.'

'Unlike me.'

He sighed. 'Aye.'

'But you didn't go in.'

'I looked up at the window. I don't know why – just a glance. And I saw ... well, I saw you. Only I didn't know it was you – how could it be? Last I knew, you were off back to your *husband*.' If he was trying to keep the bitterness out of his voice he wasn't succeeding. And then his tone softened. Softened so much that he sounded almost tearful. 'But just that glimpse – even though I didn't think it could actually *be* you – was enough to tell me I was kidding myself.' He let out a long sigh. 'I thought I was just lonely. But—' He shook his head, and she saw that there were indeed unshed tears in his dark eyes. He bit his lip. 'It was *you* I missed, Evelyn. *You* I wanted. If I couldn't have you, then there was no point. It wouldn't be fair on another woman.'

'Charlie!' She made to step forward, but he backed off, his hands up as if in self-defence.

'Don't. It's bad enough ... Don't – let me fall for you again. Not when we can't—'

She took a deep breath. 'I've left my husband.' She might as well say it. She had nothing more to lose now. 'We haven't lived as husband and wife for years. He ... he's actually a homosexual. I'm going to be divorced.' The shameful word was out, and if he was going to recoil, let him. This was the only chance she would have to explain. 'I've known for a while that he was that way. I tried not to mind, to be happy being a mother. And then Robbie ...' But she couldn't speak of Robbie. 'And when I was here before, it was like Maurice, that whole life, hadn't really happened. I *know* that was wrong – I was kidding myself, but I … well, I met you and I …' Her voice broke off and she stared at his chest, because she knew – as she had on the bridge in Durham – that if she looked into his face, she would be lost.

She shook her head and forced the words through the tears clogging the back of her throat. 'I know you won't want me now. And I … I hope you do forget me and find someone. Because you're a good man and you deserve to be happy. But I did love you. If I'd known you existed and that I would meet you one day, I'd never have married Maurice. Or anyone. But …'

Somewhere, nearby, a doorbell was ringing.

She didn't look up at his face. But, somehow, she was talking into the rough wool of his jacket.

He was holding her to him, and saying, 'I don't want someone else. I love you.'

'B-b-but I'm going to be divorced. Your religion …'

'I know.' His voice was bewildered. 'But that doesn't seem to matter as much as – well, as much as you.'

And then she did look up into his face.

When their lips touched it wasn't like it had been in Durham at all. It was much, much better: a kiss full of forgiveness, and acceptance, and hope. And – as their lips lingered, and his hands moved down to her waist and her arms tightened around him – of longing.

Then he said, 'Ouch,' and pulled away and grimaced.

She looked up in alarm.

Behind them, she heard April's voice: 'Goodbye, Jenny. That's wonderful news. We'll never let you escape now. Oh – good afternoon, Miss Dalrymple.'

'It's not you,' he said. 'It's my blasted ribs. Forgot about the buggers for the moment.'

And then April's voice again, in a very different tone: 'Evelyn! Charlie! What's …?'

Charlie took her hand – his felt rough and cool and hard, strange and familiar at the same time – and they walked back to the bureau. From the doorway, Jenny was gaping at them in surprise, April in delighted shock, and the girl in the mauve tweed was staring at Charlie with an expression that made Evelyn tighten her fingers in his.

'Gosh,' she said. 'I hope you've a few more like that lined up for me.'

'Miss Dalrymple! Why don't you go on in and wait for me? You know the way.'

With more than one backwards glance, Miss Dalrymple sashayed through the bureau door, leaving the four of them together.

'What are you wearing?' April asked, and for the first time Evelyn realised she was still in her charring uniform.

'I hadn't noticed,' both she and Charlie said at the same time.

'And,' April went on, 'what would Martha say? Kissing and carrying on at the very doorstep of the bureau?'

Then, when Charlie looked abashed and Evelyn was trying to think of something to say, she laughed.

'Och,' she said, 'I think just this once she'd understand.'

Acknowledgements

My first thanks go to the hundreds of readers who took *Mrs Hart's Marriage Bureau* to their hearts by buying it, reviewing it, inviting me to their book groups, and asking for a sequel. I hope *Miss Vey Takes Charge* is worth the wait. Booksellers and bloggers who spread the word: your support is valued so highly. And for those readers coming to Easterbridge for the first time, do go and check out April and Martha's earlier adventures! (*Mrs Hart's Marriage Bureau*, HarperCollins, 2023)

Thanks to those writer (and reader) friends who read the manuscript at various stages, offering such valuable insights: Emma Pass, Rachel Ward, Inbali Iserles, Nikki Sheehan and Elaine Fenton. And to the fellow writers who help keep me as grounded as a fiction writer can be, especially the Placers: I am so fortunate to have such wise, witty and wonderful women in my life. I miss my works-in-progress salons with Susanne Brownlie more than anyone can guess. Other friends have been tireless cheerleaders for my books, and every attendance at a book launch; every copy bought; every social media post shared; every conversation with a bookseller is appreciated more than you can imagine.

Thanks to my parents, Poppy and John Kerr and the late Davy Wilkinson, for always encouraging me to write stories, and to all the other family and friends who put up with me living half my time in a made-up world. This is often to the detriment of things like cleaning the kitchen floor, so I am very grateful that, even without the interference of Mrs Hart and Miss McVey, I found an extremely patient and helpful husband: great love and thanks to Seamus. He is also a great fount of knowledge about greyhound racing. Thanks, too, to Stroller, my retired racing greyhound, who inspired the canine characters, and to Daisy who didn't really help with anything and barks when I'm trying to write, but I couldn't mention one dog without the other.

I had the great good fortune to be invited to publish *Miss McVey Takes Charge* with Writers Review Publishing. Huge thanks, especially to Linda Newbery, for making me so welcome. Miss McVey would very much approve of a co-operative of women writers. If you haven't checked out their small but exquisite list, do have a look: Miss McVey and I are edified to be in such company.

When Michelle Griffin edited the first book in this series for HarperCollins, I really hoped to work with her again, so I was thrilled that she agreed to return to Easterbridge. Michelle has been much more than an editor: she has been project manager, typesetter, tech wizard, hand-holder and all-round publishing expert. Thanks to Averill Buchanan for her second-to-none proofreading: I felt in very safe hands with these women. Niall McCormack designed the covers of four of the books I published with Little Island, and he was my very first choice. The first time I saw his exquisite cover illustration – that lettering! those greyhounds! – I did a wee dance of joy even though I was in Poundland in Cookstown at the time.

Miss McVey Takes Charge is my twelfth published novel, and the one industry person at my side since book one has been my lovely agent Faith O'Grady, for whose wisdom and tenacity I am perennially grateful. The Tyrone Guthrie Centre at Annaghmakerrig has also been an important part of my writing life, and I was thrilled to be able to work on *Miss McVey* there in February 2024. I am extremely grateful to the Arts Council of Northern Ireland for their very welcome support in producing this novel.

Sheena Wilkinson, 2025

Find out more

www.sheenawilkinson.com
www.writersreviewpublishing.co.uk

Sign up for my newsletter:
Sheena's Writerly Musings on Substack

Writers Review Publishing

Writers Review Publishing is an author-led
publishing collaborative linked to the literary blog
Writers Review, which is hosted by Adèle Geras,
Linda Newbery and Celia Rees. Since its launch
in 2016, the blog has featured recommendations,
round-ups and interviews with authors. All reviews
are by authors or independent booksellers, with
guests including Tracy Chevalier, Patrick Gale,
Joanne Harris, Anthony Horowitz, Val McDermid,
Diane Setterfield and Jane Rogers.

www.writersreview.blogspot.com

ALSO FROM WRITERS REVIEW PUBLISHING

The Poet's Wife by Judith Allnatt
David by Mary Hoffmann
The One True Thing by Linda Newbery